Jean de Fodoas

Jean de Fodoas

by
Maurice Magre

Translated, annotated and introduced by
Brian Stableford

A Black Coat Press Book

ISBN 978-1-61227-698-4. First Printing. December 2017. Published by Black Coat Press, an imprint of Hollywood Comics.com, LLC, P.O. Box 17270, Encino, CA 91416. All rights reserved. Except for review purposes, no part of this book may be reproduced or transmitted in any form or by any means, electronic or mechanical, including photocopying, recording, or by any information storage and retrieval system, without permission in writing from the publisher. The stories and characters depicted in this novel are entirely fictional. Printed in the United States of America.

TABLE OF CONTENTS

Introduction

This is the tenth volume of a twelve-volume set of translations of Maurice Magre's prose fiction. It contains translations of the novel *Jean de Fodoas: aventures d'un Français à la cour de l'empereur Akbar* (1939) as "Jean de Fodoas" and the chapter from *Magiciens et illuminés* entitled "Le Mystère des Templiers," as "The Mystery of the Templars."

Volume One, *The Marvelous Story of Claire d'Amour and Other Stories*, contains translations of early short stories, including the collection *Histoire merveilleuse de Claire d'Amour suivie d'autres contes merveilleux* (1903) and six other stories from various sources published between 1901 and 1913.

Volume Two, *The Call of the Beast and Other Stories*, contains translations of his first three works of prose fiction in volume form, *Les Colombes poignardées* (1917), as "Stabbed Doves," *La Tendre camarade* (1918), as "The Tender Comrade" and *L'Appel de la bête* (1920), as "The Call of the Beast."

Volume Three, *Priscilla of Alexandria and Other Stories* contains translations of the original version of the story collection *Vies des courtisanes*, first published in *Oeuvres Libres* 23 (1923), as "Courtesans' Lives" plus the additional story added to the version published in volume form in 1925, and the novel *Priscilla d'Alexandrie* (1925), as "Priscilla of Alexandria."

Volume Four, *The Angel of Lust*, contains translations of the novella, *La Vie amoureuse de Messaline* (1925), as "The Love Life of Messalina," the novel published as *La Luxure de Grenade* (1926), as "The Angel of Lust," and the chapter from *Magiciens et illuminés* (1930) entitled "Christian Rosenkreutz et les Rose-croix," as "Christian Rosenkreutz and the Rosicrucians."

Volume Five, *The Mystery of the Tiger*, contains translations of the novella *Le Roman de Confucius* (1927), as "The Story of Confucius," and the novel *Le Mystère du tigre* (1927), as "The Mystery of the Tiger."

Volume Six, *The Poison of Goa*, contains translations of the novel *Le Poison de Goa* (1928), as "The Poison of Goa," and the prose poems contained in *Le Livre des lotus entr'ouverts* (1926), as "Lotus Blossoms."

Volume Seven, *Lucifer*, contains a translation of the novel originally published under the same title in 1929 and the novella *La Nuit de haschich et de l'opium* (1929), as "The Night of Hashish and Opium."

Volume Eight, *The Blood of Toulouse*, contains translations of the novel *Le Sang de Toulouse* (1931), as "The Blood of Toulouse," and the chapter from *Magiciens et illuminés* entitled "Le Maître inconnu des Albigeois," as "The Secret Master of the Albigensians."

Volume Nine, *The Albigensian Treasure*, contains translations of the novel *Le Trésor des Albigeois* (1938) as "The Albigensian Treasure," and the collection of vignettes "Communication avec la nature" from *La Beauté invisible* (1937), as "Communication with Nature."

Volume Eleven, *Melusine*, contains translations of the novel *Mélusine, ou le secret de solitude* (1941) and the collections of vignettes "Le Côte d'ombré des âmes" and "Révélation des mondes invisibles" from *La Beauté invisible*, as "The Dark Side of Souls" and "The Revelation of Invisible Worlds."

Volume Twelve, *The Brothers of the Virgin Gold*, contains a translation of the novel *Les Frères de l'or vierge*, first published posthumously in 1949.

Following the fragmentary allegorical narrative of *Le Trésor des Albigeois*, Magre reverted to the action-adventure format of *The Sang de Toulouse* and such previous novels as *Priscilla d'Alexandrie* and *Le Luxure de Grenade*. The move might well have been an attempt to write a popular book, or at least one considerably less exotic than his recent volumes, but it does have certain affiliations with its immediate predecessor, beginning in Toulouse at much the same time.

Although Jean de Fodoas does not seem to be familiar with Michel de Bramevaque, he is said to be acquainted with two of the minor characters featured in *Le Trésor des Albigeois*, Marie Cose and Isaac Andréa. Like Michel de Bramevaque, Jean de Fodoas soon leaves his natal city, but unlike him, he does not return for a long time. His journey takes him to the heart of India in the heyday of the Mogul Empire, to the court of Akbar the Great, and it is there that his adventures unfold. Like Dalmas Rochemaure in *Le Sang de Toulouse*, he is a man of action, not an intellectual, but he does not have Rochemaure's strong commitment to a cause to guide him. As a pawn in games played by others, his principal determination is simply to survive and enjoy himself as much as possible, but he does inherit Rochemaure's quasi-Quixotic preoccupation with a female ideal, accompanied whenever she makes one of her ever-elusive appearances by symbolic roses—although their kinship with the symbolic roses of *Le Trésor des Albigeois* ultimately turns out to be dubious.

Adventure and mysticism are brought together cleverly in the novel, partly by means of educated acquaintances that Jean de Fodoas makes in Akbar's court in between his periodic explosions of heroic action, but also because of his peculiar relationship with his cousin. The cousin in question recruits him to a Jesuit mission to Akbar's court, but only as an instrument, and he proves extremely parsimonious and deliberately enigmatic in gradually explaining aspects of the hidden agenda of that mission—an explanation that he appears never to complete, leaving much to the reader's imagination.

Jean de Fodoas is the least fantastic of Magre's action-adventure novels, although it contains the customary ration of visions and prophecies; its most ingenious narrative move employs the Baphomet that was once allegedly worshiped by the Knights Templar as a symbolic device, which is alleged to have served the same function for the Mongol hordes that the

Ark of the Covenant was assumed to have done for the hordes of Islam in *Le Luxure de Grenade*. That narrative employment inevitably runs into the same problem as the earlier employment of the Ark, however, because known history leaves no scope for the talisman in question actually to accomplish anything within the plot.

The recruitment was obviously an *ad hoc* improvisation, because a very different account of the Baphomet had been given in the highly speculative account of the Templars' secret mission earlier contained in *Magiciens et illumines*. I have added that relevant chapter as an appendix in any case, partly as an item of scholarly fantasy that is of some interest in its own right, and also as an illustration of the versatility of the author's imagination, which came into play with the necessary verve whenever it seemed convenient to change his mind. Unlike many scholarly fantasists, Magre did not fall for his own patter to the extent of swiftly making his inventions into dogmas, although whether that can be interpreted to mean that he never really believed a single word of any of them remained debatable.

Although Jean de Fodoas makes discoveries in the course of his idle wandering that might assist in his cousin's quests—the Baphomet is not the only thing for which the Jesuits are searching—he carefully refrains from helping him out, having become suspicious of the Jesuits' motives and the virtue of their cause. The Jesuits do not come out of the analysis too badly, however, and the descriptions of the minor members of the mission and their personal preoccupations contain more comedy than serious criticism of the kind leveled at the persecutors of the Albigensians in *Le Sang de Toulouse*.

Perhaps Jean de Fodoas' scrupulous avoidance of following up the clues he stumbles across to the location of Akbar's Baphomet and the location of Genghis Khan's treasure does not work to the melodramatic advantage of the plot, but the straitjacket of known history would have made it impossible, in any case, for the hero to achieve anything significant, even if he had followed up the leads that he discovered or passed the information on to his cousin. The private culmination that his own odyssey eventually reaches is more in keeping with the nature of the exercise, as well as with Magre's particular notion of virtue.

The philosophical elements of the novel are, however, carefully subdued and discreetly peripheral, as befits a somewhat picaresque and casually rambunctious adventure story, of which *Jean de Fodoas* is an uncommonly stylish example, requiring little more introduction than that observation, although I have included a more elaborate commentary on its somewhat cavalier relationship with known history in footnotes to the text.

The translation of *Jean de Fodoas: aventures d'un Français à la cour de l'empereur Akbar* was made from the London Library's copy of the 1939 Gallimard edition. The translation of "Le Mystère des Templiers" was made from the same institution's copy of the 1930 Fasquelle edition of *Magiciens et illuminés.*

Brian Stableford

JEAN DE FODOAS

THE HOUSE IN THE RUE MALCOUSINAT

I launched my blue épée, moving in its nudity, over the old oak table like the body of a young woman. Then I detached the scabbard from my belt, because my mother suffered secretly from the presence of a weapon at my side.

I wiped the sweat from my brow. I disguised as best I could the rip that divided the top of my doublet. It had separated into two the cross of white wool that every good Catholic in Toulouse wore on the right shoulder. I went to the door and darted a glance into the street. It was deserted, and under the bright moon, the stones, in places, seemed covered in snow.

They had not pursued me. They had lost track of me, or they dared not trouble the house where my mother was. No, it wasn't that. Could a sentiment of respect be born in those murderous souls? Assassins who had been my companions! They might have gone to have their weapons blessed at Saint-Sernin by the Bishop of Toulouse, but they were executioners all the same. Those blessed weapons had served to kill imploring prisoners or women who had just been raped.

Lord! Was I myself...but no, I didn't want to think about that. It was no time to regret what I had done. First of all, if one acts, it's by virtue of an internal pressure, a kind of volcano of the soul that one can't resist. Could I have done otherwise than go to fight when the infamous Rabastens had told me that he was recruiting noble and courageous young men to capture the fortress of Montesquieu de Lauragais from the Protestants? He had even added, lowering his voice slightly, that when it was known that I, Jean de Fodoas, was at the head of those elite young men, all the finest flower of Toulousan nobility would follow me.

That Rabastens appeared to me to be such an admirable man! I compared him to Trencavel and Arnaud Bernard! Why does infamy not burst forth on faces like a revelatory lamp? How can noble features and attitudes full of dignity be combined with the most abject baseness? Why does nature prepare such traps in sculpting the faces of men?

And I, being naïve, had allowed myself to be taken in, because there had been talk of my courage, that the nobility of my family had been exalted. It was always my pride that doomed me—my pride and my violence...rather my violence. Had I not struck the first blow? Yes, it seemed to me that I was the one who had struck first.

I tried to reconstitute the scene exactly as it had happened, for it is of great importance to justify oneself by means of solid arguments. We had told the Jews to cease their dances and their cries...all three of us were sitting...we had been drinking, perhaps too much. All three, the three leaders—for, in spite of my youth, Rabastens and Gaston de Cornusson, the son of the former seneschal of Toulouse, had been obliged to admit me to their deliberation.

It was a matter of knowing how the booty would be divided. I wasn't listening, thinking that it wasn't becoming to manifest a gross avidity. There had been enough talk on Toulouse of the poverty into which the Fodoases had fallen. And then, I had heard the sentence, inoffensive in itself but to which the tone of the syllables gave the value of a repulsive insult: "A few écus will be necessary for Jean de Fodoas."

I raised my head and I saw the faces of my two interlocutors disfigured by hideous laughter. They were laughing, and there was in the grimace of their laughter, which made them suddenly similar, the knowledge of my poverty, of the poverty of my family, and the scorn that thieves can have for an accomplice poorer than them. Not only were they scornful of me, but they wanted to make me their dupe, estimating my value at a few écus.

It was Rabastens that I had slapped, because he was closer to me. Gaston de Cornusson had made a backward movement, and my fist had only struck empty air. Already I had lost the advantage of the man who strikes the first blow. Things ceased almost immediately to be visible. A semi-naked woman, her eyes wide with fear, ran to the nearest lamp and threw it to the floor, for inferior souls think they are protected by darkness.

I heard a cry of "He's drunk!" and then "Kill him!" And I understood that from the next room, a dozen bandits who had been waiting there, seething with impatience, awaiting the division of the booty were rushing me: bandits who hated me because I had treated them as bandits, and whose companion—my God!—I had been. All the assassins of Montesquieu de Lauragais were around me and I saw their blessed weapons glinting in the smoke like lightning flashes in a storm.

By virtue of the great strength given to me as my share since birth, the table rose up like a rampart and they fell back. I struck the head of a crawling traitor with my heel, delivered a few blows at hazard, and my guardian angel, with his constant fidelity, guided me unwittingly to the door, and doubtless opened it himself, with his angelic hand, for I was suddenly refreshed by the nocturnal air and felt the pavement of the street beneath my feet.

To be sure, no one could outdistance me at a run, and I had been able to reach the Rue Malcousinat and the little house, a modest vestige of the lost splendor of the Fodoases. How blissful solitude is, especially when the respiration of one's mother floats there, like the brush of an ineffable wing.

My mother wasn't asleep. At the top of the staircase her door was open. She knew that I was there, and anxiety augmented her light breath. I heard it as an appeal, and also as a reproach. Perhaps she had not slept, and had waited for me incessantly.

My resolution was firm not to say anything about the night's events, sensible as I knew her to be to accounts of violence. I promised myself, as I climbed the stairs with the even and calm tread of a late stroller going home to bed, simply to kiss her on the forehead and go back to my room.

But when I saw her, so tiny in her armchair, so pale and so dignified, when I perceived in her features the effort to efface the anguish and replace it with a smile, my heart burst like a pomegranate under an excessively hot ray of sunlight, and I fell at her knees.

"I'll tell you everything!" I cried.

But she put her hand over my lips. "No, don't say anything; I can guess…"

What had she guessed? What had already happened a hundred times, the violence, the presence of evil that she sensed around her beloved son, and which she would have liked to chase away with the caress of her tremulous hands.

"You cross is torn," she murmured. "Leave me your doublet so that I can mend it."

I wanted to speak, to excuse myself, to tell her about the insult received, but I sensed that my explanations would be lost in the purity of her soul like boat sinking in a sea of dreams.

Then it seemed to me that my sentiments were transformed with the same rapidity as some nocturnal landscapes when they are suddenly illuminated by a ray of the rising sun falling from a mountain.

I assured her that, from that moment on, a new man had been born. While speaking, I sensed that man, full of perfections, appearing out of the depths of my soul. I saw him, I saw myself, full of kindness, pardoning offenses, incapable of anger. My entire past life horrified me.

"I swear to you that I won't go to the rendezvous with the three Pibrac brothers."

Those three brothers were ruined castellans, of which there are so many, who followed the profession of bandits and attacked travelers on the roads. They had come to Toulouse to recruit courageous men from among the bad lots of the city, and they had naturally thought of me.

But my mother, in her sanctity, had no idea who the Pibrac brothers were.

"I swear to you not to show myself in the city any more with Marie Cose,[1] and not to see her again."

With her fragile hand, my mother waved away the image of that scandalous young woman.

"I swear to you to forget that slap that I gave Rabastens, to forget the laughter of those accursed swine. I shall love poverty as you have told me to do. And even...."

I had an insensate vow on my lips. Timidly, but with patience, my mother had often expressed the desire to see me enter some religious order.

I glimpsed, as in a dream, the colonnades of a cloister, the lined-up tombstones and the broad sleeves of robes flying around me like brown birds.

Raising my eyes, I saw my mother's ecstatic face. She did not believe my promises, but my good intentions were sufficient for her. And on my forehead it seemed that a moist droplet, a little warm tear, had just fallen.

And it was at that moment, at that divine moment, that a noise coming from the depths of Hell reached me, for, as Isaac Andréa had often said to me, there is a direct communication between divine things and infernal things, to such an extent that it is not insensate to think that they have the same origin.

---

[1] Most of the names in this chapter are fictitious, but Marie Cose is mentioned in the published Annals of Toulouse as a notorious serial adulteress of great beauty who was condemned to be whipped after seducing the son of a town councilor. She is featured in *Le Trésor des Albigeois* as a somewhat raddled prostitute, although the relevant section of that novel does not seem to be set any later than the present chapter. Several other characters mentioned in passing, including Isaac Andréa and Captain Mauric, had also played minor parts in *Le Trésor des Albigeois*.

Someone was knocking on the door. They were regular blows, struck with violence, with no restraint, with no regard for the late hour and the tranquility of the inhabitants of the Rue Malcousinat.

If God sees into souls, he could take account of the fact that when I got to my feet, the syllables of my oath were still floating on my lips, and I only had the intention of shouting pacifying words through the door. I searched for a general remark about the blindness into which we had thrown drink, the necessity of sleep and forgetfulness.

What happened then? Perhaps, as I have thought by virtue of certain indications, there is a personal genius in my épée that, although deprived of speech, offers suggestions and impels actions in accordance with its nature. Perhaps the things that were being said in the street by infamous men—of which I perceived fragments such as: *Miserable hovel of beggars! His old caricature of a mother*—were of a character such that one could not hear them without a complete transformation of the living fires that circulate in the blood vessels.

The door of the house was narrow, made of stout oak, and held shut by the thick transversal beam. I understood that several men were braced against it, attempting to break it down. They were breathing heavily, and one of them said:

"He must be shivering with fear on the other side."

Gold alone, with his power of vision, can testify that my intention was simply to show those degraded individuals that I was not afraid of them. I remember that, during the moments that followed, I constantly had the sensation that my mother's tear was luminous on my forehead, like a fantastic star, the sight of which would dazzle my enemies.

I threw myself at the door and with a single thrust, I pulled away the beam that ensured its closure.

Events never happen as the imagination represents their details. I had seized my épée in my right hand, and I believed confusedly that a kind of Archangel Michael would appear to the indigenes in the street, with a star placed on his forehead.

For a second I had that illusion, for those who were shoving the door fell to the floor, and I was able to believe that they were prostrating themselves. But a fat man, whom I recognized by his silhouette as Balbaria, leapt over those who had fallen with a surprising agility.

That Balbaria had an arm longer than any other, and the right side of his face as more developed than the left. One ear almost hung down to the shoulder. At least, I saw him thus, and I had not refrained, in the course of our expedition, from laughing at such a disproportion, which no one apart from me had noticed.

He seized me by the throat with his deformed but strangely solid hand, crying: "I've got him!"

In a din of broken things, forms filled the room.

Subsequently, I was astonished by the brevity of that scene. Doubtless it was the howl that Balbaria uttered that sowed fear in souls. The cutting edge of my blade sawed through the arm near the elbow. I was able to recoil as far as the staircase. I was suddenly animated by a marvelous presence of mind.

The room was only illuminated by a night-light attached to the wall and the lunar circle that the open door made. All my thrusts must have carried. But that is not sufficient to explain that panic so rapidly took hold of the assailants. Like the waves of a tide that has reached the extremity of its force, they flowed back into the street. I was able to close the door behind them and bolt it again.

An occult intervention had occurred, and had preserved me from the complete invasion of my house by those furious individuals. But I immediately wondered why it had not occurred sooner. A minute sooner would have sufficed. What a caprice there is in providential interventions.

Everything around me was devastated. Balbaria's blood or someone else's, was forming ruddy pools on the diamond-shaped floor-tiles. The mirror had shattered into smithereens. I nearly uttered a cry on seeing the miniature of Bérangère de

Palassol that the painter Thomas Capellan had painted for me partly ripped from its frame and soiled.

I thought at first of going to give my mother an explanation. But what? The best thing was to tell her the truth. I did not have time. A rumor was coming from the street,

What was happening there? Had the chastisement been insufficient? Or perhaps too great?

As the tumult became louder, I thought that the wisest thing to do was to find out what it was. I climbed the stairs in three bounds and went open my bedroom window, which overlooked the Rue Malcousinat.

The sound produced by the shutters provoked a clamor. I was able to see that a man, doubtless traversed by an unconsidered thrust, was lying on the ground. Several others were carrying a beam for which they must have gone in search to the Rue des Changes, where there was a house undergoing demolition. I distinguished the monstrous silhouette of Rabastens and the thin caricature that was the Cornusson son. A few lights illuminated windows here and there. I recognized, on the first floor of the house facing mine, a certain Donadieu, candle in hand, who could not know anything of the quarrel, but was nevertheless turning in my direction a face full of hatred.

Only a man who weighs his intentions and know the extent to which they differ from the actions they engender can know the words that I pronounced and no one heard. They were words of conciliation. I tried to summarize rapidly the infamy of Rabastens and Cornusson in my regard and to explain that the incident that had occurred that evening was its fatal conclusion. But it seemed to me that no one was listening. Injustice possessed those frantic creatures.

Suddenly, a detonation resounded, followed by a little noise near my head. A musket-ball had just brushed me. I recoiled, but without haste, in order to show my indifference in the face of danger. Their aim was poor. But they were going to see!

I had a Spanish musket I my cupboard, of an old-fashioned form, but which I always kept ready for use. The troubled times that Toulouse was traversing required the possession of a musket. I seized it, installed the fork on the window-sill and fired, almost without taking aim.

Doubtless Cornusson merited being punished, for I saw him fall against the opposite wall. The clamors of hatred redoubled. At the same time, the blows of the beam resounded that several men were using as a battering-ram against my door.

I was astonished that the soldiers of La Maynade had not yet come. As I was struggling with my musket in the hope of firing a second shot, I heard them arriving from the Rue des Changes and the Rue du Pont, and Rabastens' band negotiated with them.

Expert in crime, Rabastens was even more so in lying. It was necessary to ward off his assertions. I deliberated as to whether I ought not to go downstairs, open my door and place myself in the hands of the sergeant of the watch. But I recognized the voice of Captain Mauric. He had come in person! The captain of the watch, in consequence of a few nocturnal quarrels, had pronounced inconceivable words in my regard, which testified to the villainy of his soul.

"That's a swashbuckler that I'll bring to account the next time," he had said to the venerable magistrate Jean de Balanquier,[2] who was a friend of my father and who had interceded on my behalf.

Now, the next time had arrived. Captain Mauric ought to have taken possession of Rabastens and his troop of bandits who were disturbing the nocturnal peace by firing gunshots

---

[2] As with Marie Cose, this name is taken from contemporary documents referring to a real magistrate active in Toulouse in the last decades of the sixteenth century and the first two decades of the seventeenth, although his title is listed in some of those documents as "Seigneur de Montlaur et de Lagarde" rather than the one with which the present text credits him.

and trying to break down the door of a house using a beam as a battering-ram. Instead of that, by the light of a torch that one of the men was holding, I saw him leaning over the recumbent Cornusson and helping him to get up, and I distinguished in the curve of his back the respectful baseness that the son of a former seneschal can inspire in a chief of police.

"Captain Mauric," I shouted, in a loud voice, "in making a pact with assassins you're becoming an assassin yourself."

I thought, too late, that that was not calculated to settle my affairs, but truthful words spring forth with the same force as water once sprang forth under the staff of Moses.

Another detonation rang out. And the wielders of the beam, who had stopped momentarily with the arrival of La Maynarde's men, recommenced striking my door with regular blows, as if they were accomplishing a just and excellent task.

Anger provokes a state of intoxication that is dolorous at first but becomes blissful at a certain degree by virtue of the total loss of the reasonable faculties. At a stroke I attained that height, at which consciousness has no place. I sensed my strength multiplied, and that is what enabled me to lift up an enormous dresser, of which I would have been incapable at any other moment, to carry it to the window and to launch it into the street. It fell with an enormous crash, and cries of rage and dolor went up. I launched all the other furniture with the same ease, until the room was entirely bare, with the exception of the bed, which was fortunately, or unfortunately, fixed to the floor and the ceiling by its columns of sculpted wood.

"They'll kill you! Save yourself, I beg you!"

My mother was beside me, and I remember having been struck by her extreme smallness, as if I were seeing her for the first time. Her hands were clasped together, and in spite of the dramatic character of the situation, I had difficulty not exclaiming at the exiguity of her stature.

"It's not my fault, I swear to you!" I cried. "There's a power that has come, which has seized me, which acted in my stead...."

I felt on my forehead the gesture of a waxen hand, which meant that words were futile.

"Don't worry about me. I recognize the voice of the Seigneur de Venerque, who loved our father so much. I've nothing to fear, since he's there."

Jean de Balanquier, Seigneur de Venerque, was the magistrate in charge of the police. I was astounded to know that he was present. The affair must be considered very important for him to be summoned in the middle of the night.

The affair was, however, insignificant in principle. Bandits drunk on wine had wanted to take me for a dupe. I had slapped one. Perhaps, in the dark, I had delivered an unfortunate sword-thrust. But I had fled, and that would not be interpreted in a pacific fashion. My house had been invaded. Did I not have the right to defend myself? Undoubtedly the blows I had struck at hazard and in the dark, blows that often strike empty space, had been directed unwittingly by a occult power—for I recognized an occult power in all of that.

But it was not the time to determine the part played by God and that of the Devil....

When one is lost in the tempest of events, a man always has a mast to which to cling, which is the appetite for life. He accomplishes mechanically the actions most appropriate to perpetuate his existence. I glimpsed in a second what it was necessary to do.

At the extremity of a kind of ladder ending in a mansard there was a skylight that overlooked the roofs. That was the route of my salvation, on condition that I acted quickly.

The sound of the beam against my door had paused for a brief interval, doubtless corresponding to the arrival of the Seigneur de Venerque, but it had resumed and I had just heard a crack that presaged an imminent yielding of the door.

I clasped my mother in my arms.

"Quickly!" she said, again.

I took a few steps, opened a door and stepped on to the ladder that led to the roof.

But without reflecting, moved suddenly by an internal force, I turned back and tumbled down the ladder. I had left my sword in the room downstairs, and, as I was about to depart without it, I had had the sentiment of abandoning an inseparable companion.

The door was about to collapse. I lost a few seconds then searching for the épée that I had left on the bottom step of the stairway. It was shining with an unusual gleam. It was longer than usual. It has a singular life. When I seized it by the hilt and replaced it in its scabbard it seemed to me that I was enveloping in a robe a maleficent creature, bloodstained but supple and beautiful, which bore evil in its substance, a fraternal creature destined to accompany me for a long time and to communicate to me the poisons nourished in its steel bosom.

I had vertigo, and it required a great effort or me to tear myself way from the attraction of the combat. Perhaps, without a further appeal from my mother, I would not have been above to tear my gaze away from the door, which flew into splinters.

Finally, I launched myself forth, I carefully closed the door behind me that gave access to the ladder. It was quite well hidden, and a few minutes would go by before anyone found it.

When I emerged on to the roofs, I felt the nocturnal air like a refreshing wave. It is a particularity of my nature to pass with disconcerting rapidity from one state of mind to another. After having crawled for a few minutes among the gutters and between the chimneys I let myself fall on to my back. A great lassitude seized me, and, at the same time, a perfect serenity. I nearly threw my sword away, but I thought about the racket it would make as it fell into the street.

To my right I saw the bell-tower of La Dalbade and the confused mass of the Château Narbonnais. To my left, Saint-Sernin projected its steeple into the sky with the unalterable patience that a heart of eternal stone gives. And in all directions I saw the stars, as far as the eye could see, and it seemed to me that they were falling like rain on sleeping Toulouse.

How beautiful they were, and how insensate I had been not to come to contemplate them more frequently! In truth, it was an ideal situation to be lying on the roof of a house in that marvelous city.

But the gleam of the stars paled. In the distance, a belfry projected a flock of brazen birds through motionless spaces. The sky became the color of ash and smoke, and in the distance, above the distant slopes of Pech David, there was a tiny solar bloodstain. What, morning already, and the end of the nocturnal delight that I was savoring! How rapid everything was, most of all the celestial colors and the fleeting gleam of the stars!

Voices wrenched me out of my torpor. My enemies were pursuing me, then, even into the sky. I recommenced crawling, but my course was limited by the abysms of the streets. In the end, a kind of vertigo gripped me, and I wondered whether the wisest thing might not be to leap into the void at random.

Isaac Andréa had often told me that every man, especially if he is a good man, has several invisible spirits that protect him. It was time for a decisive and dangerous experiment. If Isaac Andréa had told the truth, it would be easy for my spirits to sustain me in my fall.

And as I deliberated as to whether I ought to trust that uncertain promise, the spirits in question, which were perhaps deliberating in their own account as to the most favorable means of stealing me away from my persecutors, found an unexpected resource.

A skylight that I had perceived, not far away from me, like an obscure eye, opened slowly. The opening was about to increase and becoming gaping. I scarcely had any choice as to the means of getting out of trouble, and I leapt into the unknown with the greatest possible lightness.

I did not fall from a great height. A hand, moreover, helped me to get up. I was about to put myself on the defensive when, gaping with astonishment. I realized that I had before me the thin silhouette and the large-nosed face of my friend and protector, the Jesuit Du Jarric.

FATHER DU JARRIC

"My son, knowledge of the world is worth more than reading Aristotle. And in any case, you don't read Aristotle. India...if you only knew! There are glow-worms more luminous than lamps. Many times, in the evening, deprived of light, I have been able to read at my ease beside one of them. The elephant's nose is an enigma that a reasonable mind cannot succeed in penetrating. And there is an even greater enigma, which is the presence of gold. Gold is extraordinarily abundant in that distant land. Why that metal is distributed over the planet in such an unequal fashion is another mystery. The world is made of mysteries. There are human souls that are in rapport with the abundance of gold, especially the souls of powerful men, the souls of kings. If you come with me, as everything seems to anticipate, you will get close to a sovereign, the Emperor Akbar, whose soul is like a block of gold."

Thus spoke, in the disjointed fashion habitual to him, my cousin the Jesuit Pierre Du Jarric. His principal characteristic was a long hooked nose—which, according to my personal observations, always accompanies a certain evenness of character and a certain mental wisdom. In my childhood, when the Fodoases still owned a town house near the Saint Étienne cathedral, I had often listened, wonderstruck, to his paradoxical speeches. He was proud then to be the first man in France to have reached the land of India.[3]

---

[3] The historical Pierre Du Jarric (1566-1617) was indeed a Jesuit from Toulouse, but his ambition to become a missionary was thwarted and he devoted himself instead to compiling an *Histoire des choses plus mémorables advenues tant en Indes orientales* [History of the Most Memorable Things to Have Happened Recently in the East Indies] (3 volumes, 1610-1614; partly tr. as *Akbar and the Jesuits: An Account of the Jesuit Missions to the Court of Akbar*) based on reports sent back by

"The missionary who goes forth to convert the pagans," he said then, "secretly aspires to convert himself."

I had not understood what he meant until much later. When he had departed for Goa with the Portuguese Jesuits, people had bid him farewell like someone who would never be seen again. India! No one, apart from scholars, and few of them, knew where that land was situated. It evoked for me vaults of palm trees, bronzed men carrying curved sabers, and serpents sliding through jungles. One quickly gets used to no longer seeing those one knows. Pierre Du Jarric was considered as having disappeared forever. He had, however, come back, scarcely aged, and already avid to depart again. I had known of his presence in Toulouse but had not worried about it, the orientation of my life—so, at least, I believed—having taken me far away from any man who was guided by virtue.

"Look what has fallen from the sky at the moment when I believed that you were in the infernal realms," he has said to me, without manifesting any astonishment when I had leapt through the skylight of his room.

The convent of the Jesuits occupied a large quadrilateral between the Rue du Pont, the Rue des Changes and the Rue Malcousinat. Expelled from Pamiers following an attack by Protestants, the Jesuits had taken refuge in Toulouse and their community was redoubtable, unpopular and powerful. I had thought myself temporarily in safety.

I had given my cousin a sincere account of the night's events and he had listened to me, shaking his head and sometimes blinking his mischievous eyes, as if all that were known to him.

"I can keep you in my room and let you out by night without anyone knowing. But where will you go? Your house will be guarded and within a few hours Captain Mauric will

---

actual missionaries. Magre used the book as a source of materials for his narrative, but his account of events and people mentioned therein is infinitely more extravagant.

have put his hand on you, and sent you to a dungeon in the Château Narbonnais. People are hanged for less than that."

He reflected and became anxious. There was the Provincial Father. Now, the Provincial Father, although he never left his room in the convent, knew everything that was happening on earth. He knew what was happening in India. He had dissected the soul of the Emperor Akbar, and weighed, as if in a balance, the possibilities of converting him to the Christian religion, for the greater good of his Order, which would thus direct half the world. How could the Provincial Father, who knew such distant things, be unaware that a young man carrying a bloody sword had penetrated the Jesuit convent, to which no stranger was admitted, via the roof?

For one thing, Captain Mauric would come to inquire as to whether any body had fallen into one of the three interior courtyards. The brothers would be interrogated. It was necessary to know that it was a material impossibility to lie in the presence of the Provincial Father. The insensate individual who attempted to alter the truth suddenly had a thick mouth, and he saw the Provincial Father smile softly, while rubbing the table with his fingertip, as if to remove the dust of the lie and get rid of it. The best thing was to go and tell the Provincial Father everything. But what would he say?

My cousin had reflected, and suddenly he had had an idea. Thanks to that alone, I could get out of the sticky situation I was in—for my predicament was very bad. The Cornussons were all-powerful in Toulouse. They had the magistrates at their devotion. I had wounded Gaston de Cornusson, and perhaps killed him. And my bad reputation underlined that.

Sitting on the plank covered by a thin straw mattress that served as Pierre Du Jarric's bed, I had now sobered up. The cold air penetrated me. A wooden crucifix and an image of Pope Clement VIII[4] did not contribute to cheering up the walls of the room. I would rather not have thought about anything

---

[4] Clement VIII was Pope from 1592-1605.

any longer but going to bed and sleeping, but I could see with a singular clarity the contours that the moonlight picked out, the gallows outside the Porte Arnaud Bernard, in the waste ground where it was said that mandrakes moaned by night. Several times, with some of my young friends, we had gone to see the corpses swinging in the wind, and had amused ourselves throwing stones to chase away the crows that haunted the place. Would I soon be swinging from those redoubtable gallows?

Pierre Du Jarric spoke volubly.

"It isn't forbidden to a man of the world to covet a fortune. My son, the Jesuits form the greatest power on earth. Take in your hand a light cord; you will break it easily. Take in your hand twenty light cords, and you will not be able to reckon with that bond. And there isn't only India to conquer. There's Persia and the mysterious kingdom of Cathay, where men, it appears, have the custom of rolling their hair into a single tress that falls all the way to their feet. We don't have enough admiration of the Portuguese. When, from the deck of an immense ship, you see before you the city of Goa, when you see the monkeys gamboling, when you perceive that a palm tree, by virtue of the astonishing speed of growth within it, is as tall as you in the morning and shades your house in the evening...."

I fell asleep while Père Du Jarric was talking.

He touched me with his finger and he said to me, with an unexpected gravity in his voice: "Come, my son. The Provincial Father is waiting for you."

He added: "Above all, speak as little as possible. Can you content yourself with saying yes to everything he asks of you? A man is valued by his faculty of silence."

I was almost astonished by that speech from such a great chatterbox as my cousin, but it was not the time to make such a remark.

The room into which I penetrated behind Père Du Jarric was immense, with high windows, and I was immediately struck by the grandeur and beauty of the furniture that it contained. I admired the color of the carpets, the sculpted woodwork and certain mythical goddesses painted on the ceiling. A circular glance had made me think that the room was empty, and I tilted my head back in order to contemplate more easily a marvelously designed nude torso. I was about to remark to my cousin that artists all fell into the same error in lending their models contours more abundant than those seen in life, and was ready to indicate to him breasts of a shocking disproportion when I understood by the expression of fearful respect in his eyes that we were not alone and that any profane comment relative to the painting would be out of place.

There was someone behind a vast oak table, someone who could only be the Provincial Father. But he must have been very small, for one might have thought that there was only a cranium there, posed upon an object invisible behind the table, a bald cranium like an ivory ball.

And immediately, I thought of my mother. The Provincial Father must have the same stature as her. Was he a little taller or a little shorter? That was the absurd problem that took possession of my mind and occupied it almost entirely, in spite of the gravity of the interview. Why were some people so tall and other short? And what was the strange relationship that existed between the smallness of my mother and that of the powerful man that I had before me?

He looked at me, smiling. There was no benevolence in that smile, and perhaps a certain scorn. I perceived then that Père Du Jarric was trying to begin a sentence without being able to finish it.

"He's very young, but in fact…."

With that, the Provincial Father started speaking in Latin, which I did not understand, and Père Du Jarric replied to him in the same language. They were talking about me. I thought I could make out that they were talking about my stature and my strength. But they were talking in an almost commercial manner. I even thought that they were going to ask me to show my teeth, as one does with slaves. I thought that they were praising me up that I was having a great effect. At the same time, I had a flattering idea of my strength. I could, in fact, have shattered that ivory ball with a single blow of my fist. I would have been able to reckon with a dozen similar ivory balls.

Are thoughts perceptible? A flash of lightning, green in color, sprang in my direction, which chilled me to the bone. However, the conversation in Latin continued. I heard the name Akbar several times, and the word *equus*, which recurred several times. What did I have to do with that Emperor, and what did *equus* mean?

In the end, the two Jesuits were no longer paying any heed to me, and I thought it uncivil to leave a Fodoas standing up and having a long conversation in front of him in a language that he didn't understand. I started looking ostentatiously at the goddess with the enormous breasts until the moment when I saw the provincial Father rubbing the table with is minuscule fingertips as if to remove a speck of dust.

"You can thank the Provincial Father," my cousin said. "He has authorized you to depart with me and he will grant you hospitality until the day of the departure."

I recalled his recommendations and I contented myself with murmuring: "Yes," and bowing very deeply.

"It's necessary to excuse him...," my cousin began

But the bony hand on the table gave the impression of flicking another speck of dust away. The interview was concluded.

As we walked through obscure corridors, my cousin, who had recovered all his self-confidence, turned round, and I understood by his gaze that he was astonished not to see me manifesting more joy.

"How far is India from Toulouse?" I asked him.

He replied that it depended on the favor of certain marine winds that blew on the African coast and in the most distant oceans, which are vast and redoubtable.

"It's necessary to count on six month or more."

"And as many to return?"

"Naturally, the return is in the realm of possible things—but the man who is departing ought not to be thinking about returning."

I felt weak, and as we had returned to Père Du Jarric's little room, I sat down on the bed, prey to an extreme dejection.

The good priest understood my state of mind and he pronounced words that expressed the inexorable character of necessity, for he knew that one has less chagrin in a circumstance if one feels that it is impossible to modify it.

While I slept he made enquiries about the rumor caused in Toulouse by the siege of my house in the course of the previous night. The rumor was considerable. A man had died in the course of the initial brawl that had followed the slap given to Rabastens. He was an insignificant man whose end had been inscribed by Providence for that night in the register that Providence keeps of insignificant men. Everything that had followed had been the consequence of a sword-thrust that I had delivered in the dark. Then too, Balbaria's arm has been almost detached at the elbow joint. A wretched individual, that Balbaria! But it was not a matter of his moral value. Young Cornusson's shoulder had been broken and Rabastens was delirious because of a blow he had received on the head.

The magistrates had met and Captain Mauric had enumerated before them several scandalous deeds to which he had closed his eyes thus far because I was a good Christian and a Fodoas. Among the actions were several jokes, albeit scandalous, like the story of the public ball at which, in the midst of Bohemian musicians, Marie Cose had danced with me with no clothes on. There were generous ones like the deliverance of a Spanish moor afflicted with leprosy at whom the crowd were throwing stones, and whom I had permitted to flee, holding the people in respect on my own.

My cousin saw things from above, he knew how hot the blood of young men is, He himself, once.... But it was not the same for the important men of the city. The venerable Seigneur de Venerque had not dared to take my defense at the meeting of magistrates. The old Seneschal de Cornusson had promised a sum of twenty écus to the man who could put his hand on me, and my cousin was convinced that even the house of "that woman"—he meant Marie Cose—was under surveillance.

I asked what the day of the departure was. "Even if it's only a matter of a fortnight, the surveillance might be relaxed," I said.

"We're leaving tomorrow. The journey through Spain is long, and, although it seems extraordinary, the roads of that very Christian country are infinitely more dangerous than those of Akbar's empire. We'll embark in Lisbon. But between now and tomorrow you must remain in this cell. Perhaps it will be interesting to leaf through the atlas of Ortelius[5] in order to have an idea of the country to which you're going. I hasten to tell you that the atlas in question is full of errors, for having wanted to conform to the general science of Ptolemy. My superiors are counting on me to trace more accurate maps, and—who knows?—even though I'm not holding out much hope, you might be bitten by the cartographic science, and help me to correct Ortelius. In the meantime you have the good fortune to have at your disposal a world map by Mercator that you can consult entirely at your ease."

I did not think of taking advantage of that good fortune. Mercator's world map appeared to me to be a collection of hieroglyphs devoid of interest. I threw myself under the blankets that Père Du Jarric had disposed on the tiles of his room. I

---

[5] The Flemish cartographer Abraham Ortelius (1527-1598) published his pioneering *Atlas Theatrum Orbis Terrarum* [The Theater of the World], containing 53 maps, most of them copies, in 1570. It remained a standard reference work until the second decade of the seventeenth century, when it was surpassed by more elaborate and more accurate atlases, including the one produced by Gerardus Mercator (1512-1594) and published posthumously in 1595, many of them stimulated by Ortelius' example and the desire to improve on his endeavor.

took my head in my hands. I saw the face of Bérangère de Palassol, the supple torso of Marie Cose, the Place Saint-Sermin where I liked so much to stroll and watch the sunset with my friend Thomas Capellan, the painter, or with Isaac Andréa, who explained to me in his beautiful language secrets of magic that I didn't understand, but which I admired all the more in consequence.

I saw the judges assembled for my condemnation, the shadow of the gallows, the executioner and his aides, and at the foot of a pillar of the church, praying for her son, my mother, so tiny, so tiny....

Because of me the departure had been fixed for sunset. In the afternoon I had made in the chapel I know not what oath by which I became an affiliate member of the Society of Jesus, a company that had a great many lay members. At the point I was at, they could have made me swear anything they wished. I engaged myself to be a good servant of the Pope and to defend on every occasion the Order of which I was henceforth part. I had been given a rosary of a particular form as a sign of my obedience, but I remained a layman, which was the essential thing for me.

My cousin told me that he had gone to reassure my mother as to my fate and that she had accepted my departure with courage, since it was the sole means of salvation for me.

He gave me a few clothes, which I rolled around my sword and which I covered with a blanket. The whole was attached to the mule that was to carry me. I put on a monk's robe whose hood I pulled down over my eyes.

We formed a little troop of six persons, who were grouped in the courtyard where the stables opened. Behind a curtain I glimpsed the ivory ball that was the cranium of the Provincial Father. It was just at the level of the window.

Doubtless Père Du Jarric had given a password. The massive gate to the Rue des Changes opened abruptly. At the same instant, the lantern fixed to the wall in the street was extinguished, thanks to some stratagem. I had time to perceive two men-at-arms who were standing to either side of the gate. Two rays of light reflected from their breastplates were extinguished at the same time as the lantern. The mules departed at a rapid trot. My evil curiosity caused me to lower my head a second too late, for my gaze met the fiery gaze of the man-at-arms to the right, whom I recognized as a certain Dalmas, nicknamed the wolf, who was one-eyed but was reputed to be better with that unique eye than others with two.

Behind us I heard the noise of the gate. Père Du Jarric, who came out last, must have perceived the glance because he came to reassure me as we crossed the bridge.

"We're going through the Porte de Muret, a few minutes before it closes. Even if the men of La Maynarde have recognized you and they can procure horses, the sergeant of the guard won't open up for them.

As we went past the Fontaine Sainte-Claire I saw three silhouettes moving out of our way and I almost uttered an exclamation. I had just recognized the three Pibrac brothers. A few days before, they had arranged a rendezvous with me in order to engage me in the band of which they were the chiefs and which exercised brigandage on the roads.

"When brigandage is carried out by men of noble birth like you and me," the eldest had said to me, "it becomes a noble action, analogous to war."

On seeing them, I marveled at the singular play of coincidences.

As my cousin had told me, it was the hour when the Porte de Muret was closed. I heard a few joyful words exchanged with the sergeant, who cried out when we had passed him to wish us *bon voyage*.

We started galloping into the darkness. We had a long stage to make in order to reach a convent beyond Muret. A little later, perhaps because of those emotions, I felt a violent thirst. I spoke to the monk who was beside me and asked him politely to pass me his gourd. I saw a kind of animated death's-head emerge from his hood, but he did not make any reply. Thinking that he was afflicted by deafness I touched his shoulder and repeated my request. He contented himself with uttering a bizarre interjection and hastened his mule.

I was tempted to grab him by the foot and tip him out of the saddle to punish him for his insolence. I was bending down to do that, when my cousin, who was bringing up the rear of our little troop galloped up to me and said:

"He's a holy man from Flanders who prays incessantly and never says a word to anyone. As there are ascetics in India devoted to strange divinities, the general of our order wanted to show those peoples that the Christian religion also has saints completely detached from the earth."

I was about to reply that I had heard mention of certain Languedocian saints whose sanctity did not prevent them from having a wine-jug within arm's reach, but I reflected that the wisest thing was to keep quiet, and continued to ride with my thirst in my throat. I reevaluated the rudeness of the holy man from Flanders.

Late in the night, Père Du Jarric showed me a light among the trees.

"That's the convent where we're going to sleep for a few hours," he said, cheerfully.

It was then that a strange incident occurred.

I heard a voice, that of my mother, calling me by name with an anguished accent. In spite of its resistance, I forced my mule to retrace its steps. I struck it with all my strength.

"Did you hear?" I said.

My mother's voice had pronounced my name distinctly. I assured Père Du Jarric that she had followed us at a run, and I believed it in spite of its implausibility. I even discerned a black dot far away, in the shadow of the road.

"We've been galloping for several hours," the Père repeated.

He was obliged to dismount and take my mule by the bridle, in spite of my protests.

"Fatigue has troubled your mind," he said.

He was doubtless right. When I went to sleep on the straw of a barn, I had a face bathed in tears.

THE ACCURSED HOST

"There are men predestined for evil, and they recognize one another immediately."

That remark by Isaac Andréa came back to my memory in a tavern in the port of Lisbon, where I has sat down in the twilight.

My cousin Du Jarric had given me a rather tidy sum of money in order to dress myself suitably. The usage to which the Order of Jesuits destined me—a usage of which I had not been given an explanation—involved, it seemed, a certain magnificence of costume. I had been only too glad to get rid of the wretched religious robe that, for the convenience of the journey, I had worn during the long traversal of Spain. I was now clad in a crimson doublet with a tapering collar maintained by a brass wire, a claret mantle and a bronze-hued belt. The sole defect of those garments was that they attracted some attention because of their extreme splendor—but it didn't displease me to be noticed.

It was not, however, my exterior apparel that attracted the gaze of a hideous man who had a whore on his knees. A scar enlarged his mouth in such a fashion that he had a rictus of hilarity. He was tall and thin but gave the impression of being extraordinarily strong. His eyes, which had a yellow gleam, sparkled at the sight of me, and he appeared to recognize me. He pushed the prostitute away and came toward me. He sat down on a stool beside me and spoke to me in Portuguese. I knew a few phrases of the language, which my cousin had taught me while I was riding alongside him.

"You're also embarking on the *Santa-Fé*," he said, putting his elbows on the table that was in front of me.

It was not a question; he didn't wait for a response.

"It's a ship that holds well at sea, and it's better to be on the *Santa-Fé* than the *Saint-Philippe*. We have her for at least six months of navigation! And then, one is never sure of arriving."

"Perhaps we met in Toulouse," I said, seeking to rediscover his face in my memories.

He shook his head, smiling, as if to dismiss words of no importance.

"If I have some good advice to give you, beware of the Inquisitors. They have spies everywhere and there are some on the *Santa-Fé*. What a breed!"

He spat in disgust. He had had dealings with the Inquisition's tribunals several times. Those tribunals were more redoubtable in Goa and India than elsewhere. Their tyranny had redoubled since Portugal had fallen under Spanish domination. Out there, the governor and the functionaries were still Portuguese, but the Inquisitors were all Spaniards. An infamous race!

I objected that those words were very imprudent, since he did not know whether I myself....

He started to laugh.

"There are people whom one recognizes immediately," he said, "as being of one's family. I mean your family of men."

I was not flattered.

"My name if Francisco Manoël, At least, I'm known by that name. You'll see that I'll be able to render you many services."

I was about to respond that I did not like to be addressed in a familiar fashion and that I did not expect any service from anyone, but he got up and made a rather imperious sign to me to pay for that we had drunk. I did so without protest.

I followed him to the harbor. Night was about to fall. We passed negroes from Mozambique and Hindus from Goa, an entire bizarre population from Portuguese colonies, which gave Lisbon the appearance of a city of another word. I was an object of curiosity because of the bright colors of my costume and the feather in my hat. I hid my embarrassment beneath an arrogant appearance. My astonishment at everything became perceptible. For my companion said to me:

"I'll wager that you've never seen the sea."

It was true. The Tage seemed infinite to me.

There was a great dark mass in front of us. It was the *Santa-Fé*. My cousin had shown it to me on the day of our arrival, and I had wondered how, by virtue of what force, such a heavy construction was able to set forth across the waves. I had before me a cathedral with several slender towers and a multitude of windows. An extraordinary animation reigned on the deck. On the gangplank that linked the ship to the quay men were running, transporting bales.

"Do you know what scurvy is?" Francisco Manoël asked me.

I made a sign that I did not.

"Well, perhaps it'll take your teeth." And with a frightful grimace, he showed me that he had lost his own.

Suddenly, a man who had the appearance of a steward jostled us, throwing us against the gangplank. He was preceding a little group that was advancing more slowly. Several men were carrying lanterns, and I heard one of them say: "It's this way. Be careful of those ropes."

In the shadows, I thought I recognized two women in the middle of the group. One of them was fat, and was laden with packages, but the one marching ahead had a delicate and slender silhouette.

My companion tugged on my arm and I heard him snigger.

The little group hesitated for a few seconds, until a voice shouted: "Come on, the gangplank's here."

One of the servants had raised his lantern to the height of a young woman's face.

She was wearing a wimple under which blue-tinted golden hair was parted over the forehead. A shawl made pleats over her shoulders and designed heir contour. She was clutching two or three roses preciously. She half-turned, doubtless to cast one last farewell glance at Lisbon, and the arc that her gaze followed passed over me like a living light. It seemed to me that when she walked, her dress made a silken music.

"Who's that?" I asked my companion.

"I don't know. I thought I recognized, however...."

His voice had the accent of a lie, but I didn't perceive that at the time. He went on: "At any rate, that will occupy you during the voyage—if the scurvy leaves you your teeth."

He started to laugh, and I understood that he would speak to me frequently about teeth and scurvy, for when men have found a disagreeable form of facetiousness, they never weary of repeating it.

I would have liked to launch myself on to the *Santa-Fé*, but my cousin had asked me to go back to the convent of the Order, where we were sleeping, before nightfall. It was the following morning at dawn that we were to embark with our baggage.

"Would you like to have an object, a talisman that will permit you to realize all your desires, especially evil desires?" Francisco Manoël had seized my arm, and was looking at me with an uncomfortable fixity. "Give me fifty reis, which I need to liberate my trunk tomorrow, and I'll give you a part—only a part—of the one I have on my breast."

I still had fifty reis and I gave them to him, for I have difficulty refusing money. But I thought that, our acquaintance being so slight, there was something premature about that request.

We had almost reached the door of the Order's convent. My companion opened the top of his doublet wide and showed me a leather pouch that he was wearing around his neck like a scapular.

"What you take for a cord is the rolled skin of a snake, and in the pouch, see...."

He stared at me. I saw a milky disk, and I suddenly felt invaded by a great sadness. "What is it?"

"You don't know anything about anything. It's a consecrated host that I've stolen. An accursed host!"

And with that, he drew away with long strides.

THE CHIMERAS OF TRAVELERS

Pushed by favorable winds, the *Santa-Fé* had been traveling along an invisible road over the ocean for several day.

I was busy marveling at the astonishing genius of the pilot, which permitted that enormous mass to go straight ahead, with the help of sails, when my cousin emerged from the narrow cabin that we shared with two other members of the Order and came toward me. He put his hands on my shoulders and stared attentively into the depths of my eyes.

"No, your eyes haven't changed color yet," he said, "but it will come."

"Why should my eyes be subject to a change?"

"Have you not noticed that all the men sailing with us on the *Santa-Fé* have a yellow gleam in their eyes?"

I replied that I had not noticed it.

"It's because the soul is reflected in the eyes. The gold about which everyone is thinking, the gold that is the common objective, eventually fixes its fugitive nuance in the gaze of avid men. Everyone goes to India for the conquest of gold, everyone has the same desire. Once, I didn't have the gilded eyes that I have now. There will come a time when your brown eyes of the sons of Toulouse will acquire the gleam of the metal that will become the motive for your actions."

"We're traveling," I replied, "with many good missionaries, Jesuits, Dominicans or Franciscans. I've heard it said that one is going to join Père Ricci in Peking,[6] that another counts on reaching the kingdom of Cathay. All of them are talking about nothing but pagans to convert. I imagine that it's spiritual gold that is tinting their eyes."

---

[6] The Jesuit Matteo Ricci (1552-1610) was one of the key figures in the early Jesuit missions to China, and was the first European to enter the Forbidden City, invited because of his great scholarship as an astronomer and geographer.

"Evidently, evidently, there are disinterested souls," my cousin hastened to say, "but for all objectives, gold in necessary. If the Order of Saint Ignatius possessed the riches of the Orient it would be master of the world, and then.... You're very young, Jean de Fodoas, and you'll understand that a little later."

And with that, he took a little notebook out of his pocket and he gave me a sign that he was about to resume his lessons in Hindi—for I was learning the rudiments of that barbaric tongue aboard the *Santa-Fé*, alternating it with the rudiments of Persian, the language of the literate in India.

"And when you know Hindi it will be necessary for you to learn Sanskrit, which is the language of Hindu scholars— for there are pagan scholars. It will be necessary for you to learn the Persian language, in which poets write, the language of the people of the Marwari and that of the land of Gujarat, the Talenga that is full of redoubtable sonorities, the Bengali that is harmonious, Liti, Betoche, Kashmiri and the language of the mountain people that is called Pushtu or Pathan—for it seems that in the land of India, more than elsewhere, God has emphasized the division of languages."

It was a familiar pleasantry of my cousin to threaten me with all those languages to learn; and I never failed to respond: "A man who handles a sword well is always able to express himself adequately."

However, I showed an extraordinary facility for the study of languages, which amazed my cousin. Besides which, there were long hours of tedium, Great ships like the *Santa-Fé* only advance over the roads of the sea by the force of the winds, and there are absences of wind that last for several days. After having emerged from an atrocious condition known as seasickness, I had rediscovered the life that I had believed lost, and, as I could not escape my cousin's exhortations, I had made the decision to learn Hindi as quickly as possible, at the same time as I perfected my Portuguese.

In any case, the little bench where the lessons took place was situated on the second deck, in such a fashion that I could see a narrow door: the door of a cabin where, for me, the living soul of the *Santa-Fé* was.

When you go back in memory over the most significant moments in your life, you perceive that in those capital moments, absolutely nothing happened.

Of what islands were we in sight? I have not retained the memory. A bell had rung announcing the hour of the evening meal. The upper decks emptied instantly, the soldiers running forwards and the sailors toward the rear. A double rumor came from the two extremities of the ship, which seemed absolutely deserted. Very high up on a mast, there was only one man any longer, gazing through a telescope.

Why I had not got to my feet when the bell rang I don't know, perhaps because I simply wasn't hungry, perhaps because I wanted to see how the sun, larger and redder than usual was about to disappear into the ocean.

I was sitting on the little bench that I called the Hindi bench, and my eyes wandered toward the two staircases that connected the deck that I was on with the rear castle. The balustrade that united the two stairways was made of two chimeras of sculpted wood, whose heads met in the middle and whose long fish-like tails descended to the right and left along the steps—for the *Santa-Fé* was painted and sculpted with an extreme artistry in all her parts.

And leaning on that balustrade, holding the head of a chimera in each hand, was the most beautiful creature that it had ever been given to me to see: beauty incarnate.

She was not the same as the woman I had glimpsed on the quay in Lisbon—or rather, she was the same one and another at the same time. Perhaps the sea air and the contemplation of space had given her that ardent life. What color were her eyes? I sensed that question being posed within me at the same time as I said to myself: *There's a rose-bush on the* Santa-Fé!—because she was holding a fresh rose in her right hand, and she was sweeping the heads of the chimeras with it, lightly. She had a broad white collar and the wind lifted the floating sleeves of her dress like two wings.

She seemed so devoid of density that when she came down the staircase I wondered why her feet were making movements to place themselves on the steps instead of floating. Her features had an ideal expression that I had not seen on any other face. She went past me without noticing my presence, and for a second, her head was exactly in the center of the circle of the sun, and she appeared to me to be aureoled with fire, like the heads of certain saints that I had seen in stained-glass windows.

Her name was Inès de Saldanna, and she was the sister of the Viceroy of India. What was she going to do out there? Join her brother, it was said, but in the familiar conversations that took place on deck in the evening I heard contradictory assertions in her regard.

The Viceroy was only appointed for three years, and he would soon be returning to Portugal. Why was he making his sister come when he was about to depart? And a sister he had never loved. Padre Pimenta[7] had known the Saldanna family for a long time and in the evening, when we were sitting on deck, he never ran out of stories about Aryas de Saldanna,[8] the most powerful man after the King of Spain.

---

[7] Nicolas Pimenta (1546-1613) was a Jesuit missionary whose letters from Pegu [nowadays Bagu in Burma] in connection with a mission undertaken in 1599 were published, and formed one of the sources of Pierre Du Jarric's account of India. He did not take part in any of the missions to Agra, as the present text alleges, although Du Jarric mingles details from his accounts with the accounts of those missions.

[8] Aires de Saldanha (1542-1605), who was appointed Viceroy of India in 1600, was a Portuguese soldier and the son of a famous navigator who had served for a long time in Portuguese India, struggling to defend it against the encroachments of the Dutch.

When the kingdom of Portugal had become Spanish, he had immediately betrayed his own people and rendered homage to the new masters. He had an appetite for wealth to an extraordinary degree—like everybody else, in fact; like all those who were going to the Indies and were not missionaries of a holy order. But that was not in order to enjoy life, to assuage is passions. He did not drink. He scarcely ate. He only desired wealth in order to buy sculpted dressers. He had filled the Saldannas' castle with them, to the point that the rooms were overflowing with dressers; he had placed them in all the pathways in the park. A park of sculpted dressers! Padre Pimenta had no doubt that he had solicited the position of Viceroy of India in order to have more facility in obtaining dressers from China, Macao and all the Spanish possessions in the Orient.

As for the beautiful Inès de Saldanna, Padre Pimenta deemed her a proud woman. Proud! He could not find any other word. Irreproachable surely, but proud! And how could it be explained that she did not like the Jesuits and that it had been necessary to send with her a Dominican, her confessor? Were there a young woman's sins that only a Dominican could hear? And that caricature of a ruined marquise that accompanied her like her shadow! And the rose-bush that she transported with her as if the roses that flowered between the sculpted dressers of the Saldanna park were more beautiful than the flowers of India!

Padre Pimenta had a bitterness of the soul that came from his sadness in becoming fat. He had already made the voyage to India twice, he fasted as best he could and only consumed a derisory nourishment, but in spite of that, his plumpness augmented with regularity that drive him to despair. He paced back and forth along the deck of the ship with the aim of struggling against the mysterious genius that he carried within him, and labored on the incessant augmentation of his form.

The Padre's face brightened with a smile of malign satisfaction when he added, lowering his voice: "And it is, at any

45

rate, one of our friends, Seigneur Francisco Manoël, who is charged with watching over her."

The members of the Order smiled in an understanding fashion, my cousin Du Jarric made an ambiguous grimace, and I had the desire then to cry out bluntly: "Do you know that he's carrying in his breast, in a rolled snakeskin, a stolen and profaned host?"

But I did nothing, my cousin having repeated several times that among eminent religious men, some of whom are saints, the duty of a young layman is to listen in silence.

"Have you not noticed," my cousin Du Jarric said to me one day, "that the *Santa-Fé* advances over the sea even when there isn't a breath of wind?"

No, I had not noticed any such thing. I had, on the contrary, just seen the ship remain in the most dismal immobility for two days.

"That is attributable, on the one hand, to Providence, and on the other to the great winged chimeras that are in certain souls and which aid matter to move. Look at that dry little man with the weather-beaten face, Benoît de Goës.[9] He's animated by a dream of discovery. He intends to reach Agra with us, the Emperor Akbar's capital. From there, all alone, on foot, he'll start marching northwards. He'll traverse the fabulous mountains that circle India; he'll advance through pagan lands where no Christian has ever set foot; he'll skirt an ocean of sand as vast as this ocean of water that we're traversing, and he'll attempt to reach the kingdom of Cathay, where a legend

---

[9] Benoît de Goës (1562-1617) undertook an epic journey, departing from Goa in September 1602, which eventually took him to the gates of China in December 1605, travelling disguised as an Armenian merchant. It made him famous, because his journal of the voyage was brought posthumously to Mattéo Ricci in Peking, who publicized it. The account of that journey in the present story is anachronistic, incompatible with various other datable events featured therein.

says that there is a baptized king who has a cathedral for a palace and who recognizes the divinity of Jesus."

"And what if that king doesn't exist?"

"Providence will bring him back among us. You've traveled for many days along the roads of Spain with our brother Octave of the Zaalberg family. You complained of not being able to get a word out of him. He doesn't speak to anyone and lives in his dream. He believes, secretly, that God has made the bones of his face stand out and has given him that skeletal appearance in order to recall the idea of death to the minds of those who might be tempted to forget it. He lived an ascetic life for a long time in a convent in Flanders, only committing the sin of pride—the pride of having a cranium like a death's-head! But he has quit his convent, traversed France and is sailing with us to India because of a story he had heard. He is going to find the Cross of Bartholomew."

"Bartholomew? Are you talking about the apostle who gave his name to a mountain in Ariège?"[10]

"The same. That apostle is reputed to have evangelized the Orient, and particularly India. When one finds oneself among the pagans who inhabit that land, one is obliged to observe that there is scarcely any trace of that distant evangelization, but one of our brothers, who traversed India from west to east, claimed that there exists somewhere, on a mountain, a ruined church that had once been built by Bartholomew. A few savage men who live in the vicinity have retained a vestige of Christianity. Above the altar of the church there is a great wooden cross, a massive cross, carved by the hand of

---

[10] Bartholomew, one of Jesus' twelve Apostles (although he is not mentioned in the Gospel of St. John, where he is replaced by Nathanael), was reported in a history written by Eusebius of Caesarea in the early fourth century and the slightly later writings of Saint Jerome to have undertaken a missionary voyage to India after the Ascension. The Jesuit missionaries to India did indeed search for evidence to confirm those legends, although the cross featured in the present story is an invention.

Bartholomew. It was been transmitted through the ages that the cross in question has the miraculous power of converting pagans. Where is it? In what region?

"The brother who knew that must have given the silent Octave a few indications as to the direction it is necessary to take in order to find that cross. He hasn't said anything about it. He obtained authorization from the general of the Order to depart, because the latter thought, with reason, that it was necessary to show the pagans a true Christian ascetic, as true as those provoked out here by strange divinities called Vishnu or Siva. Our clergy in Goa exhibit a liking for material enjoyments and luxury, alas, equal to that of the Spanish clergy. That the Christian capital of the Orient will one say see a living skeleton appear, carrying the Cross of Bartholomew, is Octave's secret dream."

Pierre Du Jarric raised his arm toward the nocturnal sky, as if to indicate a particular star to me amid the host of stars shining through the rigging.

"Our dream, the one that is guiding us—you and me—to India, is perhaps no less chimerical."

I sensed that he was in a confidential mood.

"I'd be very glad to know," I said, "why the Order of Jesuits has determined that a young man from Toulouse, only expert in handling weapons, should cross the seas and go into distant regions , where so many valiant Portuguese apparently seem more useful. Certainly, in exchange for my life, which was preserved by the magnanimity of the Provincial Father of Toulouse, I'm ready to do whatever will be required of me, but why must my activity be employed beyond the seas?"

"Know first of all," my cousin replied, "that men on whom one can count are strangely few in number. 'He's made of solid wood,' the Provincial Father said, 'but it's necessary that the wood doesn't catch fire.' Perhaps the moment has come to tell you...."

My cousin stood up and took a few steps, but as I stood up in my turn, he made me a sign to sit down again. I understood that he only had a desire to walk because of the gravity of what he was about to tell me.

"Doubtless you know, vaguely, for your education has been greatly neglected, that the Asiatic countries have been ravaged in recent centuries by destructive hordes of Mongols, who fell on the cities and killed their inhabitants. Those hordes came as far as Europe. Their most celebrated kings were Genghis Khan and Timur, and the Emperor Akbar, toward whom we're going, is the descendant of one of those terrible sovereigns—at least he affirms as much, for one never knows the truth about royal genealogies.

"The most curious particularity of those Mongols is that they do not settle in cities built of stone, like ours. They even have a horror of cities, the sight of which has always exasperated their appetite for destruction. They always have the desire to go further on. But like all men, they have a taste for riches, for gold, jewels and precious metals. After pillaging those riches, they cannot carry them all with them. What happens to them? What could happen to them?

"Imagine what you would do yourself, if you had at your disposal the treasures of a magnificent city like Bagdad or Kambalu, and if you were obliged to leave. Yes, put yourself in the place of one of those looter kings. You're going to mount your horse, you have fifty thousand cavaliers behind you and there at your feet, all sorts of riches. What do you do?"

"In truth, I'd have filled my pockets, I'd have filled a sack that could be transported on my horse, I'd grab the most precious things, and also the smallest."

"That's right. Sovereigns disposing of fabulous riches and always obliged to depart again because of the attractions of conquest, think about condensing those riches in such a fashion as to transport them in the smallest possible volume. Genghis Khan had a morbid liking for pearls. He had a camel follow him buckling under the weight of inestimable pearls. Later, Timur reduced his immense share of booty into diamonds, emeralds and rubies, and in his capital, Samarkand, he spent his leisure hours trading precious stones for lighter precious stones but purer in color.

"The treasure of the Mogul Emperors was transmitted from father to son. Genghis Khan had it buried under the ground. Timur had it transported into a grotto. Ulugh Beg took it to Samarkand and had a fortress temple built to shelter it, to which he gave the name of the House of Purity. He called it that because of the frightful impurity it contained. But one day, lightning struck the House of Purity and Ulugh Beg saw that as a bad omen.

"He was a strange sovereign, that Ulugh Beg, simultaneously a poet, a philosopher, an astronomer and a magician.[11] He set about studying the stars in order to discover the destiny of his treasure and the place where it ought to be deposited. The stars must have announced a redoubtable destiny to him. One evening, he ran down from the top of the tower from which he was examining the sky with a telescope. He assembled his guards and, clad in the white robe that he wore in imitation of the ancient philosophers and the Sufis, he mounted his horse and departed into the night with the treasure. It's said that he only returned to Samarkand a year later, and not a single man remained of those who had accompanied him. He had hidden the treasure of the Timurids somewhere in immense India.

"It is the destiny of treasures to be so well hidden that their possessors end up forgetting where they are and not having bequeathed their secret at the moment of their death. It does not seem that Ulugh Beg's descendants entered into possession of the treasure that condensed the riches originating from pillages such as the world has never known. The Emper-

---

[11] The Timurid ruler Ulugh Beg (1394-1449) was indeed a great astronomer, and built a great observatory in Samarkand in the 1420s. The territory he ruled, centered on what is now Uzbekistan, extended into northern Afghanistan, but not India, so any treasure he might have buried is highly unlikely to have been there.

or Akbar has searched for it in vain, and after forty years of sovereignty, he is still searching. Who would dare to say that Providence does not have pre-established aims? Perhaps it is to the Order of Saint Ignatius that the prodigious power that such wealth represents will revert."

I listened to my cousin full of astonishment, and wide-eyed. As he became excited, the tone of his voice lowered, he drew closer to me, and by virtue of a curious phenomenon, it seemed to me that his nose, which as very long, was elongated in my direction.

"There are pagans," he went on, "who, thanks to us, have been converted to the Christian faith. Not many, it's necessary to agree, but in sum, there are a few. Well, one of them, at the moment of his death, revealed to a member of our order…but that is too long a story, of which the details are unknown to me, which are the secret of our general in India: a great man, a great saint, Père Aquaviva.[12] It's sufficient for the moment for you to know that you, a humble Toulousan gentleman, who are, in sum, an ignorant man with a head devoid of a brain, are perhaps called to play a considerable role."

"Me? How?"

"Those formidable sovereigns have handled the precious metals of mosques and Persian or Turkish palaces, they have scrutinized the splendor of diamonds and the purity of pearls, and have secured within a coffer of small dimension the precious essence of our planet, everything that it contains of the stellar, in order that you, Jean de Fodoas, should load that coffer on to your back and restore it to its possessors by divine right, those who ought to have the mastery of gold, those who will govern the world by means of gold."

"Was it not imprudent to have chosen for such a task an ignorant man devoid of a brain?" I was vexed by the opinion

---

[12] Rodolpho Aquaviva (1550-1583) led the first Jesuit mission to Agra in 1580-83, and was the general of the Order thereafter.

emitted in my regard by my cousin. Although I perceived its sincerity, I thought that it was devoid of any basis.

"No, because, firstly, I answered for you, and the Provincial Father of Toulouse is a man who can read souls as I read a Bible."

"But where and how am I to accomplish this astonishing mission?"

"Everything in its time. We have many marine dangers to confront before then. And remember that the mission will be carried out as much in the spiritual as the material realm—more, perhaps. The Emperor Akbar is full of curiosity about the Occidental world.[13] The true religion attracts him. Twice already he has asked the Viceroy of Goa to send him missionaries. Between the two of us, if he is not converted already it's because of the clumsiness of the Fathers who have been sent to him. They were insufficiently cultivated men. They proceeded with the Emperor Akbar as they would with a negro king in Africa who had feathers in his hair and a fly-swatter for a scepter. He needs Toulousans in his presence. That is what was thought in Rome, and rightly so. For those who succeed in obtaining influence over that sovereign might direct half the world. I've spoken to you about a fabulous treasure, but the amity of that great man is perhaps even more estimable than the treasure of his ancestors. Now, he has asked for a

---

[13] Akbar the Great (1542-1605), the Mogul Emperor from 1556 until his death, who expanded that Empire vastly by conquest, invited the Jesuits to send missionaries to Agra, partly because of his curiosity about the Occident—he was a great scholar—but in particular because of his desire to found and promulgate a new monotheistic system of belief, which eventually became known as *Din-i-Ilahi* [a Persian term for religion, although Akbar's system was not a religion in the strict sense of the term, being devoid of scriptures and priests] fusing the traditions of Islam, Hinduism, Zoroastrianism and Christianity—an ambition that attracted the wrathful opposition of orthodox Muslims

young Occidental knight who belongs to the warrior caste—for out there, there are castes. It was thought in Rome that it would be better if that knight were not Portuguese. Your lucky star has determined that it should be you. It might be the case that a great destiny is reserved for you by Providence."

I was astounded by what my cousin had told me; but I believe that there is in every man the profound conviction that he possesses an admirable and as yet unrevealed genius. The conviction in question causes him to consider the unexpected favors of fortune as simple forms of the immanent justice that is the recompense of his genius.

I straightened up before the extent of the sunlit waters. In the distance, to my left, a confused strip of land extended, which was the African coast. If my cousin had told me that it was a province of my future empire, I would doubtless have replied, simply: "Good."

Such is the folly of youth.

ABOARD THE *SANTA-FÉ*

A rather parsimonious space had been reserved on the second deck for the monks and missionaries of all the Orders and heir retinue. An extended cord delimited the area, with no one could cross without valid reason; so the first days went by without my being in the presence of Francisco Manoël.

One evening, after the diner bell had sounded, I slipped along to the place where I had seen the marvelous apparition of the young woman with the rose. I knew from experience that events have a tendency to be reproduced in a similar fashion, if one finds oneself in the same place at the same time.

That did not happen on that day. The door on which my gaze was obstinately fixed opened, but my throat tightened with disgust when I saw the horrible Francisco emerge. He was chatting in a familiar fashion with the black-clad fat woman of forbidding appearance, who resembled the idea I had of Catherine de Medici, according to the tales of people who love to talk about monarchs. They were leaning toward one another and saying secret things. They had the appearance of accomplices. There was no doubt that the affiliate of the Jesuits who was part of the retinue of the divine Inès was that man, whose physique was horrible and who must have a soul worse than his visage.

The old woman went back into the cabin, closing the door, and Francisco perceived me. He almost uttered a cry of joy. Rapidly, he came down the few steps that separated us and sat down beside me.

Assuredly, he was playing an inexplicable comedy. I could not have such a great charm. He told me that he had searched for me, that he had often thought about me, that my presence was a great comfort to him. The horrible odor of human sweat that filled the space between decks was insupportable to him. He hated the Spanish soldiers, superstitious and limited men, who filled the entire rear section of the ship. On the other hand, all conversation with the monks was impossible. He was suffering a great deal from his solitude, but it was finally about to end. He sensed in me an open mind, a mind susceptible of understanding everything. And then again, was there not another bond between us?

And with that the tapped his chest mysteriously, at the exact height at which the mysterious scapular must be.

In any other circumstances I would have slapped his face and proclaimed aloud the nature of the sentiments that he inspired in me. I even stood up in order to do so. But in a second, the instruction that my cousin had repeated to me several times came to mind, that it is necessary to dissimulate what one is experiencing and always feign a great sympathy for one's interlocutor if one wants to succeed in the world. It was insensate to insult a man who occupied a position of confidence next to the most beautiful young woman I had ever seen. And then, who knows? Perhaps my character really seduced him. Although I had often been duped, I had also encountered spontaneous sympathies. There was also a mystery to clarify in the host that he carried on his person, and of which he had promised me a fragment, without my being able to explain that improbable promise.

So I sat down beside him again, and expressed to him the satisfaction I had in seeing him.

"You're my friend, and even my relative," he said, gripping me by the shoulders. "You understand me, don't you?"

I wanted to tell him that I did not understand him at all, but he didn't give me the time.

"Hatred! That sustains life better than amour. I once wondered why I didn't die of ennui and disgust. I didn't know that I had that salt, that leaven, within me. I hate them all, and God even more, who has created them, because of that primal injustice."

I thought that he might be drunk and I breathed in deeply order to catch a whiff of it; but no, he didn't reek of wine at all. He was expressing himself for the sake of expressing himself.

"Everyone supports that injustice lightly. They enjoy it. They even do their best to aggravate it. And it's their hypocrisy, above all, that horrifies me, their comedy and purity or sanctity. Virgins and monks! Ha ha! It's almost the same thing. They're worth as much as one another. And we, whom they've taken as domestics, also have our worth."

I made an immense effort to contain the word "servant." He must have perceived that, for he repeated it, emphasizing the syllables.

"I know, you descend from a very noble and very illustrious family of Toulouse. Very noble and very illustrious but ruined. Absolutely ruined. That's why you're a servant of the Jesuits. Me too! My family...that's a whole story. If I told you the name of it you might fall to your knees and remain there instead of going to take the evening meal, as you're about to do."

"There's no name that can make me fall to my knees," I told him, coldly.

But he paid no heed to my response.

"The essential thing, in life, is to understand that evil is more powerful than good, that the Devil, or what is thus called, is more powerful than God. I understood that a little late. But you're young and you'll go a long way, followed by the invisible companion. Only, remember one thing: if one serves the angel of evil, it's necessary to render him disinterested services. He's very demanding. He wants us to do evil for evil's sake. He too wants to recognize his own."

I stood up.

He isn't drunk, I thought, *but he's certainly slightly insensate. Otherwise, he wouldn't talk like that to a man who lives with monks, even if he's recognized that the man in question....*

I was traversed by a frisson, and I don't know why the image of my mother presented itself in my mind.

"*À bientôt*—the two of us are destined to see one another frequently."

And he tapped his chest again, and winked.

I shall not recount the numerous and varied incidents of the voyage of the *Santa-Fé*, because that is not the object of this narrative, and I am not tracing these lines to remind myself of landscapes, the insignificant conversations of ecclesiastics or picturesque adventures.

I shall not evoke the dismal days of flat calm, the ardor of the sun, the fury of the tempests. I shall not attempt to resolve the enigma of the blue flame. In the topmost rigging of the ship one sees, on certain nights, an elongated flame, blue in color. Sometimes it dances and sometimes it stretches; but it is always sad. I perceived that sadness with certainty, without being able to understand why. A mariner had fallen into the sea on the first night of our voyage. He was a young man from Lisbon, and the other mariners said that it was his soul in torment that was roaming over the masts. But I didn't believe that, because the mariner, having died a short distance from his native city, would have taken advantage of the subtle lightness of his new corporeal state to return to his homeland, instead of haunting the vertiginous parts of the rigging.

I shall not describe how we encountered the Dutch carracks, how we fired cannons at them, how there was a temporary thought of a boarding, how I was politely asked by the captain to take my place among the combatants, and my great disappointment when a sudden change in the wind permitted the carracks to draw away.

I shall not describe the appearance of scurvy when we had passed the Cap des Aiguilles, the diabolical joy of Francisco Manoël in announcing to that there were more than fifty sick men on the ship and how he subsequently made a sign to me from a distance, touching his gums with hopeful laughter.

I shall not go into detail regarding the insulting words that I exchanged in the chart room, where I had gone to return a map borrowed by my cousin, with a certain Alvarez de Lima, a fat man who occupied the position of Second Lieutenant aboard the *Santa-Fé*. I shall merely report what happened the following day between him and me, because of what happened to my soul on that occasion. And it is only what happens to the soul, even in fleeting fashion, that is of any importance.

Once the insulting words had been exchanged, it was agreed that we would measure ourselves with épées as soon as an opportunity arose. It arose the following day.

The *Santa-Fé* sometimes dropped anchor close to land when there was an opportunity to renew our supplies of water. The launch was then put to sea and a crew of mariners descended on land, with a few soldiers to ensure their security. In addition to transporting the water, and if it were possible, they had to buy fruits from the natives. As that would take all day, a number of the sick obtained permission to go ashore, in order to improve their health by breathing terrestrial air.

We were in sight of a tree extraordinary by virtue of its size and known to navigators because a small stream flowed not far away from it. The stout Alvarez had been designated as commander of the launch and the water-gatherers. I contrived to be in the party that went ashore.

There were a few sniggering and menacing men on the shore who had long hair parted into long tresses, and bizarre small bones suspended from their ears. I was struck by the thinness of their legs. They were aware of the redoubtable character of firearms, for they pointed them out to one another with their fingers. They had no fruits or vegetables, but they made it understood by signs that some could be found inland, not far away, by following a shady path.

Alvarez took four men with him and followed the path, while we waited on the shore.

We waited for a long time. The sun descended in the sky. A gunshot had resounded in the distance, but we had not paid any heed to it. A signal from the *Santa-Fé* instructed us to return to the ship. The water had been in the launch for a long time, and we were very perplexed as to what we ought to do. We were about to send the *Santa-Fé* the conventional signal employed in case of an unfortunate event when, at the edge of the brushwood that rose up at the edge of the sand, we heard voices speaking Portuguese and we recognized our five companions.

We did not recognize them immediately. They were entirely naked, and the whiteness of their skin gave them, in the last rays of the sun, an appearance of repulsive larvae. It was only when they were close to us that we were certain of their identity.

They were full of fury as well as confusion. They had allowed themselves to be caught in an ambush and had been unable to put up any resistance. They had been stripped of all their garments by negroes, who had even plunged their hands into their hair to see whether it concealed any precious objet. Doubtless they had only been left alive for fear of reprisals.

Alvarez uttered many blasphemies and would have liked us all to set forth in pursuit of his attackers. The obscurity that was advancing rapidly in all directions rendered that project impossible. His fury was increased by the ridiculous quality that his nudity gave him. In spite of his rage he observed me from the corner of his eye and I did not fail to let a smile of pity stray over my face, for both the naked man and the leader who had allowed himself to be stripped without fighting.

He marched toward me, proclaiming that I must be very glad to have that pretext for avoiding the projected combat.

"The combat could, however, take place," I responded.

"Of course! A naked man against a man who might have a coat of mail under his doublet.

"What?"

I thought I had misheard, but he really had formulated the insulting suspicion.

"Arm yourself, wretch. We'll fight with equal weapons."

In a matter of seconds I had taken off all my garments, including my shoes, for he might have had a disadvantage walking barefoot over the pebbles. I took a long sword from the belt of a stupefied soldier, which I lifted alongside mine to show that it was visibly of greater dimension, and I threw it at Alvarez' feet, crying: "Defend yourself!"

I was about to make the gesture of pricking him in order to stimulate him, but there was no need for that. It was him who delivered the first thrust, powerful enough to run me through if I had not parried it.

We were at a place where the beach was not far from a barrier of trees and creepers. Night had fallen almost at a stroke, as if to give the two naked men to measure themselves at their ease.

It was then that a strange revolution was produced within me. I ceased abruptly to be myself, the Jean de Fodoas of familiar passions. I had just been stripped of my nature, as if it had been linked to my garments. My thoughts had departed with the lid of my hat. I had become a primitive man again. I had remounted the course of the ages.

That impression was so powerful that that the trees that were a short distance away were transformed, becoming a benevolent shelter, as if I were accustomed to sleep amid their branches. I was attempted to make use of my sword as a club, taking it in two hands, at the risk of cutting myself on the blade. The gesture I made was nearly fatal to me, for my adversary remained a modern man, skillful at taking advantage of an awkward gesture.

I don't know how the combat would have finished, but I was suddenly grabbed around the midriff and thrown down on the ground. I understood that in front of me, Alvarez had been subjected to the same fate.

Among the passengers who had come shore with us, there was an individual of severe and taciturn appearance, but who enjoyed a great authority over us all, and whom the captain of the *Santa-Fé* surrounded with the greatest respect. He had the title of the Grand Prior of the Dominicans of India. Seeing us fighting, he had imperiously given the order to a few soldiers to seize us and disarm us.

He criticized Alvarez de Lima severely for his conduct. The launch was waiting, we might have been attacked at any moment by the natives, and he, who was in command of our troop, instead of seeking to dress himself decently and giving the necessary orders was fighting with a young madman whose folly only merited the rod.

The rod! As I got dressed, and retook possession of my sword, I thought that it had been between my hands merely a simple piece of wood. Thus, the thing that I had considered as my own soul and of which I was so proud, was very little! It had sufficed for me to take off my clothes and find myself in the posture of a primitive man, to become that primitive man again, a savage, almost an ape! And I remembered with horror that at the moment when I was about to engage in combat with Alvarez I had darted a nostalgic glance at the trees full of obscurity—nostalgic because of my confused desire to go and caper among their branches, biting fruits and suspending myself, head down, by the tail of a beast!

I shall not describe the sterile hours that I spent gazing at the door of a cabin from which I saw the woman who was similar to Catherine de Medici emerge far more frequently than the marvelous young woman. I shall not detail all the questions I asked in order to enlighten myself as to the mystery by virtue of which Inès de Saldanna saw all the men sailing with me on the *Santa-Fé*, with the sole exception of myself, as if I had been struck by the power of invisibility. Sometimes, she stopped to say something to a monk, sometimes she smiled at a mariner agape with admiration, but when she passed beside me it was exactly as if she had passed beside nothing, a void in the air. Imagination draws strange or odious things from its depths and I set about inventing an enormous incongruity that would have signaled my presence, but fortunately, I did not realize it, and I remained invisible, as if I had been touched by some magic wand with the power to confer that gift.

I shall only recall what Francisco said when I was stupid enough to complain to him about that invisibility.

"The pure don't see the impure, those who are at the opposite pole of their nature, even if they have teeth like you and keep them in spite of the scurvy."

And he burst into laughter that had as much joy in it as hatred. My teeth were a source of constant jealousy for him and he never wearied of talking about them.

I shall not say anything about Cap Sainte-Marie and the island of Madagascar, nothing about the isle nicknamed the cemetery of the Dutch, which nearly became the cemetery of the Portuguese, nothing about our stopover in Mozambique and the visit of a Muslim king who was accompanied by thirty pirogues crowned with parasols. I shall say nothing about the Indian seas, the waters of which are similar to those of other seas, but where an old mariner who had sailed all over the world pointed out to me blue phosphorescences that are seen nowhere else.

I shall say nothing about the Sanganian pirates who attack ships with a multitude of small boats and set them ablaze with fireships that run over the waves and of which they obtained the secret from one of their people who had gone to study sciences in China. Those pirates were the preoccupation and the terror of everyone for a week, especially the captain, although he pretended ardently to desire them to appear over the horizon, certain that he could exterminate them with stones and musket-fire. That certainty made him sweat anguish in large droplets.

I shall say nothing about the coasts of India looming on the horizon, the actions of grace sung by the crew, the soldiers and the monks kneeling on all the decks when the *Santa-Fé* felt the breath of a terrestrial wind blowing the odor of trees into the sails, and when she entered the little bay of Sualis, three leagues from Surat.

I shall merely report the last words that I heard from the mouth of Francisco Manoël on the *Santa-Fé*.

Men were transporting large boxes that belonged to Inès de Saldana. Those boxes made a pile near a suspended staircase that was connected the ship a little later to the quay. I felt a great melancholy, thinking that it would probably never be given to me to see again the woman who, for long hours, had been for me the beauty of the world.

Francisco approached me and he clasped my arms while winking, as if I were an accomplice.

"Rejoice," he said. "I've labored for you. Yes, for you, for, in the final analysis, it's the young, those who have teeth with which to bite, who profit from the effort of others."

I looked at him in amazement. I was leaning on my sword, and I had the bizarre sensation, experienced before, that it was alive, that it was an animate individual that was attached to me.

"Thanks to me, the young woman with the rose-bush, the purest of the pure, is going to carry on her, on her body, next to her flesh, a tiny fragment of a soiled host, an accursed host, a diabolical host."

"But how does that concern me?"

Francisco looked at me, with a second of surprise because of the sincerity of my voice. Then he shrugged his shoulders.

"Come on, don't pretend to be stupid."

And he drew away.

IN SURAT

In reviving in memory the days of my arrival in Surat, I can measure how great my stupidity was, and with what blindness it filled me. In truth, I cannot measure it exactly, because there is no balance for stupidity; it has no weight or value. I can only consider its mass and its obscurity. But the fruit of my experience is that, from the accumulation of stupidities, honest conduct and a clear conception of things was born. So, I have set aside the regret, as a gardener removes the weeds in his garden in order to permit the cultivated plants to grow freely.

It had been agreed that, in order to rest from the fatigues of the voyage, we would spend a few days in the vast establishments, both commercial and religious, that the Portuguese Jesuits possess in Surat. I had no fatigue, and I took advantage of that time to take account of all the admirable novelties that were around me, and to perfect myself in the knowledge of the Persian and Hindi languages.

A young Toulousan thus transported to the kingdom of Gujarat is cast into astonishment by the easy and placid manner in which elephants circulate in the streets; by the strange honors rendered to miserable cows, honors all the greater the older they are and the more extensively covered with pustules; by the manner in which the seashells are utilized that serve as panes in the windows of houses, as if they were decked out in honor of the sea; by the veils that a great many women wear over their faces, with the exception of the eyes, while others allow their faces to be seen, which are sometimes of incomparable beauty.

I was particularly astonished by the order that reigned in the streets and in the places known as bazaars, where a crowd circulates every hour of every day larger than the one that gathered in Toulouse for the visit of King François I, which was the largest that had ever been seen in that celebrated city.

I ought to say that I experienced a certain mortification on seeing how perfectly organized the police were among a people that I was obstinate in believing, in spite of the stories told to me by men worthy of faith, like my people, to be more barbaric than those of the Occident. The simple guardians of the streets had sparkling suits of armor that would have filled the Cornusson son with pride if he had possessed one. They only had to raise the metal rod surmounted by a ball of steel that was the emblem of their power and people stood aside before them respectfully. I was assured that nocturnal aggressions were unknown, and that one could go abroad in the streets of Surat at any hour unarmed, even those where disreputable people lived, for it was about those of which I first sought information.

Charity, although not Christian, appeared to me to have a much greater development than it did in Toulouse and all the other cities through which it had been given to me to pass. At the principal crossroads and at the gates in the ramparts women of extreme ugliness stood, who had bags of a sort on their back. Their ugliness bore no relation to the character of their action. Those women considered the passers-by attentively. Sometimes, they chose one of them and ran toward him swiftly. I thought at first that they were the kind of creatures that one sees in all cities, and, seeing their procedure, I thought about avoiding them. But I noticed that instead of soliciting the most richly dressed men, who seemed to be to be designated to then, they only addressed themselves to the most wretched, contrary to what the strolling players and moors of Languedoc do.

I enquired as to the causes of that way of acting and learned that they were rich ladies who had made vows to gods bearing strange names and were giving poor people objects, nourishment or money. I had known charitable ladies, and my mother was one of them, but I had never seen such a large number of them choosing with so much care those who were to receive their charity, and devoting their entire day to it.

My astonishment increased when I discovered that charity was devoted as much to animals as to humans, and even extended to insects. But many travelers have described the mores of Hindus, their way of living and the beauty of their land. I refer those who are avoid to know more to the work that my cousin Du Jarric has just concluded, and for which he has gone to Bordeaux in order to reach an understanding with a skillful printer. That work will comprise three quarto volumes and will cause a great deal of astonishment. Pierre Du Jarric had made enquiries a painter in order to illustrate the historic episodes but I told him that the most beautiful illustrations are those one composes oneself with the brush of the imagination. Even the greatest Italian masters often diminish the beauty of scenes, which they represent with an excess of exactitude. He yielded to my arguments, and the book will appear without images.

There are many important facts that I am not reporting but I shall pause to retrace a minimal incident, to which I shall only attribute a significance much later. When one looks backward, one perceives that it is very trivial incidents that are the luminous reference points of existence.

I had not addressed a word to Brother Octave since the night when I had thought about seizing him by the foot and tipping him off his mule because he had responded to the request I had made him to lend me his gourd. I had not known that a great saint does not carry a gourd. Now, it appeared that Brother Octave was a great saint. Everyone repeated that on the *Santa-Fé*, but with a slight hint of irony, a suppressed smile. It was understood when one talked about him that he was slightly mad. We had traveled side by side on the roads of Spain for long days, and had been neighbors on the *Santa-Fé* without him paying the slightest attention to my existence. I had made observations about that rudeness several times to my cousin, but he had always replied that a man who can see God cannot see a young Toulousan laden with sins at the same time. In truth, his immeasurably skeletal physique inspired an unacknowledged dread in me.

The third day after our arrival in Surat, there was no talk of anything in the house of the Portuguese Jesuits of anything but the departure of Brother Octave. He should, in principle, have waited for the authorization of the co-administrator of his order, who was in Goa. Doubtless he found the time long, even though he was perpetually plunged in prayer. It seemed to me that, for such an activity, it was of no importance whether one did it in one place rather than another.

It appears that he sincerely believed in the possibility of finding the church and the Cross of Bartholomew. He had decided to head eastwards, as the saint had done at another time. He had just procured an enormous piece of wood larger than himself, and had resolved to carry it on his shoulder until he could exchange it one day for the Cross of Bartholomew.

It was morning, in front of the harbor of Surat that the Portuguese house overlooks, with its great metal portal, whose solidity had been so useful a few years before, when Surat was nearly captured by the Sanganians. Brother Octave had just made his adieux with few words, as was his custom. The Grand Prior of the Dominicans of India was there; I was going out at the precise moment when he was concluding a final futile exhortation to persuade him to remain. Brother Octave already had his piece of wood on his shoulder. I found myself face to face with him and thought too late how misplaced my presence might be in that gathering of eminent religious men.

A frisson ran through me. Brother Octave had immediately fixed me with the hollow eyes of his skeletal head, and his eyes widened. I had the sentiment that I was about to be subjected to some mortification to which it would be impossible for me to respond; and that sentiment augmented when Brother Octave dropped his piece of wood at his feet.

Suddenly, before I had time to slip away, he enveloped me with his long arms and hugged me against his breast, and I felt wrinkled lips on my forehead.

"I recognize you now. It's you, and you alone, who are my brother."

I perceived that a great surprise ran through the audience, all the greater because he had emphasized the word "alone."

When I had recovered from my own astonishment, Brother Octave was drawing along the quays with long strides. He was heading eastwards.

I thought about the sort of fraternity that Francisco Manoël had recognized in me, a man who occupied in the globe of souls the pole opposite to that of Brother Octave, and I remained perplexed.

The wonder caused by the novelty of things was not sufficient to take away a great melancholy that came to me from the sudden sentiment of my insignificance.

When I was in Toulouse and when I saw a woman whose beauty struck me with admiration I had the internal conviction that it would always be possible for me, by devoting time and obstinacy to it, to get to know her and make her love me. The nobility of my family could, strictly speaking, counterbalance my poverty, if it were a young woman of high birth, and as for the others, I knew that one arrived at one's goal by means of bold actions. The celebrated Marie Cose had dismissed, in order to receive me, magistrates and judges of the Parlement, and I possessed a little key to a hidden door to her house overlooking the Quai de la Dalbade. As for Bérangère de Palassol, I had only had to meet her gaze; I knew that when she had returned to her Château de Lauragais she would elude the surveillance of her brothers, jealous and deformed lords, in order to meet me at a bend in some sunken road or beneath the poplars of the Hers.

But as soon as he quits his city and his homeland, a man loses a power that he had thought his own, but which remains attached to places that could not accompany him. Carried on the *Santa-Fé*, balanced on the vast and unknown element that is the ocean, my importance had become almost negligible, in relation to men, and what was more serious, I had diminished in my own eyes. The young woman I had admired was placed at the summit of a hierarchy of which I occupied an inferior degree. If it had happened that the sister of the Viceroy of India had asked who the young man in the dazzling costume was that she sometimes saw sitting on a few ropes on the *Santa-Fé*, the reply she would have received was that he was a subaltern gentleman in the pay of the Jesuits. I did not doubt that the question had not been asked; but I could not doubt the character of the reply. I saw then a long ladder analogous to the one of which there is mention somewhere in the Bible, and I was sitting on the bottom rung, while he splendid Inès de Saldanna was at the other extremity, very far from the subaltern gentleman.

I knew that the young woman, accompanied by the double of Catherine de Medici, her servants, and doubtless her rose-bush, had received hospitality in the house of the governor of Surat, in the fortress that dominated the city.

The following day, as I was gazing at the accumulation of beggars and lepers not far from the port of Brampour and was wondering why they did not put bandages, or even leaves, on their wounds to prevent thousands of flies from covering them and laying their eggs in them, I heard a sound of trumpets and the noise of horses. A whirlwind of dust overflowed the zigzags of the road that ended at the fortress.

Several policemen with their sticks surmounted with steel balls parted the crowd. A man of immeasurable stature whose head was surmounted by a green turban was playing the trumpet. He was followed by thirty horsemen clad in dazzling uniforms with flat metal helmets analogous to the silver plates on which soup is served in rich Toulousan families. Those horsemen surrounded two palanquins whose drawn curtains were, doubtless by coincidence, the same color as the trumpet-player's turban. Behind them were four or five individuals on horseback with turbans of various colors, whose rich garments indicated an elevated status. One of them had a long gray beard, which he allowed to float ostentatiously, and one sensed, by the gesture favored by the wind that was lifting it, that that beard was a subject of care and pride for its possessor.

The cortege passed by rapidly. I flattened myself against the vault of the monumental gate of Brampour in order not to be jostled by the horses. The horseman who came immediately after the bearded man gave me a little amicable sign, and I recognized Francisco Manoël.

I had no need of the gift of second sight to know that the first palanquin held Inès de Saldanna, alongside—of that I was less sure—the rosebush that never quit her.

I nearly started running under the stone vaults of the gate of Brampour. The crowd of lepers had closed up behind the cortege. The insects, above their wounds, made a kind of cloud with the dust. I returned at a slow pace.

MY FIRST MEETING WIH THE EMPEROR AKBAR

The Portuguese mission was *en route* to Agra. It comprised four Jesuits, chosen from among the cleverest and most eloquent, those who had the greatest knowledge of the religions and languages of Asia.

My cousin Pierre Du Jarric surpassed them all, in my opinion, because he had a sense of the comical in life, and disguised it under a severe gravity. Now, the man is very strong who always laughs internally but never permits others to know that he is laughing.

Father Pimenta was a fat man of jovial aspect, who had in reality no joy in him, with the consequence that his external appearance constituted a permanent lie. He sensed that lie and suffered from it. Sometimes he tried to conform with his physique and gave his words a false joviality. Sometimes he abandoned himself to his true nature, which was bitter. He was talkative and interested in little things and trivia. Perhaps those who had chosen him had mistaken his qualities as a talkative man for a noble eloquence and a knowledge of the human heart.

Father Monserrate,[14] who came from Goa and had joined us in Surat, was reputed to be a saint. But were they not all saints, more or less? He was full of seduction because of the radiation of faith that animated him. His seduction also came from the desire he had to exercise it. He suffered if he did not inspire a visible and active amity in all the people he approached. A fortunate illusion led him to believe that he drew all hearts after him. He had been part of the first mission that

---

[14] The Jesuit Antonio de Monserrate accompanied Rodolfo Acquaviva on the first Jesuit mission to Agra, and wrote a commentary on that mission that was one of the sources of Pierre Du Jarric's history, but he did not return there in the early 1600s as the present narrative asserts.

had sojourned with Akbar. He assured us that he had left extraordinary sympathies in the Court of Agra. He even thought that if his arrival had been announced in advance, many great lords would come to meet him on their elephants.

The Emperor Akbar, he told us, had been on the point of converting to the Christian religion, thanks to him, and but for the incompetence of Father Pignero.... His desire to please was so great that he even had need of the amity of the insignificant individual that I had to be for him. If a taciturn expression lingered on my face he thought that I was holding something against him for some trivial cause. So, in order not to sadden him, I put a broad smile on my face as soon as I looked in his direction.

Father Antoine Pignero[15] was dominated by the idea of geography. He dreamed of nothing but the traces of rivers and designs of mountains. For him, India was a geographical map. He did not want to die without realizing a great work: the exact map of Asia. But there was an obscure region there, the kingdom of Cathay. According to the accounts of travelers, the kingdom was immense, but for some, it was confounded with China, for others it was different, a vaster neighbor of that already-vast kingdom. That was a very important difference for a designer of maps who has geographical verity as an ideal.

Father Pignero no longer had any but one subject of conversation: the confusion of the geographer Ortelius. For him, all the maps in the Ortelius atlas were erroneous. He lived with all the falsities of Ortelius present in his mind. But he had a singular form of character. He grasped with extraordinary rapidity whatever might be most disagreeable to his interlocu-

---

[15] The Father Pignero given that name in Du Jarric's history was Emmanuel Pinheiro or Pigneiro (1556-1618), who accompanied Jerome Xavier on the third mission to Agra in 1595, and spent a long time there, remaining after Akbar's death, but the character in the present novel only appears to have borrowed the surname.

tor, and said it immediately. He wanted to confound not only Ortelius but all men. Everyone had to be put in his place, he said. If a river had two outflows, it was not him who would give it three. I estimated privately that a nature so scantly conciliatory was poorly chosen for the conversion of a sovereign.

A taciturn officer was charged with accompanying us. He had doubtless been chosen because of his grave humor, because it was a matter of escorting monks. The fathers, who liked making speeches, would have preferred a more talkative man. He had a guard of six men with him. It was not a matter of defending us, because one enjoyed a perfect security on the roads. I wondered, on the journey, how the roads were maintained. They reminded me of the residues of Roman roads that I had seen between Toulouse and Narbonne. The difference was that those of India were bordered, about every hundred meters, by a heap of admirably white stones, which permitted couriers bearing messages to see their direction on dark nights. Another difference was that they were sometimes traversed by a tiger, which seized the messenger. That happened quite rarely, I was assured. Savage tigers pullulate in the region. They are courageous and extremely cruel.

Although journeys were made in palanquins carried by men or carts pulled by oxen, we were, exceptionally, all on horseback. Brother Benoît de Goes went on foot. He was not part of the mission but was going to Agra to obtain letters of recommendation from the Emperor that would favor his journey to the limits of the empire and even further. Further on was the mysterious and infinite domain that extends beyond the Himalayan mountains. He had to reach on foot the kingdom of Cathay, which might not exist. That involved a very long march, and he said that he did not want to soften himself at the outset by having himself carried by a horse. When we drew ahead of him he shouted at us to go more rapidly, in order to force him to start running.

Father Pimenta joined him and walked, holding his horse by the bridle, in the hope of getting thinner, but he stopped on the second day, claiming that he had noticed a slight augmentation of his plumpness after a day's walking.

A mule carried presents from the Jesuits to the Emperor. Those presents were simultaneously modest and splendid. They were contained in a chest from Cordova, lined inside with metal in order to protect its contents from damp. The chest was a work of art in itself. There was a Bible printed by Gutenberg's own hands, and in which the great man had written something, a kind of dedication to God. It had been bound in Venice by a great artist in bindings whose name I forget. The material of that binding, which was, I believe, skin cut from the back of a young calf, reproduced angels around a Jehovah with an irritated face and a large sword.

The chest also contained the Ortelius atlas that had appeared a few years before and had excited the enthusiasm of European scholars and navigators—with the exception, of course, of Brother Antoine Pignero.

That brother did not weary of making the slightest pleasantry. If the mule stumbled or passed over a steam he would run up with a simulated zeal crying: "Protect the Ortelius atlas!"

The Jesuits' third present was not in the chest with the Ortelius atlas and the Gutenberg Bible but in front of it; it preceded them. That was me: I was a gift offered to the Emperor Akbar.

Ought I to be humiliated by that or to glory in it? When my cousin and the Provincial Father of Toulouse had first decided to send me to India, they had spoken in my presence in Latin, an ancient and scholarly language of which I did not have the comprehension. During the evenings spent on the deck of the *Santa-Fé* the brothers who had expressed themselves in Portuguese or French had sometimes suddenly employed Latin and I noticed that it was always when it was a matter of the Emperor's gifts, the word *equus* recurred again. I had asked what the word signified. It meant "horse."

I learned that the Emperor, a great lover of horses, had asked for one of the marvelous French or German chargers of which he had heard mention. Now horses, more delicate than humans, cannot stand up to six months of navigate. Why was that, given their robust physique? I guessed that the movements of the sea, which are atrocious in nature, are only tolerable because one knows that they will come to an end. Horses placed on the deck of a ship do not know that they will arrive in a port some day, and, not being sustained by hope, they die.

Anyway, it did not matter. The Jesuits, being unable to offer a fine horse, were offering a fine man instead. Akbar was a warrior and prized courageous men. That reduced me somewhat to the level of slaves whom one compels to show their teeth and the strength of their biceps in Oriental markets. On the other hand, it is honorable to be presented as a model of strength and courage. I had told the Jesuits that I knew what my role as a substitute for the horse entailed, and that I would dispense them of the ironic delicacy that caused them to express themselves in Latin in my presence.

I aspired to show that I was no kind of slave. The opportunity to do that was promptly given to me.

It was the middle of the day, and we had just traversed the so-called city of Nader, which consists of houses with straw roofs disseminated on the sides of a mountain, amid ponds and fragments of exceedingly thick and high ramparts. One wonders what function such stone constructions can serve. Undoubtedly there was once a vast city there of which only a few vestiges remain. It is a curious custom in India to build cities with ramparts and monuments and abandon them fairly quickly, in order to go and construct others in more distant locations.

A guard with a steel ball came to inform us that the governor, informed of the passage of monks on their way to see the Emperor, was awaiting us in his palace in order to offer us refreshments.

That palace was situated outside what was known as Nader and was a kind of country house of rather magnificent appearance, the architecture of which was reminiscent of that of many palaces in Spain.

The governor received us with a great deal of affability. He was a short, thickset man with bow-legs. That defect was all the more visible because they were bare. He had us sit down in a large room covered with precious carpets, inviting us to take our places beside him on cushions. He had abundant hair gathered on top of his head, like a woman. I supposed on seeing the quality of the *objects d'art* arranged on a set of shelves and he complicated beverages that he had served to us that he was a very refined man. That was also attested by the jewels that he wore on his fingers. He must have been afflicted by some skin disease because he had a bandage on one knee and another on his arm. As soon as he was seated he took off his shoes, telling us that his feet were hurting. He expressed himself in Persian but he told the Brothers that he knew Latin.

He's a great literate, I thought.

He had only cast a single glance at me, a singular one, such as one casts at a women in order to assess her physical value, or a catamite, or even a servant. Then he paid no more attention to me. I seemed to discern a slight astonishment when I sat down.

I had experienced a surge of blood of a dolorous nature at that and had blushed, which always vexes me because I feel diminished in my own eyes. Nevertheless, I had conquered it.

All went well. Nothing could have caused the anticipation of the slightest incident. I noticed, however, that my perspicacious cousin darting a sideways glance at me in which there was a kind of recommendation.

Our host had a servant behind him with broad shoulders, who was fanning him with a peacock feather fitted to the end of a pole at least six feet long. To one side, an old black woman, her legs folded, was crushing betel leaves and areca nuts with a massive golden pestle in an ivory mortar. She worked very rapidly, took the paste that was in the mortar, made a ball of it and introduced it into her master's mouth. At each new pellet, the latter spat on the cushions—which was not the action of a distinguished man, and must have necessitated an extraordinarily frequent renewal of the fabrics. And he seemed to have the obligation to chew a large number of the pellets, for he was moving his jaw with an extreme rapidity.

Suddenly, he clapped his hands, and, leaning toward Father Pimenta, addressed him particularly as if to a connoisseur of what he was going to show him, and said to him in a low voice: "You're going to see pretty dancing girls."

And indeed, several dancers and musicians irrupted into the room.

I almost exclaimed that it was unbecoming to give monks a spectacle of dancing girls, which normally had a lascivious character. I even opened my mouth to do so. Perhaps the governor of Nader had been misled by Father Pimenta's jovial appearance. A fat man always suggests the idea of carnal enjoyment. It was necessary to inform the governor of his impolite error.

But the Fathers must have been aware of customs of which I was ignorant, for I saw them nodding their heads gravely, appearing to thank their host, who seemed to me to be very inappropriate.

The dancers numbered five and had their faces uncovered. Only Muslims are veiled. The others profess the unknown and strange religions that are called pagan. The musicians numbered three, and one of them, who was holding a minuscule tambourine, had a physique so majestic that I immediately thought of Moses, and to whom I gave that name mentally.

At first the dancers appeared to me to be ugly. Their robes were perfectly virtuous, falling all the way to the feet and not allowing the slightest gleam of flesh to show. When they began to dance, though, I saw that one of them, who must have been very young, was ravishing.

The dance appeared to me to be devoid of interest. It was more a dance of arms and shoulders than legs. The music was slow and had something ensorcelling about it. The governor seemed to take an extreme pleasure in it and leaned forward to gaze at the youngest dancer, but without interrupting the movement of his jaws for an instant. Every time a dance concluded, he clapped his hands, and the dancers resumed a new step. He never gave them time to breathe.

But what happened, all of a sudden? Was the young dancer, who was the star of the troupe, and whom I had heard named Sita, fatigued? She seemed to be giving signs of impatience, stamped her foot, said something in a language I did not know, and fell back among the cushions. There she struck a nonchalant pose and began to fan herself with a silken fan that was suspended from her belt. She supported her head with her arm and darted amicable glances, smiling, sometimes at Father Pimenta and sometimes at me.

What followed happened with extreme rapidity, and tends to make me think that the events had been mapped out in advance and were unfolding without conscious control.

The governor gave an imperious order in the dialect that the dancer had employed. She replied with two or three words that must have been of an injurious nature, and emitted a burst of insulting laughter.

He stood up, spat out a large pellet of betel and seized a large stick that seemed to emerge from the ground in a miraculous fashion. Without any restraint, he struck the dancer on the shoulder with it; she uttered a cry of pain. He was about to give her another when I leapt forward, my arms extended, and intercepted the blow, whose force I was able to measure.

The movement I had made tipped over the tray of refreshments with a great racket of breaking glass. The dancing girl, whose face was distraught with terror, attempted to flee. She was about to receive a further blow of the stick, which would have fractured her skull, but I seized the governor's wrist, tore the stick away from him recklessly, and threw it on the floor.

I immediately took account of the fact that I had done something unusual. The old man's features altered under the empire of an indescribable rage. At the same time, disorder broke out around me. The bearer of the peacock feather attempted to strike me with the long pole. The old woman threw the pestle of her mortar at me. A kind of guard, who had introduced us, obedient to a furious sign from his master, aimed a great blow at me with a curved saber that he had taken from its scabbard and which would have been sufficient to slay me if I had not stepped backwards. At the same time, he uttered a bizarre and guttural cry analogous to a war cry. Other armed men invaded the room, while the dancers and the musicians uttered howls and the Fathers surrounded the governor.

I was driven by events. I had not intended or foreseen any of it. The instinct of conservation guided my action. A few seconds later, I saw myself sustaining Sita, who was repeating: "Save me, lord!" with one arm, and brandishing my saber with the other. I had created a large void around me with a circular movement of my arm, the power of which was exercised by both the flash and the whistle. Jean Guillard, an old soldier of Pamiers, had once taught me the virtue of that circle, which he qualified as magical.

I say that I saw myself, because I had the curious sensation of watching a play; and I was a spectator suddenly endowed with an extraordinary gift of observation. Expressions on faces appeared to me as revelations of souls, and were engraved within me.

How can the governor of Nader be prey to an anger that skirts dementia, I said to myself, *and for a reason, in sum, of scant importance?*

My lucidity permitted me to comprehend that my death was imminent if I did not find a means of getting myself out of the situation in which I found myself. I had my back to a wall, and a rapid glace enabled me to see that there was a door whose batten opened outwards. I pushed it and stumbled into the steps of a stairway, which I climbed. I tried to drop the young woman who was clinging to me, but I understood that it was impossible. She was breathless, her mouth close to mine, and holding me exactly as a woman holds a brother or a husband who has, from men and God, the obligation to defend her.

I heard the governor shout: "Seize him! Kill him!"

The stairway ended at a little terrace, which was the summit of a tower of circular form. As I arrived on that tower I bumped into something bizarre and heavy, made of metal, which my instinct caused me to push toward the opening of the staircase. Fortunately, the opening was very narrow. The metallic object was displaced with a strange facility.

It was just in time. Two or three men were trying to strike me with spears. But a cry rang out: "The telescope! Be careful of the telescope!"

I then perceived that what I had shoved to form a barricade was a large astronomical telescope, such as I had never seen before.[16] It was set on wheels, which had permitted me to move it easily. It must have been exceedingly precious, to judge be the cries that were resounding. The governor's voice resumed. Imploring, almost desperate: "Above all, save the telescope!"

I understood in an instant the advantage that I could extract from that telescope, and I shouted: "If you take another step forward, I'll break the telescope!" And I shook it with enough force to demonstrate my resolution.

A cry of fear and fury responded to me from the depths of the stairway, which made me think that I had reasoned correctly.

Sensing that she was safe for a few moments, albeit very precariously, Sita pressed herself against me, and I felt her burning lips against mine. I pushed her away rather swiftly, for nothing was more inopportune than such conduct. She pronounced words of admiration in her own language, in which I distinguished that there were also promises. However,

---

[16] It is not surprising that the narrator has never seen an astronomical telescope, as history records that none existed in Europe at the time the story is set—Galileo only built his very modest pioneering model in 1609—and it is extremely unlikely that any such thing existed in India, where astronomers would almost certainly have made all their observations with the naked eye.

I was cursing her internally for being the cause of such an unfortunate adventure.

My ill humor was augmented by the proof that she immediately gave of her unconsciousness of her perversity. I looked down from the height of the terrace and I took account of the fact that I had no chance of escaping by leaping from the platform. It overlooked the road, and all sorts of people had already come running, asking what was happening.

I had only turned my head away for two or three seconds. I saw Sita, suddenly transformed into a tigress, throw herself upon a stool and deliver a blow with all her might to the telescope that as our best chance of salvation. I had a great deal of difficulty tearing the stool out of the hands of the furious woman. She had to know how much the governor cared about the object, which must be very valuable, and on which she was slaking her vengeance without any concern for our security. Such is the unconsciousness of some women!

A detonation rang out and a fragment of stone was detached from the wall. I saw a puff of smoke rise up from the neighboring garden. A man armed with a musket had just fired at me. When the smoke had dissipated, I perceived his attentive face, charged with a singular expression of goodwill. He was in the process of reloading his weapon, and doing so with meticulous care.

There were clamors in the stairwell, and I seemed to see another musket glinting there, which moved at the same time as I did. I recognized the voice of Pierre Du Jarric arguing animatedly.

At that moment, the sound of a trumpet rang out some distance from the palace, and seemed to strike people and things with immobility.

I looked along the road. As if an extremely violent wind had passed by, all the people along it were lying down, faces to the ground. The trumpeter, who was on horseback, wore a turban larger than his head and was clad in a luminous coat of mail. He had come to a halt by the gate.

He preceded a horseman in modest costume with a graying moustache and keen eyes, cleft like those of Mongols. He leapt lightly to the ground and as he inspected everything with a circular glance, his gaze encountered mine. I was leaning over the balustrade, my hair in disorder, and he must have seen that I had my naked sword in my hand. I discerned a glint of amusement in his eyes.

He threw the bridle of his horse to someone who ran forward, bent double, in order to receive it. I heard him say, in Persian: "What's happening, then?" And there was a metallic sonority in his voice that I had very rarely heard, and which invited obedience.

Sita had also fallen to the ground.

"It's the Emperor," she murmured.

I hastened to tidy my hair and put the telescope back in its place. In the garden, the man with the musket held his weapon raised, and did not know what he ought to do. I made a sign to him not to fire.

"What does it matter? We're both doomed," said Sita, still on her knees.

I did not share that opinion, but those minutes were very painful.

Eventually, I heard the voice of Pierre Du Jarric, which was calling out to me.

As I went past him, he murmured to me in Occitan, which we alone could comprehend: "Fall to your knees and above all, don't say a word."

He was anticipating the imprudence of the language of my inexperience.

I took account of the true wisdom that was the foundation of the soul of the Emperor Akbar by the fashion in which he subsequently placed the event that had just been recounted to him in its proper place among the events of the empire. I sensed that he considered the governor of Nader as a stargazer subject to eccentricities, and I admired the way, by the severe tone that he adopted in addressing me, that he spared the susceptibility of the irritable old man. However, I understood from his discourse that the latter was considered seriously in the wrong for having molested a stranger who belonged, properly speaking, to the Emperor. He was no longer chewing anything, and was darting sideways glances at the pestle, the crusher of paste, and he empty mortar.

It was with a great satisfaction that I observed that the Emperor had a desire to laugh.

"I know that in your country," he said to me, "it is not customary to beat women with a stick. They are sometimes burned alive, but only when they are not orthodox from a religious point of view."

He expressed himself in a very pure Persian that I understood very well, and in which I was able to reply to him, thanks to my cousin's lessons. Smiling, he gazed at the Fathers, who remained impassive.

A little later, Pierre Du Jarric, who had not taken his eyes off me, in order to nail my words to my lips, took me aside and said: "You'll now be delivered to your own initiative. The Emperor is delighted with our little gifts, and he'll take the Gutenberg Bible and the Orelius atlas with him."

"As well as the *equus*," I said.

"Yes. We'll arrive in Agra after you, for the Emperor is always in a hurry. Providence is visibly protecting you, for it has just saved you in a miraculous fashion. The Emperor sometimes goes hither and yon, with a few cavaliers, as a certain Caliph Haroun-al-Raschid once did, it appears, in Bagdad. But it's necessary that he was guided by an invisible hand to arrive just at the moment when you were about to perish. There is in this a combination of his curiosity in our regard and the aid that destiny wishes to accord you. Events spring forth from the encounter between what men want and the divine decision that is never absolute, and deliberately leaves a margin for the unexpected. I hope that you will continue to benefit from such a harmony. But never forget that you are the branch of a tree whose sap you received in the house of the Jesuits of Toulouse."

When we mounted up again the Emperor was lost in a profound reverie. He scarcely made me an imperceptible sign, which would have annoyed me on the part of anyone else, but which it appears that one has to tolerate on the part of sovereigns. We departed at a gallop.

I was supervising the animal on which the chest containing the Bible and he atlas was loaded, but I had time to notice among the people gathered on the roadside the face of the excellent fellow who had fired a musket-shot at me. It reflected the am attentive gravity, full of mildness.

THE BAZAAR IN AGRA

Why does one please someone? Is it because of one's own qualities or by virtue of secret affinities? Is it because of the services that one might render them? Because one flatters their defects? Because one recognizes their qualities? It was only much later that I was given a reasonable explanation of sympathies and the mystery of their abrupt birth.

I pleased the Emperor Akbar from the first day—I mean, from the first moment that he saw me. I was unable to take any vanity from that, for I knew the reason from his own mouth a short time after our rival in Agra.

I was emerging from the tent where he was sitting, cross-legged, with his minister Aboul Fazi[17] by his side, and I heard him say: "Isn't he a striking portrait of my son Mourad?" And his voice took on a hint of melancholy when he added: "In the time before Mourad had begun to drink."

Doubtless because of the memory of his ancestors, the Timurid kings, Akbar, who had a marvelous palace in Akbar with marble halls and fountains singing in the interior gardens, preferred to sleep in a tent near the ramparts of the city in the midst of his cavaliers. It's true that it was a tent to which one cannot even compare that of King François I, of which very many descriptions are made in our French provinces. It was composed of huge Persian and Chinese carpets, forming a

---

[17] Abu'l Fazi ibn Mubarak (1551-1602) was Akbar's vizier, and wrote an official history of his reign in three volumes, the *Akbanama* [Book of Akbar]. He was a great scholar and had a considerable influence on Akbar's religious tolerance; he was a principal architect of the new faith Akbar promulgated, but he also commanded his armies during the Deccan wars featured in the present story. He also collaborated with Jesuits in the education of the Emperor's second son, Murad Mirza (1570-1599), the Mourad of the present story.

sequence of vast rooms, enclosed themselves in the canvas of an even vaster tent, within such a way that the entire edifice of fabric was surrounded by a circular corridor. It was patrolled incessantly by two servants called Alaf and Kaouf, who had been his companions in war when he was young and had fought hand to hand with his enemies personally.

He said of them: "I love them, not because they are faithful to me—an elephant is faithful, a dog is faithful—nor because they are courageous, since all my soldiers are courageous, but because their hearts are pure and simple, and because they are fire-worshipers.

When I had heard him pronounce those words, forgetting that one should not ask questions in the Emperor's presence, I turned to Aboul Fazi and said: "What are fire-worshipers?"

The Emperor had started to laugh and said to me: "My child, you must believe, like all the men of the Occident, that there is only one religion that is good and true. There are many. All teach the same excellent principles, which men never follow. Behind all religions there is that same unique God, who bears a different name in accordance with the people by whom he is worshiped. The fire-worshipers have identified God with fire, the fire that burns, the fire that emerges from who knows where, which appears, destroys and disappears: fire, the unknowable mystery.

The minister Aboul Fazi was the most intelligent man that it has ever been given to me to know. Intelligence is only truly impressive when it is accompanied by an equal generosity. Generosity, in him, did not come from an impulse of the senses, as one finds in certain women. It resulted from the perfect comprehension of souls and the motives that direct them. And a hint of gaiety was combined with that comprehension—the gaiety that is always the characteristic of superior individuals.

He was a man of short stature, devoid of hair. I have noticed that the activity of intelligence often poisons the roots of the hair. He only had one pettiness, in my view, and it was very petty. He only dressed in dark clothing, as if he had established a necessary harmony between the gravity of the soul and the dark color of the garments. He did not belong to the Muslim religion and I was to learn subsequently that elevated minds devoid of fanaticism were never Muslims, for those who profess that religion think, in a more or less acknowledged fashion, that it is necessary to exterminate all those who do not have an exclusive faith in Allah.

I did not enjoy Akbar's favor immediately. On arrival in Agra he had given a man in his retinue a vague indication to take care of me. That man first had me put my horse in a stable where there were hundreds, perhaps thousands, of horses, and where I would never find my own. Then he took me through countless halls and courtyards to a place where there was a functionary clad in a long robe.

There he gave me, with an extreme volubility, indications that must have been very precise, but instead of giving them to me in Persian he changed his language abruptly, so that I did not understand anything. Then he disappeared.

I had distinguished a half-smile in his beard, and I understood that he was doing me a bad turn. I wanted to run after him, but the functionary with the long robe retained me. He had something to give me. He put over my arms a rather fine long robe, a toque and a silk belt that could be wrapped around my body two or three times. Then he turned away to other occupations. I knew that it was a custom among sovereigns and great men in India to make a gift of garments to those they wished to honor. I demonstrated great satisfaction, but what was to become of me?

I started wandering hither and yon. People looked at me with curiosity because of my costume, especially my sword, the form of which differed from the weapons of that country. "Fangui!" said one, which is the general term that designates foreigners. Eventually, I emerged from the vast dependencies of the palace.

We had arrived by night and darkness covered the city. Agra is a city as immense as any I had ever seen. From the four cardinal points caravans were arriving of camels, mules, and even elephants, laden with merchandise. Large numbers of hirsute naked men, leaning on staffs, were wandering around without seeming to know where they were going. I thought at first that they were beggars, but I recognized by the respect that was accorded to them that they were holy men, but not holy men following Allah. They professed the ancient and admirable religion of India, which the Jesuits had depicted to me as a primitive paganism and that I was only to know much later.

I was stunned, dazed and a little weary. The ordinary people did not understand Persian. I did not know Hindi well enough to explain myself, but there were some of them who expressed themselves in other dialects that seemed to me to be solely composed of guttural onomatopoeias.

I nearly stepped on a snake that appeared to have a little cape around its neck and which followed me, hissing. I watched a tame bear doing tricks, and then, after having traversed gardens, I followed a crowd that was engulfed under a stone vault. I found myself in the middle of an immense monument, which was the bazaar—or rather, one of the bazaars, for after that one I perceived the perspectives of other bazaars.

On painted slabs, all kinds of merchandise were displayed, but especially fabrics, waved by their proprietors in order to make them shine in the light of lanterns placed at the end of long poles. I saw a merchant pouring a colored liquid from large earthenware carafes. I recognized tari, which I had drunk in Surat. It is a very powerful wine made with palm juice. As various people were sitting on the ground drinking little sips from iron receptacles, I sat down among them and took a cup. It was attached by a light chain to the merchant's ambulant vehicle, although it appeared to me to be of scant value.

Supposing the merchant to be suspicious, as soon as he had filled the cup I presented my hand to him, which was filled with silver rupees and other coins of lesser value. He chose whatever pleased him and started to laugh to make me understand that that method of payment suited him. As soon as

I had emptied my cup I hastened to be served again, and did so several times.

The tari dissipated my fatigue somewhat. Time passed.

A family of tame bears nearly passed over me. A solitary cow covered in wounds was walking alone, with a great majesty, and everyone stood aside before it. The crowed diminished, and a moment came when I found myself virtually alone with the tari merchant, who continued to laugh and raise his carafe.

I then perceived that the bazaar where I found myself was surrounded by galleries with colonnades, and edifices pierced by innumerable openings, behind which merchants were spending the night keeping watch on their merchandise spread on the slabs. On looking around I saw them, motionless, almost all holding their beards in their hands, framed by countless little ogival windows. They had copper lamps by their side. A few were chanting prayers, others were reading, which made me think that they were more literate than in the Occident. In sum, though, those aligned presences had something obsessive about them.

Suddenly, as if there had been a signal, as if an anxiety had circulated from window to window, they became agitated, stood up and looked in my direction. I was now alone in the bazaar with the tari merchant, and the presence of a foreigner who had a large sword on his knees must have seemed suspect to them. Hundreds of bearded merchants had their eyes fixed on me. Some were holding their lamps at arm's length in order see me more clearly. That became hallucinatory. I hastened to leave.

I soon perceived that the tari merchant was following me, with his ambulatory vehicle. Every time I turned round I saw him laugh and hold up his large earthenware carafe. I had to hasten my pace in order to lose him.

Finally, fate favored me. A venerable man who was sitting in front of a door gave the impression of understanding what I said to him.

"The temple of the bell?" he said to me. "It's there."

My joy was keen on seeing at the end of a steep side-street a small new church surmounted by a cross.

I learned subsequently that the church was called the temple of the bell because the bell that the Jesuits had installed on finishing the church had provoked complaints from the people of the neighborhood, whom it woke up too early. I knew that thanks to Akbar's protection, two Jesuits had obtained permission to build a church and teach the Christian religion.

They ought, at that moment to be awaiting the arrival of the mission. I knocked on the door of a white house adjacent to the church. I was very surprised to be poorly received by a Father with a thin face devoid of gaiety. I tried to give him details regarding the arrival of other Fathers, but he was scarcely listening to me.

"You're not standing straight," he repeated, indicating a room and telling me that the best thing to do was sleep. He said severely, as he left me: "There's a certain odor of tari around you, which, I hope, will have dissipated tomorrow."

THE REQUEST OF BENOÎT DE GOËS

The most favorable situation for studying the human heart is to have a profound knowledge of life and to be the favorite of a great sovereign. It's true that it is not a career that one can advise a young man to follow. Destiny, even more than sovereigns, decides the choice of favorites.

It seemed that the Emperor had forgotten me during the first days of my arrival. If a favorable star was protecting me, it had flown away for a time. I could not find my way again in the immensity of the imperial stables. I did not know the name of the man who had lost me and I suspected him of having done so deliberately. Bearded chamberlains refused me indignantly when I asked to see the Emperor.

Fortunately, the missionaries arrived, and with them, the mule that was carrying my luggage. I adopted a course that had always succeeded in Toulouse. When I experienced some difficulty, of whatever order it might be, I dressed myself in the most magnificent garments, to which I added a singular detail, such as an excessively long plume or an extravagant necklace of gems. An incident always resulted from which I extracted myself advantageously. I therefore took out of my trunk what seemed to me to be the most eye-catching.

After a few days, the missionaries asked to be received by the Emperor. They took me with them into the city of canvas and carpets.

We found the Emperor sitting on his heels and very cheerful. His tent was decorated with ancient Mongol shields, on the metal of which strange heads with horns and enormous eyebrows were sculpted. There were also Chinese miniatures representing delightful landscapes. The Emperor was in the process of listening o verses that were being recited by the poet Faizi, the brother of Aboul Fazi.[18] The two brothers were sitting side by side to his right. Faizi hesitated sometimes, as if his memory failed him. He must have been reciting a famous poem, for the Emperor immediately continued in his stead. He did not interrupt himself when we entered and he made us a sign to wait until the end of the poem.

To his left he had an individual of military appearance, who was, I subsequently learned, the warrior Todor Mal.[19] He did not appear to understand anything of what was being said, but he was smiling and nodding his head. A group was standing behind him. They almost all had hooded eyes, yellow robes and black bonnets. What simplicity of costume compared with mine!

I recognized among them the man who had lost me on the day of my arrival. He was Assad Bey, a courtier who had no well-defined function but who was a friend of the Emperor. I stared at him, but I encountered in his gaze such a perfect indifference that I thought for a moment that I was mistaken.

I thought I discerned that Faizi was losing his memory by design, in order to permit the Emperor to give evidence of poetic erudition. And I also saw on the face of Aboul Fazi a clear disapproval of his brother's lapses of memory, for he was above flattery.

When it was finished, and after a few words of welcome, the Emperor pointed out to the missionaries a poorly-dressed man, a negro, who gave the impression of having been forgotten in a corner and seemed to consider poetry a profane thing of no interest.

"He comes from Cochin," said the Emperor. "He's a very erudite rabbi. He excels in arguments about the gods and about God. You're to measure yourselves against him."

---

[18] Faizi was the pen-name of Abu Al-Faiz ibn Mubarak (1547-1595), Abu'l Fazi's elder brother. He became Akbar's court poet in 1588. Most of his work has been lost.
[19] Todor Mal was Akbar's finance minister, but had previously been a distinguished soldier.

Father Monserrate's face darkened. He had not quit Agra for several years, animated by a tenacious hope. He knew that Akbar's dream was to convene a great council of priests of all religions, in order to bring out of it a unique religion, better and purer, that might serve as a means of the union of peoples. But he believed that, thanks to his power of persuasion, the Emperor would convert to the Christian religion and would extirpate the other religions by violence.

I sensed that all the missionaries were enveloping themselves in an arrogant gravity at the idea of having to sustain theological discussions with a black rabbi of wretched appearance, all the more so because the black rabbi was looking at them angrily.

Benoît de Goës hastened to explain his request. He was very timid and spoke in a low voice, but an obsession always confers strength. He explained at length the itinerary he wanted to follow, the kingdoms he wanted to traverse on foot.

The Emperor was obliged to interrupt him. He gave him all the necessary letters of credit. He even added three hundred gold mohurs of his own. And as Aboul Fazi did not make a note of it quickly enough he seized a little ivory wand that was within arm's reach and nervously gave him three strokes in the palm of his hand, repeating: "Three hundred! Three hundred!" Then he laughed softly, amused by what he was about to say.

"There is only one difficulty in this courageous missionary's journey," he said, and that is that the city of Xambalu,[20]

---

[20] Jerome Xavier, one of the Jesuit missionaries to Agra reported in 1598 that a Muslim merchant had arrived in Akbar's court claiming to have lived in Xambalu, the capital of the mighty empire of Xathai, for many years. It was Xavier's interrogation of that fantasist, who claimed that there were Christians in Xambalu, that inspire Benoît de Goës to set forth from Agra in search of the non-existent Empire of "Cathay"— which most geographers identified with China—in 1602: the author of the present story has shifted the relevant sequence of

in the kingdom of Cathay, which is, according to him, situated far beyond my states, has no real existence."

Everyone smiled and approved.

Benoît de Goës resumed speaking with an authority unexpected in such a timid man.

It was beyond a sandy ocean, vaster and more redoubtable than the great ocean with salty waves. The wind blew up waves there as high as the sky; the trails were effaced as soon as they were traced. Caravans disappeared in unknown depths. But when one had marched for a long time holding the image of Christ in one's right hand, one finally saw the city of Xambalu looming up on the edge of the desert like a port overlooking an immense sea. And above Xambalu there was a bell-tower with a cross, because the inhabitants of the city were Christians. They were distant brothers that he was going to find.

"Very distant," aid Akbar, thoughtfully. But how was it that he, the Emperor, with all the means that were in his power, had never heard mention of Xambalu and of Cathay, while Benoît de Goës, in the Occident, on the other side of the world, seemed to have a very precise knowledge of it?

Benoît de Goës lowered his eyes. He hesitated. He had a sort of modesty in expressing himself. Finally, he spoke in a very low voice.

Although he was entirely worthy, without there being any reason for it, he had been visited by certain divine inspirations. The Lord had sometimes accorded him visions. He had seen the stone walls of Xambalu, a procession in a street. He had even distinguished that the Christ that was being carried in order to appease the whirlwinds of sand had a beard divided into three points, by which the Christ worshiped by the first Christians was recognizable.

---

incidents back in time, since numerous events featured in subsequent chapters occurred prior to 1599.

By the gravity of the faces I understood that visions were respected in this milieu. Benoît de Goës raised his eyes momentarily and went on, with more firmness:

"I also know that there is a poor monk that I must save. One evening, in my cell, I saw him on a mountain, far beyond the extents that you call Gobi. I saw a little church abandoned because the tempests blow at every new moon a layer of sand that is increasing. The monk has remained beside it. He is alone and he labors all day transporting the sand away from the church. In the evening, he rings the bell. Out there, in the Occident, I heard it and I recognized that it had a tone of despair. There is, in that direction, a fir-wood of which only the treetops can be distinguished."

"Long meditations all have the same result," said the Emperor in a low voice, turning to Aboul Fazi, as if he were continuing a conversation begun long before. "Often, the images born of them have a rigorous exactitude."

"The images that Christ inspires are the only true ones," said Benoît de Goës, with his eyes still lowered but raising the tone of his voice slightly.

Father Monserrate and my cousin Du Jarric started speaking at the same time, and I saw that Father Pignero was tugging Benoît de Goës' robe. Fortunately, the Emperor's gaze settled on me. He examined me, and I saw a gleam of amusement in his gaze, almost of wonderment.

"Is that the latest fashion among Spanish gentlemen?"

Pierre Du Jarric, delighted by the inoffensive character of a conversation about fashion, hastened to say that I was French, and that in France, what was worn at Court was not always worn simultaneously by provincial gentlemen.

"But it's the young man from Nader," said the Emperor, leaning very close to Aboul Fazi's ear. And even though he was speaking in a low voice, I heard him say: "I had asked the mission from Goa to send me one of those marvelous horses such as the Dutch in Java have. It appears that horses die during the crossing, so they've given me the rider without the horse."

He must have been in a very good mood, for he laughed, as if it was funny.

The missionaries took their leave, but he followed his train of thought, and that thought related to me.

"My first judgment has always been the best," he said then to Aboul Fazi. "You can write his name in the book of friends."

I thought that was a manner of speaking. Imagine my surprise when I saw Aboul Fazi pick up a book placed next to him. It was bound in the skin of a stillborn lamb and had a golden clasp. The minister interrogated me with his gaze.

"Jean de Fodoas," I said, and added: "Chevalier," emphasizing the word in order to mark that I knew full well that I was only there was a replacement for a horse.

EMPEROR AKBAR

I had always believed that the men who occupy important situations in cities, and even nations, had only conquered those situations by their mediocrity and their similarity to the vulgar. I thought that veritable genius was only encountered among young and independent men like myself. I was obliged to revise that opinion. I found myself, in Akbar's court, among individuals who combined power and intelligence simultaneously. But of all of them, Akbar was the greatest.

He appeared to me thus because one only sensed high virtue in him as the result of a weakness that he had vanquished. He was an old man full of faults, who had drawn his elevation from inferior elements.

But I am not undertaking a life of illustrious men, or even a life of that great sovereign. I have attached myself to another task, and if it is necessary for me to report aspects of the life of Akbar, it will be in the measure that those aspects had an action on my own soul.

I lived in the palace, and after a time I even had a tent not far from the one in which the Emperor slept. He sent for me at the most various times and did not become angry when, being absent, I did not come immediately—which appeared to me to be an extraordinary trait on the part of someone who saw his slightest caprices satisfied immediately. The fashion in which I expressed myself in Persian made him laugh, but the causes of that hilarity disappeared quite rapidly because of my great facility in speaking foreign languages.

I made him laugh for other reasons. I informed him of the mores of a land he did not know, and which interested him a great deal. He had only heard it mentioned in a conventional manner by Jesuits who were only thinking about converting him, or by a few adventurers of the least order who had no other objective than to extort money from him. The private life of the magistrates of Toulouse excited his curiosity, as well as that of the judges of the Parlement of Languedoc.

He was surprised, above all, by the importance that was attached in France to women. He questioned me about the administration of cities and the comfort of dwellings. He marveled at finding in everything I said to him unexpected features of civilization. The Occident gave him the impression of a very barbaric region, and he summoned Aboul Fazi to laugh with him when I told him—with oratory precautions, of course—that for the majority of the inhabitants of Toulouse, India was a land where there was nothing but naked men, tigers and savage forests.

Several times he had me give descriptions of Saint-Sernin, and when I told him that it was the most beautiful church on earth he replied that when there were many Christians in Agra he would have one built that would be much more beautiful. He counted on building alongside it a synagogue, a mosque, a Buddhist pagoda and a temple of fire.

When I talked to him about "la Belle Paule,"[21] and the great renown for beauty that she had conquered, he contented himself with smiling and replying that there were no women more beautiful than those of Lahore, because the climate there was disposed to the forms of beauty. He asked me, however, whether had a portrait of the beautiful Paule.

I replied that I did not, but I had the imprudence to show him the miniature of Bérangère de Palassol made in paste by my friend Thomas Capellan. I always carried it on my person in order not to lose it.

The Emperor considered it for a long time, and declared to me that it was an exquisite work, worthy of the school of

---

[21] "La Belle Paule," thus nicknamed by François I during a visit to Toulouse, became the subject of a curious booklet entitled *Paulographie* by Gabriel de Minut, a supplement to his general treatise *De la beauté* [On Beauty] (1587), citing her an ideal model. She was Paule de Viguier (1518-1610), the wife of a counselor in the Parlement de Toulouse.

Ispahan, and that he would be very glad to possess it. I hastened to tell him that it was the portrait of a young woman who was very dear to me. He did not hear me, or pretended not to hear me. He put the portrait of Bérangère de Palassol in a little cupboard of ebony and ivory that was in a corner of his tent, saying: "I've tried to give it up, but I always hold on to that which is beautiful. That miniature will give me great pleasure."

I was heartbroken, but dared not persist. Commerce with the great has inconveniences of which the characteristic is to be neither foreseeable not avoidable.

The Emperor often took me hunting, which he adored. I took great pleasure in it, and the fact of savoring common joys together is always a cause for sympathy.

"You'll understand it later," he said to me, "but the Buddha is the greatest of known prophets because he extended his love to animals and all living beings. I understand that it's necessary not to kill without reason, and yet I kill for my pleasure alone. The other day, I organized camel combats within an enclosure and I've enabled you to witness duels between frogs and spiders."

I had indeed been present at that spectacle and I had found it infinitely amusing.

"The more one knows the extent of one's fault, the more the culpability is augmented. Conscience is the measure of justice."

I always listened to him respectfully, but I permitted myself to remark there could not be any fault in making animals as ugly as spiders and frogs kill one another.

"No fault for you, evidently! It's necessary that the conscience be born."

It is only from an emperor that one can hear such things being said without protesting. The idea that I had no conscience appeared to me, in any case, to be implausible.

"The sin only commences when one knows that one is committing it. And how difficult the reparation is! Thus, listen, for a time I had a mania for leopards. I wanted to have one of every sort. Every prince in India sent me some. There are now more than thirteen hundred in my menageries. And now a remorse has come to me for retaining in captivity those animals made to live in the midst of forests. That remorse was so powerful, the other morning, that I nearly had the cages opened immediately—cages that are in the most populous suburb in Agra."

He remained thoughtful momentarily.

"On has, in liberating oneself from past actions, the same difficulty as in setting thirteen hundred leopards free."

Once, he took me hunting wild donkeys. Those animals are very wily, and in order to be able to fire at them, it is necessary to approach them crawling through the undergrowth, without making a noise. One of the inconveniences of that kind of hunt is that while one is crawling one can find oneself face to face with a tiger that one has woken up. Those animals are so numerous that one night, one was pursued in the suburbs of Agra.

We were alone with Alaf and Kaouf, who were carrying rifles, and who passed them to us when, after taking a great deal of trouble, we were within range of a herd of donkeys. Those rifles were operated by a system invented by the Emperor and were very accurate—for the Emperor had a genius for discovery that enabled him to find all sorts of astonishing things. He was an excellent shot; the herd was very distant but he killed seven donkeys. When we went to see them there was one that was still alive. At the sight of it, the Emperor uttered a dolorous cry. He ordered his servants to finish it off quickly, and he turned his face away while they did so. He stayed with the donkeys for a long time, meditating. I waited alongside him.

He said to me: "Aboul Fazi claims that there is a soul—only one soul—for the entire family of donkeys. I am begging that soul's pardon."

And he did not pronounce another syllable until he returned. I thought, without letting anything show, that he simplest thing would have been not to go hunting donkeys.

"What is difficult," he Emperor said to me, "is not accomplishing good deeds. Good deeds are of scant importance. You can, whenever you want, take a handful of rupees and heap wretches with ease. The real difficulty is in the transformation of oneself."

He was to demonstrate how great that difficulty was the same day.

He happened to be residing, for a certain time, in the palace that is within the walls of Agra. That palace is formed of a series of marble courtyards surrounded by galleries with three rows of colonnades. The Emperor's apartments are in the edifices that surround the ultimate courtyard, and they overlook the banks of the Jumna. They are surmounted by a high tower, where the Emperor often went to spend his evenings, examining the stars and having their march explained to him by astronomers. At the base of the tower is a white marble hall, where every evening, at sunset, having put on a white linen robe, the Emperor meditated and said a prayer to light, which he assimilated to the universal spirit. For that, a servant, always the same one, came to light three silver candelabras, the five branches of which were in the form of a flower, the candle depicting the pistil.

That evening, the Emperor was in a somber mood. He had received bad news about his son. The rumor was running around that the Sultan Mourad, whom he adored, was preparing a rebellion against him. He forgot the hour of his prayer. He lingered with the astronomers at the summit of the tower. He came down again precipitately. I was in the courtyard when he went into the little room where he put on his linen robe. He made me a sign that he had no need of me, and I heard him murmur, following his train of thought: "Even the stars lie to us."

The servant charged with lighting the candelabras had been nicknamed in jest by the Emperor "the Pig" because of his resemblance to that animal and the stupidity of which he gave evidence. Had he thought that the Emperor was no longer coming to pray? He had extinguished the candles and had fallen asleep at the foot of the candelabras.

The Emperor went into the dark room, tripped over him and fell full length. His nose collided with a silver candelabrum, which fell over noisily.

The entire palace was aroused. It was thought to be an assassination attempt. The Emperor was bleeding from the nose, but the subtle element of wrath emerged from his soul, more abundantly. It had obscured his mind to the extent that he expressed himself in the Tchagatai language, which he never employed.

"Send for Noureddin!"

Noureddin was, with Assad Bey, one of the two Saibanis, or chamberlains charged with the administration of the palace. He was particularly precious, because he was the only one able to call all the Emirs by their names in the ceremonies. He appeared immediately. The Emperor gave him the order to leave Agra forever, and as his gaze fell upon the Pig, who was still prostrate, his forehead to the ground, he cried to his guards: "Take that to the top of the tower and throw it in the Jumna."

That was executed immediately, without any noise, for the unfortunate fellow made no protest.

Hakim Ali,[22] the palace physician, came running with bandages and dressed the wounded nose. The white robe had a long red streak. The dagger-thrust of an assassin would not have given rise to a fit of rage that took so long to appease. Other instances of negligence in service came back to the Emperor's memory, and several functionaries were summoned and threatened with severe penalties.

It was only an hour later when the Emperor asked, negligently, whether his order relative to the Pig had been executed.

---

[22] Hakim Ali ibn Kamal (?-1609), also known as Hakim-e-Gilani, was a Persian physician, one of several at Akbar's court

"But of course!" said servile voices; and one of them added: "His body was entirely smashed against the rocks."

And words rose up on all sides. The wretch! Death was an insufficient punishment. That death was an act of clemency.

The Emperor contented himself with saying: "That's good."

But I saw that his lips were trembling slightly, from a cause other than anger.

A few days later, I learned that an officer of the palace renowned for his seriousness, had been charged with an enquiry regarding a certain Mirza, son of Tahir, born in Gujarat, known in the palace by the nickname "the Pig." He was very surprised to have received from the Emperor himself the order to make that investigation.

Did the Emperor prefer that the step he took remained quiet, and did he confide it to me because he knew that I had little contact with the men of the Court? Doubtless it was for that reason, for my ignorance of the local tongue did not mark me out particularly.

He summoned me and handed me a leather bag that had to contain a very considerable sum. He gave me minute details of a little by-road where here was a very poor house, some distance from Agra. There, he said, lived an old man named Tahir, whose son had died recently. I was to give him the money without saying where it came from and come back.

That was only simple in appearance. I was obliged to have recourse to Father Monserrate in order to have a guide. He gave me a child of the only Hindu family converted to Christianity, the only one that justified the presence of the church and the appeal of the bell.

The child enabled me to find the house. In that epoch it was a great problem for me to know how certain Hindus, and even the greater number, could live without any of the accessories employed by the majority of people, such as garments, furniture, plates and glasses.

I found myself in the presence of a naked old man sitting cross-legged on a square of beaten earth between bamboos imperfectly united by the mud that formed the walls of his house. He had nothing around him that could assist him for nourishment or sleep.

He was gazing fixedly at his feet, and when I raised my voice he stared at me with a strangely clear gaze, full of meek sadness. I gave him the bag, making him a sign that it belonged to him.

His face expressed a great surprise at first. He palpated it with exceedingly thin fingers, and the rustle of metal only make him comprehend what it contained at the moment when I was about to withdrew, glad to have fulfilled my mission.

A profound disgust replaced the mildness on his face. I had already taken a few steps along the road. He spat in my direction, and threw the bag with such great force in my direction, at the same time as he pronounced a few guttural words whose meaning I did not comprehend, but among which I recognized the name of Akbar.

One cannot leave a bag of gold on a road. I picked it up and drew away.

"Great saint!" repeated the little Hindu on the way, assuredly speaking about a sanctity foreign to his new religion.

When I rendered an account of my mission to the Emperor he listened to me in silence. Then, having reflected, he said: "Power, however great it is, is limited by the evil one has caused. I might be the Emperor but I cannot modify the consequences of my actions. Thus, a man placed at the summit of a mountain, if he rolls down a stone down it, has no possibility of modifying the velocity the stone, or the bounds it makes."

THE TEMPLARS' BAPHOMET

My cousin Pierre Du Jarric asked me to meet him by sending the little Hindu of the unique Christian family. I hastened to run to the mission.

It was, in truth, a long time since I had been there. I had horses and weapons. Everyone showed me a good face because of the Emperor's favor. Only Assad Bey, the chamberlain, with whom I had dealings on the first day, feigned to ignore my existence. I had perceived quite rapidly that men are not different because they have a complexion more bronzed and beards and hair of another quality. I had recognized the hirsute Afghan lords and the seemingly savage Rajputs as similar to my comrades in Toulouse. They desired women equally, uttered cries when they were playing at archery, drank immeasurably like them and amused themselves in the evenings reciting verses. I now spoke Persian and Hindi almost without an accent. I could satisfy my love of garish costumes. I did not think about the morrow. I had almost forgotten the existence of those grave men in somber robes who lived around a deserted church and nourished a dream that I knew to be forever unrealizable: the conversion of the Emperor Akbar to Christianity.

An old Hindu with white hair introduced me into a large hall full of benches, prepared for the future catechumens. Christs and Virgins ornamented the walls. Something indefinable spoke of abandonment, of futile effort. There were muffled footsteps in the neighboring rooms. My visit was awaited. I had the disagreeable sensation of entering into a tedious domain, and that sentiment was aggravated by the sudden notion of my ingratitude.

When my cousin appeared I nearly uttered a cry, so visible did it appear to me that his nose had elongated. He still had the same fashion of being jovial without appearing to be, and passing abruptly from one subject of conversation to another.

105

That was natural to him, but he made use of it deliberately when it was necessary for his convenience.

Certainly he was glad about my unhoped-for situation, but Providence alone had done everything. He thanked it every day. No, no! All the protestations that I attempted on that subject were futile. I had come to the mission often enough, very often, in sum. It was not a matter of that. I had not shown any ingratitude, far from it.

"You see, it's me who is culpable in your regard. I haven't told you everything. I ought to have told you everything, judged you capable of understanding. I know, in any case, without you telling me, that you've been working silently for the Order. Oh, how glad I am to see you again today and to speak to you with an open heart. I even sense between us a communication that didn't exist before."

I experienced a painful sentiment, because it was exactly the contrary. The communication that had once existed between us was no longer the same. I felt a sincere pain in consequence, because I loved my cousin in the measure in which it is possible for a young man of twenty to love.

After a silence during which he had considered me attentively, he went on:

"It's because I know your character. It's only superficial in appearance. Father Octave is the only one to have understood you. Do you remember that he called you his brother? We've had news of him. He's had great disappointments. That's because it's very difficult to go abroad in the world with a skeletal physique. I say this in confidence, but I believe that Father Octave is secretly proud of resembling a skeleton. Fatal vanity!

"As he arrived one evening at the entrance to a mountain village, primitive and superstitious peasants thought they recognized in him a man buried some time before. Those vulgar beings thought themselves threatened by that phantom, and stoned him. He was able to get away, but was covered in wounds. He dragged himself through the woods for several days. But perhaps it is written that he will find the Cross of

Bartholomew in spite of the improbability that sensate minds accorded to that enterprise, for he was able to reach our mission in Lahore, where our brothers cared for him. Between us, however, it appears that he only consents to eat what is strictly necessary, so frightened is he of losing his precious resemblance to the dead.

"My child, you have been built in the most living image, and you know that the Order is counting on you to utilize those gifts. I'm sure that you have not the slightest thought of avoiding your duty"—and here my cousin Du Jarric's eyes turned to look at one of the Christs suspended from the wall— "but I ought to remind you accessorily that if you had a whim to forget those duties, it would be necessary for you to deploy a great deal of prudence."

I interrupted my cousin to ask him what he meant, exactly, and I told him that it was an unfortunate particularity of my nature to respond to threats by revolt.

He started to laugh and responded to me that another particularity of which I was unaware was the excessive promptitude of the revolt—but that revolt was as fecund as submission.

With the gesture with which one drives away importunate flies, he chased away the thoughts to which his last words might have given birth.

"Do you wonder sometimes why Genghis Khan, who only had a few pasturelands and a few men, became the greatest conqueror on earth, why his sons and generals were always victorious, and why Timur, his descendant, saw all the cities he besieged fall before him, and was master of Asia? You have never asked yourself that question or, if you have asked it of yourself, you have done what everyone else does and believed in the simplest explanations. And how Babar, Humayun and after them, Akbar, have created an empire of more than a hundred million subjects, that too has appeared natural to you, and appears natural to the majority of men. The Mongols traveled rapidly on fast horses and attacked in tight formations, that's the secret of their victory, it's said. Or else Babar and Akbar were courageous and skillful captains.

"Well, the man who reads the story of events related by those who witnessed them is obliged to search for another explanation, an explanation more probable and more secret. There is a great mystery in the victories of those conquerors, and a mystery of which once can follow the trace. Bagdad, the capital of Islam, was impregnable when Hulagu took possession of it after a few days of siege. And Delhi, the city with three thousand war elephants was sheltered from any attack behind its ramparts, so high that their like had never been seen. Delhi fell at Timur's first assault. There was an eagle's nest called Batnir, a fortress situated almost in the snows. Timur had reduced it before Delhi—it and many others, notably, all the castles that the grandmasters of the Assassins, who had succeeded one another for two centuries, had patiently erected in impregnable places.

"There is a secret to conquest that does not reside in the improvement of weapons, nor in the courage of soldiers, nor in the strategic skill of leaders. The fall of Jericho is a legend with a foundation of truth. But this is not a matter of legend. Well-guarded as the secret is, one sometimes finds a trace of it. It is reported that when the Occident sensed the threat of the Mongols, Henry of Silesia gathered all the Christian forces available before Legnica in Bohemia, in order to deliver battle to an army commanded by Kaidou.[23] He had with him the

---

[23] The Battle of Legnica was fought on 9 April 1241. A combined force of Poles, Moravians and Germans under the command of Henry II, nicknamed Henry the Pious were defeated by Mongol forces under the command of Kadan, although Medieval chroniclers often confused him with another Mongol leader, Kaidu, and that confusion is repeated by the fictional Du Jarric. Henry probably only had a handful of knights with him along with an untrained rabble of indeterminate size, and although the Mongols feigned a retreat for tactical reasons, the issue was probably never in doubt. Christian chroniclers, how-

Templars and the Teutonic Knights, the elite of the warriors of Europe. His numerical superiority was crushing and he was about to be victorious.

"At the moment when the Mongols began to disperse, a bearded human head of horrible appearance was suddenly seen to loom up in their midst on the end of a pole. It is added that around the head there were designs. And the Mongols won the victory by virtue of an abrupt reversal that had a magical character. A head! There is every chance that the unparalleled power that dominated the world had its source in a magical sign, and that sign was a head surrounded by designs.

"You know that the Jesuits believe in magic and that they even practice it in a certain measure. Not all magic is diabolical. There is a pact with God, and Saint Ignatius signed it on our behalf. It might well be that the great conquerors, those who have had an empire over the peoples of the world, were men who made use of magic and channeled the forces of the world to their advantage by means of signs."

Perhaps my face, which I was striving to render impassive, expressed a doubt involuntarily, for Pierre Du Jarric stopped. Although it was impossible for anyone to overhear us, he went to the window, and then to the door, and resumed in a low voice in order to give his words more force and verity by the faintness of his tone.

"The Jesuits utilize the virtue of signs, and they suppose with reason that those who have conquered an enormous power have conquered it by similar means to theirs. It is necessary to have experimented in order to take account of the fact that the reproduction of a certain image, a certain geometrical figure, is susceptible of directing human actions. It requires another element, of course, a will that commands. Ah, the power of emblems! You're smiling, naturally...."

I was not smiling at all. Surprise had frozen my features.

---

ever, naturally reported the event according to their prejudices and propagandistic inclinations.

"But you who are smiling, without being aware of it, are perhaps benefiting from the magic of a sign. I've given you that of our Order, and you ought to have it around your neck. If you're no longer wearing it, you are the phantom of its design, for one never liberates oneself according to one's caprice, and it is not sufficient to throw a scapular into the nettles. Our Order has attached you with its sign, you have its bond around your neck, whether you want it or not."

I made an involuntary gesture toward my neck, surrounded by a lace collar, but my cousin stopped me.

"Let's speak seriously and without detours. Our Order has saved your life. In spite of the unusual success that you have at his moment, which you only owe to yourself—let us say that you only owe it to yourself and that Providence has nothing to do with it—the Jesuits can have a great deal of influence over your destiny. You can render them a service and they know how to pay for services, be sure of that. That is what it is important to know, the first link in the chain that will lead us to the goal we are pursuing."

Père Du Jarric took from beneath his robe a scroll of cloth that he had in an interior pocket and he unrolled it cautiously. It was an exceedingly old fabric, on which something was drawn or painted, which I could not make out at first.

"Look carefully," he said to me.

I saw that it was a human head, bearded and rather ugly. The mouth was enormous and one could see teeth protruding. That head gave a strange impression; I had never seen its like.

"It's a head," I said; and I thought within myself: *How puerile these Fathers are to occupy themselves with such trifles, instead of firing bows or riding horses in excursions to which I could have the Emperor invite them.*

"Well, we would like to know whether you have noticed a similar head in the palace, and especially in the immediate vicinity of the Emperor."

I started to laugh. No, I had not noticed anything.

My uncle's eyes stared at me with the expression that one has in order to measure someone's stupidity.

"Come on, you've studied history. You've heard mention of the Templars, The Fodoas had a château in Ariège that had belonged to them."

"My father took me there when I was a child. There was a tower to the west, of the form found in all the edifices built by the Templars."

"To the west! That's the tower of conquest. They marched westwards. Well, the head that you see there is the Baphomet of the Templars.[24] There were reproductions of it in all the command-posts of their Order, but of the model, only two exist: the Baphomet of the Orient and the Baphomet of the Occident. This Baphomet was in the chamber of Jacques de Molay, the grandmaster of the Templars, whom Philippe le Bel had burned. How it entered into the possession of the Jesuits is another story, which I won't tell you, firstly because it's too long, and secondly because I only know it incompletely. A most astonishing story—incredible, even!

"There have been no conquerors on earth but those supported by a Baphomet. You'll tell me that the Templars were burned alive. That's because it's necessary to know the manipulation of the victory. And all this is linked to the riches of Genghis Khan, a story that I told you while we were sailing on the *Santa-Fé*. Try to revive your memories. You can go into the remotest rooms of the Emperor Akbar's palace. Have you not seen somewhere, even in a corner—for the Emperor might not know himself the value of the talisman he possesses—an image, a drawing, perhaps a sculpture resembling that bearded head?"

---

[24] "Baphomet" was a device invented by the torturers commissioned to extract confessions of sorcery from members of the Order in order to justify the seizure of their wealth by the financially-embarrassed King of France, Philippe le Bel, in the early 14th century. It subsequently became a central feature of occult lore and legend. The essay appended to the present novel offers a different account of it.

And my cousin brandished before my eyes the fabric curled up at the corners, on which the bearded head of Baphomet was painted, or embroidered, or painted on embroidery.

I shook my head negatively.

At the same moment I felt for my cousin a great surge of affection, with which was mingled the sentiment of my ingratitude and a sincere desire to repair it as quickly as possible. The human soul is full of mysterious turnings. At the same time, an image emerged from the shadows of my memory: another Baphomet, seen recently, appeared to me. That one was, without a doubt, an embroidered Baphomet, and very old. At first it emerged all alone in my memory. I made a slight effort and it took its normal place on the linen chemise, the night-shirt of the Emperor Akbar, to which it was stuck or sewn directly above the heart.

One morning, the Emperor had summoned me to his bedroom in order to show me an Afghan bow that he had just received and which he counted on shooting in my company. He was wearing that immaculate and very supple chemise, which fell all the way to his feet. I had noticed that remarkable face as a grotesque stain, which spoiled the beauty of the precious linen, in my opinion.

What inexplicable force had prevented the appearance of the memory on my face? I remained impassive. Several times, I said: "No, I haven't seen anything."

And I cannot explain why I did not simply say that the Emperor Akbar wore a head of Baphomet on his white linen nightshirt, over the place of the heart.

TOWARD AHMEDNAGAR

In accordance with laws of weight that are unknown to me, I have sometimes seen an object that has been thrown into water sink to the bottom, remain there for some time, and then rise up again, for no apparent reason, to the surface. Thus, the thought of Inès de Saldanna, after having remained in the depths of semi-forgetfulness, returned to the surface of my soul. For the same laws rule material and spiritual things.

To be sure, in spite of the austerity of the Emperor, Akbar's Court was dissolute. The Rajputs who were my companions introduced me solemnly to the most extraordinary old crone that I had ever known, Dgidgi Anaga, the treasurer of the harem. She had once been the Emperor's governess in the time of his infancy, and her authority was immense. The sight of young men softened her, and it was known that she favored illicit unions. That was easy for her, because she had a controlling hand on all the singers and the dancers. She had conceived an affection for me and only asked to be my confidante. I don't know what interior motive drove me not to say anything to her about Inès de Saldanna when her image reappeared within me with the force of an obsession.

Perhaps the return of that image was due to the encounter I had with Francisco Manoël. We crossed paths under the Gate of the Sun and we both leapt from our horses and simulated pleasure at seeing one another again. But in launching himself toward me he struck the attitude of someone who has something special to say.

He sniggered, and was even uglier than usual.

He put his hand on my shoulder and approached his face to mine as if to confide a secret.

"The accursed host is doing its work—you know what I mean, the host on the virginal breast. But souls take time to decompose, much longer than bodies. The slowness of their disaggregation is proportional to the subtlety of their essence.

She has asked me several times what had become of you. She's thinking about you."

I feigned astonishment, but sensed an intense burn of curiosity.

"You're young," he went on. "You don't know yet that the man who possesses and directs a truly beautiful Occidental woman can be master of India and all its kings, for it's lust that leads the world. I'd gladly tell you more, but I'm in a hurry."

He leapt into the saddle and rode away, laughing.

As the grandmaster of the police was one of the Hindus to whom one could speak familiarly—for there were many who rendered themselves inaccessible by the majesty of their nearing and their disagreeable manner—I questioned him the next day about the presence in Agra of a Portuguese by the name of Manoël.

"All foreigners are identified to me, and I'm certain that no Portuguese of that name left Agra yesterdays by the Gate of the Sun," he relied, in a tone so peremptory that I did not dream of contradicting him.

Inès de Saldanna! What had become of her? At what point of immense India was she to be found, and why? *What a mystery there is in everyone's destiny*, I thought—but I could not foresee the chain of events that was about to bring me back to her, and all that was written in the book of Destiny about me.

It began one night. I had just returned in order to sleep to the room, or rather the cell, that I occupied on the ground floor, between other similar cells where certain officers of the emperor's personal guard were lodged. I heard muffled voices; the door opened, and I was open-mouthed with surprise on seeing Emperor Akbar before me. He was followed by Aboul Fazi, his prime minister—his other self—who was holding a resinous torch.

My heart beat faster, and I immediately thought of some grave fault that I must have committed unwittingly.

There was no word of explanation.

"Look," said the Emperor to Aboul Fazi. "Lift up the torch—see whether it isn't striking."

And as I remained motionless, he told me in a tone that brooked no reply: "Turn sideways."

I saw that the resin was running in burning drops on to Aboul Fazi's hand, but that he was paying no heed to it. I saw that the Emperor was clad in the white tunic that he put on in order to sleep and on to which the head of Baphomet was sown.

"I take back what I said," murmured the minister. "The resemblance is extraordinary, and I've never been so struck by it."

I had no idea why the Emperor had come to find me by night in order to have his prime minister examine my profile. There was something stupefying about it. Nevertheless, I dared not speak.

The Emperor placed his hand on my shoulder.

"You are going to be called to fulfill a difficult mission, but you are courageous and perhaps intelligent. I hope that you will succeed."

The tone of his voice was grave and he had the kind of wrinkles around his eyes that are caused by a great dolor contained by will power.

He made a vague gesture of adieu, and on the threshold I heard him say to Aboul Fazi: "A lie is always a lie. I prefer that you should explain it to him. At any rate, leave within the hour."

In fact, an hour later, mounted on the best horses in the empire and followed by a dozen cavaliers, Aboul Fazi and I left Agra.

In order for what follows to be comprehensible, it is necessary to say a few words about the Emperor's sons. He had three of them, for whom he had a blind, inconsiderate and puerile love. Love of that sort is rarely repaid in kind. Akbar did not feel loved by his sons, and suffered in consequence.

He had had a temple built on the spot where a hermit had once told him that he would have three children and had doubtless given him some magical method of determining the make sex of those children. Alone and on foot, he sometimes made a pilgrimage to that temple in order to thank the dead ascetic, but he no longer did so with the same joy that he once had. He had asked for children, but had forgotten to ask that they should love him.

Often, he had cursed his power, wars and the métier of Emperor, everything that had contributed to separate him from his sons. He told himself that he should never have quit them; but he sensed in that separation the work of an occult force. For his eldest son, Mourad, for the second, Selim and for the youngest, Danial, the evolution had been the same.[25] Until their fifteenth year they had shown themselves to be pious, affectionate toward their father, intelligent and just, with all the qualities necessary to the sons of kings; but at fifteen they had begun to drink. The loss of consciousness caused by alcohol had been for them the greatest pleasure possible.

Their intelligence had diminished, they had become bad, and a mysterious wall had risen between them and their father. Not only did they not love him, but perhaps they hated him, When Mourad had been Viceroy of Gujarat he had thought of raising the north of India against his father. Selim had also woven a conspiracy in Lahore. Forewarned, Akbar had had no difficulty in returning his provinces to duty, and he had pardoned them. Believing that activity was necessary to deflect

---

[25] On this point and the events of the next few chapters, the present story deviates deliberately and drastically from history. The historical Murad was actually Akbar's second son, Selim being the eldest and Daniyal the youngest. Murad was with the Mogul forces that attacked Ahmednagar in 1595, but they failed to take it, and it was actually captured by forces commanded by Daniyal in 1599. Murad died in Lahore in 1599 after being replaced by Abu'l Fazi in command of an army fighting to suppress a revolt in Gujarat in 1598.

Mourad from drink, he had sent him to the recently conquered Deccan some time before, with the mission to pacify it. Mourad had installed himself in Ahmednagar, the capital of Khandesh, which he had just taken by assault, He was accompanied by Khan Khanan,[26] a former companion in war of the Emperor, charged with watching over him, and also with organizing vanquished Khandesh.

For several months, however, the news received from Ahmednagar had been increasingly bad. Enclosed in the interior fortress, Mourad never showed himself to the inhabitants of the city and even refused to see the Omrahs who requested an audience. Those irritated Omrahs were now on the point of rebellion. One of the last couriers sent to Agra by Khan Khanan requested that troops be sent urgently, at a forced march.

The Khan also announced that Mourad was afflicted by a malady whose causes the physicians distinguished clearly— alcohol, and the opium that Mourad now absorbed in large doses—but whose effects they did not understand. The Emperor's son refused to leave his room and complained of breathing difficulties. On the advice of the Khan he had made an effort and consented one day to say a few words to several great lords of Khandesh who had come to see him. The Khan had also taken advantage of the opportunity to introduce delegates of the population who had requested to be in the presence of Akbar's son. This is what had happened:

Deccan nobles, Muslim priests, Hindu Brahmins—for the two religions shared the city—and merchants' leaders had gathered in a large hall in which there was a large staircase leading to Mourad's apartments. They had been made to wait for a long time. It had been necessary for the Khan to beg him to appear, for although his dolors had ceased, by virtue of a singular whim, Mourad, who was not literate, had decided that

---

[26] Abdul Rahim Khan-i-Khana (1556-1627), usually known as Rahim, and now most famous as a poet, was one of the ministers of Akbar's court

his lector should read him the poems of Hafiz. In spite of the Khan's interruptions, for long minutes, the voice of the lector had mingled with the murmurs of the proud Omrahs, who considered that wait insulting.

Then it was necessary for Mourad to change his robe and have a pellet of opium prepared, which he absorbed. That substance acted upon him in a dramatic fashion, and generally put him in a state of benevolence and agreeable reverie. In fact, a few minutes after he had absorbed the pellet, he smiled, and asked for his ivory cane, in order, he said, to appear with more majesty before the people of Ahmednagar.

The Khan began to breathe. The doors were opened. The crowd fell silent and a part of the assembly prostrated themselves. Mourad arrived at the first step and stood still, leaning on his cane.

"I'm waiting for them all to prostrate themselves," he said to Khan. "Am I not Mourad, son of Akbar?"

A few seconds went by, and he fell asleep. The astonishment did not have time to become manifest. The ivory cane broke for some unknown cause, and Mourad, dragged by his weight, fell so unfortunately down the stairs that he rolled all the way to the bottom, his head colliding with the marble.

The details only reached Agra later; but the last message said that he had not recovered consciousness, and his physician would not answer for his life. The partisans of the old Queen, Tchand Bibi,[27] had spread the rumor of his death; the city would revolt and all Khandesh in its wake, if troops did not arrive at a forced march.

While I raced on horseback alongside Aboul Fazi and another individual with a red turban and a large moustache, I

---

[27] Historically, the female warrior Chand Bibi (1550-1599) was Regent of Ahmednagar from 1596-99, having defended the city successfully against Akbar's forces in 1595. She was assassinated by her own troops during the siege led by Daniyal following slanderous rumors that she had made or intended to make a treaty with Daniyal.

wondered what role I, a poor foreign chevalier, was called upon to play in all that.

It was the principal role.

I did not know that until the following day. We had traveled all night and most of the morning. Aboul Fazi decided that we would sleep for a few hours in the palace of the governor of I know not what town.

It was a few hours only, and then took some rapid nourishment. Although he was a Hindu Brahmin, Aboul Fazi ate with me. Hindu Brahmins consider themselves soiled if they take aliments in the company of a foreigner, but Aboul Fazi had the title of High Priest of the Sun in the new religion that Akbar wanted to reign over the world and affected no longer to observe certain rites. Those, he held out a bowl of saffron rice to me personally and explained to me what was expected of me. He did so with a certain embarrassment, in spite of his age and high position and the infimal character of mine, for it as a matter of a lie and he had a veridical soul.

"You know," he said to me, "what an extraordinary resemblance you have, in the face and bearing, to Mourad—more that I would have dared to formulate, for it is not good, it is out of the order of things, that ordinary men should resemble sovereigns. But the order of things makes detours to arrive at its ends. It is with great difficulty that Khandesh was conquered, and many men were killed in that conquest—too many men. And it is necessary that that does not recommence. Khan Khanan has caused the imminent demise of Mourad to be foreseen in his recent letter. The Emperor has seen in consequence the great evils that might result from it, evils greater than his own grief in the balance of universal dolor.

"The announcement of Mourad's death will be the signal for an uprising in the city and throughout the province. The old Queen Tchand Bibi is ready to reenter Ahmednagar. The troops at Khan Khanan's disposal are insufficient. It is necessary that Mourad should be seen, that he is believed to be alive, until the moment when that army that was due to leave

Agra immediately after our departure has arrived in Ahmednagar. Mourad is lying inanimate with a fractured skull and is perhaps in the process of dying. We will enter the city by night. You will take the place of the Emperor's son. It will be sufficient for you to be seen passing on horseback through the streets, dressed as Mourad was. You will speak as little as possible. If it is strictly necessary, you can say a few words. The luck of the Empire will do the rest."

I thought it as well to say that perhaps they were counting too much on me and my adaptation to the circumstances, but Aboul Fazi interrupted me, smiling. I understood that he did not believe my reservations, judging my pride to be immeasurable. He was not mistaken. Such is the folly of the early years. I was certain that I could play my role well. I felt that I was cut from royal cloth. No better choice could have been made. I thanked the harmony of things that had elevated me so justly to such a dignity.

I have never traveled so rapidly. We requisitioned new horses in towns and villages. We only slept for a few hours wherever night surprised us. Then the horsemen of our retinue set up little low tents beneath which we allowed ourselves to fall, exhausted. Aboul and I had the same exhaustion, and we shared it with the man with the large moustache. He was a confidant of Khan Khanan named Yacoub, a native of the Deccan. He must have had great vigor, for he had made the journey from Ahmednagar to Agra and had set forth again immediately, affirming that his presence would have a great influence and was susceptible of arranging everything.

He repeated that several times along the route, and I had a desire to reply to him that, since that was so, he would have done better to stay in Ahmednagar and pacify the city immediately. He showed me a natural antipathy, for the Emperor had not admitted him to the secret and did not understand why Aboul Fazi was accompanied by a young Christian. He must have had great courage. In the heart of the Vindhia mountains we camped in a gorge where the narrow road snaked between the walls of somber forests. The horses had been placed in the middle of four tents erected in an uncovered area, and a great fire had been lit.

We feared that the mounts might be carried away by tigers, and the men of our escort took turns to make a tour of the tents, carrying a firebrand and uttering cries that they tried to make menacing but in which the vibrations of terror were audible. As the mewling and roaring came closer and closer, they stopped going out. My two companions and I sat up simultaneously, for we had the sensation that a beast of large dimension had brushed the fabric of our tent.

That shelter was very light, but it was a shelter. Then, with admiration, I saw Yacoub get up, deposit on the ground with a rapid gesture a necklace of precious stones that he wore around his neck, take a sharp short saber that would have been similar to a Roman sword had it not been curved, and leave the tent. Did he intend to fight body to body with a tiger? Fortunately, the ferocious beast must have been frightened by the glare of the fire. Yacoub came back in, placed his weapon beside him, and went back to sleep almost immediately. It was only later, when I had seen a tiger at liberty in the forest, that I measured the insensate courage of the man.

We forded countless rivers. The governor of Aurangabad gave orders to a hundred elite cavaliers to accompany us, for the country ceased to be secure. The vanquished troops of Queen Tchand Bibi were wandering in bands, lying in wait or couriers, pillaging caravans of provisions and everything that belonged to the Emperor.

In spite of my natural vigor, I was exhausted. The scornful glances the Yacoub sometimes darted at me—for he watched the progress of my fatigue—were like an aliment of strength.

We arrived in a cloud of dust on the banks of the Godaveri. It was about midday and we witnessed a gripping spectacle. The ground and the trees were covered in crows and a certain species of long-necked raptor similar to the vultures of France. Around the ford where we were about to cross over a great battle had recently taken place in which the fate of the

Deccan had inclined in favor of the Emperor Akbar. There had been so many dead that those birds had considered that where their nourishment was, their kingdom was, the part of the earth dispensed for carnivorous birds.

They flew there in thousands and their certainty of possessing that region exclusively was so great that they scarcely moved aside in front of our horses and their wings brushed our faces disagreeably. I struck several with my riding crop, and I heard the cavaliers who had departed with us from Agra, and who were Mongols, say that in analogous cases, on battlefields, in the intoxication of feeding and conscious of their strength of numbers, those birds had not hesitated to attack humans.

"An eye is so quickly taken," said one of them.

And everyone protected is face with a flap of his cloak. But there could not be any bloody intoxication among the species there, for the bones had been entirely stripped and made innumerable white patches on the brown earth. To that, perhaps, we owed not being attacked and conserving the precious globes of our eyes.

I made bitter reflections on the immense extent of the land of India and I was despairing of ever reaching the city of Ahmednabad, when the cavalier in the lead suddenly veered sideways and quit the road. We all plunged into vast stone quarries to our right, which seemed abandoned. On the far horizon I had vaguely perceived he domes of mosques and the contours of a city.

Everyone dismounted. It was necessary to wait or nightfall. I lay down on the ground and went to sleep.

The sound of an argument woke me up. It was dark. Several people unknown to me were speaking animatedly. It was a matter of knowing whether it was appropriate to make a solemn entrance for the Emperor's prime minister, Aboul Fazi, who was famous from the north to the south of India. He was loved by the Hindus but hated by those who professed the Muslim religion. Khan Yacoub, who was a fanatical Muslim, said in a somber fashion that it would risk provoking an immediate insurrection.

Suddenly, torches were agitated. A group of horsemen had just arrived. A tall man with shining eyes and a majestic appearance, his neck entirely enveloped in a thick fur, bowed deeply before Aboul Fazi and, having seized his right hand, placed it on his forehead as a sign of respect. While he was making that gesture, a soldier who was making a metallic sound as he walked, because he was covered in plates of gold, advanced with a deliberate solemnity, holding aloft the banner of the Empire, and placed himself behind the minister, inclining the banner slightly over his head.

"I salute the Emperor's envoy, "said Khan Khanan, for it was him, bowing again, although Aboul Fazi, with his habitual simplicity, made him a sign to abridge those rites of reception.

"And I have good news to tell him," the Khan went on, raising his voice, appearing to address the audience as well as the minister. "Our Master, the Subadar of the Deccan, has almost recovered. He does not go out of is apartments, but he is much better."

I have always had a curious faculty of perceiving falsehoods by the sound of the words that express them. I was certain that that assertion was not true.

Aboul Fazi must have had the same suspicion, for instead of emoting an action of grace, he contented himself with putting his hands together and raising them slightly, thanking Providence if that were true, but participating as little as possible in the lie if it were false.

A little later he took me to one side and I knew how the idea of the lie was tormenting him.

"Mourad is dead," he told me. "Hide your face carefully, for you will be called upon to play the role that is destined for you. I had thought...I had hoped...but no, we are going to be obliged to soil ourselves with a grave lie. Know, my child, that a lie is a companion that no longer leaves you. It is to save the lives of many men that the Emperor has decided to organize the lie of which we are about to be the actors. Do not forget that, in a certain measure, one is free of the responsibility for one's actions, in not losing sight of their utility and refusing to obtain a personal advantage therefrom."

I only knew very vaguely then about what is called Karma in the Hindu religion, and I only grasped the meaning of those words poorly. I nevertheless approved them with vivacity, for I respected Aboul Fazi.

We were in the shadows, at the foot of the smooth wall of the quarry, and the only light that reached us was that of a torch that seemed to be about to go out. Aboul Fazi was anxious, not so much because of the death of Mourad, who had always nourished an active hatred against him, as because of a prevision of the events that were about to ensue. I perceived that his principal cause for anxiety was the unease that my nature caused him.

"Khan Khanan," he went on, "is naturally in our confidence. An old woman who was caring for Mourad and his physician witnessed his death, but there is nothing to fear from them, it appears. The Khan has done everything necessary. Thanks to you, we shall gain the necessary time. But it's for you that I'm afraid."

He looked at me intently. He was about to say something else, but we were abruptly interrupted. A face was stuck close to mine. It was that of Khan Khanan.

"It's true. The resemblance is prodigious."

And abruptly, he snatched from his shoulders the brocade robe that, in spite of the extreme heat, had a sable collar, and he threw it over my back. Once, a fakir had predicted that he would escape the death delivered by a sword thrust thanks to the thickness of a sable fur that he was wearing around his neck. Since then, the Khan had not taken off that fur, in expectation of the sword thrust in question.

He raised the collar over my face and almost over my eyes

"When he has the costume he will be the Subadar in person."

The clink of weapons was heard. All eyes were fixed on Aboul Fazi. The bearer of the imperial banner had approached. The horses were brought.

"How long do you think it will take for the troops to reach Ahmednagar?" the Khan asked.

Aboul Fazi reflected.

"That depends on the rain, the heat and the difficulty the cavalry has in crossing the rivers. Twelve days, perhaps fifteen."

I sensed his anxious eyes passing over the Khan's sable that I was wearing.

I was about to be a king for a fortnight!

THE FACE OF DEAD MOURAD

Now that I can look back with serenity on the events of the past, I have no difficulty in absolving myself of the insensate actions that I am about to relate, for I can see the chain of causes and effects, and how small a part my will played therein.

No, I am not responsible for what happened. Was it me who demanded that liquor composed of sagre, a kind of black sugar mixed with the juice of baboul bark?[28] I didn't know what sagre and baboul were. Would I have been able to think of having that tari brandy extracted from two kinds of palms, the codgiour and the coconut, brought to me, and demanding that the proportion of codgiour be greater than that of the ordinary coconut?[29] Was it my fault if someone placed before me, in a massive golden casket, pellets of opium prepared by a Chinese physician, and if I swallowed several with simulated avidity in order to play the character that was imposed on me? Was it my fault if, in order to dispel the somnolence that the diabolical drug in question procured, I was obliged to absorb the essences of baboul and codgiour that make inflamed anger surge through the veins?

Mourad's last lucid words had been addressed to his confidant and friend the Macassar Aurend Bey. He had given him an order to have reduced to powder the fragments of the ivory cane that had broken under his and caused his fall. He wanted to punish that object, or rather, the spirit hidden in its sub-

---

[28] The Baboul or Babul tree, more commonly known as the gum Arabic tree, is *Vachellia nilotica*. Its bark was long used in herbal medicines.

[29] There is a reference to the codgiour palm in the oft-reprinted *Histoire générale des voyages* assembled by Abbé Prévost in 1751, where Magre presumably found it, but it appears to be idiosyncratic to that collection.

stance, for the evil intention that it had manifested, and he intended to smoke the ivory dust in his pipe. Then he had asked for the various palm alcohols.

That was on the day of our arrival. He drank during the morning and had been seized by a crisis of furious delirium in the course of which he had died. Khan Khanan, hearing his cries, had come running and had found him lying on the flag-stones. He had immediately had his door sealed up, without informing anyone. The thought he might gain us the two days necessary for the repair of the walls of the fortress, in which the Emperor's partisans could enclose themselves and defend themselves until the arrival of troops if the revolt burst forth

But in order for me to be able to take Mourad's place usefully, it was necessary that there should not be the slightest suspicion of trickery, that I was scarcely glimpsed, that I was not betrayed by the accent of my voice or some excessively persona gesture. It was also necessary that I adopt, in a sense, the course of his ideas. I had to demand the various liquors and drink them. I even had to smoke the ivory dust of the cane.

Everything went well to begin with. Did the Chinese physician have a heart of stone or was he nourishing old re-sentments? He manifested for the death of his master a mute indifference. Perhaps he was proud of participating in a State secret. Or did he know from his experience of the great men of the earth that his life depended on his obedience? He could acquire from a Chinaman of Ahmednagar everything that he required to preserve Mourad's body from putrefaction and await the definitive embalming that could take place in a mat-ter of days.

We had arrived during the night, through the great breach in the ramparts made a year before by the imperial cannons. We were preceded by the banner and ten trumpet-bearers who were not playing. It was not necessary to wake the inhabitants, but to show those not yet asleep that the trum-pets were there and that they could have been played to an-nounce the arrival of the Emperor's minister. I followed the

Khan to reach the interior of the fortress. Workmen were toiling on the ramparts by the light of torches. Men of wretched appearance surrounded them and were shouting insults at them because they were working. I was gripped by an atmosphere of insecurity and hatred. I think that a stone was even thrown at us and hit a soldier.

We traversed the three enclosing walls, skirted some ponds and climbed a steep pathway that led us to a stone vault that seemed to me to be very ancient. We went through halls with exceedingly high ceilings that resonated beneath our footsteps. It seemed to me that bats were colliding with the walls and I saw a huge lizard ambling slowly over one wall, and was immobilized by the light.

In front of a metal door, Khan Khanan gave various orders, and all those accompanying us withdrew respectfully, with the exception of Yacoub, who took a step forward and twisted his moustache angrily.

The Khan took a torch from the hands of a servant and made a respectful sign to Amoul Fazi to go through. I marched behind them. The door closed again.

"Those are the women's apartments," said the Khan, indicating a sequence of rooms to the left where I could still perceive a flock of bats. I remembered how many times in my childhood, in the vicinity of Toulouse, I had heard it said that those creatures were a bad omen.

Those of Toulouse perhaps, but not those of India, I said to myself, so much was I in need of optimism.

Aboul Fazi had seized my arm and he squeezed it with an eloquent gaze that meant: *I have confidence you in spite of your youth.*

The experiment that it was about to be given to me to make is rather rare—rare and frightening—and I was often to repent of it subsequently.

The Chinese physician must have been waiting for us. He surged forth like an apparition. He must have originated from northern China, for he was of tall stature. He gave the impression of a philosophical executioner. His eyes were invisible beneath his eyelids. At the sight of me he remained immobile for a few seconds and I saw a green gleam flicker in his eyes and then die out. I perceived then that the Khan's fur had slipped.

The Emperor had been struck by my resemblance to his son, but other people had assured me that the resemblance was almost non-existent, for faces lend themselves to the interpretations, and resemblances are relative to the desire one has to discover them. But the Chinese physician certainly had the sensation of once again seeing alive the man he had just seen dead.

There had been neither any transition nor any preparation. At the back of the room there was an area elevated by three steps and covered by a mosquito net suspended from the ceiling, narrow and tapering at the base, so that, in the torchlight, one might have thought it a great maleficent goddess whose face could not be seen. The Chinese physician had approached it, and with a gesture that was both simple and theatrical he threw back one of the undulating sheets.

And then I saw myself. I saw myself as I might have been, deformed by evil passions, violence, remorse and the desire to kill my soul. There was a black ribbon sustaining the jaw and cutting the yellow waxen block of the face in two. The forehead was swathed in a bandage on which had been posed, like a crown, a necklace of turquoises that he had the habit of wearing. The physician had not had time to dress him again, and had hastily thrown over him a gold lamé cloak whose sumptuousness was lugubrious. I recognized myself, and was sad to recognize myself such as I might be in death, if I had allowed to develop in me that which resembled that debauched son of a great Emperor.

I bowed profoundly and stood aside, gripped by horror.

In a shadowed corner, what I had taken for a heap of cushions stirred, and I saw that it was an old woman, praying. The Khan said a few words to her in a low voice. It was necessary not to waste any time. The rumor of Aboul Fazi's arrival had spread rapidly and almost all the important men in the city, friends and enemies, were filling the halls of the palace. At the same time as the imminent arrival of troops, Mourad's recovery was about to be announced, and a glimpse of him would be allowed.

The old woman had drawn away and she came back carrying what is known in Agra as a cadeby, a brocade coat with broad sleeves, which Mourad had the custom of wearing, tightened at the waist by a broad Persian belt of white silk. I experienced a great repulsion in putting on that coat, as well as a green turban that was to conceal my hair, more abundant that Mourad's, but it was too late to back out.

The Khan picked up the necklace of turquoises and held it out to me.

"Is that necessary?" I asked.

"The Subadar never took it off. He wore it over his turban."

I felt one of the turquoises touch my temple. I had such a sensation of a burn that I could not help reaching up to it with my hand, and I suppressed a cry.

I had to lean on Aboul Fazi's shoulder, and accompany him to the top of the staircase at the bottom of which the officers of the army and the notables of the city had gathered who had come to render homage to the Emperor's minister. I would appear for a few seconds, and the door would immediately close on me again.

Reassured by Aboul Fazi's gaze, full of wisdom, I started walking by his side. It was then that an unforeseeable event occurred.

We had passed through two interminable halls and I had just noticed, with an internal smile—for it is necessary to divert oneself in the most difficult situations—that the Khan had hastily put on his cloak with the sable collar, as soon as I had taken it off, when I heard footfalls behind me and a sigh that might have resembled a sigh of great joy or of sudden alarm.

I turned round. A woman had just run up behind me. She had emerged from the door that had been designated to me as the one leading to the women's apartments. Her face was unveiled. It was of great beauty and revealed a delightful ingenuousness, at the same time as the distress of dolor. She had been running. She stopped, open-mouthed, in front of me.

In the haste to arrive, the Khan had not talked to us about Miriah, the daughter of Ali, one of the masters of the Deccan, a friend of Akbar, whom Mourad had married two months before. He had only loved her for a few days and had then started drinking again. After his accident, he had immediately asked not to be cared for by her. Khan Khanan had had great difficulty in persuading her to withdraw to a fortified house that her father had twenty cosses from Ahmednagar, and to which news of her husband was sent every day.[30]

Now, mysteriously informed of the death of her husband, or under the influence of an imperious presentiment, she had come running during the night, and was considering, with eyes widened by the inexplicable, the caricature of the beloved individual that I was for her.

I saw her take a step forward, and she held out her hand as if to touch me and thus assure herself that my form was material and that I was not a vain simulacrum. But she dared not carry that experiment through to the end, She uttered a loud heart-rending cry.

"A preta! It's a preta!"

Pretas are, for the Hindus, the miserable dead wandering in the afterlife in quest of evil to accomplish.

At that exact moment the great door leading to the staircase opened slowly, and I heard a murmur of distant voices.

"But can't you see that it's not him! It's a demon that has taken possession of his body! Expel that demon! Mourad is dead!"

The Chinese physician, who had come running, seized her by the arm and started running, carrying her away.

"Close the doors!" cried the Khan.

---

[30] A coss was an East Indian measure of distance approximately equivalent to a kilometer.

"Mourad is dead! Expel the demon!" The young woman's voice seemed to grow louder as she drew away.

Then there was a silence.

Have they heard? we asked ourselves.

THE NIGHT OF THE CHINESE PHYSICIAN

A saint, an authentic saint, would not have been able to resist, and if I resisted for two days, it was only thanks to the tari alcohol and the opium pellets that the Chinese physician gave me, which made me sleep for fourteen hours. But I felt so ill when I woke up that I swore not to touch that poison again and that I would content myself with the effect of the alcohol, which was at least familiar to me.

The physician, the old woman and I were prisoners in vast apartments where two taciturn eunuchs brought us our meals and tari alcohol, and renewed the water in the alcazaras suspended near the windows in order that they retained their freshness. My two companions knew that their lives depended on their silence and their immobility, and they had no thought of budging. In the Chinese physician at least, however I sensed an interior anxiety as to what might happen to him later. We quickly sympathized, for he thought that my destiny had points in common with his, and that they would not fail to get rid of me as soon as my role was concluded.

We were able to converse in Persian, a language that he knew better than me. But when I told him that I was trusting my lucky star to get me out of the adventure, he did not understand me, either because I expressed myself poorly or because the notion of a star shining for an individual was known to him and he expected no other protection than that of his own cunning.

I learned that his name was Lao Yang. His parents had large domains in China, but the taste for science as well as that for adventures had driven him to leave his homeland. He had gone into the regions of northern Asia, pushed by a chimera. Far beyond the kingdom of Xambalu, in the mountains of Hai-Lin, there was a region surrounded by great wild forests that covered in snow most of the time. There was nothing there but red wolves, white leopards always drunk on blood and

Houndhouze pirates as cruel as the wolves and the leopards. But he had believed that there was also a root there that has a human form and which cures all maladies and even confers a relative immortality. He had found that root but had not been able to keep it because one cannot get out of the Hai-Lin mountains without being despoiled by the inhabitants, who keep watch on the passes and rob travelers.

He had learned, however that there were mountains in India where the little green flower produced by the Gin Seng root was also found. Lao Yang had traversed the Himalaya and had gone as far as Delhi. The cures he had achieved in that city had given him a certain celebrity and Mourad, who was then the Viceroy of the northern provinces, had summoned him and had attached him to his person.

"How were you able to get out of difficulty in the midst of all the dangers that you have traversed?" I asked him, for the physician, expert in knowledge, was not a man of war like me and I thought at that time that a man who did not know how to strike a blow at the right moment is badly served in life.

But he smiled like a strong man talking to someone weaker than him.

"I got out of difficulty thanks to this," he said. And he took out of the folds of his robe a kind of flute, which he began to play. But in doing so he drew nearer to the room in which the imperfectly embalmed body of Mourad lay.

"He considered the sounds of my flute more highly than my medicines," he said, when he had finished.

Now, that door closed poorly, and our preoccupation was to know whether the decomposition of the body might be active enough to poison the atmosphere.

I had the surprise, on the first night, of being woken by the sound of Lao Yang's flute. He was playing right next to the door, almost stuck to it, as if he wanted the sounds to pass through the cracks.

Seeing me sitting up he murmured in a low voice: "Music, with the aid of the will, might stop the decomposition of the molecules of the body.

Sometimes, Aboul Fazi or Khan Khanan came. Then, leaning on the arm of one or the others, I traversed the large halls, where I always had the surprise of encountering a flock of bats, and walked like a convalescent under the colonnades of the gallery that overlooked the monumental staircase of the palace. It was sufficient for a few people to be assured that the Emperor's son was still alive to take away the pretext for the revolt that was brooding in Ahmednagar, so great was Akbar's prestige.

"What is the purpose of that gong?" I asked Lao Yang, pointing at a gong whose ball was a massive block of gold.

"My master, the Subadar Mourad, stuck it three times when he wanted to summon his servants."

I had no other thought than that of distracting myself. It was a day of optimism. I estimated that the comedy that was being played was too enormous to be understood by anyone.

I made the gong resonate. Lao Yang simulated fear, but I sensed in the gleam of his little eyes that she shared the amusement of my action.

The servants were figures of stone lent to the most servile obedience. In a terrible voice—for Mourad was harsh with everyone—I gave the order to bring me he various alcoholic beverages from which the son of Akbar drew his preferred intoxications.

I was surprised by the number and color of the bottles that I was brought. I was examining them with a severe eye when, without being summoned, a stout and rubicund individual of short stature, undoubtedly a eunuch, arrived. He must have been one of Mourad's intimates, because he was not at all frightened and had a broad smile on his face.

He handed me a casket of precious wood encrusted with gold, which I took negligently, making a gesture signifying that I was satisfied. I was to discover shortly afterwards that it contained a green paste, which the physician told me was Persian hashish. The eunuch had not gone away and he continued to stand before me. In the end, lowering his voice slightly, he said: "The Ethiopian is awaiting orders, with the young women and the musicians. The house is two cosses from the city."

I made another sign that I was quite satisfied, while Lao Yang winked at me. The eunuch went away and I thought that it was necessary to do honor to the various beverages that had been brought.

I did them honor, to such an extent and so well that when Aboul Fazi appeared, my soul had emerged mysteriously from the limits that reason had assigned to it. I conceived life differently. I no longer had the same respect for the wise minister and for wisdom in general. I was joyful, and above all full of curiosity. I could not bear the idea that I was in the bosom of a vast and picturesque city, without being able to enjoy the sight of it.

"It's necessary that I make a tour of the city," I said. And scarcely had I pronounced those words that the idea imperiously took possession of me, chasing away all others. I added, negligently: "It's dark. No one will recognize Mourad. And if anyone does recognize him, won't that be for the best? The rumor will immediately run around that he's entirely recovered, that he can ride a horse and put himself at the head of troops. It's surely in the Emperor's interest that I'm seen passing by on horseback."

And without waiting for any response, I seized the golden ball, which was within arm's reach, by its copper handle, and made the gong resonate.

The eunuch appeared.

"Have two horses saddled," I shouted, in a tone that brooked no reply. "Lao Yang will accompany me."

Night had fallen. As we went along the exterior walls of the ultimate enclosure, we heard the sound of arms and horses.

"An escort is certainly being sent after you to protect you," Lao Yang told me.

"Or to murder me. Who knows?" I replied.

"An accident might happen to a Chinese physician," he replied. "That is of no importance. But the son of the Emperor Akbar cannot die until the imperial troops are in view."

The lights of shops were illuminated on all sides. We had turned a corner and entered a street bordered with bazaars and swarming with a crowd of people who were almost all clad in nothing but a loincloth and wore their hair long, knotted down their back.

"This is the Hindu quarter," Lao Yang told me.

It was immense. A year before there had been fierce fighting here. The Omrahs of the Deccan had put around the rumor that of Mourad succeeded his father he would suppress the worship of the gods of India to the profit of Mohammedanism, for which he sometimes had fits of fanaticism. So Hindus had been killed in large numbers, and the streets through which we passed had large holes left by houses that the Mongols had burned. The streets were very narrow; our two horses could hardly get through them, and were obliged to go at walking pace because of the crowd.

"The pillage of all the Hindu houses was organized in spite of the Emperor's orders," my companion told me. "It would be unfortunate if anyone recognized this evening the man who had allowed it to happen."

I smiled, I was drunk on my reconquered liberty as much as on the palm, alcohols mixed with sagre. I showed my sword, which was suspended at my side, and which I had passed hastily through my belt at the moment of departure, although its unusual form clashed with the rest of my costume. In truth, I was another man when I wore it. Without my daring to admit it to myself, it exercised a superstitious influence on me. I attributed a power to it, and almost a personal activity, that sometimes thwarted my will and drove me to certain evil actions that I would probably not have accomplished without it. But it was, above all, a pledge of victory.

That evening, the sword might have saved my life. It was already improbable that the Emperor's son was circulating in a popular street without being preceded and followed by an escort, but how could he be carrying that strange weapon of elongated form instead of a curved saber with the hilt of precious stones, the distinctive sign of every warrior of Mongol origin?

People stood aside with an ill grace and considered me with a visible hatred. The splendor of my costume designated me as one of the execrated conquerors. And when a passing camel train obliged us to remain motionless at a crossroads for a few minutes, there was a murmur around us of sinister augury.

"Do you know how the people of this country hunt tigers?" my companion said to me, doubtless to dissipate an anxiety that I did not have.

I shook my head negatively.

"They go to lie in wait in the jungle near its lair, when they discover one. They place themselves facing it, having no other weapon than a short, sharp dagger like the one that man over there has, who is looking in our direction. And when the tiger leaps upon them they flatten themselves on the ground and raise the arm holding their weapon. The firmly-held dagger opens the belly of the tiger along its entire length. Then they run away. If the blow has been skillfully struck, all the beast's intestines are spread on the ground and hook on to plants and roots before it is able to overtake the hunter."

"Why are you telling me that?"

"Because there might be hunters of that sort in this crowd: very nimble men, almost acrobats. They might leap on to the rump behind us in a single bound and stick the dagger destined for the tiger into our back."

Nothing is more disagreeable than the sensation of an attack from behind. I made my horse rear up. The cries around us increased, but we were able to reach other streets, less animated.

I enjoyed the sight of things, in spite of the inopportune story of the tiger hunters and the enumeration of their qualities. Night had come but the moon was making the domes of the mosques resplendent, and singular pagodas guarded by stone monsters. We galloped along a broad avenue bordered with palm trees, where there were monuments to the right and left with columns, which must have been the sepulchers of saints. The more rapidly our horses went, the more my intoxication increased in seeing new things and filling my lungs with the air of the starry night.

"I also like life," said Lao Yang, suddenly, as if our sensations were common. "One does not seek in vain for the root of the Gin Seng. It's necessary not to hold it against me if I demonstrate that I want to live."

I did not pay any heed to those words. With a joyful tone, he showed me several side-streets where we would be able to dismount from our horses.

"This is the Chinese quarter. There are Chinese everywhere."

"And this?" I asked him. I pointed across the square where we were at a dilapidated construction that had the appearance of a very ancient palace that had been repaired in haste.

"Your compatriots the Portuguese"—Lao Yang thought I was Portuguese, and in any case, all foreigners were reckoned to be Portuguese—"bought that old dwelling and tried to chase away the night birds. If those Portuguese have not been exterminated in the course of wars, a few of your priests might still be there, the ones wearing the black robes."

"Is that possible?" I exclaimed. And I pushed my horse as far as a low wall, half-demolished, which preceded a courtyard. "But there's a window illuminated!"

I raised my head and I saw that a rose-bush with roses in flower was draping its branches along a balustrade over which the flap of a mosquito-met hung. At that moment I heard the sounds of a guitar and those of the melodious voice of a woman who was singing, but in a very low tone, as if the singer was afraid of being overheard.

"In Heaven's name, Lao Yang, tell me what this means!" I cried. "To whom does that rose-bush belong?"

I did not receive any reply. I turned round. My companion had disappeared. I saw that his horse was taking a few hesitant steps across the square. I raised my voice and shouted: "Lao Yang!"

Suddenly, I remembered what he had said to me a few minutes earlier about his love of life and what he had told me the previous evening about the danger there was in possessing a State secret. The Chinese quarter was nearby and that experienced man must have judged it wise to lose himself therein. No, I didn't hold that against him.

I suddenly felt strangely alone. As I was looking round I saw a group of cavaliers emerge into the square, whom I recognized by their uniform as imperials. The officer uttered a cry of joy at the sight of me, and advanced respectfully to my side. It was necessary to put on a brave face against fortune.

"What is your name?" I asked him, abruptly.

I understood by his surprise that he ought to be familiar to me, so I didn't insist, and pointed at the riderless horse, in order that it could be brought back. I launched myself at a gallop, followed by my escort, along the avenue of palm trees and sepulchers, promising myself to find out how that rosebush had flowered in that window of an ancient palace.

THE CONSEQUENCES OF HASHISH

It was the dread of a conversation with Aboul Fazi that caused me to absorb a little of the green paste that the eunuch had brought me in a casket covered with incrustations.

Perhaps, I thought, it's good to taste what the Emperor's son consumed. Mourad wanted to forget life, so I might forget the remonstrations of a wise man.

I would not advise anyone to spend a solitary night after having absorbed without measure the paste of hashish in an apartment where bats are flying near a door behind which there is a cadaver that one knows to be only imperfectly embalmed.

A thought had taken possession of my head and did not want to abandon me. *How do sovereigns who possess unusual wealth consent to inhabit palaces through which large lizards wander, where nocturnal birds fly and where rats of some sort with tails like plumes scurry along the cornices?*

Hashish suppresses—I have made the experiment—the notion of dimensions. I thought that the bats were brushing my face when they were at the ceiling. And in the morning, when I summoned the officer that I had met the previous evening and tried to place an amicable hand gesture on his shoulder, I only groped empty air, for he was still near the door when I thought he was beside me. And that lasted all day.

That officer, Omar Ali, had appeared to me to play a preponderant role in the palace. I gave him curt and severe orders—curt, especially, for I feared being betrayed by my accent or some fault in the Persian language, which I only spoke in a mediocre fashion. Mourad must have had the habit of talking to that officer in the Tchagatai language, because it was in Tchagati that he replied, and I was obliged to lose myself in my thoughts in order not to let him see that I had not understood.

Nothing incites an ordinary man to devotion like being an accomplice in a desire related to women. When Omar Ali understood that I was interested in a woman and that he was to be my confidant, he was entirely acquired.

The orders I gave him consisted of having armed guards placed at all the doors of the apartments I occupied. Those guards were not to let anyone pass.

"But if...."

"I said anyone."

The minister Aboul Fazi and Khan Khanan were, without being named, tacitly included in that prohibition. I knew how that would upset the palace, but hashish distances thoughts as it does objects and deforms their real value—with the result that as soon as I had given that order it retreated in my memory and quickly came to seem infinitely distant. Sometimes distant and sometimes imperious was the thought of the rose-bush and the woman who had been able to place it on a window in a house belonging to the Portuguese. Surely, the woman whose voice I had heard could not have anything in common with the one of whom I dreamed? What could the sister of the Viceroy of Portuguese India, the powerful Aryas de Saldanna, be doing in a semi-ruined house in the city of Ahmednagar?

I interrogated Omar Ali and this is what I learned.

Several years before, Portuguese merchants from Goa had been installed in the half-destroyed ancient palace before which I had arrived. Monks had joined them. The old Queen Tchand Bibi, who professed a rigorous Mohammedanism, had given them the order to leave. When Mourad's troops had besieged the city, fanatical Muslims had taken advantage of it to pillage the house and the trading post that had been installed here, but Mourad's victory, which had presumed the same tolerance as his father, had brought back the Portuguese.

Recently, an important individual had arrived, with litters, an escort, horses and carts charged with bales, who was said to be an envoy of the Viceroy of Goa. Omar Ali remembered his name: Juan de Barbosa. He had come to the palace and made a great noise here. He complained and made promises by turns. He wanted to be received by Mourad in person. But he expressed himself in Portuguese and no one had understood very well what he was saying. "I'm a Barbosa," he repeated incessantly, putting his fist on his hip in an imperious manner. It seemed, however, that he had magnificent gifts for the son of the Emperor Akbar. But he had come on the unfortunate day when Mourad fell asleep on his ivory cane and it had broken, causing him to fall down the stairs.

A noble inhabitant of Ahmednagar who made frequent voyages to Goa and whom I summoned gave me some information about him. He was a debauched man doomed by debt and the damned soul of the Viceroy Aryas de Saldanna. He lived in Goa in usual luxury. Only a powerful motive could have made him submit to the discomfort of traveling. That motive was known. The Marquis de Barbosa talked recklessly and did not try to hide anything. He wanted to create narrow links between the Viceroy of Goa and the future Emperor of India, Sultan Mourad. He had no doubt that the Emperor Akbar was near death. He had that from a Jewish astrologer who was never mistaken in his predictions. He counted on announcing that news to the man who was presently only the governor of the Deccan but to whom the stars promised an imminent sovereignty. He counted on giving him the presents of his friend the Viceroy. And then he never failed to wink.

Presents of a particular kind! For the men of the Occident—those of base extraction, at least—exploited the attraction exerted by the women of their country, women with white skin. They ordinarily brought the most degraded, the daughters of Seville—but it seemed unimaginable that the Viceroy of Goa could have recourse to such a base means!

Now, that day, the hashish and the alcohol were acting with more force on my brain. They had given me a strange activity that succeeded a period whose duration I cannot evaluate, doubtless several days, which had passed in alternatives of sleep and divagation. Perhaps because of that, Aboul Fazi had decided not to pay any more heed to me.

The noble inhabitant of Ahmednagar was about to retire, with genuflections, when he thought it appropriate to add a further detail to what he had said. The powerful Yacoub, the lord of a city in Khandesh—a man, in truth, always tempted by desire—had found beauty in the woman, or one of the women, in the Portuguese house—he did not know whether there was one or several—and had linked himself with Lord de Barbosa. He went there often. Oh, if one knew that Yacoub! It was necessary to feel sorry for anyone that he succeeded in taking to his city, even in the capacity of his first wife.

The name of Yacoub made me remember the scorn that he had shown me, and everything in my head spun: the rosebush, the Chinese physician, Inès de Saldanna and the mad idea that that exceptional creature might be close by and might need my help. Mourad's necklace suddenly weighed heavily upon my head. But events became precipitate and did not leave me time to regret the days that I had just wasted.

Forgetting my quality as the Emperor's son and Subadar, before Omar Ali, who was scarcely surprised, so accustomed was he to the singularities of the real Mourad, I had accompanied the man who had just given me that information through the halls. Omar Ali was about to open the last door. I then made an abrupt gesture, doubtless to extend my hand in accordance with the custom of my own land, to the man I wanted to thank. But, by the fault of the hashish, I miscalculated the distance that separated me from him. I thought he was distant and he was close by. My gesture shoved him.

He tried to lean on the handle of the door, which opened. He fell to the ground in the midst of the guards who were standing at the top of the stairs. He uttered a cry disproportionate to what had happened to him. The guards thought it was an aggression on his part from which I had just defended myself. They threw him down the stairs brutally, and if Omar Ali had not run forward to intervene, one of them, the most zealous, descending the steps behind him, would have pierced him with his spear.

Now, at the bottom of the stairs, behind another guard of Mongol soldiers, there was a crowd of people—noblemen, delegates of merchants, solicitors of every sort—some desirous of assuring Aboul Fazi of their fidelity, others animated by evil designs coming in search of a pretext to manifest them.

The inhabitant of Ahmednagar who had come to inform me, and whom I had recompensed so poorly, went down groaning and was lost in the crowd, but a buzzing circle formed round him. I was on the threshold and I perceived the accents of a voice expressing itself in Portuguese.

I saw a man of tall stature with a graying beard and a plume of several colors in his hat, dressed in the Occidental style, who was waving long arms in front of a functionary with hooded eyes and folded arms. The latter was listening impassively, and his attitude showed that he did not understand. The individual was speaking very loudly; he was almost giving orders. It could only be the Marquis de Barbosa.

And it seemed to me—I was almost certain without being able to certify it to myself, for all sorts of people were incessantly pressing—that, standing beside the Marquis de Barbosa was Francisco Manoël, in an ostentatious costume. Although I could hardly see him, I had the impression that he had the attitude of someone who would like to see a situation that he was responsible for calming down become envenomed.

I took a step forward and I shouted in a resounding voice to Barbosa that it was not becoming to talk so loudly but that, in any case, I would see him immediately.

The retreat in which I had been living for some time and the sight of so many men gathered together, combined with the poisons I had absorbed, suddenly gave me a state of mind of benevolent and almost affectionate disposition. I advanced as far as the first steps of the stairway and I shouted that all those who had a request to make, that all the inhabitants of Ahmednagar who wanted to address themselves to the son of the Emperor Akbar, had only to advance and climb the stairs.

Scarcely had I pronounced those words that I was conscious that I had just done so in French, a language that was not known to anyone!

Perhaps I was in the same place where Mourad's ivory cane had broken and where his fall had taken place. I saw Omar Ali launch himself in front of me, his arms outspread, as if to prevent me from falling.

I felt so favorably disposed toward all humankind that if Barbosa, beneath his plume, had climbed the stairs, I would have hugged him in my arms. I made a sign to the crowd to come toward me, and I was ready to make use of my power to grant all wishes. But it is written that love is always poorly recompensed.

Darting a circular glance over the stone galleries I suddenly saw Aboul Fazi surge forth from a lateral door, as well as Khan Khanan, enveloped in his fur. Both of them pointed me out with their fingers to a troop of armed men, who stated marching rapidly in my direction. The genius of security that inhabits my soul with an eternally attentive eye informed me in a second that those men had received orders to seize my person without delay.

At the same time as that notion of imminent captivity replaced the mild benevolence for all humankind that I had just experienced, I felt close to my right ear the wing of a bat. It had gone past me with surprising speed, surpassing the possibilities of a bird through the air. I turned round and I saw a large arrow fix itself, whistling, in the woodwork behind me. At the same time, a savage clamor burst forth from the crowd at my feet.

The forgetfulness I which I lived had prevented me from knowing that the revolt had became increasingly imminent as the news had spread that an imperial army led by Akbar himself was advancing at a forced march toward Ahmednagar. I was to learn little later that the enclosing walls of the fortress and the reception rooms of the ground floor were full, that day, of a crowd of people more numerous than usual, who were hiding weapons beneath their garments and were supposed, at nightfall, to massacre Aboul Fazi and the partisans of Akbar. The incident of the man I had shoved involuntarily had only precipitated events.

I saw the stupefied Marquis de Barbosa borne away by a human whirlpool on which his plume as floating like a boat with multicolored sails. But the wing of the first arrow had sobered me up. I launched myself backwards. In a matter of seconds I tore off the mantle in which I was enveloped, the brocade coat and the white belt, and threw away the green turban with the necklace of turquoises, all the ornaments of my ephemeral royalty. I seized my sword, pulled it from my scabbard, and was possessed by the joy of being merely a man holding a weapon, who is about to do battle.

I don't know whether the men who had the mission of arresting me recognized me, but they followed me and obeyed my voice. Through the clamors, the gunshots and the disorder, I understood that the essential thing was to throw out of the doors all the inhabitants of Ahmednagar who had penetrated the fortress. I discovered subsequently—for I have not retained a very precise memory of what happened—that it was thanks to a sort of frenetic genius deployed by me that we were able to arrive at that result.

The revolt was two hours in advance, and a trumpeter was supposed to summon armed men who were stationed in the houses near the fortress. Hazard caused me to notice the signaler in question. His instrument resembled a horn of plenty and he was climbing a watch-tower that was backed up against the main gate. I launched myself toward him. The watchman had been killed. I nearly tripped over his body. Having almost reached the platform, I found myself facing a man who had one knee on the ground and was raising some kind of rifle-cannon that I had never seen before. They are redoubtable weapons that fire a packet of grapeshot, and which are only manufactured in Kabul.

The man, who was there to protect the trumpeter, had a broad smile on his face, doubtless because of the surprise that he was about to cause me by a sudden death. I advanced bold-ly. The shot did not depart, and it was him who was stupefied to receive a great blow from my sword on his head. I snatched the trumpet away at the moment when it was about to resound, but I had a scruple about putting to death a man who was perhaps only a musician, and with a shove I caused him to fall off the tower.

It was around the gate that the principal combat unfolded. Someone shouted: "There's a cannon in the square!" A steep road extended from that Gate to the Meidan-Chah, or Royal Square, surrounded by low houses with arched arcades, in front of which there was a market. The rebels had amassed an enormous quantity of vegetables there, from which a cannon, transported the previous night, had just emerged unexpectedly.

I heard Khan Khanan cry out beside me for someone to bring him a horse. The powder of gunfire formed a dark cloud around us. In that mist a few cavaliers surged forth, in whom I recognized the Mongols who had left Agra with Aboul Fazi and me. One of them dismounted in order to give his horse to the Khan. With one bound, I was in the saddle.

"I'll take charge of the cannon," I said to the Khan. And I made a sign to the cavaliers to follow m, if they could. I perceived hesitation in their faces because, although we could leave the enclosure, the difficulty would be getting back in. I launched myself forward, striving to scatter the crowd. There were whistling sounds in my ears but I knew that it was only a matter of bats.

It was not until I had arrived in the middle of the square that I perceived that seven or eight horsemen were around me. With their long spears, those Mongols carried out an extraordinary massacre of all the men surrounding the canon. I was obliged to stop them. More than me, they had lost their reason. A principle of security that never quit me reminded me internally that if it were possible to close the gate, they would do so without any concern for us.

I succeeded in rallying the furious men. One fell face forward with an arrow between the eyes. Two others, seized by the foot, disappeared into the crowd as if into a sea. I have no idea how we were able to reach the gate just as they were about to close it.

Being in battle is nothing, but it is necessary not to reflect after a battle. It is necessary not to hear the groans and the cries of those who are being finished off. For me, that day, an absolutely new event of an interior order occurred. No one was fighting any longer, but the Mongols pierced with their spears all those who had taken up arms. I had blood on my face and on my hands, and I was sickened by its insipid odor. I had just sat down on the steps that descended toward a waterless pool situated between the first and second enclosures.

A large insect with a damaged wing landed on my foot and I was about to crush it when I was retained by the thought that it would be a pity to destroy that delicately organized and colored work of nature. I touched the unknown insect and I put a little blood on its spindly body.

I felt a sharp regret. I would have liked to wash it. It seemed to me that I had soiled an object of a divine order, superior to me. Then the cries that I heard became strangely heart-rending. I looked at my sword with its blue-tinted blade as one looks at a snake with poisoned fangs.

What! I said to myself. *I've just killed those men, who were savant organizations of the Creator, and I'm suffering for having put a drop of blood on the light body of that insect!* That little stain must have made me understand how much I had soiled myself.

I heard footsteps beside me and I got up precipitately on recognizing Aboul Fazi. He considered me with severity, but with the acuity that comprehension gives. The light of reason had returned to me and I made the gesture of falling at his knees, but he stopped me.

"It's the Emperor who will judge you if we see him arrive. I'll leave you the means of showing between now and then that you are his faithful servant, and who knows? It is always permissible to hope, even if one has merited death by one's folly."

THE DISAPPEARANCE OF THE ROSE

The three breaches in the fortress made a year before by Khan Khanan's mines had only been repaired imperfectly. It was there that the battles took place. As I had no title in the imperial army, no fixed post had been assigned to me in the defense, with the result that I was everywhere on occasion. The Khan did not trust me. I was seen with a jaundiced eye by almost everyone because of my quality as a foreigner and I only owed it to my striking actions of the first evening that I was not shackled by an iron chain in the depths of some subterranean prison where a few enemies of the Khan fought with the rats and the darkness.

Mourad's death had been officially announced. There was no exhibition of the body because of the state of siege and the imminent danger in which we found ourselves. Naturally, the comedy I had played so badly, and in which I had magnified my role immeasurably, had not been able to remain secret, but those who knew about it said nothing. I was grateful for the consideration that they showed me—consideration mingled with an affectionate interest because they judged me summoned to a very rapid death that would be of an inexplicable character. They did not know that a favorable star shone for me and that a strange curve of destiny was traced in the book of human beings on the page concerning me.

I did not know that either, but doubtless I had received an interior notification of it by an invisible message. It was the receiving of that message, I now believe, that had caused the insensate courage of which I gave proof. Those who brave death are, most of the time, those who have been informed, without their knowing it, that the death in question is still distant. Nevertheless, there are some who are mistaken, or have received bad information, since I have seen many courageous men die, as perfectly insouciant of danger as I was myself.

Omar Ali was my companion. He retained a certain respect for me, although it was well-established in his mind that I was only a young foreigner without a fortune who had no other title than that of the Emperor's favorite—a title now severely compromised. He was the same age as me and listened with admiration to everything I said. There was only one point on which he differed and showed, when we talked about it, a singularly bad character. He claimed that his sword of curved form, with a broad and heavy blade, was infinitely superior to my long and straight épée. Contradiction on that issue irritated him to the point of fury.

He was a Muslim convert to Hinduism. Emperor Akbar favored that kind of conversion, but in spite of that there were very few, so great is fanaticism. That was in Omar Ali a sign of moral superiority. I had even remarked after a very short time the immense difference that separated the Hindus from the Muslims and, in addition, from believers in all other religions, including mine. In wanting to unify religion, Akbar, although he was a Muslim, wanted to make Hinduism dominant, because he considered it to be the most elevated of beliefs.

One night, we were sitting on the round path of the ramparts, and Omar Ali was talking to me about his new faith with a mixture of naivety and ardor. We were guarding a demolished tower whose base plunged profoundly into a pool of stagnant water. The fortress, with its courtyards, its tables, its hangars, its troughs and its wells, was larger than the entire Saint-Sernin quarter of Toulouse, which contains an immense basilica and a no less immense monastery, with its cemetery and its dependences. Only one part of the troops was enclosed there. The others had been distributed to guard the ramparts of the city, and their fate as unknown. We hoped, without being sure, that they had been able to enclose themselves in the various towers erected beside the gates. The vastness of the enclosure was disproportionate to the number of its defenders and Omar Ali and I had the entire length of the pond under our responsibility.

The city was full of rumors, for Akbar' partisans and those of the old Queen were fighting in many places there. We saw a conflagration burst forth in the direction of the east. I seized my companion's arm and asked him whether it was not in that direction that he had encountered me, a few days before, when he had been sent to search for me.

"The blaze seems to me to be exactly there," he replied.

And he added a few details that he had not yet given to me.

The palace in front of which I had stopped had initially been occupied by Capuchins

"They were as lugubriously clad as the Jesuits, they have the same religion and they pursued poor Hindus likewise, in order to convert them. They obtained no more results than one another and it's difficult to understand why they hate one another. Capuchins were the first buyers of the house Afterwards they sold half of it to the Jesuits. Quarrels followed, and they increased in violence when the Marquis de Barbosa came to install himself in the Jesuit residence, with an entire caravan."

My companion scaled the highest part of the tower we were guarding and declared that he was almost sure, according to his knowledge of Ahmednagar, that it was the dwelling of the Portuguese that was burning.

My resolutions are abrupt but difficult to extract from my brain. I was determined to go and see. At the place where we were standing there was a rudimentary stairway carved into the stone. At the bottom, a little boat was moored, with its oars. The night was dark. On the other side of the pond was waste ground, where I could land without being seen. I would go to take stock and come back.

I put down my sword and belt, which would not have failed to provoke the astonishment of anyone I encountered. I was in my jerkin. While protesting against my project, Omar Ali wound his own turban around my head in order that my silhouette, in the shadows, would be that of an ordinary man. He recommended that, once on the other side of the pond, I should follow the bank, avoid on the right a caravanserai in which dogs might snap at my heels, descend a sloping street bordered by shops and, after crossing a little bridge, I would find the long avenue along which I had galloped, which led to the Portuguese dwelling.

One is sometimes led in the most singular fashion, as if an invisible guide had taken you by the hand. I have often been pleased to imagine that I have an invisible protector, and I confess that every time that conviction has been profound and certain in me, I have been protected, and the protection has been mathematically proportionate to my conviction.

I was serene and tranquil. I knew that I was not to disappear obscurely but to confront the judgment of the Emperor. I traversed the pool in spite to the weeds that I initially mistook for snakes, and which rendered the manipulation of the oars very difficult, especially for someone used to rowing in the running water of the Garonne.

Hindu cities have a nocturnal animation unknown in the cities of France. In Toulouse I passed for a debauched young man because I took pleasure in living by night. There, the extreme heat gives the most virtuous inhabitants the habits of the young debauchees of Toulouse. There were many shops illuminated. I do not know whether their lights served as points of reference for my invisible guide or whether it was able to steer in complete darkness, but I arrived without difficulty before the burned house, which was indeed the one I supposed.

The fire was almost extinct and already, the curiosity-seekers that the event had summoned were going home. I had noticed that the conflagrations do not trouble Hindus. They regard them as manifestations of destiny and they expect, ordinarily, that destiny will depart as it has come.

The courtyard preceding the house was full of people. Two monks were arguing, and almost ready to come to blows. Sometimes they took as witnesses impassive naked men who must have been servants. I understood that a Capuchin and a Jesuit were at odds. The Jesuit was accusing the Capuchin of theft, rapine, lèse-majesté and a crime against God. I heard the name of Yacoub several times. In the end, the Capuchin, who was a thin, pale man and who was affecting a calmness he did not have, said: "You are an envoy of the Devil, then."

And to attenuate the gravity of that remark by generalizing it, he turned to the audience and repeated: "The Jesuits are envoys of the Devil."

As if that word had the power to make him emerge from the earth, a man appeared in the frame of the door and I recognized Francisco Manoël.

"The horses will be here in a moment," he said to someone who was following him, and in whom I recognized by his plumes the Marquis de Barbosa.

"I'll bring you up before the Kotoual!" cried the Jesuit. "You'll be pursued for the abduction of the young woman."

"Have you no shame," interjected another monk. "Before these pagans! You're dishonoring the religion of Christ."

To my great surprise, I saw Francisco Manoël's eyes fixed on me. In spite of my turban and my modest appearance, he recognized me! He made a semblance of finding my presence normal, and he said to me in a low voice: "Follow me."

I raised my head and observed that the rose-bush was no longer on the window where I had seen it.

"Was there not up there…?" I began.

But Francisco Manoël laughed and took me into a ground-floor room that had not been touched by the fire.

"Barbosa's waiting for me," he said. "Here's the best tari in India." He had just taken from a cupboard an earthenware jar covered in wicker and glasses. "For once, the Jesuits have been rolled over by the Capuchins. It really is a good story. It will oblige me to a pursuit and adventures in order to catch up with the stake in the game. The stake is a beautiful fairy-tale princess. You know something about that!"

He sniggered and pushed a glass toward me.

"I never drink," I said, coldly.

"Oh, really! But it's a matter of the best tari in India."

He was the image of temptation. I wondered how he had been able to recognize me when I had played the role of Mourad. He emptied a large glass, passed his tongue over his lips and spoke at hazard. I thought that he had drunk a good deal before my rival.

"One doesn't get bored with Christian monks. Can you imagine that the Capuchins have stolen the Viceroy of India's gift from the Jesuits. And what a gift! A pure young woman who has an accursed host between her breasts. They imagine that one arrives at governing men by the intermediary of a woman. What folly! How it happened I have no idea. I've been played myself, although I believed myself to be very strong. And I don't know who set fire to the house ether. Perhaps that Yacoub, perhaps the Capuchins—for it's to the lord of the city of Almaner that they've delivered the pearl originally destined for Mourad."[31]

Francisco Manoël had poured another glass of tari.

"That Yacoub! I wonder how the Emperor Akbar could have such a companion. They're not the same family. There are those who hate and the others. Yacoub is one of those who hate. And that poor fool Barbosa imagines that by invoking the name of the Viceroy of Goa he might be able to enter into possession of the lost treasure. Have you ever heard of an owl returning a little bird that it's in the process of devouring?"

The voice of the Marquis de Barbosa interrupted him. He was calling Manoël by name. We could hear the whinnying of horses.

"He hopes that they won't be able to get far because of the darkness of the night. We scarcely have four men at our disposal. And what weapons!"

Barbosa appeared in the frame of the window and shouted that it was no time for drinking, but for departing without losing a minute.

"Do you at least have pistols?" Manoël replied.

---

[31] The original has "Almaner" here but sometimes substitutes Amalner subsequently, which is the name of an actual Indian city, but certainly not the one featured in the present story, bearing no resemblance to it. I have preserved Almaner to emphasize the difference.

"They're unnecessary. Those we're pursuing now belong to the Emperor. I shall speak in the name of the Emperor."

Manoël shrugged his shoulders and headed for the door.

"You know the stake. Come with us. I have an idea that it's better for you to run over the roads than wait for the Emperor's arrival." To Barbosa he said: "We have one man more."

But the latter did not look at me, doubtless thinking that the authority of his presence was more than sufficient.

A Jesuit with graying hair was already in the saddle. "The difficulty," he said in a low voice, "will be having the northern gate opened. But I know the man in command there. I've even cured his daughter. Let me handle it. I hope to succeed."

A horse had been brought forward for me. An internal combat was engaged within my soul. We left. I was the last of the troop that we formed.

I do not know what would have happened if we had taken another road than the one I had followed myself. It was necessary to traverse a part of the city in order to reach the northern gate. When we were going along the little wall of earth that marked the limit of the caravanserai, I perceived the water of the pond vaguely and I thought I could see the contour of a human silhouette on the other side, on the rampart of the fortress.

It was almost without reflection that I let myself drop from the horse and started running toward the place where my boat ought to be. Perhaps it was the same invisible guide that permitted me to find it immediately. Who knows? Perhaps it had been guarding it in my absence. Who can ever know the power and activity of those guides?

SINCERITY

My soul had lost all its customary lightness when it was announced to me that the Emperor had given me an order to appear before him.

The camp extended beyond the northern gate and the entire city of Ahmednagar was decked with the Emperor's banners. The city had abruptly changed its appearance when the trumpets of the Mongol advance guard had resonated. Thus, it appears, other trumpets, before Jericho, destroyed the walls of that ancient city. The rebels had abruptly dissolved. All the inhabitants were unanimous in their love for their Emperor. They formed corteges in the streets, which descended to the camp in order to manifest their fidelity. A triple row of guards was necessary to prevent them from penetrating into the tangle of tents.

It was an entire city of fabrics, brocades and hides that unfurled in front of me when I emerged from Ahmednagar at sunset behind Omar Ali, who was marching in silence, his head bowed. The streets were delimited by high standards and painted canes surmounted by the tails of yaks. To the left were the bazaars of the merchants who followed the army no matter how rapidly it marched. They were arguing about the emplacements and their cries and demands could be heard in all languages. To the right was the elephant park and that of the camels, and the wind blew a pungent odor of animality toward me. Men were lighting fires with animal dung, of which they were making heaps. Others were unrolling straps to hold up the tents of Omrahs whose importance was recognized by the height of the standards that flew at their summit. The night passed over like a tide. The men posted as nocturnal guards commenced shouting: "Kaberda!"—which is to say "Look out!" The dust fell back like a immense lid, confounded with the impalpable element of the first shadows.

157

"There's the Agacy," said Omar Ali. "It's just been lit." The agacy is an exceedingly tall mast with a lantern, placed in front of the imperial tent. "May it be a good omen!" But he pronounced the words in a lugubrious tone.

Omar Ali, as an officer in frequent communication with Mourad, had been summoned immediately by the Emperor in order to give him the details that he knew about his end. He had overheard a few words spoken in my regard and had not drawn favorable conclusions therefrom.

"Above all, don't admit to having drunk the tari liquor," he said to me in a low voice. "Remember Kouli Sultan."

The Turkman Kouli Sultan had been condemned to death a year before my arrival in Agra for having brought that same liquor to Danial, Emperor Akbar's youngest son. Danial had been locked up in a castle in Gujarat with theologians and sages in order to cure him of his mania for absorbing poisons. He took, indifferently, opium, hashish, Arab preparations bought back by pilgrims from Mecca, aphrodisiac mixtures that came from China or Malaysia, plants from the island of Macassar that exasperated the nerves, and also the tari liquor.

That was the least violent of the poisons. The desire to forget life was so imperious in Danial that he had once swallowed crushed rubies because a charlatan had assured him that he would obtain a certain appeasement therefrom. But the Emperor, who, according to his intimates, absorbed opium in the evening, either aspiring it through a hollow bamboo stem or eating it in pills, had a prejudice against alcohol. He said that the fermentation of plants or fruits engendered hatred, which is an evil liquid known s au-de-vie. He had therefore prescribed the death penalty for anyone who introduced it into the castle of Sourban, which he had filled with tedious and pious old men. He thought that wisdom could be substituted for poisons.

Danial had simulated a desire to hunt birds on the terrace of the castle and sent his young comrade Kouli Sultan to fetch a choice of rifles from the city of Surat, where there were a number that had come from Holland and Portugal. All would have been well if the young man had bought back rifles of a normal form, but by virtue of zeal, he had bought three weapons with enormous, tapering barrels of a kind never seen in India, which were an object of curiosity. When he entered the castle of Sourban, the governor wanted to handle such strange devices. He had perceived that the barrels served as a receptacle for the forbidden alcohol, Kouli Sultan was imprisoned and only owed his life to the intervention of his grandfather, who spent a fortune in order to contrive his escape.

Yes, I remembered Kouli Sultan. I had often been told his story. It was present in my mind when we went through a group of Gourzeberdars, cavaliers of tall stature who never quit the Emperor when traveling. I sensed the necessity of lying, in spite of the horror that it has always inspired in me.

Omar Ali made a gesture that seemed to be that of an eternal adieu and I traversed the line of tents that led to the Emperor's.

Contrary to his habit, the Emperor was not seated. He was pacing back and forth, his head bowed. Aboul Fazi was at the extremity of the tent with a visage clad in impassivity. Through a partly-raised door-curtain, I glimpsed as in a dream, in the tent next to the Emperor's, a catafalque that seemed to me to be enormous and around which mullahs were standing in prayer, as if made of marble. I knew that Mourad's body had been transported during the day, before it departed for Chapour, where it would be buried.

As I was about to prostrate myself, the Emperor stopped me with a gesture. He stopped very close to me. I had the strange sensation of having no material weight and that I might be able to fly if I made an intense wish to do so.

"What is it that made you lose your reason?" he said to me, in a very low voice.

I had a bizarre sensation of being a stranger to what was happening.

"Reply," he said, without impatience. "Were you acting under the influence of opium, hashish or alcohol?"

The alteration of the truth suddenly seemed to me to be an absolute impossibility.

"I was acting above all under the influence of alcohol," I said.

And, seized by an unexpected facility of narration, I reported the events that had unfolded in Ahmednagar, as a historian might have done who had wanted to depict my soul, but a partial historian, exaggerating my weaknesses and my errors and glossing over that which was meritorious, or even passing over it in silence. In particular, I did not mention the incident of the cannon and other valorous actions.

The Emperor had to know about them, but he had the appearance of sweeping them aside with a gesture.

"I know that you're courageous. But everyone, or almost everyone, is courageous. Have you ever heard mention of one of my soldiers who was not? And I have a million soldiers. There is a courage other than that in war."

When I had said everything, I fell silent. I did not pronounce any word of regret. That was not out of pride, but because I sensed that it would be futile. My fate depended on something else. The Emperor's thinking was above my own sentiments.

He was looking at me, but it was not me he saw. He saw his son Mourad, and also his other two sons, Selim and Danial, whom he had loved the most in all the world. He was scrutinizing the mystery that had separated them so profoundly, without anyone being able to explain why, from goodness, generosity and all the human virtues. For all three of them had been transformed in the same fashion. They had followed an inexplicable spiritual curve. Until their fifteenth year they had shown elevated qualities, nobility of soul, and above all, they had loved their father. And at fifteen, as if an evil wind had passed over them, they had changed, their virtues had ceased to grow, they had gone bad. That was manifested by abuses of power, injustices, a mysterious appetite for the cessation of thought, for stimulation by alcohol, for plunging into dreams by means of opium.

But all that would have been lost in the infinite forbearance of Akbar's heart—except that the three sons, as if they had been subjected to an inhuman influence, had also become detached from their father, had shown him animosity, and then hatred. He had responded to that hatred with untiring forgiveness; but it had been so great that they could not always disguise it. Mourad had taken advantage of a war in the north and the distancing from his father to put himself at the head of a revolt. Selim had done the same.

Certainly, the Emperor had had no difficulty in reestablishing order. His sons were not of his stature. He would have preferred it had it been more difficult and they had at least demonstrated some grandeur, even in revolt. And when they had come to beg his pardon, they had done so with tight lips, knowing that it was granted in advance. And the third son, to whose love the father had clung desperately, had followed inexorably the same path of evil transformation.

Unhappy Emperor! By a curious phenomenon, that infinite misery of a great man only appeared to me in its verity at that moment, when I appeared before him after having enjoyed his confidence. He was gazing at me with a desperate curiosity. I was like the living image of one he loved and whose love he could not attain. I showed him the face of the bad son, and by an inexplicable twist of my nature, or that of hazard, I, who was nothing, was not begging his pardon.

He was still staring at me, and I understood that he was looking into the past. He was seeing again the time when his children, at a young age, were obliged to love him because they were not yet conscious. He was wondering why that love had died when their intelligence was born: a profound law of destiny, a punishment, the bad advice of their entourage, or simply alcohol and all the poisons that deprive humans of consciousness? Or the corruption of power? He had just given the illusion of it to a man who was standing before him, he had enabled him to play the role of a King, and that actor had lost his reason and had almost overturned the stage that had devolved to him in the drama of life.

For an instant, I saw passing over his features the wrath that certain excessively accurate portraits produce, the portraits of beloved beings who are far away, that one cannot attain. One sometimes breaks those portraits. Then it disappeared. Wretched play of passions! That thought was in his gaze. Wretched humans! That shadow of anger gave way to a great serenity, a sad serenity in which there was resignation to the incomprehensible laws that direct human destinies.

From a great distance, from high above, I heard his voice, another voice than his own, murmur: "Go, poor child."

I tried to open my mouth. Was it not necessary to stammer a phrase in which there were words of thanks and pardon? I could not do it. Aboul Fazi made a sign that meant that the interview was concluded. Was the Emperor not accustomed to silence and ingratitude?

Outside, I marched at random through the rows of tents. It was the month of Ramadan and the heat was extraordinary. I passed my hand over my face several times, as if to remove the mask of the man I resembled. I sensed a flaw in myself. I resembled someone else.

I suddenly bumped into a guard with a long beard who was walking around a tent, bearing a great curved sword on his shoulder as one carries a musket in France. He shoved me away without interrupting his march, and said "Kaberdar!"

Yes, it was necessary to look out for one's soul, for which evil passions were lying in wait: the human soul, ever tempted to go backwards.

THE MONSTROUS HORSE

Almaner, Yacoub's city, is fifty cosses from Ahmednagar, surrounded by sheer mountains. I would require two days on horseback and a guide in order to reach it. I asked Aboul Fazi for authorization, I found a guide, and I departed.

I had not been able to forbid myself, before setting forth, a puerile desire. Strolling in the bazaar with Omar Ali, I had seen a prodigious gold lamé cloth for making a turban, and I had bought it for fifty rupees. It was so heavy and well-woven that I was unable to wind it round me head without my friend's collaboration. Beneath that turban I walked like an idol and I had difficulty making my head oscillate either to signify yes or no. Furthermore, once my guide was paid, I no longer had anything in my belt but than five gold pieces, all that remained of a sum rapidly handed over by Aboul Fazi when we left Agra.

"That's only on account, for traveling expenses," the powerful minister had told me.

There had been no more question of the full sum. I had noticed that powerful men who dispose of great wealth forget promise sums more easily than those who are poor. In India, as in all the lands of the earth, all the actions one accomplishes have a counterweight in local coin, and one has exactly the same difficulty as elsewhere in procuring that counterweight.

While riding behind the guide, a timorous Hindu, I remembered what I had learned on the subject of Yacoub. That man of vulgar appearance, whom I had seen ready to fight bodily with a tiger, the man whose hairy arms and legs I had noticed with disgust when I had been sleeping in the same tent, belonged to the most ancient nobility on earth!

He was the cousin of the venerable Queen Tchand Bibi and the uncle of Bahadur,[32] the pretender to the throne of the Deccan. He belonged to the family of Farrukhis, who descended from the emperors of Byzantium, and also the ancient emperors of Persia, the same sovereigns that had combated Greece twenty centuries earlier, in illustrious wars. I would never have believed that such an ancient family could exist in the world; but it was said that a tableau engraved on marble and conserved in the city of Asir carried the design of that unprecedented genealogical tree, whose roots plunged into the very sources of humankind. It gave proofs of the crossings and descendances, and the people were able to admire it and assure themselves of the antiquity of the royal blood. What were the Kings of France compared with such a nobility? What were the Fodoases, of which I was the unworthy last branch?

Yacoub's father had converted to Islam and had been held in suspicion by his relatives because of that. Yacoub himself, a former companion in war of Akbar, was seen badly by everyone because he gave his passions priority over everything that it was customary to respect: amity, religion and duty. Abruptly seized by a desire, he had invaded the house of the Portuguese monks and had taken possession by force of a young woman of great beauty, it was said, whom the Viceroy of Goa had sent to Mourad under the guidance of the Marquis de Barbosa, as a present of amity, doubtless in the hope of seeing him ascend his father's throne. What had been given to Mourad became, after his death, the property of his father. Yacoub had therefore stolen from the Emperor, and he had fled with the fruit of his theft at the moment when those who believed themselves to be his friends, the partisans of Akbar, were besieged by the rebellious inhabitants of Ahmednagar. A singular man, that Yacoub, who was reputed to have once accomplished great deeds, to be a traitor, to be by turns unscru-

---

[32] The historical Bahadur Shah, Chand-Bibi's nephew, was a child when she was appointed as regent to reign on his behalf, not the mature man featured in the present story.

pulous and full of generosity: a violent man full of eccentricities, and incomprehensible.

I had learned that the Marquis de Barbosa and his retinue had come back without having been able to penetrate into Almaner, and that had given me an even keener desire to attempt an adventure whose goal I could not have defined precisely.

My guide only spoke a few words of Hindi and made long speeches in a dialect that I did not understand. He was so importunate that I was obliged to threaten him in order to make him shut up. Every forest inspired a particular terror in him. He announced to me before traversing one of them that we would undoubtedly be attacked by extremely cruel white owls. Another was full of snakes that fell from the trees like leaves: small, slender red snakes and whose bite was fatal. The first time I held the pistols that Omar Ali had prepared for me before departure in my hands, but there were no owls, black or white, and not the slightest trace of a snake.

Twice, I had to sleep in the cabins of Hindus, extraordinarily timid and good men, in spite of the savagery of their appearance. The village where I stopped on the evening of the second day was situated at the base of a sheer mountain at the summit of which there as a quadrilateral of lights. That was the ancient city of Almaner. With the aim of defense, Hindu cities are situated in the most inaccessible places.

I would have been able to reach Almaner that same evening, but it resulted from a few words that I exchanged through the intermediary of the guide that since Yacoub's return the gates of the city were closed at sunset and arrows or gunshots were fired at travelers as soon as darkness fell.

I awoke soon after an icy night, spent on beaten earth. My guide had disappeared. The Hindus who had offered me hospitality offered me goat's milk and gesticulated with guttural cries while surrounding me. The meaning of their mime and their exclamations was clear. They were advising me not to go up to Almaner. They showed me their little pagoda, half-destroyed, near a pool that was sacred to them. Yacoub the

Muslim doubtless persecuted those simple folk who worshiped other gods than Allah. That made me think that he had put himself completely in revolt against the Emperor, who, under severe penalties, prescribed to his Omrahs to tolerate all religions, especially the ancient worship of Brahma.

I should, reasonably, have listened to them. But when a folly takes possession of the soul, it is very difficult not to obey that joyful tyrant. A very old man who must have been the village Brahmin extended his fleshless arms before me as if to prevent me from passing. I went around him; I thanked him in French, for it is always necessary to express oneself, even with the certainty of not being understood, the spirit being in he sounds, and I set forth up the zigzag mountain paths.

The city had high ramparts with towers, and when I drew close I saw several silhouettes of warriors who had the appearance of watchmen. One of them shouted to me from a distance something that I did not understand, and similarly, entirely naked peasants who were emerging from the village and riving two donkeys ahead of them, said something to me in passing whose meaning eluded me. They must have brought forage or bananas to the city, for their donkeys had empty baskets on their back. That gave me a familiar sensation of security, which comforted me, for since I had been climbing, the city, within its silent walls, and the enigma of its altitude, had had a sinister appearance.

But that sensation was not durable. Something abnormal must have been happening. The sound of trumpets, like signals, resonated behind the ramparts. The entrance gate opened between two square towers, and there were already beggars sitting there, as there are before all city gates. They got up as I arrived and started to flee, some outside the city and others inside. Was that because of me? I was pained by being an object of fear, and I shouted to a man eaten away by ulcers who only possessed one foot that there was no need to be afraid of me; but he continued running. A few camel-drivers with their camels also went past me very rapidly. They looked at me with a bewildered curiosity, and one of them shouted something to me, but I could not tell whether it as a threat or a plea.

A man wearing a metallic garment with a large saber by his side was standing beside the door, gravely. I asked him what that signified. He contented himself with agitating his beard, and instead of replying he went into the tower.

Then I went through the gate and looked around. I was in a small square where everything was heaped up, as in cities that are too tightly-confined within the enclosure of their walls. There were a few shops, whose proprietors were making haste to close them. One of them abandoned an entire row of watermelons and made a sign to a child who was helping him and had picked up one of the largest to leave them and come inside as quickly as possible. On a terrace, a haggard woman who had a goiter leaned over, and, raising her arms, cried: "God protect us!"

That was nothing. But she added, while looking at me and looking at the heavens by turns: "God protect him!"

I turned round, and I then saw two men pushing the entrance gate of the city, which was reinforced with iron and bristling with nails. It closed, with a deafening noise.

Gripped by a vague anxiety, I made my horse take a few steps backwards, wanting to ask why the gate had been closed at such an early hour, but the two men had disappeared and I seemed to glimpse them shortly thereafter at the top of the rampart, beside the man, who was holding is beard and laughing, but laughing without hilarity and ferociously.

The square, in the morning sunlight, was now deserted. In order to be more able to decipher the enigma that I sensed around me and to try to interrogate one of the inhabitants, I dismounted and led my horse by the bridle.

I followed a street, and then another. Sometimes I gasped behind the walls a phrase expressing the terror of a danger that must be close at hand. Several times I heard the words: "Wild horse!" and also: "The monster!"

Was it my inoffensive mount of which there was question? Was I among ignorant and naïve people who had never seen a horse and who mistook mine for a monster? I passed my hand over its neck to show how little it was to be feared. But my own naivety became manifest. It could not be that; Yacoub was an accomplished horseman and he must often have ridden through the streets of Almaner with his two hundred warriors that his title of the Emperor's Omrah obliged him to equip and maintain.

I distinguished above the houses several tower that appeared to me to be in the center of the city. One appeared to belong to a mosque, but another, which seemed to be clad in porcelain, had an oval window, and I believed that I could see in its frame the contour of a feminine silhouette with a white collar, a vestimentary ornament that is not normally worn by women in India. I took a descending street that appeared to me to head in that direction. I lost sight of the tower and when my eyes found it again, the human creature had disappeared and a metal grille had been pulled over the window.

As I stopped in the middle of a larger street, anger seized me, and I called out to the mute house around me: "Are all the inhabitants dead? Is there no one to reply to me?"

I shouted that, or something like it. The silence that followed seemed to me to be extraordinary. Then, suddenly, like a mysterious response to my words, there was a terrifying noise, never heard before, a sort of distant snigger that was reminiscent of both the cry of a tiger in the forest and the whinny that certain horses utter when their riders beat them At the same time I perceived that somewhere, on the paving-stones of a street, footfalls of an impressive nature were resonating.

I experienced an anxiety that was localized in my throat in the form of dryness and the desire for a cool drink, for what is unknown kills the most reliable courage.

At that moment I heard a noise to my right. A large door that must give access to a courtyard opened. In the gap I saw a little man with a cunning face who made me a sign to approach with his hand. He wore garments that merited being signaled and were evidence of a certain importance.

"Come in," he said, "and hurry. Bring your horse through quickly. It exposes you to certain death."

I did not have to be begged. I penetrated into a narrow courtyard.

"Tie it up there," said the small man. "Do you think it might start to whinny? What if we were to put a cloak over its head? I'd like to block its ears."

"Why do you want to block the ears of my horse?" I asked him, amazed.

He looked at me with a similar amazement.

"Perhaps you've just arrived in Almaner. I'll explain."

He made me a sign to follow him, and I went behind him into a small room that overlooked the street, and where he stuck his ear to the closed window.

He must have been a subtle man, because he divined my thirst and poured me a large cup of milk. He was extremely ugly. His hair, knotted over his back, was not very abundant. He gave an impression of timidity and inner peace.

"I recognize you," he said. "You're the Christian who was part of the Emperor's retinue. He took you hunting with him."

He expressed himself in a very pure Persian, with an affectation of speaking well.

"I too lived in Agra. I was one of Kwaji's secretaries, but misfortune dictated that the lord of Almaner requested a great literate, one of the great literates of the Court, someone who could recite Hafiz and all the poets."

The Tartar Kwaji was occupied with the administration of the Empire's finances, and did indeed have the most knowledgeable men in India around him.[33]

"And note this: that descendant of emperors of Persia has no desire to hear verses recited. He only summoned me once,

---

[33] The Tartar Kwaji Aeïas is named as Akbar's director of finances in *India and its Native Princes* (1878) by Louis Rousselet and Charles Randolph Buckle, but that version of the name seems to be idiosyncratic to that volume.

and everything that I was able to tell him filled him with ennui and, I think, anger."

The literate went to stick his ear to the window again.

"I'm listening to see whether the monster is approaching. I don't know whether you've been told the story, but there's a monster that roams around Almaner on certain days."

I waited impatiently for an explanation.

"For me, it's a matter of the mystery of reincarnations. Certain men are linked with certain animal species. By virtue of what? It's a great problem. My master Yacoub is linked to the equine species. He has an inexplicable love of horses. He, whose human lineage is lost in the night of time, the ultimate product of humankind, secretly regrets not being a horse! And he also regrets that the horse does not have the same cruelty as him, the man. I'm telling you all this in confidence, for I'm risking my life in telling you."

"But I don't see...."

"So what has he done? He has rendered a thoroughbred as cruel as him. He chose one of enormous size. He has nourished it exclusively on flesh. I wonder whether he has even thrown certain prisoners to it as fodder. He has made a monster more redoubtable than a tiger. And on certain days, as he, a Muslim, hates the Hindu inhabitants of Almaner, fearful, pious, inoffensive people ignorant of the prophet Mohamed, he launches his ferocious horse into the city."

"And it was that horse whose footfalls I heard?"

"Yes. It breaks the backs of children with a single snap of its teeth. It also kills with its hooves. One only has the resource of barricading oneself in on being warned by the sound of trumpets that the monster is in quest of prey. The strength of the beast is unimaginable. The Brahmins have gone in vain to plead with their master. He has remained insensible. I believe that he does not enjoy all his reason. Then again, perhaps he can do nothing because a powerful demon now inhabits the body of his horse. It's necessary to inform the Emperor, but who would believe such a horrible story? And think that if your horse begins to whinny, that will exasperate the monster.

170

It will lay siege to my house, and break the door down with blows of its hooves.

I felt my blood circulating in my veins with ardor under the influence of indignation. "What would the Emperor think of a servant who told him the story of such a cruelty, without adding that he has immediately punished it?"

The literate put his hands together fearfully. I had drawn my sword. "At any rate," he cried, "that weapon will be insufficient."

I was mortified to have been frightened by a horse. I opened the door to the street and ran outside, without paying any heed to the fearful cries of my host.

The city had the same aspect. I arrived in a square that had to be the center of Almaner. It was there that the tower stood that had appeared to me to be made of porcelain. There was a very ancient palace beside it, which must have been restored. Two great lions were crouching in front of a pagoda, but they were made of stone. Sparkling water was emerging from a fountain in the middle of the square. Grass was growing between the flagstones. It was a place full of peace and sad grandeur. Eagles were flying in the distance.

I suddenly had the sensation that behind closed windows, people were watching me. Perhaps they were laughing on seeing me walking beneath my immense turban, sword in hand, looking to the right and the left. They were laughing at my fear! Perhaps there was no danger. I put my sword back into its scabbard precipitately, and began walking like a stroller, curious about temple and new dwellings. I regretted not having a swagger-stick to twirl negligently.

It was when I had almost made a circuit of the square that I abruptly found myself in the presence of the creature that all called the monster. It was at the corner of a street, in the shadow of a wall. Its stature was so tall that I might have mistaken it for an elephant but for the evident absence of a mobile trunk. I was struck by the sheen of its black coat, the twitching of its ears and the formidable rows of teeth that its

171

lips uncovered. Such teeth were well-suited to a monster of creation. It was looking t me as if it were laughing.

I took three paces backwards, having a great deal of difficulty in not fleeing, and I drew my sword from its scabbard without haste, for I had heard it said that savage animals charge when one makes a abrupt movement. But was I in the presence of a savage animal or a wily demon?

To my great surprise, the monster did not hurl itself upon me. It made a semblance of sniffing some grass, it cased laughing and it took a few steps over the square, drawing away from me.

I thought again about the ironic spectators who were following me with their eyes. What if I had been deceived by a pusillanimous literate? It is not customary to draw one's sword when one runs across a dog or a horse in the street, even f he horse is gigantic in size, with a dentition of a phenomenal order.

What followed happened in a matter of seconds. The horse had almost made a slow tour of the fountain in the center of the square. I thought to myself: *Decidedly, it's inoffensive.*

It came toward me at a gallop, its jaws open to bite me, and I only just had time to bound sideways.

All my anguish disappeared in the action and gave way to a perfect lucidity. I had folded myself up. I saw the horse loom up above me and I had time to say to myself: *Why, there's another horse whinnying nearby. It seems to me that it's mine.*

The monster lost a quarter of a second listening too, and that saved my life. I plunged my sword into a white patch that it had on its breast, remembering the words of a Toulousan groom who had told me that such patches often coincide exactly with the location of the heart. And I recoiled precipitately in order not to be crushed.

The beast did not get up again. It gripped the pavement with its feet, uttered a frightful cry, and after its body had been agitated by spasms, it expired.

The entire city must have been behind the windows, for an immense rumor filled the houses. There were voices and appeals as I wiped the blade of my sword and inspected the point to see whether it had suffered any damage. I raised my head. I was outside the porcelain tower, and the metallic trellis of its window had just closed.

I did not have time to reflect on the range of the homage. The door of the old seigneurial dwelling in the center of the square had just opened wide. I recognized Yacoub coming down the steps. His face was furious. His long moustache was agitated. He was surrounded by armed men.

"Who gave you permission to kill one of my horses?" he cried.

And without waiting for any explanation, he added all sorts of insults, among which I distinguished the words *dog* and *Portuguese beggar*.

At the same moment I heard a distant sound of trumpets. The bearded man that I had seen at the gate of the city arrived at a run, and without paying any heed to the dead horse he approached Yacoub and spoke to him in a low voice, like someone who has to confide an important secret.

"Well," replied the latter, "do you not have orders? Fire the cannon. Sweep the road with grapeshot. Yes, even if Miran is at their head."[34]

One does not kill a monster with impunity. My action had given me an unusual verbal abundance. I was fortified by having just accomplished an exploit of which he Emperor would have approved. I have no exact memory of what I said, but there was a poisoned dart in my words for Yacoub's pride. He stopped with a gesture those who wanted to hurl themselves upon me. He wanted to punish me himself.

---

[34] Miran Mubarak Shah was the ruler of Khandesh, who sought an alliance with Akbar in the 1560s, obtained it when one of his daughters entered the Emperor's harem, and remain closely associated with him thereafter.

I was still speaking. Before that day I had never under-stood so well the heroes of Homer and their interminable speeches. Certain texts need to be lived in order to be ex-plained. I said that I scorned the Emperors of Persia of olden days and their decadent posterity, that it required to be particu-larly devoid of courage to fight tigers with a dagger, and many other follies.

He thought at first of traversing me with one of the long arrows that are the ancient weapon of Mongol warriors. He took the bow that one of his companions was carrying and drew one from his quiver, but he must have found the form of the arrow too short.

"Have you a longer one?" he said.

He changed his mind, fortunately for me, and threw the bow to the ground. Then he drew the enormous saber that he had at his side.

I darted a circular glance around. I saw the faces of peo-ple who were about to witness an interesting spectacle, but who were not palpitating, because the outcome was certain. Doors banged. The square was full of people who were show-ing one another the dead horse, and exclaiming, but muffling their exclamations because of the presence of Yacoub and his warriors. I recognized the literate and was surprised by the sincere expression of sympathy for me that his fearful face expressed.

I no longer had more than two or three minutes to live: that was the general sentiment that I perceived, and which impressed me disagreeably.

Yacoub measured me with his gaze. Did he have the chivalric thought of equaling the combat or did he want to satisfy the spectacular taste of the audience by having the ap-pearance of equalizing it? With a rapid gesture he unhooked from the belt of a thickest man who was next to him a saber similar to his own and he threw it at my feet.

I had a desire to cry to him that to equalize the combat it was necessary that he took off the thick tanned leather breast-plate that covered him to the waist. I contented myself with kicking away the saber and raising my excellent épée toward him slightly, making a sign that it was sufficient for me, in spite of the difference in weight and length by comparison with my adversary's weapon. That provoked laughter. I threw my turban to the ground in order to be freer in my movements and everyone laughed again. I was vanquished in advance, and hence ridiculous.

At that moment, a drum-roll resounded, which had to come from the gate of the city through which I had entered.

"The Nakar" said several voices in the audience.

The Nakar was the great war-drum of the imperial armies. It was carried on the back of an elephant, and two men struck it in turn.

"Quickly," cried Yaoub, "go throw his head to Miran, since they're sending me Miran."

Miran was an army leader honored by the Emperor for his great wisdom.

And as a sharpshooter shows a target before firing, Yacoub said to the thickest man, loudly enough for his performance to be well-established by everyone: "I'm going to cut it just there, where he has a black cord."

I had a widened collar, and the black cord of the Jesuits' scapular had ridden up on my neck and was tracing a black line there, which I could not see but suddenly began to feel.

The blow that Yacoub struck would certainly have cut off my head if, during my childhood, a skillful master had not taught me the art of giving and receiving trenchant blows and alternating them with thrusts of the point. The features of Bertrand de Latourmadour, who had instructed me in the art of combat suddenly reappeared before my eyes.

"Victory in single combat," he had said, "comes from the concentration of thought in the blow that one is about to deliver."

In order to obey that precept, I immediately chased that image away, and my first riposte would certainly have wounded Yacoub but for his leather armor. The thickset man saw that and, taking a spear from the arms of another warrior, he attempted to strike my wrist with the shaft in order to break it, crying out several times: "It's vermin! It's necessary to crush it."

The Nakar resonated in the distance, and, because of the necessity of finishing it quickly, all of Yacoub's warriors would doubtless have thrown themselves upon me, but one does not belong to the oldest nobility on earth with impunity. Kings dating from the primitive formation of societies doubtless intervened confusedly in Yacoub's soul. Then too, his pride and confidence in his enormous saber assured him in his mind of victory over a young man he considered as a despicable Court favorite.

He launched an imperious order. The circle widened, doubtless in order that he could send my head flying entirely at his ease.

If I had reflected then on the situation in which I found myself, alone in that closed city, fighting with an experienced warrior in revolt against the Emperor, I would have despaired of my fate, and that thought would have diminished my strength. Often, thought is a bad thing. I banished it from my mind and concentrated on the blow to deliver, in accordance with the recommendation of my master Latourmadour.

My head did not roll on the ground, and I saw on the face of my adversary a rage even greater than his surprise. I noticed then how Yacoub's face, divided by long moustaches, had a pair of short and graying side-whiskers, which I had never seen. Death was suspended over my head, and I thought: *Haven't those side-whiskers just grown abruptly? And why are his side-whiskers gray while his moustaches are black?*

Fortunately, I said to myself immediately: *I'm doomed if I occupy myself with his side-whiskers.* And I chased away such absurd thoughts.

In such a combat, salvation depends, most of the time, on the quality of the blade. Mine was undamaged in spite of the blows it received. Yacoub, in truth, was a master in the art of fighting with the Mongol saber, but, like many combatants on earth, he was to perish for not having estimated his opponent at his true value.

He renounced the exploit of making my head fly off my shoulders when he understood the difficulty of that enterprise. He was in a hurry. He was awaited on the rampart. As I had broken before his furious attack, he took advantage of the fact that my heel bumped into the saber that he had thrown me—and which still lay on the ground—to precipitate himself upon me with a bound that I would have thought impossible for a man of that age. At the same time as he released his saber he seized the little dagger known as a ginda, which every man of quality wore in his belt. I was saved by the instructive rapidity that permitted me to seize his arm, letting go of my sword and taking from my own belt the ginda that was suspended here.

Nature, in the distribution of strength, had been generous to me and, without giving it the external appearance, had gratified my body with an uncommon force. I had the sensation of bending a tree in one hand and delivering a mighty blow with the other. The circle of spectators had widened when we seized one another bodily, and a rumor had spread. It was not yet terminated when my adversary lay at my feet, his heart traversed clean through the leather breastplate.

I had not withdrawn the weapon. No blood came out of the wound. The certainty of death came from the inexorable immobility. A strangely long silence weighed upon everyone, and great birds that were flying, and whose wing-beats could be heard, suddenly began to glide.

In the silence, I picked up my sword and simulated the greatest calm

Will they hurl themselves upon me en masse? I thought, carefully wiping it and examining the cutting edge, while watching the thickset man from the corner of my eye.

But no one budged. I also picked up my turban, and replaced it on my head.

Interest spoke in souls and informed them that the revolt was dead, that I was a creature of the Emperor and that his soldiers had just made their drum resound at the gate of Almaner.

There was a tumult in the square. I recognized Miran on horseback. He was a celebrated individual. His bridle was being held by the literate who had greeted me. He was trotting beside him, and giving him explanations in a breathless voice. I saw him pointing his finger at me. Miran's face, framed by a black beard in a fan, remained as impenetrable and severe as a philosophical enigma. Everyone moved aside respectfully before him.

He dismounted and remained standing in front of Yacoub's body, as immobile as him. He had been his companion in war and his friend, and it was because of that amity that the Emperor had sent him. But their destinies had separated; one had been possessed by a madness of cruelty, the other had marched toward wisdom and it was said that he had attained, it in the solitude of his soul.

The crowd was attentive and silent. Finally, Miran made a movement and turned toward me.

"The Emperor orders you to return immediately to the camp at Ahmednagar," he said.

I uttered a sigh.

"I have it from my venerable master Kwaji," said the literate then, as if he were continuing his interrupted speech, "that in spite of his young age, he has his name in the book of friends, his name written by the hand of Aboul Fazi."

"We are all in the book of the friends of God," said Miran gravely, as if speaking to himself.

And as I had bent down and was searching the ground attentively, he added in a curt voice: "The order is: without any delay."

"Do I not have time to pick up a rose?"

"No."

I hastened to go away.

"I'll return your horse," said the literate, accompanying me.

I did not know how to thank that man, to whom I owed a great deal. I measured the effort he must have accomplished to vanquish his timid nature in informing a chief as taciturn as Miran.

I asked him what I could do for him. He smiled.

"The man who has received from God the gift of writing verses is so complete that he cannot desire any other favor."

How different the poets of India are from those of France, I thought, drawing away.

As I went through the city gate I turned round. The tower was outlined against the sky. The grille of the oval window had disappeared. I saw the contour of a woman's upper body. She seemed to be leaning in my direction, but I was too far away to be entirely sure.

THE SIEGE OF ASIR

"My son, mistrust any man wearing red boots. Even if the boots are black and only the lining is red, be suspicious. You might well be told that red boots have been in use in Kashmir at all times. Once, the Uighur cavalry only wore red boots. It might be that you are dealing with an inoffensive Kashmiri on someone observing the customary costume of the Uighurs, but all the same, believe me, if a man who has red boots approaches you, be on your guard."

Thus spoke Pierre Du Jarric. He called me his son, although I was only his cousin—but he loved me more than one loves a distant relative.

"But it seems to me," I replied, "that the ancient Emperors of Byzantium, and after them the Doges of Venice, wore red brodequins in their ceremonial costume."

"That's possible. And that's not only a matter of coincidence. When one thinks of the roles played by the Emperors of Byzantium and the Doges of the predator city that as Venice, one wonders...."

"But what would be the significance of the choice of that color of footwear?"

"There's no certainty, but the Orient is such an enigmatic land! What I can tell you might appear risible, and have the effect on you of a fanciful tale. It might be that it is a fanciful tale. But after all, why should a certain category of men not have found it convenient to have a simply sign of recognition? Fundamentally, there are good ones and there are bad ones. And if one admits that the bad ones act consciously, that they are linked together by the interest of enabling evil to triumph, they need to have a sign of recognition. That sign might perhaps be in the color of their boots. So, I say to you: mistrust a man who wears red boots."

"But I imagine that you haven't made the long journey from Agra to Asir in order to give me that advice?"

180

"No, not only for that. But Father Aquaviva thinks that the moment to act has come. Once the city of Asir is taken, Emperor Akbar will be the greatest sovereign on earth.[35] The Jesuits ought to reign through him. I have spoken to you about a great treasure to conquer, but that treasure is only a symbol, the exterior sin of power. It is the Emperor's soul that it is necessary to conquer. We'll have all the rest as surplus. Now, we have a method of conquering souls, and through you...."

My cousin launched into long explanations concerning that method. It was a question of a magical chain of which I was to be one of the links, and a host of things that surpassed my understanding. In the end, I was only listening with a distracted ear, and thinking about something else, but I felt a shock on perceiving this sentence:

"Do you remember Inès de Saldanna? She will be the second link in the chain."

I was ready to demand explanations. Certainly, I would have liked nothing better than to make a link in that incomprehensible chain in such company; but at that moment someone lifted up the flap of the little tent that I occupied in the midst of the tents of the officers of the imperial retinue. The Emperor was asking for me urgently.

My surprise was extreme. I thought that I had lost the favor that I had enjoyed. Since the siege of Asir had commenced, I had not been able, in spite of my requests, to be

---

[35] This entire episode is fictitious, but appears to be based on a paragraph in Du Jarric relating to the siege of "Syr." The reference is probably not to a city, although there are references to a city of Asir, but to the fortress of Asirgarh, the so-called "key to the Deccan," which Akbar besieged, eventually capturing it in 1601 (a date inconsistent in the present story with the dates of earlier events, such as the death of Abu'l Fazi.) According to Du Jarric, Syr was surrendered because its commanders were bought off with gold, but Magre's lurid account of the climax of the siege is infinitely preferable in the currency of melodrama.

designated among the troops that had attempted assaults against ramparts. We had been there for several months, and the rumor had begun to go around that the city of Asir was decidedly impregnable and that the imperial army would be obliged to resume the northward route, not because of the value of the defenders of the Deccan, but because of the height of the walls of the ancient city.

My cousin came out with me and he indicated to me, among the inextricable host of tents, the direction in which he was camped, with two other Jesuits and the priests of different religions who always followed the army.

As he drew away, I noticed, not without astonishment, under the hem of his floating robe, red sandals that I had never seen before.

There was need, for a hazardous enterprise, of a man whose courage almost extended to folly. They had thought of me.

The siege of Asir was becoming eternal. The city enclosed behind its ramparts the elite of the Deccan armies, provisions for several years, immense riches and certain pagodas so ancient and sacred that the gods of India were reputed to inhabit them when they came to earth in human bodies. On an isolated rock in the Satpura chain, with its citadel framed by precipices, its fortified walls, its vaulted galleries and its hills guarded by three fortresses, connected together by lines of ramparts, Asir gave the impression of a great geometrical figure in granite. For centuries, the kings of the Farrukhi dynasty, in anticipation of the coming of the men of the north, had hollowed out subterrains, built arsenals, elephant parks and interior courtyards for livestock. The city was vast in spite of its stone limits; every house had reserves of nourishment in the depths of its cellars, just as every tower had shelters for archers on the platforms of its terraces.

Bahadur, the descendant of the Farrukhis, had only just mounted the throne of the Deccan. He had been cloistered in a remote castle until his thirtieth year, in accordance with the custom of the sovereigns of India, for only thus could royal heirs be preserved from assassination. A Brahmin sage had instructed him in divine things but had not thought that a future King ought to know the things of the earth.

Abruptly snatched from his solitude, he had received the supreme power at the moment when Akbar's armies were entering his kingdom on all sides. The Omrahs of the Deccan, the old regent Tchand Bibi and her Abyssin ministers had ceased their quarrels in order to gather the unanimity of resistance around him. Ten thousand armed warriors had solemnly come in search of the son of the ancient kings. He had been found clad in white in a garden of laurels, in meditation alongside his aged master.

At first he had refused the offered royalty. He only believed in the efficacy of prayer; he did not want to quit his white robe, not to abandon the man who had instructed him and who had made a vow to die in the shade of the fig tree under which he was sitting. "That won't stop it!" had been the reply. The uprooted fig tree had been carried away on an elephant's back, the old Brahmin in its shade, and him, in the same ascetic's robe, to pray for his people—but the men of the Deccan would know that the legitimate descendant of the Farrukhis was in impregnable Asir.

To the astonishment of everyone, Bahadur of the innocent heart had seized the reins of authority with a firm hand. He had kept his linen robe, he had had the fig tree planted, he had sat down beside his master, but he gave orders that were peremptory, albeit mysterious. He was the one who had decided the resistance to Akbar's armies, in spite of the advice of the minister Abyssin Nahang, but an unexpected resistance. He had had a meeting with Aboul Fazi and had learned how benevolent the domination of Akbar would be if he submitted. He had returned to Asir and had closed the gates. God alone would decide, he had said.

The siege had begun, but he had given orders to the operators of thirteen hundred artillery pieces and mortars lined up on the ramparts only to fire in the night in the direction of the stars. In the same way, on the bastions, the boilers had been heated in order to launch boiling oil at a pure loss when there was no attack. The army would withdraw of its own accord, he said.

It had not withdrawn. At the first attacks, the sovereign's pacific orders had been violated. The war had been exercised with its habitual fury.

Eleven months had gone by.

And now Akbar and his chiefs were wondering whether they would ever succeed in taking Asir. It was the month of Zilhidja, which we call July. The heat was overwhelming. Epidemics had broken out among the troops. The earthworks could only be carries out at night. The cavalry was useless and the horses were dying in large numbers. Certainly, many deserts assured them that the city of Asir had become an inferno, that there were many partisans of surrender, that the mortality among the discouraged inhabitants was so great that the dead were no longer being buried. Sometimes, the wind blew a reek of the charnel house from the city as far as the besiegers. But they were sure of nothing. The fury of resistance is rooted in souls and the defenders of Asir might have to be killed to the last man.

Now, one man who had escaped from Asir by night and who was being kept out of sight near Aboul Fazi's tent had come to make a proposition. He alone knew, he said, of a narrow passage through the mountains departing from the ditches and ending inside the city wall, between the populous district of Takhati and the fort of Malgarh. He offered to lead warriors along that passage. The man was employed in the bunkers where the powder was stored. His name was Bahagum; he seemed trustworthy.

Emperor Akbar did not want to risk a troop in that hazardous enterprise. He consented to risk the life of one man, who would take account of the condition of the city and the possibilities of an attack by that route. I was to be that man.

"I would have preferred him to be less ugly," I said, when I saw Bahagum.

"It appears that it was an accident," said the officer who had accompanied him. "Once, when he was sleeping in the open, a hyena tore away a portion of his face."

"And why is he betraying his own people?"

"Like all traitors," the man, who was full of experience, told me, "for money. He has asked for a lot of money. And like all traitors, he says that the money is not for him but for his wife and children."

I had hair long enough to be knotted over my shoulders. I stripped down to my underwear, over which I put a kind of cotton smock, so that I looked like just anyone, neither poor nor well-off.

Bahagum had arrived shortly before dawn and it was necessary to wait for the end of the following night, for the surveillance relaxed during the hours preceding sunrise. Aboul Fazi wanted to accompany me as far as the limits of the camp. He gave me the name of a notable inhabitant of Asir who had been won over to the Emperor's cause and by whom I could have myself recognized.

As he was about to quit me he hesitated for a few seconds, and then called me back in order to say in a low voice: "Be on your guard. While interrogating that man it seemed to me several times that he was not entirely in his right mind."

We traversed the dried-up ditches thanks to the moonless night, avoiding the patches of light cast by the torches attached to the round path of the ramparts. The entrance to the passage to which my companion led me opened at the foot of one of the bastions of Fort Malgarh.

It was necessary to crawl under the thickness of the wall. Then we found ourselves in a kind of tunnel, which broadened or narrowed, doubtless in accordance with the form of the rock under which we were moving. My companion preceded me with a lamp. When we arrived in a kind of room where I could almost stand upright, he turned round in order to say: "The crocodiles of the ditches once assembled here in heaps. Now there isn't a single one."

He seemed to regret it. Then we took a rudimentary staircase that rose up in a spiral. I imagined that such a passage must have been contrived when that tower of Fort Malgarh was constructed. It was the most ancient. I had heard it said that it was prodigiously old, built before known epochs by a race of giants. The stairway was, however, so narrow that it seemed rather to be made for the usage of dwarfs.

It was necessary to crawl again. Suddenly, my companion stopped, extinguished his lantern and made me a sign to come alongside him.

"We've arrived," he said.

I could only see darkness in front of me, but I was bathed by cooler air..

"The passage opens into a well," my companion murmured.

"Into a well?"

"It's dry, and corpses have been thrown into it. That's how I discovered the passage. I came down with a rope in order to see what the dead had in their pockets."

Bahagum uttered a bizarre sound that must have been laughter. "One is always robbed in such cases, but I get my revenge by biting them in the good place."

"What is the good place?" I asked, troubled by his strange words.

He touches my cheek with his finger drawing a circle.

I shivered, imagining that horrible being biting dead men in the depths of a well. The idea of a fall chilled me with horror.

"How are we going to get up?"

"A rope might have given an alert, although the place is solitary. We'll hang on to the stones. But in order to distinguish them it's necessary to wait for sunlight to begin to appear."

That could not be long delayed. We remained still. I sometimes felt a draught that brought us nauseating odors. In the end, I began to get drowsy. I was woken up by a warmth against my cheek and I moved my head back instinctively. I bumped it on the stone and I heard a noise of jaws snapping shut. There was a silence, and then my companion said: "Let's go—there's enough light now."

I crawled behind him, feeling my cheek.

I heard him murmur again: "You put your foot to the right."

He was above me, and I was tempted to seize his leg and make him fall to the bottom of the well, but I made appeal to my reason. I hoisted myself up behind him without too much difficulty.

The sun had risen. We were in waste ground. The sound of trumpets could be heard in the distance. We took a few steps and stopped at the foot of a few stunted palm trees. It had been agreed that I would see all that it was possible for me to see of the city, its defenders and their armaments. I had to spend my day doing that and meet my guide again at sunset. He would then take me back through the subterranean passage we had just followed and into the heart of Akbar's camp, and would receive the promised recompense thereafter. He had an interest in nothing happening to me, so he made me all sorts of recommendation.

"There are places it's necessary not to go," he told me. "Death passes there. It's almost always invisible and those it touches die suddenly without anyone being able to explain why."

He had already said that the previous day, but we had not believed him. We knew that a terrible epidemic was rife in Asir, but we could not add faith to those instantaneous deaths."

"What are those places?"

"The side-streets where the poor live. The poor are always stricken first."

It was no time to deliver oneself to considerations of divine justice. I started walking rapidly, orientating myself as best I could. I had prepared an entire story in case I was interrogated, but when I reached what I judged to be the commencement of the city, I saw that no one was thinking of paying any heed to me.

I was struck by the pestilential odor. It must have been emanating for a long time, for all the inhabitants and soldiers that I saw were holding pieces of cloth under their noses. I thought of engaging someone in conversation. I saw a family on the threshold of a house of good appearance. A large balcony cast a shadow over a tall old man who was in the middle, legs crossed, between two children. A woman a little further away was semi-recumbent, and I supposed that she must be looking for something on the ground. I slowed my pace and approached them. I got ready to offer my services to find whatever it was the woman was searching for so attentively.

I commenced a phrase, but it stopped on my lips. The old man had responded to me silently by way of the stony grimace that was fixed on his features. He and his kin had been overtaken by death. How long ago?

I passed soldiers in disorder. I went down a streets that ought to have been lined by bazaars, but whose shops were closed, and I arrived in a narrow square where several pagodas were facing one another. Hazard had dispensed me of long research. I recognized from the description that had been given to me the location of the dwelling of the rich Miram Adil, Akbar's partisan, who had been prevented from quitting Asir by concern for his property.

I was struck by the sounds of an orchestra, which had to be inside an ancient palace, doubtless the dwelling of Miram Adil. People sitting cross-legged in the square were listening to the orchestra with ecstatic faces. I wondered whether they were dead or alive; the movement of their respiration indicated to me that musical ecstasy was the sole cause of their immobility.

I penetrated into the palace without difficulty. Disorder reigned there. I climbed a staircase and, guided by the sounds, I arrived in a large room where the musicians were playing. There were dancers who were drinking and eating. Some were getting ready to leave. It was the end of a night of music and dancing. It was infinitely surprising in such circumstances, but I had acquired the habit of not being astonished by anything with the Hindus.

When the music stopped playing, a few aged men who were sitting on cushions got up and took their leave of a tall individual who had to be the master of the house. I had seen his gaze settle on me without surprise. I understood that anyone could come in, and that all precedence had been abolished in the universal disarray. I thought involuntarily of what happens when a fire ravages a forest and causes all the wild animals that ordinarily flee from one another to fraternize.

I approached Miram Adil and said to him in a low voice that I had been sent by Aboul Fazi. He did not manifest the surprise that I expected. Perhaps he did not believe me at first. He contented himself with making me a sign to wait until we were alone.

I rapidly undid the corner of my garment into which I had sewn a ring that Aboul Fazi had give me at the moment of departure and of which he made use as a seal. There were various overlapping designs engraved on it, which were the symbols of the various religions in which he believed equally. Mira Adil examined it very attentively and contented himself with saying: "The water of the sapphire is very poor."

And instead of returning it to me he carefully put it in an inside pocket of his garment.

"It's a pity that you didn't arrive sooner. You'd have seen the most extraordinary dancing girls that you'll ever see. This evening they'll all be dead."

I explained to him rapidly that, in accordance with the information that I was going to take back to the camp, a general assault would be mounted on the city of Asir.

"It will be too late," he told me. "You've arrived a day too late. Asir will be burned and the Djohor constructed beforehand."

The Djohor was a horrible custom of ancient wars in India. When a besieged city was on the brink of being taken, its defenders built a huge pyre and burned all their women and children thereon. Then they had themselves killed in combat. The Djohor of Asir was what the Emperor feared most. For centuries the Deccan had furnished sacred dancers to a part of Asia. There were several celebrated schools there, which had retreated to Asir in order to preserve them from invaders. There was not a warrior in the imperial army who did not dream about the beauty of those dancers. Akbar had given severe orders for the dancers to be protected. In the case that the city was taken by assault, it was his personal guard that was to surround the pagodas in order to defend them. I knew that if the Djohor took place, even the greatest military victory would be considered as a disaster.

"But I thought that Prince Bahadur had to an extreme the great respect for life that the religion of Brahma teaches!" I cried.

"It was thus, but evil engenders evil. On the tower of his palace, the Prince never ceases to implore his ancestors, the solar Devas. Since his master died and the fig-tree under which he sheltered has also dried up, his soul has changed and he allows his Omrahs free rein."

"Is there no means of preventing the execution of this crime?"

"No. The decision has been made. And what would be the point? Death is born of death, and death is everywhere. It appears here spontaneously, as if it were in the paving stones over which one walks, in the air that one breathes. Look."

He went to the window, making a metallic sound with every movement, which made me think that he must be carrying all his jewelry sewn into the lining of his garments. He showed me all of the western part of Asir.

"Out there are the dead that have not been buried, and of which great piles are being made. That cart drawn by oxen, preceded by a guard ringing a bell is laden with rice for distribution. No one, or almost no one, is taking any. The reserves are so great that the entire population of Asir could be nourished for some time. It is more terrible to die without cause than to die of hunger. That began with the elephants. Then the livestock followed. Perhaps they were too densely crowded in the parks. First the vultures came in thousands. They must have been visible from the Emperor's camp. They died in their turn."

Beyond a succession of stairways, behind walls of earth, Miram Adil's hand showed me the livestock pens. There was no longer anything but one vast charnel house in which designs of animals gleamed in places, traced in bones. Vultures were lurching around them.

"Death has come to the beasts," he went on. "There is a pagoda into which it penetrated when the crowd filled it and everyone was stricken simultaneously. Who knows whether it is not a supernatural intervention, whether the Unique, who orders everything, in response to Bahadur's prayers, has not sent death, as the best mediator between his children and him?"

I looked at that man, with the puffy face of a sybarite, whose sparkling eyes and plump lips revealed a mixture of intelligence and sensuality. Something that was foreign to him seemed to be fluttering around him. His natural love of life and its pleasures had given way to a strange lassitude.

"The Djohor!" he murmured. "Perhaps it's the expression of a divine thought. Our ancestors believed that. An exceptional beauty that is revealed in the rhythm and form of women, a traditional art augmented by the genius of the creatures that exercise it, ought to be destroyed rather than soiled. Is not fire the hidden breath of the supreme force?"

"But don't you think that if Akbar's troops succeeded in entering Asir today, the Djohor might be prevented?"

Miram Adil shook his head. "The situation is desperate. More than a third of the defenders and more than a third of the inhabitants have died of the epidemic. If Akbar attacked on every side at once, there would be a weak point that lacked men. But he doesn't know that. You can't inform him in time, and when you do inform him, the suicide of Asir will have taken place."

A resolution had just taken possession of me.

"I'm going to try to save the women of Asir from the pyre," I said. "I'll go back to the Emperor's camp as soon as possible. I might fail, but I might succeed. Don't you want to come with me? It's the best chance you have of saving your life."

Miram Adil had a melancholy smile, and his gaze, in scanning me from head to toe, seemed to say that I must be very young to suppose him possessed of such a great love of existence.

"I've made three journeys to Bagdad to bring back Persian miniatures that I contemplate every day because of their perfection. They are, with the beauty of dancing girls, my reason for being on earth. Now, there are other lovers of Persian miniatures in Asir. I would only have to leave my palace, and few hours later, my treasure would have disappeared. My miniatures are my children. I carry two of them, the most ancient, on my breast, but I can't carry them all."

His eyes had become brilliant. With a rapid gesture, he took a little scroll from beneath his robe, seemingly from the same pocket in which he had placed Aboul Fazi's ring. He unrolled before me an ancient piece of worn silk on which were painted, in faded colors, individuals, which might have been birds, sitting in an arbor. Everything was very indistinct and seemed to me to be devoid of beauty. I would have liked to make him see how contradictory his conduct was. His treasures would be destroyed if Asir was burned; by fleeing, he might save at least a part of them. But I had to act quickly and I sensed the futility of anything I might say.

It was not until I was in the street that I envisaged the difficulty I would have in getting out of Asir immediately. I only had a rendezvous with Bahagum at sunset. There was little chance that he would spend the day waiting for me at the well in which the subterranean passage opened. He had told me, moreover, that he had a beloved wife in Asir that he counted on bringing with him. He would certainly be with her. I did not envisage without apprehension the idea of finding my own way, alone, through a maze of dark corridors. Subterranean obscurity has always had a paralyzing influence on me. I had wondered, a few hours earlier, by means of what signs my guide took one route in preference to another. I had slipped a briquette into my belt, but it would not be much use to me if I were lost.

While making these reflections I followed the street that I had taken before. I seemed to perceive an animation that it had not had previously. Suddenly I heard cries. Women were fleeing. I saw armed men who were blocking a street to be right. Doors were banging. I started to run. Doubtless I took a wrong turn, and I arrived at a rather vast square. Was it there that the Djohor was to take place? A pyre was being built there. There must be a shortage of wood, because I saw men in the process of removing the doors from a large house. Others were throwing furniture out of windows, which was crashing down.

I almost ran into a group of people engaged in animated discussion. In the middle, a tall man, absolutely black in color, with wooly hair, was talking incessantly. That negro was majestic, and I thought that it was Nahang, the Abyssin minister, a wise and cunning man who had arrived at governing the Deccan by virtue of his oratory power. It was learned subsequently that he had always been a partisan of the surrender of Asir, but that the violence of the Hindu Omrahs had triumphed over his will. He was surrounded by silent warriors whose terrible and impassive faces I remarked. They were listening to the Abyssin's words but they were not shaken in their resolution.

The city was too narrow within its ramparts for one to be able to go astray there. I orientated myself in the direction of Fort Malgarh, which dominated it, I went back to the stairways that I had descended, still crossing the path of people running in an indescribable disorder. In the end I recognized a wall of earth that I had crossed. The well ought to be a little further on.

I was suddenly grabbed by the arm so forcefully that I nearly fell. It was Bahagum.

I remember that my first thought was to thank Providence. The second was to say to myself: *There, is therefore, a Providence!*—something that I had frequently doubted in confrontation with the incoherence and illogicality of events.

I made him a sign that there was no time to lose, and pointed in the direction of the well.

He burst into extravagant laughter.

"The well is blocked," he told me. "We're condemned to burn in Asir."

He explained to me that Abyssin soldiers, the only troops in Asir that were still disciplined and continued to fight methodically against the epidemic and death, had gone past that morning carrying bodies to the abandoned well. Then they had finished blocking it with earth.

Bahagum added that it mattered little to him. He was no longer thinking of fleeing. His wife had been one of the first to be taken for the Djohor. She was now penned with other women, to be burned a little later.

It would have laughed myself on any other occasion at the excessively sudden faith that I had placed in Providence. With lightning rapidity, I was traversed by the thought that it was my overly hasty thanks that had brought misfortune and had determined the event that would cause my doom. But I reflected immediately that the well must have been filled in long before my thanks could have reached the divinity that I blessed and cursed by turns. And I remembered that, in the vicissitudes of life, it is not appropriate to occupy oneself with divine things, but to seek in human reason the best means of getting out of trouble.

I remarked that Abyssin soldiers, recognizable by the blackness of their faces, were emerging in large numbers from a covered gallery than ran along the ramparts and heading in an orderly manner in the direction of the city. A little further on, the gallery was interrupted; there was an uncovered esplanade on to which a cannon of gigantic proportions had been dragged. That cannon was famous, and had a name, like a person. It was called Abdallah. I had perceived it in the distance on arriving and had noticed the silhouettes of the black men who were guarding it. Now, however, the esplanade was deserted. I remembered that Bahagum had been employed transporting munitions from the bunkers to the forts.

I seized his arm in my turn as he was about to draw away, no longer occupied with me.

"Perhaps there's a means of preventing the Djohor and saving your wife from the pyre," I told him. "A dangerous means—but at the point where we are, it's worth taking a few risks."

He looked at me in bewilderment. He did not seem to understand. I explained to him, regardless, the plan that had just hatched in my brain.

Abdallah, the enormous cannon, had been placed in a location where the mountain had a dip and where the rampart, being lower, had more chance of being taken by storm. If an explosion occurred inside the rampart, it might, if it were sufficiently powerful, open a breach from which Akbar's troops would immediately take advantage. I knew that the eventuality of an attack at that point had been examined several times. But where were the powder stores? Were they confided to the Abyssin soldiers that we had just seen heading for the city? What was the ordinary surveillance? Did Bahagum think that he might be able to get me into the bunkers?

At first he remained silent. Then, instead of responding to me in Hindi, the language in which he had conversed until now, or in Persian, which he spoke badly but in which he could make himself understood, he started speaking in the dialect used in Khandesh, of which I had only learned a few words in Ahmednagar.

That exasperated me to the point that I grabbed him by the shoulders and shook him. He pulled away and proffered a few incoherent remarks, still in the same barbaric dialect.

I thought that violence could only make things worse. I summoned up all my calm and, in the name of the wife that he loved and might save, I begged him to respond to my questions in Hindi. I added that I would take all the responsibility, and that he would only have to facilitate my entry, which ought to be possible for him, since he was an employee of the arsenal, and in view of the general disarray.

He finally decided to respond. It was, in fact, to the Abyssin soldiers, who were the best artillerymen and the most disciplined troops, that the operation of Abdallah and the mortars in that section of the ramparts had been confided. Emir Togrul was their chief. He had not seen him come out, but he thought that the bunkers must have been abandoned, everyone, or almost everyone, having been summoned for the Djohor. The plan might succeed.

He spoke slowly. He did not have the appearance of a man whose wife was about to be burned and who found himself in such a dramatic situation. His eyes had become astonishingly vague. He was unhurried, He seemed possessed.

"What's the point" he said. "Isn't it better to die?"

"No, no!" I shouted, forcefully, "it's better to live." And I shoved him in front of me, without knowing for sure whether that was the right direction.

It happened that I was not mistaken. We went through a vaulted gallery, and he made me a sign to go down a stairway behind him. We marched along a corridor only illuminated by loopholes. Everything seemed deserted. At the entrance to a room, a voice that seemed to emerge from the ground called to us. I saw in the gloom a man who appeared to be a cripple, with a saber across his knees. He was a guard whose disability doubtless prevented him from carrying women to a pyre. Bahagum, who knew him, said a few words to him in a low voice, pointing at me.

"Is it here?" I asked.

"No, the stones for the catapults are here. The powder is in the other room.

I saw a wooden gutter running at head-height. It was presently empty. I thought that it was a precaution in case of fire. Water could not have been circulating there for a long time, for the tree-trunks forming the conduit were dislocated and falling in places. There was an odor of mineral substance,

a damp so penetrating that I thought involuntarily that the atmosphere of tombs must be similar.

"The powder stores are in front of you," said Bahagum.
"But the Emir Togrul might appear at any minute."

His voice was imprinted with respect. Large crates bound
with iron were piled up one atop another. He added: "Those
that are to be sent up first are always opened in advance."

I had not prepared anything, and I could see that it was
necessary not to count on my companion, who as giving signs
of the most intense fear. He might even hinder me. I made him
a sign that I would act alone, and he drew away rapidly by
way of the corridor along which we had come.

My belt terminated in a fringe. I tore a strip off it and
wound it into a fuse. How easy the work of destruction is to
accomplish, by comparison with creation, which takes so
long! One spark, and everything would be finished! The difficulty consisted of saving my life. It was necessary to make a
calculation regarding the duration of the combustion of the
fuse. I had a point of comparison in the wick of my briquette,
but that was consumed with an extreme slowness. I suspected
that the one I had just fabricated would burn much more rapidly. I had to calculate the time that would be necessary for me
to regain the agglomeration of the houses of Asir. If the fuse
burned too quickly I would be doomed. If it burned too slowly, someone might come.

I fixed it between the planks of the lid. I hesitated, and
then I lit it.

At the precise moment when I gathered my momentum
in order to flee, a thunderous voice resounded.

"Who are you? What are you doing here?"

At the same time, I perceive a shadow that was blocking
the corridor.

I was tempted to tear out the fuse and crush it underfoot.
Then I thought: *By the grace of God!* The silhouette that was a
few feet away from me seemed to be gleaming with weapons.
I looked around and perceived one of the hollow trees that had
served as a gutter for the flow of water. It was enormous but

my strength is great and it was multiplied tenfold. I seized it and delivered a formidable blow to the head of the man, who collapsed. I noticed his irritated expression and his forked beard. A metal helmet rolled under my feet. Like an arrow, I traversed the space that separated me from the light.

It was my instinct that made me leap over the cripple, of whom I was no longer thinking. A blue flash passed beneath me. I heard the whistle of his saber, with which he doubtless tried to cut my hamstrings.

A clamor was rising up from the city of Asir. How beautiful the sunlight streaming over the towers of the pagodas seemed! How desirable life was! That perception took possession of me involuntarily while I raced forward. I stumbled over a crouching individual, who stretched himself out and gripped me around the neck with his hands. It was Bahagum.

"The fuse is burning!" I cried. "We only have a few minutes—perhaps a few seconds."

But he did not let go. I heard the sound of his jaws. He was trying to seize my cheek with his teeth. He had the face of a madman.

"It's better to die!" he shouted. "We're going to die!"

I struggled with him desperately. Had emotion diminished my strength while the madness that possessed my adversary had augmented his? It seemed to me that his torso and arms were made of granite. We had fallen to the ground and he was holding me beneath him. Before my eyes, the silhouette of the enormous cannon Abdallah was outlined. Gripped by a bizarre disinterest, I examine its details.

I was only thinking of protecting my face from the teeth of the madman, which were drawing incessantly closer, and at the same time, I said to myself: *But he's right! It's better to die!* And everything that I had just done appeared to me to be utterly futile. The struggle was long and unending. It lasted so long and appeared to me so atrocious that I ended up wishing that the fuse would be consumed and that an explosion would put an end to the combat.

Suddenly, I thought: *The cripple will have gone to help the man whose skull I fractured; he'll have seen the fuse and will have extinguished it.* My head touched the ground; I was holding Bahagum's jaw at arm's length, and I could no longer see anything but the blue sky. *How near it is!* I thought. *Perhaps nearer than we believe!*

And it was at that moment that an unknown but agreeable force lifted me up and projected me into the air, detaching me from the horrible grip of my adversary as if by magic. At the same time, a deafening but harmonious detonation resounded and I lost consciousness, penetrated by a sentiment of delight, for there is a mystery in great catastrophes that transforms human terror into joy.

The explosion opened a breach in the rampart, as I had foreseen, and Akbar's troops precipitated into Asir. The Djohor did not take place, but there was only a change of sex in the quality of the dead, for the garrison was exterminated in defending itself. The immense riches of the family of the Farrukhis, accumulated over centuries in the citadel, fell into Akbar's hands. Prince Bahadur only retained the fief of the Deccan nominally.

If a guardian angel watches over me, as I have always believed, it manifested the interest that it had in me that day. It prolonged my unconsciousness while the Mongols mounted the assault ad launched themselves into Asir, or I would certainly have been killed if I had attempted to have myself recognized.

It only reanimated me toward evening, and in the midst of the general disorder it guided me to the Tchagatai warriors of the Emperor's guard, whose companion I had been during the long nights of the siege. They took me to Aboul Fazi, to whom I gave an account of my mission.

Certainly, I thanked the guardian angel, for having protected me in that way. But since it was able to do what it did, it had to have a certain power over material things, so why had it not made use of that power to aid me in my struggle against

Bahagum and permitted me to escape the explosion? The man who says that destiny has played with him employs an expression full of verity, for there is a game that escapes us, a kind of cosmic chess game in which we are only derisory pawns.

THE STAR OF INDIA

The Chinese astronomer Li Tai was celebrated in the
court of Agra for having translated into pure Persian the book
of *The Perpetual Concordance with the Stars*. He had studied
the stars in Peking with the Jesuit Ricci, of whom he flattered
himself of being the friend. He had been obliged to flee China
in consequence of an imprudent horoscope of the son of the
Emperor of that country and had traversed the Gobi desert,
recognizing the route by the skeletons of humans and camels
that bordered it. He was a very savant astrologer, but he had
had the unfortunate custom of only learning from the planetary
signs about impending misfortunes of a horrible nature. He
had a love of catastrophes and he announced them incessantly.
Thus, he had advised Emperor Akbar that a certain formal
indication originating from Mars permitted him to affirm that
the city of Asir would never be taken. He was, however, not at
all confused when the event contradicted him. He was a jovial
man and, although he scorned the vulgar things of life, he
drank a great deal.

Like many men and a few women he had wanted to meet
the man who had blown up the cannon Abdallah, had been
launched into the sky along with it, and had fallen back almost
intact, while the cannon, made of thick bronze, had been pul-
verized. We had sympathized in spite of the difference in our
ages, and he had drawn up my horoscope.

My future was very somber. I would never see my homeland again. I would be bitten by a cobra and my limbs would
be paralyzed by it. The glory I enjoyed would not last long.

Astrology is very important in India, and was especially
so at Akbar's Court. I noticed that, there as everywhere else,
the errors of astrologers fortified the faith people had in them
even more than the predictions that were realized, Li Tai had a
great authority because he knew how to manipulate misfortune, which he gladly distributed in a lavish manner. Then too,

201

the fact that he was Chinese added to his prestige. One day, he made me a strange revelation.

We had gone out together on horseback to go see a celebrated ascetic whom everyone, including Emperor Akbar, held in great veneration. I had allowed myself to yield without restriction to my liking for magnificent costumes and I remember that I was wearing a long boucaran cloak lined with silver, which floated behind me. Boucaran is a precious fabric that came from Arzingan in Armenia, and which only the sons of the richest families in Agra dared to wear. I had a turban so vast, and knotted in such a manner, that it was sufficient to protect Li Tai from the sun, to whose right I was riding.

"Have you ever seen the star of India?" he asked me, while we were on the road.

"What star?"

"A star that only shines over the land of India. It's enormous and blue. I believe that one only sees it once in one's lifetime.

The existence of such a star had an implausible character, even for an ignorant young man., but I thought that the affirmation of its existence came from a great Chinese astronomer. I never knew, moreover, whether he wanted to make fun of me.

Sri Narinda, the ascetic we were going to visit, lived in the ruins of an abandoned fortress. He had been traveling for years when, on an indication he read in the sky, he had know that he had to stop. A few disciples had come to live with him and had installed platforms in the large trees nearby, like those that are fitted over the roads for travelers in case of tigers. Unlike the majority of ascetics, who are difficult to approach, Sri Narinda liked to converse with men and did not show any pride in the wisdom he had acquire. He was an exception among sages.

Li Tai and he talked for a long time in my presence, but it was in one of the numerous language of India that I did not understand. I ended up getting bored, and perhaps my foot was tapping the ground impatiently. That was involuntary, for I deem that it is necessary to respect wisdom, even in its incomprehensible manifestations.

Sri Narinda then perceived my presence. His gazed was fixed upon me. I felt a singular impression then. I understood that he said something to Li Tai about me, in which I caught one word because he repeated it several times.

"A Kshatrya! Is that possible?"[36]

They exchanged a few remarks, and Li Tai said to me: "Sri Narinda is going to make you a gift."

I waited in silence. I was surprised. Then I saw that Li Tai was bowing respectfully in order to take his leave.

"What is his gift?" I asked. For I expected to receive some object—an object of scant importance, but an object.

"It's done," Li Tai told me. "Don't you know that Sri Narinda can give a quality, as the Emperor can give you a sword, in a fashion just as real."

"And what quality have I received?" I asked, without taking account of the favor off which I was the object.

"Detachment," he said. "The seed of detachment, for qualities take a long time to germinate. The earth of the soul is hard."

I nodded my head, but I had difficulty not making my indifference to the liberality of that seed manifest.

As I bowed, in the same fashion that I had seen Li Tai do, Sri Narinda, turning toward me a visage filled with amicable irony, said to me in Persian: "When you put on the yellow robe, remember that that robe ought not to be made of a single piece, but of fragments that you have found yourself, of old fragments sown together."

When we were some distance away, I said to Li Tai: "Thank God I'm not thinking of putting on such a robe."

He smiled.

---

[36] A kshatrya or kshatriya is a member of the second Hindu caste, below that of Brahmins, the warrior caste.

I am not a historian and I have not undertaken to write the history of a great sovereign and the unusual intrigues that were woven and unraveled around him. I am recounting my personal history, which is, in sum, only of interest to me. And there, the great events, instead of being wars or treaties between peoples, are merely the appearance of a face, a rapid conversation, the memory of the homeland returning without a reason on such a day, at such an hour. I am only mentioning Kings, ministers and famous Jesuits because they passed through my life, most of the time in spite of me, and I am aware of the shocking vanity there is in giving myself the leading role in a drama in which characters like the Emperor Akbar or Aboul Fazi only play episodic roles; but I am only writing for myself, and in order to satisfy the strange appetite for storytelling that comes to a man when he has surpassed the age of passions.

How many scenes I can relive in my mind without being able to make out why I resuscitate some in memory and why others remain buried in the darkness of the soul!

I see myself in an extravagant costume, on horseback, in the middle of a troop of young men emerging from Agra through the northern gate. My conceit has become so great that I am only preoccupied, when I am in someone's presence, with knowing whether he is taking sufficient account of my merit. We are going toward vast buildings that the Emperor has had constructed on the bank of the Jumna. There, races were held, and javelin-throwing contests; one witnessed combats of elephants and all sorts of wild animals. There were marvelous gardens in the pathways of which tents had been erected in which the harems have just been installed of the Emperor, his son Selim and the great men of the Empire. Those tents like the ones that follow the Emperor in his travels, were extraordinarily high and extremely sumptuous in their colors.

We were overtaken on the road by a cavalier who sounded a special trumpet, the sound of which meant that it was necessary to move aside to allow women of quality to pass by.

We got out of the way immediately. The custom men accustomed to the manners of the Court dictated that one should look away ostentatiously. Once that rite was accomplished, one gazed, impudently, and made gestures to the women, who did not fail to respond with laughter.

A great elephant from Pegu passed in front of us. It was clad in silk and there were Tartar and Kashmiri maidservants in its howdah belonging to noble families. We knew them, and they parted the curtains of the howdah to make us signs of amity. The reserve imposed on Muslim women no longer existed in Akbar's Court, where Aboul Fazi strove to combat the prescriptions of a religion whose importance he wanted to diminish. I had, as a principle of seduction, an extreme coldness toward women, which went as far as insolence, for I had noticed that it was the best attitude to please them. I strove to look straight ahead of me and not to notice the Pegu elephant, whose enormity, celebrated throughout the Empire, ought to have rendered my apparent distraction impossible.

A Gourzeberdar in the Emperor's guard, a cynical and talkative individual, started to make his horse prance, while making absurd comments.

We then saw a chadoul covered in crimson silk drawn by two small white elephants. It was the carriage of Djidji Anaga, the great administrator and treasurer of the harems, a lady of high virtue and vast intelligence. She was not alone, as usual, with the mahout, who wore a turban and a robe of the same pale color as the hide of the little elephants. A woman was beside her, whose features I would have been able to distinguish, for I felt her gaze upon me, but for my stupid method of indifference.

"Isn't that a few rose petals falling from Djidji Anaga's chandoul?" asked the Gourzeberdar.

"It seems so," said one of his companions.

And the talkative fellow said, sniggering: "A woman is being brought by Djidji Anaga in person. It can only be a new favorite of the Emperor."

"But I thought that the Emperor…?" I said.

Laughter interrupted me. That question was often discussed at Court. Did it still happen that the Emperor had preferences for one of the women in his harem? Did he spend every evening in the study of sciences and religions? Or, as had been claimed, did he spend them playing Tchandal Mandai making use of his women as pawns?[37]

"I believe," said a taciturn young man belonging to the family of reigning Princes of Amber, "that it's rather a matter of a favorite of the Sultan Selim. I recognized her. It's an Occidental woman. We Rajputs wouldn't touch an Occidental woman with a fingertip under any pretext."

He looked at me from the corner of his somber eye. I felt a solidarity with creatures of the Occident, but I did not want to pick a quarrel. Then again, it was disagreeable to me to hear talk of the Emperor in such an irreverent fashion, for I consider pleasantry to be like an acid corrosive of the idea one has of respectable men.

And it was because of another comment regarding the Emperor that my destiny was to change course. I mean my material destiny, for that of my soul had its path marked somewhere, on a map of souls, and that course could not be modified.

Emperor Akbar had the habit of conversing with God. Everyone does that, or ought to do n it, to some extent, but without witnesses. He did it voluntarily in front of his entire Court. He devoted himself to invocations, asked for advice and for support for his people. That was because he considered himself as the representative of the divinity on earth, as a man

---

[37] The game of Tchandal Mandai, similar to but not identical to chess, is mentioned as having enjoyed a brief fashionability at Akbar's Court in Victor DuBled's *Histoire anecdotique et psychologique des jeux de cartes, dés, échecs* [An Anecdotal and Psychological history of Games of Cards, Dice and Chess] (1919).

invested with a particular mission by virtue of a special disposition of God himself.

That gave rise to many criticisms. I heard those of my
friends the Jesuits when I saw them. But I heard above all
those of orthodox Muslims grouped around Selim, the Emper-
or's son and pretender to the throne. For my part, I thought
that there is a great pride in wanting to communicate directly
with God, but as I loved the Emperor and I had sworn fidelity
to him, not only did I not allow anything of my sentiment to
show, but I said, as many times as I had the opportunity, that
Akbar's conversations with the deity were proven and indubi-
table.

At sunset, in the gardens that were staged on the banks of
the Jumna, the holy Agingir was brought forth on a large slab
of white marble and placed on the water's edge. The Angingir
was the vase in which the sacred fire was conserved. It was
sacred because it had been it solemnly at a certain hour fixed
by the astronomers and to which particular virtues were attributed. The Muslims said, of course, that it was just any fire.
Twelve candles were lit around the marble. A cantor with a
lantern in his hand that he raised toward the setting sun, chant-
ed a very pleasant prayer whose words were taken from the
Vedas. The Emperor knelt down, his hands joined, and he
listened to the advice of God.

The entre Court gathered around him, and when the
chant died away and the candles were extinguished, it was
impossible for those who saw the emotion on his noble visage
not to think that something extraordinary had taken place in
the spiritual domain.

One evening, after that ceremony, I was returning to the
palace with Omar Ali and I overheard the words that Selim,
the Emperor's son, said to one of his confidants. He had just
given hypocritical signs of adoration kneeling behind the Emperor and touching the ground with his forehead. Recently,
with the rebel Rajputs, he had attempted to take possession of

the Empire.[38] Akbar had pardoned him. But his faithful Omrahs would have liked him to designate as his successor his grandson Khosro, who, in spite of a slow intelligence, seemed to have inherited his grandeur of soul and religious tolerance, while Selim dreamed of following the letter of the Koran in which it is said that it is necessary to kill anyone who does not think like you.[39]

It was a well-established custom among the Kings of India to designate their successor while alive—a deadly custom, for as soon as his successor is designated, by virtue of another well-established custom, instead of thanking their benefactor, who is generally their father, they hasten either to have him poisoned or to imprison him in some remote castle. Akbar hesitated between Selim and Khosro, for he loved them both tenderly in spite of the ingratitude of one and the insignificance of the other. Selim dissimulated, and one sensed that he was nurturing dark projects.

That evening, for some unknown reason, he allowed his sentiments to burst forth.

He was addressing a ridiculous and effeminate individual from whom he was never separated. He was a Rajput who wore a trailing robs, several valuable necklaces and who was fat and jovial. He always had a ring whose setting was a large mirror in which he contemplated himself incessantly. He in-

---

[38] The revolt headed by Akbar's eldest son, Salim, occurred in 1599, while Akbar was busy fighting the Deccan wars.

[39] The historical Khusrau, Salim's son and Akbar's grandson, was born in 1587. Although there does not seem to be any historical foundation for the plot device employed here by which Akbar might have thought of nominating him as his heir, he was Akbar's favorite grandson, and he was still in his teens in 1605 when he led an revolt against his father, who was by then the Emperor Jahangir. Daniyal died in April 1604, more than a year before Akbar's death in October 1605, so he would not have figured in a discussion of the succession during the final year of Akbar's life.

spired a great terror for everyone knew the authority he had over Selim. That authority came from the fact that he was the brother of the beautiful Nour, whom the Emperor's son adored and wanted to separate from her husband, Shere Shah, the commander of the Emperor's guard.

"What a comedy!" said Selim, in a loud voice. "I believe that my father's falling completely into infancy. Don't you think so?"

Assuredly, I should have put on a semblance of not having heard, or found some lively, biting and unexpected repartee, in which there was a measure of wit. I found nothing, and, moreover, did not search for anything. As a dog bites when its master is attacked, I pronounced in a loud voice the perfectly banal remark: "The Emperor Akbar, the master of us all, is the greatest sovereign on earth."

Reported thus, such an affirmation might seem very anodyne, but if one pictures the servility with which Selim was surrounded and the habit he had of never being contradicted, it was a personal insult.

All of us had stopped. That only lasted a few seconds. With an admirable timeliness, Rajoura, Selim's fat companion, sought the last ray of sunlight, and by angling his ring, projected it into my eyes, which blinded me for a few seconds. That was a pleasantry familiar to him.

Omar Ali dream me away, making objurgations in a low voice, and I heard Selim say, raising his voice further as I drew away in order that I could hear his words: "That's the man who killed Yacoub. My father should have condemned him to death at that moment. Why is he still alive?"

He said other things that I did not hear. We drew away with the ray from Rajoura's mirror dancing around us.

"Beware! He's going to have you murdered," Omar Ali said to me, when we were some distance away.

But it was not me that Selim had murdered; it was the minister Aboul Fazi.

I sometimes went out alone, on horseback, along the banks of the Jumna, and I liked to stray into the middle of jungles and woods in spite of the continual danger posed by the presence of tigers. Those redoubtable animals were, it appears, very numerous, but as they did not allow themselves to be seen, I did not think about them.

One evening, I was surprised by a storm. It promised to be extremely violent. Ion looking around, I saw the ruin of a monument on a ridge and hastened to reach it in order to take shelter there. By virtue of the position of the sun and the course of the Jumna I realized that the monument was what remained of the tomb of a Muslim saint, which had been mentioned to me, and its solitude and abandonment identified. A place of pilgrimage several centuries before, no one went there any longer since a slaughtered pig had been found on its threshold. *Stay away from the tomb*, I had been told, *it's a tigers' lair*.

I had made a bad decision, but when I became conscious of where I was, night had fallen and cataracts were falling from the sky. I could not think of reaching any human habitation. It was necessary for me to wait for the next dawn. I tied my horse to the trunk of a centenarian eucalyptus and unrolled its leather leading rein sufficiently for it to be able to lie down in a room that had conserved a part of its ceiling, and into which I penetrated myself. *Thus*, I thought, if a tiger comes, *it will attack my horse before attacking me, and—who knows?— perhaps it will leave it at that*.

I chased away various birds and cut down some plants with my sword; then I examined the interstices between the stones to see whether they contained any snakes or scorpions. Afterwards, I made a bed with my cloak and lay down to sleep, having set my naked sword within reach of my hand, as well as the little flask that I always carried with me. It contained a mixture of bezoar and wild hemp, which one has to drink immediately if one is bitten by a snake, and which will preserve you from death.

My sleep was light and consisted of number of short series, separated by abrupt awakenings. The apprehensions inseparable from darkness kept me awake for a long time. I heard the voices and calls of a host of nocturnal animals but, contrary to my expectation, nothing happened. Morning arrived, and the event was of an order that I had not expected.

On picking up my cloak and shaking it, I saw that the stone on which I had slept was a slab larger than the others and that there was a figure crudely hollowed out in the left-hand corner. I scraped away the earth that prevented me from seeing the design and observed that it was that of a bearded head that bore an extraordinary resemblance to the Templars' Baphomet, the head that my cousin Du Jarric possessed, and which I had seen one morning on Emperor Akbar's linen nightshirt, in the place of the heart.

The desire for a meal, for I had not had one the previous day, prevented any examination. I departed at a gallop for Agra, which was a long way away.

On the way, in spite of the veil that great appetite casts over reasonable thoughts, I made the following reflections.

If that sign was a sort of talisman, a password of protection, it was not without reason that it might be on the slab of an abandoned monument. And since the Mongol kings had possessed that talisman and one of them had gone to hide an immense treasure in a secret place, was there any more perfect hiding place than the tomb of a saint, especially if many pious manifestation on the part of humans has been driven away by the pollution of the blood of a pig? In truth, it was an unusual stroke of luck that had led me that very night to the treasure of which my cousin Du Jarric and is Jesuit colleagues had come in search. But was it really luck? Was it not a sort of indication of my destiny, which wanted certain things of me without my knowing what they were?

I made those reflections, and I was astonished not to feel a greater joy at the thought that I might be capable of discovering a fabulous treasure. That treasure, I might, for one thing, keep for myself. Thus, all difficulties relative to money might disappear—for those difficulties had never ceased to exist for me. I was inscribed in the registers of the grand treasurer Kwaji and, on the day of the full moon, I was to receive the salary of an officer in command of a hundred men. As I did not, in fact, exercise that command and I belonged to the Emperor, my salary was doubled, but those payments were always made with long delays, for it is a particularity of India entire that the greatest luxury is always mingled with a certain meanness. There is no rich man's house that is sumptuous from the threshold to the grain-loft—like, for example, that of President d'Assézat in Toulouse[40]—and no entirely generous rich man, since custom dictates that one can only approach a powerful individual with presents. I was incessantly running after my salary, and my expenses, in any case, far surpassed that figure.

And yet I did not think of keeping those riches, if they existed—although my imagination made me consider that was certain—for myself. I would go to recount what I had seen to my cousin. Had he not saved my life? Had he not brought me to India? It was to him that I owed my fortune. Yes, I would go to see him and I would tell him everything.

Assuredly, I would go to see him…but would I really tell him everything?

Just as I was about to go to the Jesuit house, the rumor of Aboul Fazi's assassination spread through the imperial palace and the city of Agra.[41]

---

[40] Pierre d'Assézat is named alongside Jean de Balanquier in the list of Toulosan magistrates from which Magre presumably took both names.

[41] The historical Abu'l Fazi was assassinated on 12 August 1599 while returning from the Deccan by the Rajpuut chief Vir Singh Deo, also known as Vir Singh Bundela, on the orders of Salim, who knew that the minister was opposed to his accession to the throne.

He had been coming back from the Deccan, and when he passed through Siroudj, the traitor Gospal Da, the governor of the town, only gave him a feeble escort composed of particularly pusillanimous men, assuring him that the road was perfectly safe. A considerable troop of Rajputs, who had Nar Sigh for their chief, had no difficulty in putting that escort to flight in a solitary valley. Only a few warriors fought heroically. One of them distinguished himself by extraordinary courage; that was a certain Thabouk, a Turkman with whom Aboul Fazi had been discussing philosophical subjects since the departure. He had quit the métier of arms to become a fakir and to meditate naked on a rock. He had recognized that that was an error and that a mediocre employment was more appropriate to a sage. He had become a cook's aide in Siroudj, and while he was cooking bananas Aboul Fazi's eagle eye had picked him out. At the moment of the attack he had seized the sword of one of the cowards and had fought like a lion. It was not until he fell that a Rajput was able to traverse with his spear the body of the wisest man in India.

If only I had been beside the assistant cook! Two heroic men have more than double the strength of one heroic man, even though that seems contrary to the laws of mathematics. I was certain that with the valiant Thabouk, we would have saved Aboul Fazi. But it had been decided otherwise.

That fatal day was the fourth of the month of Rabr.

The Jesuits had started ringing the bells of their church as a sign of mourning.

"You see," said my cousin Du Jarric, "We have gathered all the Christians of Agra." The unique converted Hindu family was in the interior courtyard of the house.

The Jesuits were gathered in the main hall, talking about various things. They scarcely paused when I came in. For a long time I had been a cause of irritation and jealousy for them.

Each of them had his personal preoccupations and thought about them incessantly. Father Pigenro was exultant. A Jesuit who had spent several years with Father Ricci in Peking had arrived in Goa from China, and news had been sent from Goa to Agra to bring news of Benoît de Goës. He was dead. That death, certainly, filed Father Pignero with sadness, but indirectly, it brought him great joy. From what was known of Benoît de Goës' journey, it resulted that all the map of Asia in the celebrated Ortelius atlas were false, and his own maps were confirmed.

The courageous and admirable Benoît de Goës, dressed as an Armenian merchant, had initially followed the annual Kashgar caravan. He had reached a town called Charikar, had crossed the Gobi desert and had entered China through the Jade Gate. After a thousand adventures and a thousand dangers he was no more than a short distance from his brothers, the Jesuits of Peking, and it was then that he had died. For a strange and rigorous law dictates that certain men are not to be able to carry through the realization their dream and that, by a derisory order, they shall fall just as they are about to reach their goal.

Father Pimenta thought he had made a discovery that troubled him greatly. A malign demon had penetrated into him, in order to aggravate enormously a plumpness that had always been his most serious preoccupation. He was the victim of the machination of a certain bearded magician who lived in a nearby house. He had had an argument with him on the subject of the delimitation of a small garden of the church. The pagan had sniggered like a man promising to avenge himself and some time thereafter, the Father had glimpsed him striking a tambourine and devoting himself on his own, to a sort of dance. That was not a sufficient reason to accuse him, someone objected, but Father Pimenta was sure of what he said, for the magician was striking with his left hand, sometimes his tambourine and sometimes his belly. That gesture was an indication of magical action. It designated the part of the body threatened. Now Father Pimenta's belly was augmenting incessantly. He demanded a ceremony of exorcism.

I had prepared an oratory effect that I thought assured of success:

Good Fathers, it is wrong for you to have thought me in-grate. I have not forgotten that your Order had saved my life and that I was affiliated to it as a lay member. I am bringing my contribution to the common effort. The Jesuits have among their goals the conquest of material power in order to arrive at spiritual power. I might perhaps hold the thread leading to immense riches and I have come immediately to place it in your hands.

To take the floor in a conversation there is always an opportune moment. That was the moment for which I was waiting. Father Monserrate was speaking just then about the repercussion that the death of Aboul Fazi might have on their situation.

"It is a thing worthy of admiration to see how Providence skillfully causes good to come out of evil. I know, by virtue of one of the interior certainties that are never mistaken, that the Emperor Akbar has profound spiritual affinities with me. The law of sympathies and antipathies is the most mysterious in the world. As a river flows from its source to its mouth, sympathy flows from the Emperor's heart to mine. Perhaps that is because of a gift that God has given; I won't insist on that.

"Thanks to me, I'm certain that the Emperor Akbar would have been converted to Christianity had he not been turned away from it by his minister Aboul Fazi. The unrealizable and insensate dream that consists of combining all the gods of all the religions in one unique temple was that of Aboul Fazi. Now in that imagination, which is certainly demonic in one aspect, Our Lord Jesus Christ is placed on exactly the same footing as their Mohammed and their Buddha.

"It required a particularly erudite Brahmin, knowing Greek and Plato, to make the Mongol Akbar dress in the white robe of Julian and make him light the same sacred flame that comes from the first Zoroaster. That Brahmin is no more, that high priest of the sun has been slain by another pagan. We have rung the bell of the church as a sign of mourning, but in the depths of our hearts let us recognize that that has arrived for the greater glory of Jesus Christ."

I was sitting by the door. I got up quietly, and I have no idea whether my departure was even noticed.

Many things have astonished me and have appeared mysterious to me, but none so much as the movements of my own soul. Perhaps the human soul, with its tidal changes and currents that come from who knows where, is the most incomprehensible thing there is in the world.

I paid no further heed to the head of Baphomet engraved on a stone in an abandoned tomb. I wondered, when I happened to think about it, whether it was not to the Emperor himself that it was appropriate to mention it. But I knew how dangerous a secret relating to wealth might be in regard to an all-powerful sovereign, and I always put it off until later.

In any case, the Emperor spent the months that followed the death of Aboul Fazi in a profound sadness. He had charged the noble Rai Raian,[42] a very faithful but cunning man, with the punishment of Nar Singh and those who had participated in the assassination, Rai Raian set forth on campaign with an elite troop, but it was necessary to endure a pursuit through the mountains. The Vindhi Mountains are full of wild forests. The rainy season arrived. Rai Raian could not find any Rajput capable of indicating who had set the bandit Nar Singh in motion. Those who approached the Emperor at the moment of Rai Raian's return, all saw that his feigned anger disguised the conclusion of a great anxiety.

Aboul Fazi was not avenged. Alaf and Kaouf, the two former war companions of the Emperor, who never quit him and served him as slaves, received the order one day to light a little fire of a few dry branches on the stone balcony of the palace facing the direction of the setting sun. They reported that the Emperor deposited in the midst of the flames a little book bound in the skin of a stillborn lamb, which was the

---

[42] Rai Raian is named in a *History of Hindostan* translated into English from Persian by Alexander Dow in 1802 as Akbar's "secretary of state."

book of friends. He sat alongside it, stoking the fire himself, and watched the leaves of parchment as they were consumed. Several times he repeated: "Aboul Fazi!" as if he were calling to his friend, and raised his head, as if he thought that he could see his face somewhere, in the sky. The binding took some time to be consumed, but the Emperor remained there until the fire was extinct and there was no longer anything of the book but the golden clasp, blackened and deformed, in the middle of a small heap of ash.

Was there a European woman in the Emperor's harem? Or did she belong to Selim's harem, or that of some high dignitary of the Court? I could not find out. The palaces reserved for women were immense and there was no possibility of penetrating into them. Fortuitous encounters could only take place in the Summer Palace, in the shade of the gardens of the Jumna. The amity that I had inspired in Djidji Anaga might have favored one of those encounters, but the epoch of great rains had begun and the Court had deserted the tents for the stone palaces of the city.

The same inertia that prevented me from going to lift up the stone marked with the seal of the Templars in the abandoned tomb of the Muslim saint, also prevented me from hastening my steps to discover Inès de Saldanna. I sometimes astonished myself by my incomprehensible inertia. In the minutes when one jokes with one's own conscience and mocks certain traits of one's character as if they were those of a stranger I said to myself: *Is it not the invisible gift of the ascetic Narina that is acting on my nature and contributing to detaching me from what was once the object of my passions?*

And I surprised myself, in the evening, searching the sky to see whether I could discover the extraordinary star, the star that, according to the astronomer Li Tai, only shines on the land of India and that everyone only perceives once in his lifetime.

THE DEATH OF AKBAR

It was midnight. It is notable that far more dramatic events occur at that time than at any other hour. I have never been able to grasp the reason for that, but I believe that it must relate to astrological causes, and that only those who have a knowledge of the planets and their influence can explain it.

The room that I occupied at that time in the palace overlooked a long stone gallery. It was situated between other similar rooms where officers, literates and other intimates lived.

"Good evening! It's midnight!" said a low voice in the distance.

I was not asleep because of the extreme heat, and, seizing a blanket, I was about o lie down on the gallery, along the balustrade. At that moment my life changed course and without my having anything to do with it, I was precipitated on to a new and unexpected slope.

I tried to go to sleep but I could not succeed in doing so. Anxiety kept me awake. Emperor Akbar was very ill and Hakim Ali, his physician, had emerged from his room with a somber visage and without wanting to say a word. Furthermore, an old elephant, named Lone, which had once been Akbar's war elephant and which he often rode, started trumpeting desperately in the courtyard where it was penned, and no mahout had been able to make it shut up. The nocturnal palace was filled with its voice, in which it was easy to discern a mortuary plaint.

I heard footsteps in the gallery. Several men were marching without lanterns. They were speaking in low voices and as they advanced toward me, this is what I heard:

"It requires a few men of low intelligence but without scruples and courageous."

"That one is entirely indicated."

"Especially, having a hatred of Mohammedanism."

218

"Oh, he can't even know what it is. He's a Christian. It's him who killed Yacoub in single combat. That's his room."

I recognized Assad Bey, the man who had once lost me in the imperial stables on the evening of my arrival in Agra. He had always manifested a scorn for which I would have chastised him if he were not an old man. He was with Man Singh[43] and Miran, the sage, the Emperor's most faithful friends, the last of his generation.

Man Singh, who was in the lead, stumbled over me. I stood up, surprised and troubled by the presence of those considerable men. What could they be doing at midnight in a gallery that only led to the rooms of individuals who were subaltern, at least by their situation.

"Come," said Man Singh.

The door of my room was ajar. They went in. I followed them. Assad Bey closed the door carefully. I apologized for not having a night-light, and lit one.

"Darkness is better for what we have to say," said Miran.

"I hear that it requires unintelligent men," I could not help saying, as I turned to Assad Bey. "I'm at your orders, and the Emperor's orders."

It was Man Singh who spoke; his voice was grave and emotional, and from his first words I was ready to do what he was about to order me to do, because I knew that he loved the Emperor.

It required unintelligent men, but courageous—he hesitated—and unscrupulous. That meant, he explained, without religious scruples. The Emperor might die at any moment. Who would succeed him? He had not absolutely designated his son Selim. He had thought about his grandson Khosro, a weak young man, not daring to accomplish any action because of the hatred it might excite. Selim had revolted against his father. The magnanimous Akbar had pardoned him. But it was not a secret for anyone that he hated his father. Those who

---

[43] Man Singh I (1550-1614), the Rajah of Amber, was one of Akbar's most trusted generals.

loved the Emperor wondered whether the abrupt illness that had struck him, and which resembled a poisoning…but it was better not to think of that. If Selim reigned, Akbar's work and the work of Aboul Fazi would collapse. Selim was a limited Muslim who had often said that the Koran was right in prescribing the death of those who did not believe in the true God. He was a cruel man. He had just flayed one of his servants is horrible conditions. A group of fanatical dervishes had already prepared the persecutions that the Hindus were about to suffer throughout the Empire. Foreigners, even the Emperor's friends, would be massacred.

He stopped. There as a silence. It was Miran who spoke. In the semi-darkness I could see his white beard like a circle of light.[44]

"It's Khosro who must be Emperor. We've put all our hopes in him. Khosro must be Emperor, even against his will, for the good of men. Just men will govern in his stead, if necessary. If the Omnipotent withdraws our master Akbar tomorrow, we'll proclaim Khosro. Except that it's necessary to prevent Selim…."

There was another silence. The wick sizzled in the oil of the night-light. I wanted to reanimate it. Miran stopped me with an abrupt gesture.

"No, no light, above all."

Assad Bey started speaking in the tone of a man who thinks: *It's necessary to finish it.*

"At the moment when the Emperor renders his last sigh, all those who have loved him and loved Aboul Fazi will cry 'He has designated Khosro! It's Khosro who is Emperor, by the will of his grandfather.' It's then that it's necessary to make sure of Selim. He also has partisans. Among ours, many who ardently desire his fall won't dare to raise a hand against him. He is still the son of the man who represented God on earth. And the fear of reprisals! The Gourzeberdars are with

---

[44] Miran's beard was black when he was in Almaner, but this scene is probably set some four of five years later.

us; they will cry: 'Khosro!' But touch Selim! You would dare. You know full well that if Selim is Emperor you'll be among the first victims. And he'll reestablish the tortures abolished by his father, like impalement, which causes suffering without killing for an entire day.[45] And you can be sure, whatever happens, that no one will reproach you for anything. Even...."

"No, I have no need of recompense for carrying out an order of arrest, even the arrest of Sultan Selim."

The night-light went out, and I firmly believe that Miran had blown it out.

"There are duties that are without glory," he murmured. "In any case, the anger will be great."

Three Gourzeberdar officers were, as far as was possible to place themselves behind Selim at the decisive moment, and were to throw themselves upon him at the same time as me. I was told their names. I would have preferred that they had not chosen three despicable men given to drinking and ruined by debt. I sensed that more was expected of me than them.

"There are others as well," said Man Singh, "but you, who are a warrior, know the importance in any action of the man who dares to strike the first blow."

I could no longer see the whiteness of Miran's beard. My three interlocutors went out like phantoms.

Alone in the shadows I wondered to whom I ought to address myself in order to know what I ought to do. I remembered my prayers of old, and a certain clarity that filtered over me through a stained-glass window on a Sunday afternoon when I once went to kneel in the little church of the Minimes near Toulouse. But Aboul Fazi had spoken to me about so many gods, all very good and very powerful. He had even told me that they were only one with Jesus Christ, But they were

---

[45] The historical Salim, as Jahangir, did indeed restore the punishment of impalement, and had all the supporters of Kusrau's revolt impaled, with Khusrau looking on, before he had Khusrau blinded.

confused in my mind. They were too numerous. I did not know to whom to address myself.

I went to sleep.

The Emperor had had a marble hall built, surrounded by columns and refreshed by air currents, for the burning sands that surrounded Agra were the cause of an ardent heat. It was there that the throne made of precious stones was, where he received the Kings who were his subjects. He had himself taken to that hall and his bed was placed at the foot of the throne.

The rumor immediately went around that he was getting better, and was accredited all the more because he wanted his intimates, of which I was one, to gather around him. Nevertheless, the physician Hakim Ali, a modest man suddenly clad in an immense authority, demanded that they keep their distance—which was possible, given the size of the hall. The morning went by in the greatest optimism.

Selim only came to see his father momentarily. He had a distracted air, and recoiled if anyone came too close to him. He kept his right hand in a broad belt, in which the hilt of a dagger could be seen. He pretended to believe that his father was almost cured and looked to the right and left as he withdrew.

"He knows that the game is lost for him," Omar Ali said to me in a low voice. "He's secretly preparing boats in order to flee with his intimates on the Jumna if his father dies."

The Emperor loved perfumes; aloe wood and certain essential oils whose formulae he had devised himself, were burning perpetually. He gave an order to have them extinguished. Then he demanded that the objects necessary for smoking tobacco be brought to him. That caused great surprise, and it was thought that the request was occasioned by the presence next to his bed of the physician Hakim Ali and of Assad. Several years before, Assad Bey, returning from an embassy to Bijapour, had brought back tobacco, then unknown, with wooden pipes. It was by way of a curiosity. The pipes came from China and had been brought to Bijapour by the Dutch. A great discussion had taken place. Hakim Ali considered the novelty to be dangerous. Assad praised it. But the Emperor, having tasted it, had not liked tobacco.

The old argument nearly resumed—but the Emperor was no longer thinking about it. That desire augmented the general optimism.

"He wanted to smoke," everyone murmured—and that rumor spread out of the palace and was repeated throughout the city of Agra.

But in the course of the afternoon, the Emperor made a sign to Assad that he had an order to give him. His special function, for years—a function that conferred upon him the title of first Saibani—was to go and fetch Emirs to whom the Emperor wished to speak. He had the order repeated twice. The Emperor ordered him to fetch Mouzaffer Khan.

Now, Mouzaffer Khan, a great administrator of the Empire, a man devoted to Akbar, had been dead for many years.

In his embarrassment, Assad took a few steps, hesitated, and came back. He adopted the attitude that he habitually struck when he wanted to announce an Emir. The Emperor lowered his eyebrows gently and smiled in satisfaction. He made another sign to Assad. This time he asked for Todor Mal. Todor Mal was a man of war who had often fought beside the Emperor. He had been elevated to the highest dignities, because of his fidelity and also, it was said, because of his Buddhist faith. But he was dead.

Assad undertook the same pantomime, and thus the Emperor summoned and seemed to see grouped around his bed many faithful companions of his youth: friends, warriors and philosophers that he had loved, and whom the inexorable separator, death, had stolen from him. Thus appeared the mullah Azamuddin, who had instructed him in matters of religion when he was a child, and old Bayard, who walked on crutches, and Mounim Khan, who had the stature of a giant and had taught him to shoot a bow. There was Bairam, who had been with him at the siege of Tchitor, had run by his side through explosion of mine, had stood to his right when he had killed Djamal the Lion, had lent strength his soul before the pyre on to which the vanquished had precipitated the Rajput princesses. There were the Brahmins who had taught him the mysteries of Siva and the Parsees with whom he had measured the relationships that might exist between the element of fire and the divine spirit.

Every time that Assad received an order he took a few steps, and could not help repeating in a low voice the name of the man requested by the Emperor, and that name was repeated by the audience, who stepped back, as if to make way for the invisible newcomer.

There was also the ascetic Tchichti, celebrated for his sanctity.[46] Often, alone and on foot, Akbar had gone in pilgrimage to the village of Sikri and he had meditated with him, sitting on a stone burned by the sun. Now the ascetic came in his turn to find the Emperor. When Tchichti's name was pronounced, it was if a breath of veneration had blown between the colonnades of the hall, everyone bowed and made the taslim prescribed in the ceremonies for the greatest individuals.

Then the Emperor face brightened very slightly, and he had the appearance of listening to words that did not resonate. He had spoken the name of Faizi, the poet who had spent many evenings reciting fragments of the Mahabarata to him, and other sacred books of India. Faizi was the brother of Aboul Fazi, and it was Aboul Fazi, his friend, his adviser, almost his brother, whose measure, wisdom and sense of justice had guided him, that he named last. Aboul Fazi had been the intelligence of the Empire, and when his name had been pronounced, all heads bowed.

A great void was made around the Emperor's bed; but it was only an apparent void. It was filled by all the companions

---

[46] The Sufi saint Salim Chisti (1478-1572). Akbar thought so highly of him that he had a city, Fatehpur Sikti built near his home and moved his Court there for a while.

who had followed the Emperor in the course of his long life. And everyone understood that a choice had presided over their summoning. There was not one Muslim among them. All of them were among those who, although penetrating to a greater or lesser extent the meaning of his work, had aided him to realize it. All of them, including the warriors, had had a human love of the ideal. They had wanted, with their master, to suppress hatred by suppressing the barrier of religions.

Some had aided him with their weapons, others with their intelligence, the poets by means of the meaning of their poems, the administrators by the exactitude of their accountability. And in designating them to witness his final hour, in pronouncing in a low voice the names of those he had judged good and just during his life, the Emperor had designated his successor. He had set aside his son Selim, the enemy of his work, and given the crown to Khosro. All the witnesses of the scene understood that, at the same time as they perceived the silent gathering of invisible friends.

In the hours when the soul is about to quit the body definitively, a man must already find himself in a region where the difference between the living and the dead is already not very sensible, if it even exists. The Emperor's face had taken on an expression of calm quietude. The cares that tormented him had disappeared. All those he had loved were around him and his circular gaze contemplated them in turn as if to thank them for having come at the hour of his final deliberation.

The presence of the dead was so real that I had the sensation that they were crowded in the space that had been reserved for them. I headed toward the officer in command of the Gourzeberdars in order to indicate to him the urgency there was in moving back a little further the living grouped around the Emperor's bed. But I stopped before reaching him. I had the perception that something had just happened. I was not the only one to take account of it. Assad quit his official attitude as the announcer of Emirs before the throne. I saw that Miran, who had kept his head bowed, raised it now and passed his hand over his long beard, wiping away the brilliant droplets that speckled it.

The summoning of the dead was over. The dead had come. They had grouped around the man who had summoned them. But, doubtless by virtue of a different custom and another conception of the measure of time, visits are infinitely short in their world, and they had departed as rapidly and as silently as they had come.

I considered the Emperor's face. It had lost the tranquil peace that it had had before, and even its benevolence. He was no longer looking around. His eyes were fixed much further and much higher. He was already participating in a mode of life unknown to us. But what was distinguished was not, as is announced by the age and the just, a very seductive promise; nor was it a threat. He must already have glimpsed things absolutely foreign to human conceptions, incomprehensible things, toward which the soul only launches itself because it is borne by the unchangeable rigor of the law.

"What admirable serenity!" someone nearby said. It was less by virtue of serenity than a limited vision.

"At present, he can see the Unique God," said a Parsee philosopher, mechanically raising toward the sky the shaft of a long golden pipe from which he was never separated, and which he had hidden in his garments.

For myself, I thought that it was not the Unique he was seeing, but that he was searching for a path in an immense dusk. And that dusk was floating, so far as I was concerned, above a desert of stone strewn with stunted cacti, exactly similar to the desert of Thar, where I had accompanied him in the course of an antelope hunt and which had made him say: "How lugubrious this desert it! I wouldn't like to cross it."

For in that unknown world, perhaps there are great deserts to cross.

But I did not have to search any further. The scene changed abruptly, as if another face of life and souls appeared after the stroke the invisible wand of death.

Hakim Ali, who had not ceased to hold the Emperor's hand, put it down with infinite precaution on his breast and, turning toward the nearest witnesses he raised his arms slightly and made two or three movements of his head that signified: "It's over." Grief possessed him, but I would have sworn that at that moment, he was not penetrated by any other sentiment than the importance of his role.

A mortal silence ran through the fall like a wave, a silence that no one dared trouble and was strangely prolonged.

No one could tell how long that silence would have lasted, so much did everyone feel the impossibility of breaking it. Suddenly, a frightful cry rang out, at the same time as an old man fell to the ground as he uttered it. I recognized that cry; it was that of a hyena, in the evening, in the jungle. Kaouf, the old servant who accompanied the Emperor everywhere, imitated perfectly, and his master often asked him, in jest, while hunting, to utter it. There was an eddy around Kaouf, who was carried away without him ceasing to utter the cry of the hyena, a desperate snigger announcing the ineluctable victory of evil.

A few had run to Akbar's beside, but the majority left the hall in haste, and it was visible in their gleaming eyes that they were hastening toward material interests more powerful than vain grief. I remembered then the role that I was to play and I searched with my eyes for the Gourzeberdars who had been designated as companions. I perceived near the door the tall stature of Abdullah, nicknamed the hirsute, and headed toward him. I had thought that a bad choice had been made in selecting him, for he was a Muslim and very pious.

My soul was full of excitement. I was about to collaborate in keeping alive the thought of the great man who had just died.

Glory to courage! Glory to the spontaneous impulse that victory gives! I do not regret anything, and if time went backwards, I would accomplish the same actions.

I took a few steps toward the courtyard paved with mosaics, where jets of water were making an unusual sound, and I cried, as had been prescribed:

"Khosro is our Emperor! He has been designated by his grandfather!"

I do not know why my words seemed not to spread, and to fall back in pieces around me. I saw Miran beside me and I searched for his gaze, but could not find it, and was surprised to see him drawing away rapidly, hiding his face in a large blue cloth, suddenly exaggerating the sobs by which he was shaken.

"Shut up"!" Abdullah said to me, as an order. "The moment has not yet come."

It was, on the contrary, the decisive moment. But it passed.

"They've gone to fetch Sultan Selim" said another of the Gourzeberdars who had received the same order as me, in passing, and he made as if to draw away. But when he had taken two or three steps he came back toward Abdullah and me. His face, broadened by large side-whiskers, had taken on a cunning expression.

"Why are you still there?" he said to us in a low voice. "Believe me, the wise thing is to disappear."

I was about to cry that his duty was to stay with us, but there was a great movement at the other extremity of the courtyard.

Selim had just appeared, surrounded by his friends and other unknown courtiers. He was standing very straight, with a deliberate majesty; a false grief caused him to make a grimace. He cut obliquely across the courtyard as quickly as possible, like a son who is running too late to a dead father, a beloved father. Weapons glinted all around him.

Everything happened in a matter of seconds. I darted a glance at Abdullah, at the same time as I braced myself to run.

"God is one and Mohammed is his only prophet!" He cried, raising his arms toward the sky, with an inspired expression.

The stupor of hearing such an inopportune speech but, faithful to my original promise, I cried again: "Khosro is our Emperor!"

And I precipitated myself toward Selim.

He did not even see me. Twenty arms seized me and threw me back. While I struggled, a great rumor rose up, and I heard nothing but the name of Selim repeated a hundred times over.

A man dressed in a crimson brocade robe with a mantle of the same color made a great solemn gesture and with a voice whose timbre was enormous, to which he skillfully gave an official character by the monotony of the intonation, as if he were rep[resenting the entire land of India and all the sky that covered it, he said:

"In accordance with the ancient usage of the Tchagatai Tartars, and in accordance with the will of Allah, the living son receives the heritage of the father, and Selim Shah becomes our Emperor."

The voice was so powerful that it must have been audible far into the distance.

Half-fallen backwards, I saw a Mongol with a long beard who raised a sword above me as broad as that of an executioner. I drew my épée and parried the blow.

"Grief has rendered him mad! Leave him! I'll guarantee his fidelity to Selim!" cried someone who threw himself between me and my aggressors.

It was a man who had traversed the courtyard to Selim's left and whom I had not seen.

With amazement, I recognized Man Singh, who had renewed his orders to me an hour before.

"Lower your weapons!" he said, imperiously. "It is appropriate to meditate and not to fight."

"God is one and Mohammed is his only prophet!" cried the Gourzeberdar Abdullah, raising his arms—and for the first time, in spite of the gravity of events and the death suspended above me, I noticed the astonishing stupidity of his features.

"God is one!" was repeated on all sides. The courtyard filled up. There were prayers, cries of dolor, and conspiratorial discussions. Dusk was falling rapidly. I lost myself among the groups and started running as soon as I was out of the court-yard.

My ideas were dancing in my head like insensate cavaliers in an obscure grassland. Where could I go? During the day, Man Singh had gathered the few men who were to lay their hands on Selim. He had recommended us, in case of failure, to go to a recently-constructed hall at the extremity of the palace and the gardens, where a few hundred soldiers were hidden, all Hindus, forming part of the elite troops who bore the sign of future Omrahs on their foreheads and were faithful to Khosro. The Daroga was to command them personally. There, all the Omrahs determined to impose Akbar's grandson as Emperor would gather. That troop was to spread through the palace as seize all Selim's partisans.

While I was running I sensed on all sides the manifestations of a strange and new life, made of dolor and the hope that all transformations give, even when they are bound to be unfortunate.

On the pacing stones, alternately black and white like a chessboard, I saw several Brahmins in yellow robes, arms raised in an ecstatic pose. They must have fallen into prayer at the news of Akbar's death and they were still there, like the pawns of a mysterious game that God alone could move.

At the entrance to the garden, where two large white marble elephants stood guard, servants were arguing. Custom dictated that at sunset, two large lanterns placed on the elephants' foreheads, should be it. The servant responsible had just lit one. He was one horseback under the neck of an elephant. But another was affirming that it was sacrilege and that mourning should be manifested by darkness. He picked up a stone and tried to break the lighted lantern.

A little further away, behind the walls of gray earth, real elephants were trumpeting strangely and agitating, as if they had understood the grandeur of the event that, if it did not trouble the life of the elephant population, was about to render more miserable the life of the human population. And above the walls I saw their trunks raised to the heavens as if for a funereal adieu, an animal prayer whose uncertainty rendered it more moving.

"Hakim Ali is a wretch!" said a grave man near to whom I passed, and whom I recognized as a physician from Delhi.

He was arguing with an old man who never ceased stamping his foot and repeating: "He gave him Ganges water every day, I witnessed that!"

"Yes, but it's necessary that the Ganges water be passed through a saltpeter filter," replied the physician from Delhi, sniggering. "The wretched Ali didn't even know that Gages water only has all its powers if it's poured into a silver jug."

"Ganges water ought to be drunk without preparation!" said the old man, at the peak of exasperation.

"My master the Emperor Selim has already fixed the fate of the ignorant Ali."

"Khosro is our Emperor!" I cried, in passing.

I launched myself into the great avenue of palm trees that bordered the circular canal that the Emperor had recently had dug, and on which junks had been placed for evening excursions.

I saw the two battens of the entrance door of a hall reserved for musicians open. With a solemn air they formed a cortege. The trumpeters placed themselves at the head, then came the cymbal-players and drummers, and the great ceremonial drum appeared last, with its guards. Where were they going and under what order?

I knew that Mourtazan Khan, a considerable individual, and the high functionaries of the Empire determined to raise Khosro to the throne, had gathered a large number of warriors in the city and ought, as soon as the news of Akbar spread, to appear at the main gate of the palace and make their entrance with Khosro. Perhaps I had only witnessed one episode in the drama. It was the arrival of Mourtazan Khan and the Omrahs accompanying Khosro that would decide everything. Perhaps they were already masters of all the exits and summoned the musicians for I know not what ceremony.

"Who has been proclaimed Emperor?" I asked a man with a bird-like head who seemed to be leading the musicians.

He looked at me attentively.

"Who knows!"

"Where are you going?"

"Who knows?"

I continued on my way.

The canal was always furrowed by junks carrying the women of the harem, who hid behind colored veils disposed at the rear, but this evening it was deserted, or nearly so. A single junk was gliding slowly there is the declining dusk, and came to the shore near me, at a place where an oblique path lined by strange stone figures formed a communication between the canal and the palace where the harem was.

I ran. I nearly collided with a woman who was emerging hastily from the junk. The state of agitation that I was in did not permit me, at the time, to measure the audacity of her gesture—the abrupt, willful gesture with which she moved aside, or rather ripped away, the light fabric that hid her face. I had seen it for a second. It was Inès de Saldanna.

Consciousness requires an interval of time in order to make sure of the reality of an event. That interval went by while I continued running. I stopped. I went back. Perhaps I had been deceived by an apparition. The oarsman of the junk was striking the water with regular strokes and drawing away. The silhouette of a woman was running between the stone forms. I saw her turn round. I believe that she lifted a hand that held something, perhaps a rose, and she disappeared into the palace. I heard the door close.

I was only a few paces from the hall of the rendezvous. It was an immense room adjacent to the observatory of Li Tai and the court astronomers. It had been constructed with vast dimensions in order to contain a large telescope, on which Chinese workmen were laboring. Those same dimensions had caused it to be chosen for the assembly of Khosro's partisans. It ought to have been vibrant with the presence of a numerous troop. It was, on the contrary, silent.

I opened the door. Instead of the armed host that I should have seen, I perceived in a corner, leaning on a pike, a thin old man whose tall stature seemed further elongated by the presence of a narrow white beard, formed in a tress, which fell almost to his feet. He darted a terrible gaze at me and spoke a few severe words in a dialect unknown to me. Through his parted robe, I saw that he had a wooden leg.

I had such a need to speak to someone that I uttered a sigh of relief when I saw Li Tai appear. He was the one who spoke first, and in abundance.

There were conjunctions of planets that announced abortive projects. His personal method, based on rigorous calculations, permitted him to evaluate with exactitude the equilibrium of good and evil. Now, that evening, the equilibrium had been destroyed and evil had triumphed. There was a star, the mysterious star that only shines over the land of India, that was about to disappear. It could still be perceived intermittently, then it would enter into slumber; it would go to place itself in the unknown and very distant region where the stars sleep.

Fortunately, he was interrupted by the old man with the wooden leg. He seemed irritated. He struck the ground with his pike and decided to go away, having said more things that we did not understand.

"He's a Pathan," Li Tai told me. "A few others have come like you and gone. It's never the courage that is lacking. When the stars are contrary, it is the direction that is at fault. Whatever the force of the wind might be, the vessel turns according to the tiller."

My disarray was so great that I told Li Tai the story of everything that had happened to me since the moment when Assad, Man Singh and Miran had come to find me during the night.

"Do you know Mourtazan Khan?" Li Tai asked me.

I had heard mention of that powerful Rajput, a friend of the Emperor, but I had never had occasion to see him.

"By the description you've given me, I'm sure that it is him who is accompanying Selim and that it is him who was the first to proclaim him Emperor. He is the only one to possess a voice of such resounding timbre, the power of which is to play a role in influencing souls."

I saw that he was considering me gravely.

"If you are wise," he said, "you will prepare yourself for death."

"What?"

"The first thing of which Selim will think is making sure of his power by making all the overly zealous partisans of Khosro disappear. He will not go against that custom of all sovereigns. But death is very little and it is even necessary to rejoice when it comes."

Doubtless my visage did not express any joy, for he went on: "Think of the new worlds that you will contemplate. You must often have asked yourself questions about the state that will follow death. Your curiosity is finally about to be satisfied."

I replied that my curiosity was exercised far more over things of this life than on what might happen in an uncertain existence in which one is deprived of the precious support of form. I hoped moreover—I only said that to reassure myself—that the powerful men who had pushed me would not fail to defend me. Man Singh was renowned for the grandeur of his soul and the wisdom of Miran was discussed throughout India.

"Child!" said Li Tai. "Man Singh has acquitted himself with you, since he defended you, Miran has become too wise. Courage decreases as wisdom grows. First of all, you are a foreigner, which is an entitlement of death at this moment. Then, those great individuals will feel that in order to maintain themselves among the other great individuals, they ought to show manifestations of disloyalty. A new period began to unfold the moment that Akbar's soul drew away from the earth. Believe me, prepare for death."

I objected that after drawing up my horoscope he had announced that I would be bitten by a cobra and that it would lead to paralysis.

He had completely forgotten the cobra. He shrugged his shoulders and in a tone of confidence, he said: "Death is by far the best solution. But it is necessary to prepare for it. My own life is hanging by a thread. The study of the stars is contrary to Muslim orthodoxy. The fanatical mullahs are going to demand my head. I've been preparing for death since this morning, and I'm joyful. Through a telescope, the stars remain extremely small. I'm certain that the soul can fly a long way, as far as the conception of infinity permits. Mine is immense."

I listened distractedly. A prodigious appetite for life possessed me. I deliberated within myself as to what it was appropriate to do. I went to the door and studied the palace and the gardens. Night had fallen. Lights were wandering here and there, others vaguely illuminating the mashrabiyas screening the windows. I thought that I was in the one place where it was inappropriate to remain. Selim's men might have caught wind of the rendezvous arranged for this hall, and it was at risk of being surrounded at any moment.

I heard furtive footsteps and saw a shadow coming toward me. I uttered a sigh of relief on recognizing Omar Ali.

"Come," he said to me.

I said a rapid adieu to Li Tai and I followed him outside, but he only took me a little further than the astronomer's house to a place where the banks of the Jumna limited the imperial gardens. While walking he brought me up to date rapidly.

Selim was Emperor, even though the Court and the people were unanimously in favor of Khosro. The fear that people had of him had brought him to the throne more easily that love would have done. That fear had paralyzed all resolutions and I was the only one to have attempted to realize what had been decided. They were searching for me. The wretched Rajoura had put armed dervishes at all the doors. I was to be slaughtered without explanation. It was necessary to flee, to quit Agra immediately.

We descended a stone stairway accommodated in the slope of the bank. I saw several boats without lanterns lined up in succession. On the water, where a few stars were reflected, they made long patches of shadow. I found them surprisingly beautiful because of the speed that their slim form revealed.

"They've been prepared at hazard, in case of fighting and defeat. The boatmen belong to Man Singh and they'll take you as far as you desire. Man Singh also instructed me to bring you this."

He handed me a small package wrapped in leather, which, I judged on touching it, had to contain gold. He approached a boatman standing on the sand and spoke to him in a low voice. Then he returned to me.

"There's no wind. You have only to allow yourself to be carried by the current. Don't stop at Tawah, whose governor will have been alerted. Much further on, you'll find a small village called Kalpi, where there's no garrison. But it would be better to quit the Jumna before then and try to reach Goa or Surat. There are Dutch trading-posts in Lahore, and even Jesuits, who might hide you. Think about the best course to take."

One never gives thanks for the great services on which life depends. The word thanks represents trivial currency that one uses for petty transactions. I climbed into the boat silently. There were two oarsmen and a third who detached a mooring-rope and rolled it up with disconcerting slowness.

I was suddenly seized by a desire to lie down on the ground and await events. That discouragement came too late. I felt a shock, as if a large bird had fallen on me. Omar Ali had thrown me his cloak.

"The night will be icy," he said to me. "You'll be glad to have it at midnight."

Was there a charm in that cloak? All my combative strength returned. I put my hand on the hilt of my sword. I had a desire to go back, to run to the palace and hurl myself at those who did not respect the will of the great dead Emperor, the admirable Akbar.

The boat started to move slowly. I felt Omar Ali's arms around my neck.

"May God protect you," he murmured.

THE TOMB OF THE SWORD

God protected me in accordance with that wish. He did even more. He penetrated me and transformed me. Like the warrior in the *Iliad* of whose name I am unsure because of my incomplete studies, whose body, steeped in a marvelous water, became invulnerable, he gave my soul the invulnerability of detachment.

The boat glided noiselessly. Skeletal rocks loomed up on both sides of the Jumna. The beauty of the world appeared to me as hard and cold as the destiny I had before me. A fortunate arrangement of human nature dictates that when one loses certain goods, they immediately cease to be indispensable. The contrary is also true. But perhaps the words of Li Tai were acting within me. I thought seriously about death, for in weighing up the pros and cons I estimated that my chances of living were quite slim. Rajoura would be unable to forget me. He was both fat and perverse, and hated thin men of normal mores. Selim was scarcely emperor when he had started a search for me. I only had one night's start. Couriers would depart the next day and wherever I went I would be recognized by my costume, the sumptuousness of which would cause my doom. And I envisaged above all the necessity of having myself killed while defending myself, in order to avoid certain tortures, like that of impalement, the idea of which was unbearable to me.

On the other hand, I said to myself, was it wise to die abruptly and without preparation? Li Tai was right. Death is not very redoubtable, on condition of entering the new region whose doors one is opening with a firm soul exempt from regrets.

There was a little water in the bottom of the boat. There always is, in the boats of all lands. And I wondered why those who occupy themselves with boats do not render them absolutely watertight. That problem, insignificant by comparison with those that preoccupied me, nevertheless contributed to sending me to sleep.

I woke up with a great mental lucidity, feeling that many graver problems had found their solution while I slept, as if they had been examined by a nocturnal sage who had a secret existence within me.

Dawn was about to break. The Jumna appeared to me to be narrower, between higher banks. Clumps of palm trees formed isolated groups here and there, which seemed to be making signs. In the bottom of the boat the water was no more abundant. Had someone emptied it out? It would have been puerile to make enquiries.

The sage that makes decisions during the night had settled on a plan.

The brilliant young man who had conquered the favor of Akbar was condemned. He had to disappear. The people of India have other divisions than those of Europe. There are, at the summit, those who dispose of wealth, arms and costumes and who travel on elephants or in bizarre ox-carts. They recognize one another by their facial features or the houses they inhabit. But below them, there is an immense multitude of naked men who have no house, sleep under the trees and are eternally traveling on the pretext of making pilgrimages. They live on mendicity and no one knows whether they are simple beggars or ascetics who are thinking about God. It sometimes happens that they are both, for the profession of mendicant is considered as infinitely honorable, and certain beggars are superior to the highest dignitaries. I had heard the great Katoual, who had the entire police of Agra under his orders, say that many criminals could not be apprehended because they had rid themselves of everything that made them a particular individual and become one of those anonymous naked men. I resolved to disappear into that human ocean too.

The sun appeared and the heights that bordered the Juma lowered as if it had melted them. I perceived the low houses of a village in the distance. I made a sign to the boatman that I wanted to be set down there.

I deliberated for a moment as to whether I ought not to divide between them the entire contents of the little leather bag that I had received the previous evening. I rejected the thought. A sudden and excessive fortune could only trouble those simple creatures, I gave them a gold mohur to share and they prostrated themselves, touching their heads to the sand of the shore. The word Akbar was in the words of thanks that they pronounced, and I took a bittersweet joy from that.

The blade of my épée was chipped several times against stones while I was digging. That would have afflicted me at any other time, but in digging that tomb, it no longer had any effect on me.

For it was a tomb that I was digging: the tomb of my sword.

I thought about the Rue des Couteliers in Toulouse and Jean-Baptiste Phalipon, an extraordinary artist in steel and the possessor of ancient secrets relative to that metal. It appeared to me for the first time that Phalipon had a diabolical visage. He never sold a dagger without saying: "You can open your man in two with a single thrust."

Are not sharp and trenchant weapons instruments of evil, since, as soon as one makes use of them, one causes dolor and death?

And while digging, an extraordinary sentiment took possession of me. I had been accompanied by an evil sand cruel spirit of nature, whose body was that sword, of which I had been proud for such a long time. It had only served me to kill. It was a companion of perversity, the agent of an immense force that had delegated it to me. That companion had driven me to many evil actions. It had stimulated my pride and my violence. Why had I not rid myself of it sooner? The moment when I was about to separate myself from it was blessed among all.

When I had dug a sufficiently deep hole, I placed my épée therein, and the bag of gold coins. I threw over them my splendid turban, which had been the astonishment of men, my belt and all my garments. I cut my hair but kept, temporarily, the sandals that I had tied crudely with string, for my feet would have been too rapidly lacerated by the brambles of the path. Then I replaced the earth that I had removed and trampled the soil in order to erase the trace.

Then I felt a great calm, and a kind of joy that I had never experienced before descended into me. I had just buried the evil genius of my life. I was alone and I was free. I would have liked to thank someone, but I did not know who and I postponed until later the elucidation of the problem of the spiritual benefactor who had guided my actions and orientated my destiny.

I went back down to the bank of the Jumna and I disturbed the birds that were fluttering over the water. They must not have been accustomed to humans, for they did not fly far. I covered my hands with mud and I threw it over my face in order that the mud would have effaced my features when the sun had dried it and no one would be able to detect my age I had seen certain ascetics wearing that mask and observed that it rendered them more respectable. Then I coated my hair and the rest of my body.

The sacrifice of my cleanliness was painful to me at the time, but on seeing myself in the water, so different from myself, I was filled with satisfaction at having achieved the result that I wanted.

When I passed the tomb of my sword again, I was not surprised to see an enormous scorpion of particularly hideous appearance wandering next to the stones I had thrown over it. Nature is full of such singular correspondences.

And suddenly, the spirit of the new man that I was, by external appearance, was occupied by a single image, that of my mother. I sometimes thought about her, but, without taking account of it, I rejected the thought of her, feeling that it was inappropriate to mingle it with the life that I was leading. Was it because my life had changed direction? It seemed to me that she was beside me and that she replaced the evil genius that I had just quit.

What had become of her? Was she still alive? Was she waiting for me in the house in the Rue Malcousinat? At the moment when I was about to leave Surat I had confided to a Jesuit who was about to embark for Cadiz and was to return to Flanders via Spain, the mission of taking her news of me. He had promised me to turn aside from his route and pass through Toulouse. But had he done it?

I had such a real sentiment of her presence that when I found myself in the presence of two paths that took different directions, I thought I saw her on one of them making me a sign to follow her. That was the path I took. The one I left behind me was the one that led to the village I had seen. I did not get far without regrets, because I was beginning to feel hungry and wanted to experiment with the resources of the estate of mendicant.

I was to learn subsequently that that decision had saved my life. Soldiers sent in my pursuit arrived there the following day and I would have had every chance of being captured.

I endured great suffering. I knew hunger and thirst and the torment that insects make you endure, the search for shelter in the bleak extends of sand, the fear of ferocious beasts and the wait for the first ray of sunlight after icy nights. I encountered poor folk so charitable that I cannot think of them without being moved, and others who chased me away, throwing stones at me, and giving as a reason the sign I had traced on my forehead with charcoal, without knowing its meaning.

Prudently, in imitation of mendicant ascetics that I had seen on the roads in Agra, I simulated a vow of silence. At first I did so timidly, but I had perceived that it caused no astonishment and assured me almost everywhere of respect and a bowl of rice. Thus, I did not have to respond to any interrogation, indicate any place of provenance, nor goal of pilgrimage. I traveled impenetrably in my robe of mud. But the nights were so cold, the rains so abundant, that I was obliged to recall the words of Sri Narinda, to whom Li Tai had once conducted me.

Remember that your robe ought not to be made of a single piece but of old fragments that you have found yourself and sewn together.

Then I searched among the ordure, on the edge of villages, for whatever cloth I could find. But I could not succeed in sewing the shreds together. It was an old man who saw me struggling with those rags who did it for me, with a long thorn, of which he also made use to scratch his head.

"O Gautama," he said to me—and that word returned incessantly to his lips, which had not made a vow of silence—"I do not see on these fragments of cloth any trace of the putrescence of the dead. A veritable Gautama ought not to wear as a garment anything that he has taken from a cadaver."

And, so saying, laughing, the old man turned the meager face of a joyful specter toward the sun. For it is a great enigma that one cannot resolve without having lived it, that the most miserable life incites the greatest joy.

I always headed toward the direction in which the sun set, because I knew that Goa was in that direction, and other cities in which there were trading-posts of men of my race.

And time passed.

THE AVATAR

I had just traversed, in a mountainous country, jungles intercut with forests. Some distance away, I perceived a large village, and I was tempted at first to go around it, for I thought that I could see from afar an inexplicable agitation there. I had even seen the reflection of sunlight on armor. But everyone ought to march without hesitation toward his destiny.

"There he is! That's him!"

Such were the cries that I heard when I arrived at the first houses. All the inhabitants of the village were assembled on the road. They were shouting and agitating. It seemed to me that there were the silhouettes of cavaliers behind them.

I'm doomed, I thought.

But flight would have been futile, all the more so as my lacerated feet would not have carried me very far. I therefore continued to advance, simulating the greatest indifference.

I marched with my eyes lowered. When I raised them I saw that the crowd was kneeling around me. Many foreheads were in the dust. A woman touched my ankle and rapidly withdrew her hand, as if it had been burned, but her face had an ecstatic expression. An old man who was holding a garland of flowers hesitated as to whether to launch it around my neck, and consulted with his gaze another old man who shook his head to express that it would be a lack of respect. I heard the word *avatar* repeated frequently.

A man who was wearing a turban and a chemise with a belt, who had to be the village chief, addressed several phrases to me in a local dialect that was unknown to me. My absence of response did not astonish him and he began marching in front of me.

As we passed in front of several modest shops I saw men dressed as soldiers of the Emperor who were leading a horse to drink. They expressed themselves in Hindi, and as they were marching close to me I overheard their conversation. This is what I was able to deduce from it.

Some time before, an astrologer had announced to the inhabitants of the village that on that very day, between sunrise and sunset, an avatar incarnate in the body of a Jain ascetic would pass before their houses and attract great blessings to them. An avatar, as I was to discover, is a man into whom a little of the divine being has descended in order to aid souls in emerging from their miserable darkness.

Now, the inhabitants had been waiting since dawn, and the sadness of disappointment had begun to take possession of them, all the more so because a child had just been born, and if the avatar did not pass through until the following day, because of some delay, it would not be blessed in the same fashion. A fortunate combination of circumstances, with which I had nothing to do, had caused me to trace the sign of the Jains on my forehead. The sun was about to set. I could only be the avatar.

The headman of the village led me to a centenarian banyan some distance from the house. There, they had deposited milk, fruits and rice for the avatar. I sat down in the middle of a respectful circle.

I experienced a certain emotion on seeing a man in European dress accompanied by an officer of the imperial troops. He had to be a Dutchman. He was stout, with little cunning eyes, and must have had a ruddy complexion before being bronzed by the sun. In general, Europeans lend one another mutual assistance in India, although the Portuguese and the Dutch never forget their rivalry. But I was French and not Portuguese, and I wondered whether if I might be able to interest the Dutchman in my fate. I was retained by the obsequiousness that he was manifesting in regard to his companion. The crescent that the other had on his turban indicated that he was a Muslim.

They had come to see me out of pure curiosity, but for a Muslim and a Christian a Hindu ascetic inspires a certain respect, for they are supposed to possess powers of sorcery.

I heard some of what they were saying.

"One of the rules of the Jains," the officer explained, "is not to kill any living being. Even if the ascetic feels a cobra on his body, and even if he is bitten by it, he does not move."

"Is that possible?" exclaimed the Dutchman.

"We can make the experiment," the officer went on. "There's no danger, for it's well known that snakes don't bite saints of that sort."

Saying that, to my great terror, he lifted up a stone that was nearby. Fortunately, there was no snake underneath it.

"This category of religious individual has an incredible power of fasting," said the officer then. "I'm convinced that if we came back tomorrow morning we'd see that none of these aliments had been touched."

They conversed further about various subjects, and I understood that the officer was returning to Agra after having searched or months for a dangerous foreigner who had attempted to assassinate the Emperor on the same day as the death of the great Akbar.

"An avatar, if I understand tightly," said the Dutchman, "is a prophet of sorts."

"No, a prophet preaches and this one is silent. An avatar is, in sum, the divinity himself who has incarnated himself. These poor Hindus don't reflect that the divinity wouldn't make the choice of such an ordinary body to come and enlighten humans."

Problem of theology were foreign to the Dutchman, a founder of commercial enterprises. He stared at the ground. "However, look at Jesus Christ...," he began, slowly and not without a crude logic.

The two men drew away. I resumed my route the same night, for I had found a particularly piercing character in the Muslim officer's gaze. And then, is not the destiny of an avatar to travel eternally?

I was to experience a surprise no less great in another village, but it was after having traversed it and as the sun was about to set. It is noticeable that an entire order of events chooses the end of the day to present itself to humans, as a sort of present or chastisement, according to whether the event is fortunate or unfortunate.

In that village cotton cloth ornamented with colored thread was fabricated. Some sheets were painted and were hung out on ropes in order to dry. They appeared to me to be agreeable to see and reawoke in me the attraction of vestimentary sumptuousness that I have always experienced and which was only asleep within me.

The artisans worked on bamboo looms in the depths of small, dark low-ceilinged rooms sunk in three or four feet of earth like basements or cellars. I wondered as I passed why those men, who could have had the enjoyment of the beautiful celestial light, were condemned to weave in the shadows. By the same token, even though they could have dressed in light colored fabrics, they only wore sordid rags.

But there was something more surprising in the village. All the inhabitants that I encountered had one leg visibly stouter than the other. I could not help noticing it. It was usually the right leg, and that deformation was innate, for I noticed it in very young children playing in the dust.

Seeking a shelter in which to spend the night I took a little path that seemed to lead to a ruin behind trees. It was on that path that I saw an apparition, extraordinary because it was real, while having a phantasmal character, at the same time as it enlightened my mind in a fulgurant fashion.

Advancing in front of me was a skeleton carrying a cross—a skeleton that was laughing. It was not entirely a skeleton, for parchment-like skin maintained the bones grouped in accordance with the law that regulates bodies. I recognized him immediately, and, what is more marvelous, he recognized me in spite of the difference there was between my present appearance and that of old. It was Brother Octave that I had before my eyes, whom I had last seen in Surat, at the moment when he was departing, without knowing exactly where he was bound: Octave de Zaalberg, who had departed in quest of the Cross of Bartholomew, the apostle of Christ who had come, according to pious legend, to convert the Hindus.

Brother Octave deposited the cross that he had over his shoulder, which appeared to me to be very heavy, on the ground and took me in his arms. He gave me a kiss on the forehead, and it seemed to me that I was receiving it from Death itself, or, rather, a statue of death made of gnarled wood, but whose substance was not at all repulsive and had something of a vegetal character.

Then he considered me, still laughing. His joy was great on seeing me, and I understood immediately that he no longer had a very solid head. For my part, I savored a keen satisfaction in expressing myself in French, which I had only been able to do with my cousin Pierre Du Jarric since arriving in India.

"Come and see the church of Saint Bartholomew," he said to me.

A little further on, half-buried in the vegetation, there were indeed the ruins of a Christian church. How had he discovered it? What genius had led him, in immense India, to the only place where Christians, in an era we could no longer determine, had built that church? Was it Nestorians who had come that far, or Portuguese anterior to the first conquerors who established themselves in Goa? Did the church date from the time of Bartholomew? I could not learn anything from Brother Octave's incoherent words. He said a thousand astonishing things, but had he not invented them?

He had found the apostle's cross lying on the vestiges of the altar. That cross, made of exceedingly hard wood, was worm-eaten and seemed very ancient. It was awaiting the courageous Christian who would seize it and utilize its virtues, for that cross had a power of conversion. It gave faith to those who did not have any. Had I not noticed in traversing the village a strange particularity in the physical conformation of the inhabitants?

I replied that I had indeed been struck by the thickness of certain right legs.

Brother Octave laughed for a long time, longer than is appropriate to a Christian when it is a matter of a punishment imposed by a God of forgiveness. Saint Bartholomew had been stoned by the inhabitants of the village and, by way of punishment, they were to be born for a indeterminate duration with one leg stouter than the other. Why the right leg? Because the first stone of the lapidation had broken the saint's right leg.

I did not point out the contradiction there was between the fact of being stoned by pagans and that of possessing a cross that converted. The unutilized power of the cross was, however, the greatest concern of Brother Octave. He considered the inhabitants of the village as converts. A stranger to the study of languages, he only knew French and Flemish, and it was in those languages that he had instructed them. He had been well understood. He saw the proof of it in the rice and bananas that people came very day to deposit on a stone with his intention.

But a village was nothing. It was the whole earth that it was necessary to convert. If he had not departed it was because God had not wanted him to accomplish that work, but me. His strength was being taken away. It withdrew a little further every day. It was only by virtue of a great and painful effort that he was able to put the cross over his shoulder, and when it was there he was no longer capable of making the tour of the little church on the path that he had traced himself, and followed every evening at sunset. It was to me that the glory of the conversion of humankind would belong. He told me in confidence that those it was necessary to convert first were the Christians, and especially the priests.

The cross was still in the place where we had met. I was obliged to carry it to the church, for Brother Octave's strength was exhausted. He even told me, quite simply, that he would die the following day. He showed me a kind of deep pit that might have been an ancient tomb, which he had discovered behind the altar. He had thought that it was the tomb of Saint Bartholomew, and he had emptied it of the earth that filled it.

It was there that he desired to repose. He made me promise to place him in it when he was dead and to cover him with enough stones for the jackals to be unable to disinter him.

"Bones are sufficient for those filthy animals," he told me, with disgust.

For obscure reasons, or antipathies with regard to certain animal species, Brother Octave had a horror of jackals.

"On the other hand, I like monkeys," he said, pensively.

I took that as an eccentricity of a deranged mind, but of all the things he told me, those relative to his death were the most veridical. He did, indeed, die the following day.

THE CROSS OF BARTHOLOMEW

I would have sworn that the monkeys came to dance by night on the tomb of Saint Bartholomew, which was also that of Brother Octave. Why were there monkeys and not jackals? Is there a difference of hierarchy between animal species? Some eat fruits and others nourish themselves on carrion; but one does not judge the superiority of beings over one another by the quality of their nourishment.

That problem occupied me, as well as others more serious. Until then, I had never asked myself questions. Everything appeared natural to me. And suddenly, the world was, for me, filled with enigmas.

I don't know what force made me stay in the ruins of the church. Every evening I put Brother Octave's cross on my shoulder and I followed he path that he had traced. I was accomplishing a duty. It was not in conformity with the one he had prescribed for me, since he had counted on me to convert humankind. It was, however, a tribute that I was rendering to him. I was accomplishing a pious ritual. I have no idea what the inhabitants of the village thought if they perceived a silhouette different from the ne they knew, but I found aliments sufficient for my nourishment every day, on the same stone.

Perhaps it was the transportation of that cross that determined in me the curious phenomenon, entirely new for me, of reflection. I began to meditate on things about which I had never thought: the creation of the world, what a soul was, and what might become of it after death. Until then, I had thought that those questions had been resolved by the knowledgeable and religious men who had studied them, but in remembering the conversations that the Jesuit fathers had had together on the deck of the *Santa-Fé* and all the discourses that I had heard in Aboul Fazi's entourage, I was obliged to conclude that those problems had not received a definitive solution.

What were the laws that regulated sympathies and antipathies? Why was one drawn toward one person rather than another? Why was I, who had known many women of great beauty, unable to forget Inès de Saldanna? Why were there monkeys on Brother Octave's tomb, sometimes dancing round and sometimes sitting in melancholy attitudes?

It was in wanting to make sure of that fact that an even of great importance for me occurred, although I cannot characterize it and I still wonder, even now, what its nature was.

The tomb in which I had placed Brother Octave was behind the altar, but as there was no kind of vault in the church and the roof had collapsed, the tomb was in the open air. One night, therefore, I went to sit down on a section of all that formed a bench of sorts, and I contemplated the night, which was particularly serene. I felt intensely a need to have a certainty regarding God and a need to appeal to him by a name.

But what should I call him? Jesus Christ, evidently, but that was only apparently logical, and because I had been raised in the Christian religion. I had known in Agra many men full of science and wisdom, as virtuous as the best Christians, who honored other prophets and gave God different names. From afar, I had called them pagans and thought, like all the inhabitants of Toulouse, that there was no other valid religion than that of the Pope. But since it had been given to me to hear them, a great perplexity had entered into me.

What was the reason for the hatred that men bore for religious reasons? It could only be the same God that they worshiped under different names. What importance did that name have? Was it not normal that the unique God had had different prophets, according to the time and the country? Was it not wise, for anyone who wanted to approach the Unique God, to invoke him under all the names that he had been given and to ask for the support of all the prophets successively?

That is what I tried to do, with a sincere heart. I pronounced the same of Ahura Mazda, which I had heard so often on the lips of Emperor Akbar; that of Allah, which the mullahs cried from the top of mosques; that of Jehovah, whose wrath quivers in all the pages of the Bible; that of the Brahma of the Hindus; and I even found in the memory of my childhood studies a forgotten invocation to Olympian Jupiter. I also appealed to the mediators, those who had given themselves as messengers or sons of God: Zoroaster the Persian; Krishna, whom I imagined playing the flute among shepherds; Buddha, seated under a tree; Jesus Christ, walking on the water; and Mohammed, guiding a caravan of camels through an Arabian desert.

But I don't know whether my appeals were heard and whether marvelous presences populated the ruins in the midst of which I was sitting. I don't know whether it was to those presences that I owed the interior light that illuminated me. I cannot help thinking, if I want to be just, and in spite of the implausibility of the assertion, that the principle cause of what I saw was in the curiously fixed gaze of a little monkey that was kneeling, with its hands clasped together, and which never took its eyes off me. I believed, for a moment, that after asking itself the same questions as me about God and the prophets, it had started praying, and it was exhorting me silently to do the same.

I don't know whether it was a dream or a real image that passed before my eyes. I saw with the color of life the treasure of the Mongol sovereigns where I imagined hat it reposed, in the tomb of the Muslim saint not far from the steep banks of the Jumna some distance from Agra. I was conscious of the force that kept it prisoner beneath the stone. It was a magical force issuing from a higher and vaster power, which embraced the entire earth, the power of evil. It was symbolized by the bearded head of Baphomet, the sign of the Templars, which had also been that of the Asiatic conquerors, the one that Akbar bore on his linen chemise, and the one that the Jesuits utilized secretly. And it was only the sign of evil under one of its aspects. Under another, it was the sign of force, under yet another that of the authority from which order, organization, peace and even good stem. The treasure was simultaneously good and evil, evil in its origin, by virtue of the evil that its conquest had engendered, good because of the immense possibilities hidden in it.

One by one, with the gravity of Kings evoked by gods, I saw those who had been the possessors of the treasure emerge from the stone tomb. I saw Genghis with his bow larger than himself; Batou the cunning, the master of the Golden Horde, who wanted the steel of his buckler to be as limpid as the water of the lake of Ala Houl; Tamerlane the cavalier; Ulugh Beg tormented by celestial things: Babar the writer; Humayun of the arched back; and Akbar, the friend of the sun. Depositaries of wealth and strength, none had on his face the calm peace that disinterest and the satisfaction of the conscience give. Somewhere, in the unknowable beyond, there was still something that was the representation of those dead men. Perhaps it was neither a form, nor a contour, nor a vague design; but something unknowable that had no resemblance to any known aspect of matter was linked to that treasure and experienced suffering by virtue of the radiance of its attraction.

Those powerful men were suffering because of their powers, those Kings were bound to their royal past. They had loved the representations of enjoyment that are riches, and those riches retained them with the imperishable force of their attraction. Gold and precious stones exercised a power from which death had not delivered them. The more those men had sought their possession, and the more they had enjoyed it, the more they were enchained. Liberty was the price of detachment. And that lesson had been given to me by I know not what invisible instructor, with the living image of Kings saddened by having been Kings.

Those Kings passed by and disappeared into the shadows. I understood that they had no reality of their own. They were only the illustration of an open book, one of the verities of which it was given to me to understand: that of the necessity of detachment. That verity was linked to others that I perceived poorly, perhaps because they did not have an explanatory image for me as yet. But I understood that detachment was an inexorable law and that the man who was not wise enough to detach himself while alive was condemned to suffer after death, in the measure to which he had been attached.

Why were such things seen by me that night, rather than another? Had it a connection with the invisible gift that the ascetic Narinda had made me, and which I had taken at the time for a joke? Was the cross that I had transported the authentic cross of Saint Bartholomew, and did it contain a virtue communicative of sanctity? For sanctity is nothing but a capacity to detach oneself from the pleasures of terrestrial life.

But what is the good of asking questions that never receive a response?

It seemed to me that the monkey raised its hand toward the sky as if to deliver itself to an invocation, and then it launched beneath the thickness of the trees a round object that must have been some kind of nut or fruit, and started running after it. Did it mean that something was coming to a conclusion?

I stood up and started walking. There had never been a night as serene. A snake slid through the stones, and he sound it made had an amicable resonance. A bird perched on a branch, which seemed to be in ecstasy, drawn by the weight of its dream, almost fell to the ground. A few luminous insects took flight in a spray.

A sensed a great exaltation take possession of me. I would have liked to run, to utter cries, to reach the sky, or at least get closer to the luminous stars. How bright they were up above, but so far away! In order better to distinguish the mysterious figures they form and to which astronomers have given mythological names, I wanted to lie down on the ground, face upwards, and turned toward them. But the ground was hard and bristling with stones. I lay down on the cross of Saint Bartholomew, which was beside me, and in order not to let my hands trail on the ground, where scorpions live, I extended my arms along the lateral branches of the cross.

Then, directly above me face, I saw a star that had certainly just appeared while I assumed the elongated position. It was so luminous that it made those surrounding it pale. It spread a light such as I had never seen. It was an animate light, which communicated a sentiment of delight and peace to me, which made me find the world more beautiful.

I only received the contact for a few seconds, for surprise and the desire to make sure with certainty of the presence of that star caused me to sit up; but, no matter how hard I looked, the star had disappeared.

THE MAN OF EVIL

I had just made a tour of the church carrying the cross of Bartholomew on my back when I saw a silhouette through the trees. I had felt that I was observed for a long time, but had continued to follow the course of my thoughts. I heard a burst of laughter and the man who was observing me marched toward me. I was stupefied to recognize by the form of his hat and that of his sword that he was a European.

The laughter resumed, a laughter that had a tonality of bitter scorn. The man who was before me was Francisco Manoël.

With the tip of his foot he touched the bowl of rice that he found on a stone. The rice, dried by the sun, formed a crackly paste, not very appetizing.

"It's not as good as the Emperor Akbar's feasts," he said. "What a change!"

And he strove to laugh again.

After so many days of solitude, one does not see a man of one's own race without a keen pleasure. I set down my cross and almost held out my hands to him. But he laughed as one strikes with a whip. I asked him by what unusual hazard he had reached me.

"It's a very ordinary hazard. I was looking for a saint with a cross on his back. I've found the cross, but the saint has been replaced by another. I had no difficulty in recognizing you, even though you haven't changed to your advantage."

He stated laughing again.

"The Jesuits learned that their beloved Brother Octave, the one who was mad, was in the vicinity of this village. Their situation is already difficult enough with the new master of India. They do not want to lose consideration because of the extravagances of one of their number. They charged me with bringing him back. For myself, I'm still at their service. Unlike you, I haven't had the luck of becoming a Court favorite."

I couldn't help asking him why he was laughing in that singular fashion.

"I'm laughing at seeing you. You're like a wolf disguised as a sheep. How thin you are! You'll no longer seduce the beautiful Rajput princesses. All the same, you still have your teeth."

As he spoke, he showed his empty jaw and a rictus in which I discovered an immeasurable hatred, all the more so because it was without reason, apart from the jealousy that my teeth seemed to inspire in him. He experienced the need to let his triumph burst forth.

"Luck comes and goes from one to another, by turns. One might have thought that you had taken possession of it, to your advantage. I'd like to know what you did to gain the good graces of those Hindus with the incomprehensible souls. It's true that it hasn't done you much good. They're beginning to believe you dead, but your head has a price on it and represents a hundred gold pagodas to the man who can bring it to the great Katoual. Apart from your cousin Du Jarric, the Jesuits are even more furious with you. And to think that if you'd listened to me.... There are two routes in life. You only had to put on the red boots. So much the worse for you."

I noticed that the lining of his boots was red.

"What connection has the color of boots with a man's success?"

"You continue to play the simpleton. But with me, it's futile, especially at the point you've reached. You don't know that throughout the Orient, from Constantinople to the depths of China, there's a category of men of the same family who recognize one another by the color of their footwear? They're the brothers of the left hand. One can, if one wishes, call them that. You didn't want to be frankly one of ours. You see where it's led you. And even now, you think you can get out of it by means of the cross, by putting yourself hypocritically in its shadow. One can serve the cross. There are many who do. We're paid, you and I, to know it. But I wonder whether, on your part, there isn't a little bit of sincerity."

He looked at me with an expression on his face in which hatred and curiosity were mingled. While he was speaking I sensed the thought that was within him, and had no connection with what he was saying. That thought had been born a few minutes before when he had evoked the reward promised by that great Katoual for my head. He was thinking that it was possible for him to collect that reward, either by delivering me or by killing me right away, and he was examining those eventualities internally. His words were slower. He was gaining time in order to reflect. For my part, I was obliged to exhort myself to calm, for it is difficult to hear scornful words without reacting.

"Here you are, covered with vermin, and as you're nourished on the nourishment of beggars, because you've become a beggar, you've lost the physical strength in which you gloried. For you're the man who killed Yacoub! The man who killed Yacoub is reduced to this state!"

He was mistaken about my strength, for I had proved that it had not been diminished by my thinness. I had a desire to tell him so, but thought it was better to maintain silence, and I thought that it was fortunate for my interlocutor that a new man had been born in me.

"Listen," he said to me, with a significant intonation— and now that we were going to talk about serious things, he drew closer to me. "Perhaps all is not lost for you. Although not having had your success, I nevertheless have a certain credit. We're not far from Lahore, where there are many people from all the lands of Europe. The Jesuits never abandon their own. Although you've made too much noise for their liking, they'll still seek to utilize you. But what you can do for them, why not do for yourself and for me? They've been put on the track, I don't know how, of one of those chimeras that will eternally be the goal of all the adventurers on earth, whether they depart from Lisbon or Rome: a treasure. That treasure is, it seems, worthy of those who are searching for it. It appears that your situation at Court allowed you to have indications in its regard?"

I shook my head negatively.

"Tell me what you know. I'll save you and we'll share."

"It is, in fact, a matter of a chimera."

"You don't know anything about a bearded head?"

"Nothing."

He repeated his question several times, and he could not help shouting insults. Anger rendered his words unintelligible and he spat disagreeably as he spoke. Then he resumed his forced laughter.

"Already, the first day, when I met you before we embarked on the *Santa-Fé*, I had the feeling that you thought you were of another species than me. You were nothing at all then, less than nothing. You were fleeing Toulouse, where you would have been hanged for I know not what crimes. You're just a criminal, like me."

I was not unaware that patience was, among the virtues, one of the most difficult to acquire. *Fortunately*, I said to myself, *I'm a new man. I've succeeded in vanquishing my natural violence.*

"I could consider you as being one of ours. You surely are. I'm wondering why you haven't accepted what I proposed to you."

"I have no memory of it."

"I offered you a fragment of a profaned host. You should have thanked me on your knees. I, who am speaking, who don't believe in anything, believe in the power that sacrilege communicates. A power in evil, of course—in what is conventionally called evil. I've made the experiment and I've seen the effect on others."

At that point he burst into laughter so insupportable that I made the gesture of putting my cross over my shoulder in order to draw away.

"But that's what interests you the most. You haven't asked me what became of Inès de Saldanna."

I had the belated sentiment that I had allowed the interest that suddenly animated me to show by a stupid widening of the eyes. At the same time, in the back of my mind, I had knowledge of his thinking. He couldn't get anything out of me. He was going to take his revenge with the bile of words, and then he was going to deliver me in order to collect the promised reward. If some divine power had touched me with some grace, it was the same power that had sent that man to me in order to prove myself and permit me to exercise my empire over myself. I had to show myself worthy of the grace received and touch without indignation the utmost depths of human evil.

"Inès de Saldanna carried, on her swan-like neck, a fragment of the soiled host. I had made her believe that it was a fragment of the holy cross of Jesus Christ. Certainly, she was a miserable prey destined by her brother to the lubricity of Hindu sovereigns, for they love to have beautiful foreigners among their wives, but the host communicated to her a power of lust that good Christians qualify as demonic. She has abandoned herself to it entirely."

"That is the most frightful of lies!" I cried, betraying by the sound of my voice the heartbreak I experienced.

"And do you know who it is that she has demanded, among many others, the man who pleased her most of all, because he was of her race, and also because of his incomparable seduction?"

He began laughing again, and I had the weakness to show him how he had triumphed by crying out in a strangled voice: "Who was it?"

"It was you. Ten times she begged me to go and find you. But you were so occupied! You, the seducer! Ten times, I told her that you refused to come."

I continued to read Francisco Manoël's thoughts. *He's a miserable rag devoid of reaction*, he said to himself. *I'll collect the hundred gold pagodas, but I'll poison his soul beforehand.* I noticed that he had put his hand on the butt of a long pistol of a model that was unknown to me and must be recent.

And as the mind, when it is overexcited, seems multiplied, at the same time as those perceptions, I had the sensation of an interior voice that said:

261

"Remember the star, the face of your mother, the violence that you have rejected."

Francisco Manoël was still laughing. In order to fire it, would it be sufficient for him to pull the trigger of the pistol, or was it necessary to light a wick?

"Anyway, what would you have done with her? A woman who has been everyone's? That was good for me, and more!"

The body sometimes acts as if it is not directed by the mind at all, absolutely autonomously.

My arm had extended with great force and struck Francisco Manoël in the face. I don't remember whether it was with the flat of the hand or a closed fist, and that problem is, in any case, unimportant. The blow was such that he took two or three steps, stumbled and almost fell. His hat rolled on the ground.

He straightened up with a growl of joyful hatred, and he extended his pistol toward me. There was no wick to light. The joy was greater than the hatred. He had me at his mercy and he had, in his own regard, an excellent reason to kill me and collect the hundred gold pagodas.

I saw the contraction of his finger, and, by an instinctive movement, I held out the cross between us. He fired, and my fortune dictated that the bullet hit the wood of the cross. It made a little dry click. There was no disappointment. He was a man of war. In the same second his hand dropped the pistol and drew the long sword that he had at his side. Also in the same second, I dropped the Cross of Bartholomew on his head. He collapsed, with the inhuman cry of those struck by death.

Then I drew away with long strides. I reached the road and marched in the direction of Lahore.

THE MUD OF THE TAPTI

It is very agreeable to be a beggar, on condition of only addressing oneself to very poor and very simple folk. They have a noble charity that magnifies both the mendicant and the benefactor. It is also necessary to possess a wooden bowl and to content oneself with a nourishment of crushed millet and boiled rice. But the estate of the mendicant becomes humiliating as soon as one approaches a city and its corruption.

I reached Lahore, the city of pagodas, and the first evening, in the courtyard of a caravanserai where men and camels were piled up pell-mell, I approached a group of men sitting around a fire of palm-branches. The flames were high and bright and illuminated laughing faces. A man with a long beard was recounting joyous stories. He was gesticulating and speaking with such great rapidity that I had difficulty comprehending him. However, I distinguished a few features of the following story.

When the great Akbar died, the marble of the ceiling of his palace opened and the people gathered there saw Devas in festival costumes who had come to conduct him to the blissful Svarga. He rose up lightly into the sky. But there was a Portuguese in the Court who was out of his mind. His taste for colorful costumes, turbans and strange belts had informed perspicacious minds that he was a reincarnation of a bird, for the habit of a colorful plumage in a life as a parrot gives the desire for sumptuous clothing in a human life. That insensate Portuguese had wanted to follow Emperor Akbar in his rise into the sky and he delivered himself to disorderly leaps at the very moment when the Emperor's son came to weep over the body of his father. People had tried to catch him, but he had run into the gardens, and those pursuing him had been utterly amazed to see him leaning over the branch of a tree above the Jumna. He had resumed the form of his past life, and no bird had ever been seen with such sparkling plumage.

I did not hear any more. A foreigner of noble appearance who was standing in the crowd of listeners had just drawn away. I followed him, pushed by I know not what presentiment, and it was with a certain regret, for I would have liked to know what had become of the parrot. But it is always necessary to respond to the signs of destiny. The sign, on that occasion, was the fugitive gleam in the man's eye.

He was a rich Venetian who had arrived from Delhi and had just confided his merchandise to the guardians of the caravanserai. His name was Nicolas Matteotti and he was the man who had founded the first European trading-post in Lahore. I had known his name for a long time but that evening, he was merely, for me, some traveler emerging from a caravanserai.

When a life has almost no value anymore and is at risk of being taken away from its possessor at any moment, one does not hesitate to gamble with it. I gambled mine on a single card, and I won.

By his appearance, the gleam in his eye and the way he carried his head I estimate that the unknown European in question had sufficient grandeur of soul to learn who I was and not deliver me to the great Katoual of Agra.

"Lord," I said to him, "I am the insensate parrot whose story you have just heard."

He invited me into his house, and there finished that period of my life. I have no more to add but the final episode.

Nicolas Matteotti devoted himself to commerce in everything, but above all that of furs and precious stones. He needed courageous men, for his principal transactions took place with the Sanganian pirates who cruised the coasts of Gujarat and certain Rajput lords who had fortresses in the mountains so inaccessible that even the great Mogul could not capture them.

Only a few months had gone by before he thought of replacing his principal employee with me. That man, named Arzigan, under the pretext that his ancestors belonged to the tribe of Oirotes and had the privilege of drinking the milk of the thousand white mares of the great Kubla Khan, was unreasonably proud. He only ate onions, wore a wretched woolen robe and labored from morn till night, but he affected the arrogance of a sovereign. He had amassed a vast fortune at his master's expense. Matteotti wanted to replace him with a less laborious man less avid for wealth. It was agreed that I would go to Europe to regulate various business affairs, as many in Venice as in France, and that when I returned I would occupy the position he destined for me.

It was me that had suggested that voyage to the Occident to him, which was not an imperious necessity. I had made it following a dream, or, rather, an apparition during the period that precedes sleep. I thought I saw my mother surrounded by light and making me a sign to join her. I had not been surprised by that, for since the day when I had buried my sword on the bank of the Jumna, the sentiment of her presence had always been in the back of my mind.

I therefore left for Surat in order to embark on a Dutch vessel. For some years, Holland had surpassed Portugal in its commerce, and its ships made the voyage to the Occident in a shorter time and in greater security.

The city of Surat is situated three leagues from the bay of Sualis, which serves as its port and where vessels of large tonnage drop anchor. To reach them, one goes down the Tapti on great flat barges on which merchandise is heaped. The one that carried me was entirely covered with crates of every sort containing silk and spices. A tornado of unexpected violence burst forth while we were descending the Tapti, and, having departed in the morning we only arrived at sunset. The banks of the river are formed of vast extents of liquid mud. The wind whipped up that mud and caused it to fall on the deck of our barge to the point that everything thereon, men and things, was entirely soiled and covered in a thick layer of mud.

It was with a great deal of difficulty that we reached the Dutch ship. It had shifted on its anchors and everything there was in the greatest disorder. In the midst of the people who were running hither and yon on the deck and the general emotion, I understood that it would take a long time to find the functionary charged with the allotment of places, and I sat down on a crate of elongated form that belonged to the cargo of the barge that had preceded mine on the Tapti. A vestment of mud covered it, like myself. Furthermore, around me, officers mariners and passengers were unrecognizable under the mask of primal mud that the egalitarian breath of the tempest had put on their faces.

An old man who was wearing I know not what uniform, unrecognizable under the wood, came to sit beside me. He had a desire to enter into conversation.

"That is what we are, we humans: mud, nothing else."

And as I did not reply, affecting a philosophical cynicism, he continued: "Do you know that we're sitting on a coffin? A coffin, after a tornado on the Tapti, resembles a crate of pepper or ginger. This coffin is that of Inès de Saldanna, the sister of the governor of Portuguese India.

With one bound I was on my feet. The man got up too.

"You didn't know? She died a few days ago, and this ship, which is due to call in at Goa, will place her body in her brother's hands. Personally, I'm Dutch and despise all Portuguese. Why do you think that Aryas de Saldanna sold his sister to the Mongols? It wasn't to enrich himself; he's going to inherit an immense fortune. It was to have old furniture, which he collects. Look, there are sculpted dressers that he'll receive at the same time as his sister's corpse."

Around me, there were, indeed, several large somber items of furniture, decorated with Ganesha gods, half-elephants and half-human.

But I did not have time to meditate on the play of destiny that had determined that I would rediscover under terrestrial dirt the remains of the person who had been the secret motive of my actions, the goal of my dreams, the ever-present ideal of beauty. I heard my name pronounced by a familiar voice. My cousin Pierre Du Jarric was before me. He seized me in his arms and I felt, while he embraced me, a tear moistening his long nose.

He had not lost the habit of passing from one subject to another. He had been very ill and needed to rediscover the poplars of the Garonne. Then again, he sensed that in India, the game was lost for the Jesuits. Anyway, Père Pignero attributed all the merit of the new geographical maps in which he had collaborated to himself. But he would turn the tables in his fashion. His great work on *The Marvels of the Lands of India* was nearly finished. A friend of his youth had a printing press in Bordeaux; he would take him his manuscript. But he would not yield to new fashions. No illustrations! His book would not include illustrations. He swore to that. I could be reassured on that point.

He stopped suddenly, like someone remembering something important. His face was suddenly filled with gravity.

"My son, I have some dolorous news to give you. I know that you do not lack courage. I received during my illness a letter from a Jesuit in Toulouse, which informed me that your mother is no more. I should have, immediately…but…."

A misfortune only afflicts the soul some time after the knowledge has reached it. I remembered the dream that I had had a few months earlier. It was not in the house in the Rue Malcousinat that my mother was making me a sign to rejoin her. Where she was, the Dutch ship could not take me.

I knew that Nicolas Matteotti would be happy with a change of plan that left me by his side. Night fell and the disorder redoubled under the lanterns that were illuminated here and there.

A voice was taking a roll call of passengers. It cried: "Pierre Du Jarric!"

He replied: "Here I am!"

I hailed a boat that was on the point of returning to the quays. I let myself slide down to it on a rope.

The land of India was enveloped in shadow as the oarsmen beat the waves to take me there. But I knew that somewhere in the vastness of the heavens that covered it, there was a star that shone for it alone, and I did not despair of seeing its light one day.

THE MYSTERY OF THE TEMPLARS

THE INITIATES OF ACTION

It was prescribed for the Knight of the Temple, in the regulations of the Order, not to retreat, and to fight to excess before three enemies; it was commonly said during the twelfth and thirteenth centuries that a single Templar knight was sufficient to vanquish ten Saracens.

The essential quality required of a member of the Order was courage, personal valor, and the ensemble of those combined courages was intended to procure the power of force, material domination.

The Templars were the initiates of action, the messengers of the sword. They marked a new check to the Oriental initiative to pacify and cultivate the Occident, crushed by the grip of the Church. Previously, in Athens and Alexandria, that Church had annihilated the initiates of knowledge that the neoplatonists were. The last survivors of that marvelous school, the disciples of Ammonius Saccas, who had dreamed of bringing the world to perfection by philosophical knowledge, had been obliged by persecutions to flee into Persia to the protection of King Khosrow.[47]

---

[47] The Sasanian Emperor Khosrow I (501-579), known as the Philosopher King, whose reign began in 531, immediately welcomed many refugees from the Eastern Roman Empire who had fled when the Emperor Justinian closed down the neoplatonist schools in Athens in 529.

At the moment when the Order of the Temple arrived at its apogee, the initiates of love, the Cathars and the Albigensians, who had discovered the secret of immediate perfection, conquered in this life by the road of purificatory poverty and fraternal love, were exterminated to the last man, and from the Atlantic to the Mediterranean it was impossible even to discover a stone on which the sign of their sublime tradition subsisted.

The initiates of the Order of the Temple attempted to make the verity of sages triumph by the sword. They followed the third of the three paths open to human beings, after that of knowledge and that of love, the path of action. Their success was dazzling at first. The elite of society, seduced by the ideal of chivalric courage that they raised like a banner, came to them from all parts. All the valiant young men of Europe dreamed of collaborating with the defense of the Holy Land in the phalanx of those glorious veterans of the Crusade.

However, the directors of the Order glimpsed a more magnificent goal. In their eyes, the Holy Land only enclosed the tomb of one prophet among the prophets, and not a God. It was a question of making the entire world a Holy Land. It was necessary first to take possession of the world—and that was possible. The Order of the Temple attempted it, and it might have succeeded. The eleventh and twelfth centuries saw the development of that enormous dream, that gigantic and secret chimera: the conquest of Europe and Asia by a valiant and well organized minority—but a minority ignorant of that goal, directed by a group of initiates.

Success would have meant the reestablishment of the ancient priestly hierarchy of Egypt. Behind the kings and their warriors there would be sages, simultaneously priests and scholars, who would have imposed a will for justice and oriented the world toward perfection.

If one does not find in the rules of the Order texts that give proof of that goal, one cannot be astonished. A project as vast as the fall of kings and the leveling of religions, the constitution of a unique civilization simultaneously Muslim and

270

Christian, could not be confided to any parchment, and could only be revealed to the great priors of the secret council when their ambition and sagacity had been carefully measured. No knight revealed at the time of the trial the purpose of the Order of which he was only a blind instrument. The members of the inner circle, those who knew, only confessed under torture the exterior rites, scandalous to the profane, but which did not touch the very essence of what the Temple really was.

Doubtless Philippe le Bel and Pope Clement V were not unaware of the danger that the papacy and royalties were running. The extraordinary avarice of the King of France was not a sufficient lever for him to pry up a stone as heavy as the Order of the Temple and to break it. He could not have succeeded and would have been broken himself. He would not have decided on that audacious action had there not been a vital question for his throne. Previously he had tried to be admitted among the knights of the Temple and, to his great surprise, had been rejected. He suppressed those who would have suppressed him a little later.

The papacy would only have been attacked long afterwards, because the Order had need of the ecclesiastic organization for its domination. Nothing would leak out, either in the interrogations or the judgments, of the force that had almost destroyed the social edifice in order to reorganize it on a more perfect plan. Its enemies were content to convict the Templars of having spat on Christ, of having committed and even recommended sodomy, and of having adored the idol Baphomet—all things that were proven in the letter but unknown in the spirit. Stupefied peoples saw the glorious and celebrated Order condemned and did not know the true cause of it. After them, history remained as ignorant.

The most prodigious actions can be accomplished by believers. Faith can not only move mountains but can launch them into the sky and juggle with them. And it is not necessary that the faith in question be in good, in God, or any other sublime chimera. Faith in egotism has just as much power; but it collapses quickly. It is necessary that the element of faith be the basis of action. When men cease to believe in their goal, their armor falls away, and they cease to be invincible. That is what happened to the Templars.

Wealth entered into their plan of conquest, and with a vertiginous rapidity they became the bankers of the world. The knights charged with accounting showed even more zeal than those charged with fighting, who were reputed to be the most illustrious combatants of their epoch. Wealth corrupted them, as it corrupts all those who possess it. They perished for having become too rich, and with them expired the dream of a civilization reconciling the Orient and the Occident, and replacing the power of kings with the government of an elite of intelligent and just men.

HUGUES DES PAYENS
AND THE ORDER OF ASSASSINS

It was in 1120 or thereabouts, in Jerusalem, that the magnificent dream appeared in the mind of the genius who founded the Templars, Hugues des Payens.

He was a poor knight from Champagne who had followed Godefroy de Bouillon in the crusade and had remained in Jerusalem. Pillages had left him devoid of a fortune. History shows that whenever a city, no matter how vast it might be, was taken and pillaged a mere three days sufficed for there no longer to be a single house to rob or a woman to rape. From Antioch to Jerusalem, Hugues des Payens must have spent the first three days thanking God for the victory. It is possible that the founder of the richest Order in Christendom was a disinterested man.

When one dreams of the kingdom of Christ, what is a Moorish house with women around a fountain and negro slaves in vermilion doublets? He had neither a house nor women. He believed himself to be a good Christian, but he liked discussing heretical doctrines with his companion-in-arms, the Toulousan Geoffroy de Saint-Adhémar,[48] who, like all the men of his race, was imbued with Catharism. They were young and poor, as befits builders of immense projects and prompt realizers of chimeras.

The Orient, with its architectural beauties, the voluptuousness of its women and the mysticism of its philosophy, transformed the men of the Occident with surprising rapidity. Baldwin II, who had become King of Jerusalem, set the example. Taken prisoner by Emir Balak in an ambush, he remained in the power of the Saracens for a year. When he was liberated, he continued to make war with the same ardor, but he spoke of Emir Balak as a sage with whom he had been glad to

---

[48] Author's note: "Not Saint-Omer, as is often written."

converse. He dressed in a robe in the Oriental manner, affected to follow their usages, and married a young woman who belonged to an old Arab family. He was the protector of the first Templars, to whom he gave as accommodation, perhaps intentionally, the part of his palace that had been constructed on the site of the ancient Temple of Solomon.

Hugues des Payens and Geoffroy de Saint-Adhémar, who were combatants as well as mystics, were struck with admiration by what the Orient revealed to them in the order of ideas, which preoccupied them the most. They heard nothing recounted but the stories of saints of Islam who imposed their mystical conceptions by force, or even the memory of a certain misunderstood prophet. All of them employed a similar method. They founded a secret society, simultaneously philosophical and military, with different degrees of initiation and a hierarchy of members, based on the hierarchy of nature in accordance with the ancient principle that what is at the bottom is like that which is at the top.

In Persia there had been Mastek, Kermath and then the Rawendis, who taught their initiates that souls transmigrate from body to body. They had heard mention of "the ones clad in white" of Mokanaa the masked, who always wore a golden mask on his face, and Sasendeimah, "the man who disposes of the moonlight," so called because, in order to dazzle his disciples, he caused a dazzling light to appear above a fountain by night, which he assimilated to that of the divine spirit.

There was also the founder of a secret Ismailite society, Abdallah, son of Maimoun, who had succeeded in mounting the throne of the Caliphate of Egypt. Since his accession there had been in Cairo a society of wisdom of which the Caliph was the grandmaster and who had his "house of wisdom" and his "house of science" full of instruments of astronomy and books, in which ink, parchment and quills were distributed gratuitously and to which the physicians, poets and scholars of the Orient flooded.

Hugues des Payens and Geoffroy de Saint-Adhémar heard at that time in Jerusalem the echo of a great events, the temporary closure of the "house of science" in Cairo following a riot, and they were astonished by the importance that matters of the intellect had in the Orient, which they had believed to be barbaric when they were living in their stone châteaux enclosed by sad ditches in the land of France.

Most of all, the destiny of Hassan Sabbah, the Old Man of the Mountain, and that of the sect of Assassins, which reigned by terror over Persia, Syria and Egypt, and even over the crusaders, must have occupied their long conversations during hot nights in Jerusalem.

Hassan Sabbah had been an ambitious man as well as a mystic philosopher. Educated in the great university of Nishapour with the poet and astronomer Omar Khayyam, and Nizamolmouk, who was to become the prime minister of the Caliph of Bagdad, he was initiated into the sect of the Ismailites of Egypt and had founded a sect of which he was proclaimed the grandmaster. That sect had nine degrees of initiation and reposed simultaneously on absolute obedience and the intellectual knowledge of philosophies.

The disciples rose in the hierarchy of the sect in accordance with their intelligence. After knowledge it was necessary to arrive at faith in the superior God common to all religions. At that degree they practiced the ecstasy of the Sufis and saints. But the final degree informed them that for humans there is neither punishment not recompense, that the world is directed by an indifferent law and that individual egotism is probably the final word in life. Only a few directors of the sect reached that ultimate degree.

There must have been a degree superior still, which was the prerogative of the first grandmaster Hassan Sabbah, the anguish of which he did not reveal to anyone. He must have doubted his own philosophy and the ultimate superiority of egotism. His disciples reported that he spent thirty-five years without emerging from the library of the castle of Alamut, where so many books were accumulated that it had become the largest in the world after that of Bagdad. During that interval of thirty-five years no one recalled having seen him appear on his balcony, except twice. A man who bears an absolute certainty within him recognizes the vanity of books as much as one who is possessed by faith; he expects nothing of the dust of parchments and he is not content only to see the light of the sun twice in thirty-five years.

Hassan Sabbah had found an ingenious means of becoming the foremost individual in the Orient—that of levying taxes and governing sovereigns thereby. Anyone who resisted his will was assassinated by one of his emissaries. If one of his emissaries was captured before carrying out the murder, he sent another, and then another; and Hassan's disciples stopped at nothing. They converted to Christianity if it was necessary to kill a Christian. There were some who adopted the appearance of ravishing women and had themselves sold as slaves in order to get close to a suspicious and lustful emir and stab him in the hour of caresses.

To fanaticize his disciples and obtain from them the sacrifice of their lives, Hassan possessed a personal method that he bequeathed to his successors. Like his father Ali Sabbah, who was already nicknamed "the skeptic" and "the atheist," and whose knowledge he revered, he had studied plants in his childhood. He had found a manner of preparing hashish and mixing it with henbane that gave a self-confidence that provoked an unshakable mental firmness. Those he sent carried with them, in addition to a short triangular dagger, the absolute certainty of success. Perhaps, as related by Marco Polo—all of whose other stories have been confirmed—Hassan gave his disciples another mixture of hashish that procured them, in the gardens of Alamut and amid their fountains, delightfully blissful dreams and made them believe that he had sent them to paradise by virtue of his divine power.[49] Obedience was easy to obtain for someone who disposed of such a recompense. It was from there that the members of the sect took the

_____

[49] Author's note: "A part of the castle of Alamut was named Meimoun-Diz, the fortress of happiness."

name of Assassins, or hashishins, eaters of herbs. The Old
Man of the Mountain was called the possessor of Hashisha.[50]

At the moment when Hugues des Payens and Geoffroy
de Saint-Adhémar were dreaming of a power conquered in
imitation of Oriental intellectuals, Hassan Sabbah died. But
his sect lost nothing of its strength, thanks to the mechanisms
of its organization. The two Frenchmen would have had no
difficulty in seeing that, even more than the daggers obscurely
raised above heads, what made its power were the castles that
it had methodically acquired and fortified, the impregnable
castles guarded by small contingents of well-disciplined
troops.

And the dream became precise. It would be possible to
master Europe if one disposed of castles distributed throughout its kingdoms. In order to have those castles it was necessary to be rich, but religion led to everything, especially
wealth. How many men had renounced their fortunes on join-

---

[50] Author's note: "Certain overly grave minds please themselves removing from history events that present themselves
dressed from head to toe in legendary fantasy. Facts are often
flat and boring, but at other times sublime and poetic, without
anything being added to them. In his interesting work on chivalry, Monsieur Victor-Émile Michelet says that deriving 'Assassin' from 'Hashishin' is like deriving 'cheval' from
'equus,' and he seems to think the usage of hashish unworthy
of Hassan Sabbah. The etymology I give is proven abundantly
by Sylvestre le Sacy, Hammer and several other historians. In
any case, many Persian, Hindu and Chinese secret societies
have employed and still employ today beverages based on
hashish, opium and many other plants in order to favor the
emergence of the astral double and attain the first degrees of
ecstasy." The reference is to *Les Secrets de la chevalerie*
(1930) by Victor-Émile Michelet (1861-1938), a symbolist
poet, prose writer and a leading contributor to the later phases
of the French occult revival, with whom Magre had much in
common, and must have been acquainted.

ing the Crusade, exchanging wealth for the pardon of the Church! The knights of Christ would drain the gold of Christianity. As for the terror, the power of assassination that had been Hassan's first lever, that would rediscover in a religious word of command a virtue given by faith.

That word of command was brought to them by the Oriental initiation that they received from Theoclet, the patriarch of the Gnostic sect of Johannites.[51] That sect was attached to the evangelist John and claimed that he was the founder of the true Church. The Church of Rome as not the legitimate Church. The missionaries of Peter had altered the thought of Jesus in going to preach it among barbarian peoples. According to the Johannites, it was a blasphemy to say that Jesus had been put on the cross, for the son of God could not be crucified. Since John, the Johannite patriarchs had succeeded one another without interruption. The latest was Theoclet. He wandered obscurely in Palestine, but if he found defenders, his Church would triumph over the false churches and his successor would be the most powerful man in Christendom.

Hugues des Payens gathered around him seven knights, and founded an Order of Chivalry whose apparent objective was to protect the pilgrims coming to the Holy Land. He called it the Order of the Temple because his mystical and secret goal was the reconstitution of the Temple of Solomon, a symbol of perfection. That symbol had been buried in the ge-

---

[51] The assertion that the alleged Templar heresy was linked with hypothetical ancestors of the Johannite Church that had been founded by the French priest Bernard-Raymond Fabré-Malaprat (1773-1838) in 1804, through the mediation of someone named Theoclet, although invented by Fabré-Malaprat, was more widely popularized in by declaration made by Pope Pius IX (1792-1878) while fulminating against various contemporary heretics. It was enthusiastically taken up by various participants in the Occult Revival, but evidence of the existence of any such sect or any such thesis prior to the nineteenth century is exceedingly difficult to find.

ometry of stones; it was the pursuit of divine wisdom and its realization by order and harmony under the hierarchical direction of the initiates. Material power would be the means to elevate the Temple.

The material power in question was acquired with a rapidity that surpassed all the dreams of the founders.

In 1128, Hugues des Payens came to France and had the rules of his new Order approved by Saint Bernard. It was ascetic and military. If it bore a strange resemblance to the rules of the secret societies of the Orient. no one knew it. The Templars were divided into three grades: the knights, armed servants and affiliates. They obeyed the Grand Master but they had an interior order composed of seven members who remained unknown and who perpetuated the primitive tradition.

Their costume was a white robe with a red cross on the left side. They were exempt from taxes and military service to kings. They could only be judged by the Pope. The number three played a particular role in their rites. When a candidate wanted to be admitted as a knight he knocked three times at the door of the church where the ceremony was held and was asked three times what he wanted. Each knight had to have three horses, make three long fasts and take communion three times a year. Those who had committed a sun were flagellated three times. They made three vows.

Only a few years went by before they had immense wealth and formed an ever-growing force in the midst of the European nations and in the Orient. That chivalric strength was accrued from their financial operations.

During the hundred and eighty-four years that the Order existed the goal was never lost to sight and it was pursued with an obstinate determination. They had castles everywhere, numbering as many as nine thousand. They made incessant progress. In fighting the Egyptians, the Syrians and the Order of Assassins they learned about their mores, their military organization and their doctrines. When they built fortresses, they were modeled on Saracen fortresses, and could thus be distinguished easily from those the Hospitallers, their rivals.

Narrow relationships, in the form of alliances made and then broken, often united Templars and Saracens. They betrayed Frederick II for the Sultan of Babylon. Another time, they refused to fight the infidels to the profit of Leon, King of Armenia. After taking Damiette, Imbert, a Maréchal of the Temple and confidant of the papal legate, Cardinal Pelage, who was in command of the Christian army, abruptly quit that army, bogged down in the Nile floods and went over to the Muslims. If it was a Knight of the Temple who prevented the Grandmaster of the Assassins from converting to Christianity and killed his ambassador, as was said, it was doubtless because he did not believe in that improbable conversion and only saw it as a strategic ruse.

All of that proves how many affinities the Knights of the Temple had with the enemies they were fighting. They did not hesitate to betray Christianity if it was in there interest, and when they took Muslim prisoners they were only seen to accord them mercy, or to release them without ransom. That was because, for them, the only verity was the increase in their strength.

Over the years the grandmasters became more powerful and were all the more ambitious for it. Under Thomas Béraut they made war against the Hospitallers with at least as much ardor as they had against the infidels. But human life did not count in their eyes; one cannot realize a great material project without killing one's friends and enemies indifferently. Nothing counted, not the authority of the Pope, from whom they were liberating themselves further every day, nor moral laws, nor chivalric laws. We will give a significant example.

The Christians had been expelled almost everywhere from the Orient, where for more than three centuries they had been destroying the monuments of Arab art, burning libraries—notably that of Tripoli, which contained more than a hundred thousand volumes—and spreading a desolation that can only be compared to that inflicted by the Mongols.[52]

Sultan Khalil had laid siege to Saint-Jean-d'Acre, whose defense had been confided to the Grand Master of the Temple, Guillaume de Beaujeu. After several months of conflict, he was killed on the ramparts, and as the besieged city contained the number of senior priors necessary for an election, his successor, the monk Gaudini, was proclaimed immediately. He was an intellectual and a philosopher rather than a warrior. He hastened to negotiate, but too late; the city was pillaged.

The wives and daughters of the nobles of the city, numbering three hundred, had taken refuge in the Templars' fortress, the towers of which were beaten by the sea, and still permitted resistance. Night stopped the fighting and pillages. The Knights of the Temple, summoned to surrender, would only consent to do so if they were given the liberty to withdraw the next day safe and sound, with the women what had taken refuge behind their walls.

The sultan consented to that, but it was agreed that a few hundred Muslim soldiers would occupy one of the towers to make sure that the articles of the capitulation were observed. Unfortunately, that tower was the one in which the Christian noblewomen were accumulated. The Muslim soldiers, intoxicated by the victory, were unable to resist the sight of the women; they dragged them all to the church of the Order and raped them.

---

[52] Author's note: "I cannot explain the admiration with which history books are filled for what is called there 'the great mystical movement of the crusades.' Behind French chivalry there were the dregs of the Occident that ran to pillage the Orient. Saint Bernard depicted accurately the crusaders whose enthusiasm he had stimulated: 'What was charming in the crowd, the torrent, that flowed to the Holy Land is that you saw nothing therein but scoundrels and the impious; but Christ made a champion of an enemy.'"

The knights, alerted by the screams, ran to warn Grand Master Gaudini of the treason, the evil that was being accomplished and the vengeance that it was necessary to take. The latter shrugged his shoulders and replied: "Well, Messieurs, I'm no less afflicted than you, but what can one do in such sad circumstances?"[53] And he hastened to embark with the archives of the Temple and a dozen of the senior officers of the Order on a boat that was able to escape by favor of the darkness and reach Cyprus. What, indeed, did the rape of three hundred women matter, as long as the few men who had in their hands the conquest and organization of Europe were saved?

The Templars who remained massacred Khalil's lustful soldiers, but perished the following day along with the dishonored Christian women; the tower of the Temple where they were defending themselves collapsed at the moment of the attack, burying the victors and the vanquished alike.

A few years later, under the mastery of Jacques de Molay, all the proud towers of the Temple erected at the crossroads of Europe crumbled at the same time.

---

[53] Author's reference: "Pierre [actually Claude] Mansuet, *Histoire critique [et apologétique] de l'Ordre des Chevaliers du Temple* [1789]"

THE DENIAL OF JESUS,
SODOMY AND THE BAPHOMET

It was the time when Philippe le Bel had just depreciated French coinage to his advantage. In spite of those depreciations he remained needy. He received a letter from the governor of a château in the Languedoc near Béziers. The governor told him that a bourgeois of the city named Squint de Florian, who had been condemned to death, had asked to speak to the King before being subjected to the penalty, assuring him that he had a secret of unusual importance to reveal to him. The governor had postponed the execution.

Impelled by curiosity, the King had Florian brought to Paris. Florian threw himself at his feet and asked for his life in exchange for the secret, which was granted to him. This is what he revealed.

Florian had spent his days in prison in the company of a Templar apostate similarly condemned to death. The Templar, on the point of being executed and unable to obtain a priest, had confessed to his companion. He revealed to him that when he was supposedly an honest man and a member of the Order of the Temple he had committed crimes much greater than that were presently sending him to his death. Those crimes were also committed by the elite of French chivalry.

The Templars denied Jesus Christ and spat three times on the cross at the moment of their reception into the Order. They practiced sodomy, not for occasional pleasure, but with an official permission and as a praiseworthy and recommended action. Finally, they consecrated themselves, by a magical rite that involved a rope wound around their loins, to a strange bearded idol named Baphomet.

One can hardly believe that Philippe le Bel, so little respectful of the Pope of the Church to which he had recently delivered a slap by the intermediary of Nogaret, was indignant about the heresy and the adoration of Baphomet, or against the practice of sodomy, so current in those times and in all times. It is probable that something was revealed to him of the Templars' ambitious ideal of conquest.

That ideal, known only to the interior group of senior priors, must have filtered out, whispered as an uncertain legend, and did not have enough reality to figure in the accusations of the trial. But his knowledge must have made Philippe le Bel reflect on the extraordinary power that was constituted in his kingdom and over which he had no authority. He must suddenly have understood that an immense danger might be looming up before him, and told himself that if he destroyed that danger abruptly by means of an audacious coup, he could simultaneously enrich himself with the immense fortune of the Order of the Temple.

That dread, which was only supported on vague testimony, of which there was no formal proof, is the sole excuse for the greatest crime, after the massacre of the Albigensians, that the Pope and the King of France committed in collaboration.

For the great realization of the Order, the time had perhaps come. The Muslims had expelled the Christians from Palestine and Egypt. With what would the formidable activity of those warriors, for whom combat was a vital necessity, be employed? The maintenance of forts and Oriental possessions devoured almost all of the Order's revenues. With the cessation of the war against the infidels, enormous sums were about to become available.

A Templar named Roger de Flor had thought that the moment had come. He had just been expelled from the Order for having stolen a part of its treasure at the time of the fall of Saint-Jean-d'Acre, and for having abused Christian women who had taken refuge in his galley. Alone, at the head of Spanish adventurers, he had attempted the foundation of a Mediterranean kingdom. He escaped the pursuits of the Pope and the Order, gained an immense fortune and obtained from the Emperor of Constantinople the hand of his niece Marie and the title of Caesar.

But Jacques de Molay did not have the scope that would have been necessary. Everything found him sympathetic. Honesty and mild qualities were dominant in him. That did not take him very far. One sole clue can permit the supposition that the Temple judged that the moment had come to play a major role in Europe. When the Pope, in accord with Philippe le Bel, summoned Jacques de Molay to meet him in Poitiers he instructed him to come incognito, almost alone. Jacques de Molay left Cyprus, where he was, accompanied by an immense retinue, the elite of the Knights and the treasure of the Temple. That might well indicate that he judged that the Order's field of action was henceforth to be in Europe and that he was about to have need of all his combatants there.

With skill and hypocrisy, Philippe le Bel showered Jacques de Molay and the Templars with all sorts of marks of amity and favors. On the other hand, Clement V could refuse him nothing. He had been elected Pope thanks to the King of France. Public opinion was forceful, and for the first time, the university and the people had to be asked to approve a royal decision. But the very character of the accusations was calculated to render the coup popular. Rumors had been circulating for a long time about disappearances and the mysterious deaths of people who had imprudently witnessed a secret ceremony of the Temple.

The Templars were hated very widely. "They were, it was said, notoriously in rapport with the Assassins of Syria. The people remarked with alarm the similarity of their costume with that of the followers of the Old Man of the Mountain. They had welcomed the Sudan in their houses, permitted the Muslim cult. In their furious rivalry against the Hospitallers they had gone so far as to launch arrows against the Holy Sepulcher."[54]

It was thought scandalous that the Grand Master's court was more numerous and more beautiful than those of kings.

---

[54] Author's reference: "[Jules] Michelet, *Histoire de France*, [19 vols, 1867]"

The occult character of initiations to the Order was criticized. People spoke in low voices about magic and the ritual murder of children. Philippe le Bel was to find auxiliaries in the indignation and hatred caused to the people by everything that they do not understand.

On the night of 13 October 1306, Jacques de Molay was arrested with the Knights that were in Paris. Orders had been given in advance to the provinces for all the Templars in France to be imprisoned simultaneously. Torture rapidly obtained more than a hundred and forty confessions. On searching the house of the Temple, however, the archives of the Order were not found, nor its true and primitive rule, not the rote of initiation. Jacques de Molay, motivated by rumors that had run around a few days before regarding a danger that threatened the Order, had had then removed from the Temple and hidden in a safe place. They were never found.

The Templars were accused of renouncing Jesus Christ and spitting on the cross three times at the moment when they made the oath of fidelity. That accusation has been discussed endlessly, and various explanations have been found for it. The one to which many sensate minds rallied, notably Michelet,[55] is that that form of reception as borrowed from ancient mysteries. In order to make the perfect purity of the initiate more obvious after initiation, the initiate had to demonstrate that he had attained the ultimate degree of irreligion. He denied Jesus. The Order rehabilitated him all the more because is fall had been more profound. At the time of the Templars' trial the rite was practiced but its symbolic meaning had been lost.

That explanation is a trifle infantile. How could an action that must have appeared monstrous have been asked of them without giving them a reason, since that reason was so simple? The question must have been asked incessantly, for the anguish of the pious knight admitted to the Order and invited to spit on what he had learned to worship must have been pro-

---

[55] Author's note: "In spite of the explanation he gives, he remains horrorstruck by the magnitude of the impiety."

found. His conscience could easily have been calmed and a response so easily obtained would not have been forgotten.

In reality, the numerous knights who declared that they had begged their initiator to dispense them from the ceremony of the denial of the cross, or who tried to escape its consequences by a mental restriction, could not have had the veritable explanation without also knowing the secrets of the Order, and those secrets were reserved for another initiation, on entry to the interior order.

The action of spitting on the cross signified the deliverance of the Templar with regard to the Roman Church, which he would not longer serve henceforth in spirit. In the same way that the Assassins, enemies of official Islam, prescribed to their disciples of the first degree the rigorous observance of the Koran, the Order of the Temple preached a Christianity rigorous in form. But in spirit, the link that united each member of the Order to the Church was broken by the initiatory ceremony. He was attached to a higher Church, to a Christ who could not die on the cross, and there would come a day, when it was necessary to fight the Pope of Rome and his bishops, when each of them would be obliged to remember his initiation as a living act.

The Templars were, in fact, so detached from the Catholic Church that they did not make use of consecrated hosts in the mass, and they received the confessions of their visitors and preachers, who were often laymen.

The accusation of sodomy weighed as heavily against them as that of heresy. It is not that sodomy was not very widespread in the Middle Ages. It seems to have been more so than in Greece and at least as much as in our day in the society of London, Berlin and Paris. "In the eighth century, according to Alcuin, and probably in the following centuries, every elected bishop had, before being consecrated, to justify himself with regard to these canonical demands: 1., whether he had been a pederast; 2., whether he had been in criminal commerce with a nun; 3., whether he had been in criminal commerce with a four-legged animal."[56] And he had to swear thereafter not to practice any of these "criminal commerces." In order for a candidate bishop to be interrogated insistently on such actions, they must have been in current usage; but as in our day, everything was tolerated, permitted and encouraged on condition that it was kept quiet and hypocrisy covered it with its mantle of ashes.

A large number of witnesses deposed that at the moment of their entry into the Order they were recommended by their superior to give themselves to sodomy with one another and to neglect the amour of women. That revelation aroused great indignation in society, but that indignation in not really justified. Complete chastity was proposed as an ideal, but that ideal could not be realized at length. Sodomy was a first step, an attenuation of the excitement of the senses. Then again, the Templars were primarily warriors, takers of castles and cities. The custom, at the time, was to rape the women when one entered anywhere as a victor. Those who resisted were killed, and sometimes those one had had and of whom one was weary. That custom was so well-established that a special order of chivalry was founded in the twelfth century for the preservation of women during the marches of armies and the taking of cities. It was perhaps with an objective of human economy that a sage Grand Master of the Temple recommended sodomy as a last resort of carnal desire.

There are analogous examples in the history of mystical sects. Those which deem material life irremediably evil are logical in refusing to perpetuate themselves. They deflect their senses, therefore, by means of rapid actions that bring them a minimum of pleasure and are deprived of consequences. In India about thirty years ago there was a certain sensation when proceedings were instituted against a philosopher who gave advice of a similar nature.

---

[56] Author's reference: "Frédéric Nicolai. *Essai sur les accusations intentées aux Templiers et sur the secret de cet ordre* [1783]."

In reality, the cause of all the misunderstandings comes from the enormous importance that religions and society give to the physical relations of individuals with one another. Those relations, the interest of which varies with the age and intelligence of individuals, ought only to matter in the measure to which they develop the sentiment of beauty and love, in the most elevated sense of the word.

But a rule like that of the Order of the Temple supposed in its adherents a sense of moderation and a minimum of spiritual development. It took no account of the baseness of instincts and the total absence of rudiments of spirituality in the great majority of men. The majority of the Templars saw only saw therein permission to take a pleasure previously considered as forbidden. All the Order's rites were debased.

The kiss on the lips given to the candidate at the moment of reception, which was the communication of breath and strength, as practiced in the Oriental secret societies, became a sign of pleasure. The reception of the knight was very often the pretext for caricaturish and obscene scenes in which the defenders of the Temple and lovers of symbolism cannot discover a hidden meaning under any pretext. During the interrogations in Cahors, a knight named Arnaud reported that as soon as his reception "when he had been made to suffer criminal kisses, the superior who received him had immediately abused him."[57]

In Carcassonne, the young Jean de Cassagne confessed that "while a priest of the Order read a psalm, the superior kissed his mouth and lay down on the bench where he was sitting, that they exchanged other kisses, and that the ten knights kissed his navel. Then the superior took a bronze idol from a box...."

---

[57] Author's reference: "[Anon] *Histoire de l'abolition de l'Ordre des Templiers*, 1779."

The third accusation was concerned with that idol. It was named Baphomet.[58] The one found in Paris had a serial number, because there was one in every chapter of the Temple. It was made of bronze, with a long white beard. It was depicted variously, because the knight only saw it for a few moments at the moment of is initiation. It was said that it was a sort of marionette, that it had the face of a cat and also that it represented Satan. Those puerilities contributed to providing a basis for the suspicion of heresy that hung over the Temple. The Knights were convicted in public opinion of worshiping an Oriental divinity.

In reality, Baphomet was a sign of Gnostic origin, destined to summarize the doctrine of the Temple and to remind it of its goal. They worshiped therein neither the image of Jupi-

---

[58] Author's note: "A word derived from the Greek, the meaning of which is 'the baptism of the spirit,' (Hammer)." The reference, presumably taken from a secondary source, is to the Austrian Orientalist Baron Joseph Hammer (1774-1856; known as von Hammer-Purgstall after 1835), specifically his intensely peculiar *Mysterium Baphometus Revelatum*, the sixth volume of his *Fundgruben des Orients* [Mines of the Orient] (1818). Magre also appears to have taken some inspiration from Hammer's imaginative history of the Assassins. The word Baphomet is more commonly supposed either to have been derived from Medieval Latin, or as a corruption of "Mahomet," and various adaptations of it have been gleaned from documents contemporary with the crusades, in Latin and in Occitan, but its meaning therein remains stubbornly unclear. It was, however, taken up by the extravagant pioneer of the French occult revival who called himself Éliphas Lévi, who applied it to the "goat of the Sabbat," a key symbol in his writings, and many of those who followed in his tracks did likewise. Some modern Johannites, having adopted the assimilation of the Templars to their imaginary history, have suggested that the archetype of the idol might have been the head of the apostle John.

ter nor that of Mahomet, as was said and believed, but force: the force directed by intelligence that was the ideal of the Temple and was always represented in ancient symbolism by a bearded man wearing a crown. That bearded man is found on seals and medals that had belonged to the Templars. It was for them what the rose in the middle of the cross was to the Rosicrucians, the symbol of the superior idea to which they had devoted their life. The linen cord that was given to the new knight, which he was recommended to wear under his garments, must have touched Baphomet, because it represented the chain that linked the man to his ideal.

THE FALL OF THE ORDER

I shall not recount in detail the proceedings instituted against the Templars, which lasted seven years. Torture had immediately extracted the expected confessions of heresy from a large number of them. Even the Grand Master had not been able to resist it. His confessions must, however, have been falsified by the three cardinals who heard them, for he did not recognize them when they were read back to him, and he declared that he preferred the procedures of the Saracens "who immediately cut off the head of the accused."

Clement V appeared resistant at first before the grandeur of the injustice, but he was linked by interest to the King of France. He also coveted the spoils of the Templars, in order to satisfy the demands of the beautiful Brunissende, Comtesse de Foix.

What is particularly striking about the trial is the terror inspired by the King's justice. No one dared to raise his voice to defend the Templars. After two years of equivocations and preliminary tortures, a pontifical commission is solemnly installed at the Archbishopric of Paris and sits there every day to hear the defense. Every day an usher appears on the threshold of the Archbishop's palace and cries to the people: "If anyone wants to defend the Order of the Militia of the Temple he has only to present himself." But no one does. The days go by; the ceremony is repeated for four months.

Finally, a man clad in black traverses the silent crowd and asks to be heard for the defense of the Order. A shudder runs through the throng cluttering the streets. The commission stands up, in great emotion. The man is named Jean de Melot. He has been a Templar for ten years. He has a great many things to say; he is going to demonstrate the Order's innocence. When attention is at its peak he declares that he needs immediate nourishment, that he is poor and that he hopes that someone will come to his aid. It is perceived then that he is simple-minded. He is given nourishment, and the commission then renounces hearing any defense of the Order of the Temple.

That defense was never to be produced. It seems that all the knights have become simple-minded, Even the Grand Master declares that he is a man of war, incapable of debating logically. After two years of captivity he asks for a week to reflect and authorization to have a chaplain, who says mass for him. Perhaps the fear of torture threw a veil over the minds of the accused? Perhaps all trace of human intelligence has been suppressed from the interrogations. What remains mysterious in the trial of the Templars is the incapacity of the knights to find a reasonable defense.

Finally, after seven years, Clement V appoints a council to study the affair and judge it. But as the members of the council ask to hear witnesses, to be informed of the case and they seem to want to exonerate the Order, Clement V, by his own authority, declares it suspect of heresy and abolishes it.

A large number of knights were kept in the royal prisons, Philippe le Bel hastened to have condemned to death, by a tribunal under the presidency of the Archbishop of Sens, the brother of his minister Marigny, on whose ferocity he can count, all the Templars that had retracted their initial confessions.

"Near the Abbaye de Saint-Antoine, fifteen or twenty pyres had been lit, not in flames but like as many beds of ardent coals, to burn the culpable individuals gradually. Fifty-four knights were thrown into them."[59]

The Grand Master, Jacques de Molay, and the master of Normandy had been condemned to perpetual imprisonment. At the last minute, however, before the Archbishop of Sens, they abruptly withdrew their confessions. They declared that "the Order was pure and holy, and that they were ready to die to sustain that verity." They died the same day. Philippe le Bel

---

[59] Author's reference: *"Histoire de l'abolition de l'Ordre des Templiers."*

293

had them taken to an island in the Seine situated between the King's gardens and those of the Augustins, where two pyres had been built. The two Templars, says the historian, "had become hideous by virtue of the effects of such a long captivity." An immense crowd watched the torture.

There was no thick smoke to stifle them, with the consequence that they were burned slowly. As Jacques de Molay was partly consumed, tradition reports that he cried: "Clement, iniquitous judge, I summon you to appear before the tribunal of God in forty days time, and you, Philippe equally unjust, in a year."

Forty days later, Clement V died of lupus near Avignon. The King of France only survived him by eight months. A Templar from Beaucaire, when he was about to be burned, having encountered Nogaret, the king's counselor and instigator or the proceedings, on the way, also specified the date of his imminent death for him. Florian and the prior of Montfaucon, who had denounced the Order on his evidence, were murdered within the year.

Those coincidences have been seen as evidence of certain powers of magic that were lent to the Templars. It cannot be explained, however, why those powers were not manifest during the seven years that the proceedings had lasted. Perhaps there is an inferior magic that can only be employed for vengeance.

A legend of the Midi says that in the church of the little Pyrenean village of Gavarnie, nine heads of executed Templars have been preserved. Every 13 October, the anniversary of the Order's fall, at midnight, a voice resounds in the church and says: "Has the day of the deliverance of Christ's tomb come?" and the nine heads blink their desiccated eyelids and reply, in a whisper, with their mummified lips: "Not yet!"

The deliverance of the tomb of Christ was originally intended symbolically as the deliverance of the spirit. That legend shows that in the land of the Albigensians, the goal of the

Order had been understood, and that even after its destruction, people did not despair of the promised deliverance.

For the papal bull only rendered the Order of Templars secret thereafter. In his prison, Jacques de Molay had designated as his successor Jean-Marc Larmenie of Jerusalem. Thibaut d'Alexandrie succeeded him and since then, the Order has continued to exist, "and the succession of its grandmasters, which includes many illustrious and influential men, has never been interrupted."[60]

De Beaujeu, the nephew of Jacques de Molay had received his ashes and possessed the archives and the secrets of the Order. Followed by a few Templars he went to Scotland, where Edward II had conceded lands to them. That little group recognized as leader the master of the freemasons Henry Fitz-Edwin and he formed the Edinburgh lodge. Others went to Sweden. In the centuries that followed, the Templars mingled with freemasonry and played an active role in its development. But the study of that role and its action on the French Revolution is too vast a subject for me to treat it here. I shall only report the last act of the drama, which indicates, if it is true, that the Templar filiation existed in a vivacious fashion among the first elements of the Revolution and that there is a direct relationship of cause and effect between the death of Jacques de Molay and that of Louis XVI.

At the moment when Louis XVI's head had just fallen from the guillotine, a man who had been seen in all the street demonstrations since the taking of the Bastille ran toward the scaffold, took royal blood in his hands and made the gesture of throwing it over the crowd, crying: "People, I baptize you in the name of Jacques de Molay and liberty!"[61]

Jacques de Molay was avenged. Perhaps the Order had no longer had any other gal for five centuries than that venge-

---

[60] Author's reference: "[Jean-Emmanuel] Le Couteulx de Canteleu, *Les Sectes et les sociétés secrètes*, [1863]"
[61] Author's reference: "Story recounted by Éliphas Lévi and reproduced by Stanislas de Guaita."

ance. It has only been glimpsed since then in an enfeebled form. At the beginning of the nineteenth century, some of its members attempted to reconstitute it, but in an imperfect manner.

That attempt was made with the assent of Napoléon, who reserved the possibility of extracting the best from the Order and perhaps becoming its Grand Master, when the Order had recovered a measure of social importance. He sent an infantry regiment to form a line in front of the church of Saint-Paul Saint-Antoine in 1808 when a funeral ceremony was held for the anniversary of the death of Jacques de Molay. The new Templars were gathered in that ceremony and they sat on thrones in the church. They wore a chlamys edged with ermine and had pectoral crosses, epaulettes, armbands, fringed belts, and white boots with red heels. Their first concern, after the distribution of titles and dignities, had been to compose sumptuous uniforms. That is, alas, a characteristic of many sects that pretend to seek true spirituality to believe that an initiate ought to wear a costume and that the sign of the elevation of the spirit is proportional to the diversity of symbols, and the choice of colors and fabrics. One finds the search for that facile superiority in academies, philharmonic or mutualist societies, and other groups in which human vanity is expressed.

The new Order of the Temple was modified a little later under the direction of the physician Fabré-Palaprat, who attempted to restore the Johannite religion. In that he was in the true Templar tradition of Theoclet and Hugues de Payens. He based his beliefs on a mysterious manuscript he had found, called the Leviticon, which supposedly contained the secret doctrines of the Templars of the thirteenth century. But nothing resulted from his effort, except that new dignities and uniforms were distributed.

The Order of the Temple has now disappeared, and that disappearance marks the complete failure of its high aims. The Church of John, the true Christian Church, has lost its heroic champions. The deliverance of the spirit, the organization of the world by a group of initiated sages, as well as the attestation of the nine dead heads under the brick and slate of Gavarnie, was not and never will be realized. The men in white mantles who had a red cross over the heart and who might have attempted it perished in the royal prisons of Philippe le Bel after having been dishonored by the interrogations of Dominican Inquisitors.

But the Spirit could not be delivered by the Templars. A grand design cannot be accomplished by that which is founded on hypocrisy. The Order of the Temple instructed its knights in the practices of the narrowest Catholicism, as the Order of Assassins did for the rules of the Koran. Both orders wanted, however, to destroy the church that they venerated in appearance, in order to erect another, more perfect, on its debris. A lie is never solid. The Mongol horsemen of Hulagu and the foresight of Philippe le Bel put an end to those two great forces of the Orient and the Occident.

If the Templars had triumphed, history would have been modified in an unforeseeable manner. They had understood the necessity of the union of religions. Their narrow links with Islam and its philosophers had taught them to respect the civilization of their enemies and even to adopt it. They embraced in their social projects the elevation of the third order. Who can tell what might have become of the states of Europe in the hands of that aristocratic army? Perhaps they would have been transformed by an element of sublime progress. Perhaps—and it is more probable—they would have been curbed under the iron tyranny that those who possess strength always exercise.

It was the mystic knights of the First Crusade who had received the message to begin with. They had wanted to transmit it by the sword. By the noble verities that they had learned in Jerusalem were incomplete. They did not know that the word loses its virtue with the vapor of the blood that is shed on its behalf. There is a certain light of the spirit that dies on contact with the metal of a breastplate and the steel of a sword. And if the person who wants to transmit it is enveloped by the magnetism of gold, that light becomes shadow. Certain verities, in order to keep their original purity, need to be expressed by the lips of poor men, and their annunciatory sign ought to be made with a hand blanched by asceticism and long invocations.

Whether the corruptions of which the Templars were accused were true or false, and whether the initiations had degenerated into the scenes of collective amour that one finds in so many mystical sects, is of little importance. It does not matter whether the eyes of Baphomet were luminous carbuncles, or whether the denial of Christ affected one form or another. Their true crime was not enunciated in the proceedings. How could it be? It was committed on a daily basis by Philippe le Bel and Clement V.

Having lost their initial ideal, the Templars had mistaken the means for the end. Those exterminator monks became thereafter bankers, acquirers of châteaux, moneylenders, seigneurs of vassals and lands. How could they retain the divine delight of the years of their youth, when they were running among the shores of Lake Tiberiad for the defense of pilgrims? They were so poor then that they only had one horse between two of them. That was in the times when they kept Jerusalem for the Christians. When each of them had several caparisoned horses and squires to lead them, they were expelled from Saint-Jean-d'Acre.

The secret of their strength was in their courage and their faith. But they took wealth for an ideal, in the same way that the Albigensians had taken poverty. They wanted a Christ superior to the one that the vulgar worshiped, but they had not heeded the parable of the camel and the needle's eye. They believed that a great work could be accomplished by making use, with impunity, of the weapons of evil. So the message was lost, their work was consigned to oblivion, as with all those who do not have as a first principle a perfect disinterest.

298